Born and raised in Dublin, Ireland, Alistair Anbard began putting stories together at a young age. Encouraged to both read and write by their parents, they developed a knack of conjuring up characters and worlds which consumed whole notebooks. They studied literature at university, by which time the mountain and its residents were already taking shape. A lifetime of being absorbed by science fiction, fantasy and horror, together with a passion of travel, culture, cuisine and mythology, eventually helped to form their scraps of writing into one complete project.

They continue to live in Dublin with their family and dogs.

To those we have lost.

Alastair Anbard

THE MOUNTAIN AT THE EDGE OF SPACE

AUSTIN MACAULEY PUBLISHERS™

LONDON * CAMBRIDGE * NEW YORK * SHARJAH

A CIP catalogue record for this title is available from the British Library.

ISBN 9781398483460 (Paperback)
ISBN 9781398483477 (ePub e-book)

www.austinmacauley.com

First Published 2022
Austin Macauley Publishers Ltd®
1 Canada Square
Canary Wharf
London
E14 5AA

Thanks to the multitudes of people who have encouraged me to pursue my passion, who gave me the confidence to put pen to paper. To those who discouraged me, who coaxed the fire in me. To the people I have met in life who have planted the seed of a character, or even an entire race in my mind. And of course, to the people whose works came before, whose worlds and tales I lost myself in, who taught me how to shape my own visions.

Table of Contents

I

Duncan bit into the apple with a loud *crunch*, showering her hand in slobber and half-chewed chunks without much consideration. Crim tried to adjust her grip, momentarily taking it out from between his teeth in an act of boorishness that brought on a bout of angry braying from the old mule. He even stamped his hoof at her.

"Oh shut up, you old codger!" She shot back, wiping her sticky fingers in her patched brown trousers and offering the apple again. He near bit her finger with it this time, and Crim was certain he meant for her to feel the fleeting pinch of his oversized incisors. He relaxed as he chewed, giving her a minute to look around again. This was a pleasant little village, nestled on a rather flat hill in a shady valley surrounded on all sides by rocky slopes. Despite the heat, the mountains were high enough to don white caps, their feet covered in coarse grass and sparse foliage.

A broad stream, which she suspected could become a torrent in wet weather, ran from north to south, hooking around the hill as it passed. The village itself had grown down the easier slopes over time, with the church, a few municipal buildings and this large square at its heart. Today was Sunday, and the Sunday market was in full swing with people milling around the clusters of tents, stalls, carts and weighed-down blankets.

Crim took in a long, rather unnecessary, breath through her nose and allowed her concentration to flow outward, washing over the crowds and the buildings and the rustling queuna trees. Outwards and inwards she went; into the hearts and minds of passers-by. Just a glance—not enough to be intrusive. Into the houses, where more people sat in the shade eating or sleeping or just living their daily lives. Into the treetops to find the creatures that dwelt there. She took it in, all of it. After all, the shadows of the mountaintops were lengthening, and she hadn't much time left.

The mule tossed his head, bumping her in the face hard enough to bring her rushing back into her own mind. Her hood fell, and Crim yanked it back up in a panic, checking her hands and arms so make sure her illusion had not faltered. Once certain she still looked like the same gangly mortal girl, she glared down at him, but he only flicked his ears and swished his tail at the cloud of flies gathering round his rear. Crim swatted them, too; bad as the cranky old ass was, he was allergic to most bites, and his mood was probably being made worse by the growing patch of irritated skin now visible on his tail.

"I can give you something for that." A man in a battered grey hat shuffled out from the shelter of his porch to the shelter of the large tree she sat under. "My horses get the same, and it makes them grumpy too."

"I'm fine, really. I asked my friend to get something for him."

She stood on tiptoe to scan through the throng and, spotting a headful of dark curls, pointed to Sunshine, who was currently chatting with one of the shopkeepers and his wife, debating the price of bread. Crim had to smile at this; no matter what price they settled on, Sunshine was sure to give the couple double their original ask, for she only enjoyed the game of bartering and had no real need for the money. Sure enough, when she dropped a handful of coins into the husband's hand, his wife slapped his arm and told him to give it back, but Sunshine was already moving away, laughing and telling them to use it on the roof.

They would not be the only ones with a little extra in their pockets today; Duncan's cart was already piling up with baskets of fruit and vegetables, parcels of fresh meat, wheels of cheese, jugs of milk and the local brew, tins and jars and bags of whatever spice or herb or ointment or medicine that tickled their fancy. And they still had the satchels to fill. There would be nothing left to buy before the day's end. Not that they needed any of it; they would try to eat most of the purchases in the coming days, the rest would be used as offerings.

"Yes…" The man said, watching with her as Sunshine now moved on to the next seller, who greeted her with open arms. "Don't misunderstand me—I'm not selling. Let me give it to you."

He offered a small metal tin full of a creamy, rather lumpy paste, which she supposed was a simpler version of what they themselves usually made. Crim took it and smiled her own lopsided smile, not nearly as radiant as Sunshine's.

"Thank you, but…here…" She fished in her purse and produced three shining coins. The man's eyes went wide, but he did not take them.

"No, I couldn't, miss. It's not worth that much."

"I want you to have this much."

"It wouldn't be right."

"How many children do you have?"

"Five, miss."

"And another on the way?"

"How did you…?"

"I want you to have this much. All of you. Take it."

Without another word, he took the money.

"Don't stare like that, please, someone less honest might see. Put them in your pocket."

He did so, and with the next move of his hand swept his hat off his head. He was not old, but already his black hair was thinning. Attempting to pat down the wisps, he offered: "If you'll not take that, miss, at least let us treat you and your friend to dinner. There's plenty would be happy to put you up, I'm sure, and we've not much space, but my wife, she cooks—"

Crim kept her expression in check. "Of course, thank you."

He grinned now, looking less worried. "It's our pleasure, miss! And you can stay the night, if you need!"

"*Perfect.*"

Sunshine punched her in the shoulder, laughing as they unhitched the cart from Duncan and fished their packs out from the day's winnings.

"You sly rat!"

"What? He offered, I accepted!"

"Oh? And you didn't put the idea in his head?"

"I did not discourage him."

A snort. Her friend tossed some of her curls about, studying her. Crim stared back, wordlessly pleading for her to take up the offer. "Fine. But just one night! And you can explain this to Mentor when we get back!"

"Just one night. And I'll take the blame, of course."

Another punch, harder this time.

"Ow."

*

Dinner was served on a large table, though not quite large enough to accommodate the thirteen people that gathered round to eat. Besides Miguel (their host) and his bubbly little wife, there came their five children; three boys and two girls, some charging, some skipping, one crawling. The toddler sat and was fed on his father's knee, leaving a seat free for his grandfather, who was rather deaf and relied on his wife to relay everything directly to his one good ear. Miguel's wife's elder brother sat opposite them, smiling shyly in sharp contrast to his stout frame, and spooning generous portions out to their guests and his teenage daughter before he let a morsel past his own lips.

Crim dug into her food with genuine enthusiasm; Loretta and her mother, with some help from her niece, had prepared whole platters of sliced plantains and potatoes, fried vegetables, and a strange meat which Crim very much suspected was guinea pig (a hunch she did not share with Sunshine). Everything had been carefully seasoned and cooked to perfection; even the guinea pig (presumably) had been cut up to resemble thin strips of chicken, so that Sunshine did not question what she was eating even once.

When they were done, the table was cleared and they were led outside, where they sat and drank well into the night. Neighbours came by to look at the guests, and some asked rather a lot of questions, which they struggled to answer. Questions about who they were and where they had come from, their friends and families, the toughest of which Crim left to Sunshine. After a while, however, her companion tired of this and invited her input.

"Where are you from, girls?" One middle-aged lady asked, coming to sit in Loretta's chair (their hostess had long since retired to bed).

Sunshine poked her in the ribs, and Crim stammered: "Can't you guess?"

Not used to deflecting, she thought this a rather good response. Sunshine groaned and tugged at her baby hairs. Luckily, the woman took the bait, and named a country whose name had not changed much in millennia. Crim beamed at her.

"Yes, that's right!"

"It must be very cold this time of year!"

"Very!"

"Lots of snow?"

"Lots!"

"Ahh. We only get snow high in the mountains."

Emboldened, the woman took a long look at Sunshine, and said something which neither of them understood. Sunshine just nodded.

"Yup!"

Their inquisitor clapped and proceeded to tell them all about their own homelands. Crim and Sunshine, firmly trapped within their lies, could only nod and smile and agree with every presumption she blurted out. For this world was entirely foreign to them, and what they knew of it belonged to antiquity.

*

Despite their hosts' insistence that it was not a bother, Crim and Sunshine politely declined the invitation to commandeer two of the older children's beds for the night. They had bedrolls in their packs, and insisted that the couches in the living room would be more than enough to sleep on. The adults all seemed rather perturbed by this suggestion, to the point that Sunshine subtly persuaded them that it was more than fair. Much to the delight of the children, who were not thrilled at the idea of squeezing in together in the summer heat.

Though they had both taken the spare bedding, and promised the couches would be comfortable enough once they had been made up, Crim ended up spread out on a blanket on the floor, wondering how Sunshine fought the urge cast off most of the coverings they both had so enthusiastically crawled under when the grandmother came to check on them. Even this far up in the mountains in the middle of the night it felt like an oven. She closed her eyes and tried to pull some of the cold out of the floor tiles. This helped a little; enough to convince her that she might sleep.

"Hey," Sunshine whispered, and her eyes snapped back open. She rolled to find her hanging over the edge of the couch, one slender brown arm reaching to scratch the ear of one of the house cats, who peered out from under the couch with glowing green eyes.

"I know," Said Crim, sighing. "We leave first thing tomorrow."

"No. Well—yes, that too—but that woman has me thinking—"

"Don't hurt yourself."

"Very funny. Anyway: How long do you think it's been? Since we were taken, I mean?"

"Uh…" Truth be told, Crim often wondered about such things. How long had it been since she was mortal? Who were her family? Where did she come from? But she had little to no memory of her life before, and now she was timeless, so her estimations were pure guesswork. "A while. I suppose…A couple of centuries, at least."

"Hmm…" Sunshine set the cat purring by scratching his chin. "I can never tell. Not that I've been let out often. Sometimes the places we visit seem familiar. Others…I don't know."

"I know." She might have said more, but her lids were drifting shut again, and it was much too confusing to think about, anyway. Sunshine apparently sensed her disinterest in the conversation and rolled back against the cushions. The cat opened his eyes a crack, glaring at Crim indignantly.

Her dreams came; deep, hazy dreams that came in snippets as she tossed and turned in the sweltering night. Another meal with another family. They sat around a fire pit and picked at bowls full of boiled vegetables, taking the occasional piece from the fish slowly roasting over crackling flames. The dogs sniffed about, only to be shooed away. They came back as quick as they retreated, and were rewarded with scraps behind the backs of the children.

*

Morning came, hot and dry and golden over the peaks that surrounded the flattened hilltop. The adults in the house woke with it, greeting their guests one by one as they shuffled into the kitchen. Crim and Sunshine had been up well before dawn to make sure their disguises had not slipped away as they slept— with good reason, too, as part of Crim's hair had turned bright red while she dreamt, and her complexion had needed adjusting. Loretta soon passed by and they followed; she laid out plenty of fresh bread, butter, cheese, avocado, olives, plates of fruit and dried meats for all. They helped themselves, and were also treated to mugs of a hot black liquid, which neither knew. It was bitter, and they both choked on it at first, but Crim persevered enough to drink both cups.

As they had both agreed, they gathered their things to leave immediately after eating. Miguel, though disappointed, conceded that it would be best for them to get moving before noon, as this day was already promising to be hotter than the one before. Still, they could not depart without packets of cheese and ham being pushed into their hands. Sunshine eyed Crim suspiciously at this.

"*This time,* I did no convincing!" She swore.

"Did you remember, at least?"

"Of course. I left it under the rug." The purse full of their remaining coins would hopefully feed the family for a few weeks. "But let's get going before they notice."

Miguel and his eldest son insisted on escorting them to the northern gate, back the way they had come. Crim willed no-one to ask why they were returning to the heart of the range, when any other direction would lead them to far more favourable territories.

"You should make it under that ridge before the sun is fully up," Miguel told them, pointing to where a sharp spear of rock overhung the road snaking up the nearest slope. "My advice would be to siesta there until it moves over the western peaks. Behind that mountain there is a ridge which the road follows. You can cut straight over the valley to…to…"

"Yes, thank you, Miguel," Sunshine cut in. "We should make it home before sundown."

"Right," He replied, blinking. He was beginning to get confused and his son, who had been listening the whole time, was a breath away from asking exactly *where* they were going. She could hear the notion rattling around in his head. Feigning calm, Crim gave Duncan a smack on the rump and began to lead him off.

"Thank you for dinner!" She called back. "And the roof over our heads!"

The man and his son, looking more and more perplexed, tried to grin. Tried to wave at who they presumed had been visitors to their little village, but eventually forgot why they were there, and looking to one another for a reason, both shrugged and turned back homeward.

"Thank you!" Sunshine skipped backwards, waving and smiling that dazzling smile. Then, under her breath, she added: "You won't remember us, but we will remember you."

II

They reached the shelter of the outcrop just a little after midday. This was mostly due to Crim dragging her feet the entire way up the dusty slope, and partially due to the strop Duncan threw after a particularly unpleasant bite, that looked more like a sting. They rubbed the last of Miguel's balm over it, talking sweetly to him, but he still refused to move forward until they offered him another apple.

The sun was bright and scorching, Sunshine turned her face to her namesake and spread her arms wide. The heat and the light coursed through her, filling her from head to toe. A warm, rippling current.

"Invigorating, isn't it?"

Crim, trudging over the steepest part of the incline and dripping with sweat, grumbled incoherently. Duncan snorted in agreement.

She laughed, and finding a wide, flat rock out of the shade, spread herself out on it to bask. Crim collapsed in the darkest corner of the shelter and guzzled water, pouring entire bowlfuls out for their mule, who sucked noisily and blew bubbles.

"You're both dramatic."

"And you're insane."

"You're going to hide in there all afternoon?"

"And you're going to fry over there. To each their own."

Sunshine guffawed. They both knew such feeble rays could not harm her. Her skin drank them in, feeding their energy to her limbs. "You know, if you ever paid attention to your lessons, you could cool yourself down."

"I know how to cool myself down!" Crim snapped. "But all everything around us is boiling. I need a reference. A nice cool rock, or—"

"Or a section of shade?"

"…Oh." Crim scooted further into the shadows and, folding her legs under, began to meditate, pulling the chill from the stones and the dirt around her.

Eventually, cold trickles began to run down her face and arms, and Sunshine knew she had found a water source deep underground.

With her companions quiet, Sunshine had time to look up at the sky. She had forgotten just how blue it could be, how the stars and moon were veiled during the day leaving this endless ocean above everything. Puffs of white cloud sailed across it, winding their way between the sharp peaks. She remembered, from somewhere deep within her mind, the ones laden with water, that dragged their heavy grey bulks overhead, only to drench the land. After that, the grass would turn green, and the trees would bud. The herds that had moved to greener pastures would return and in turn be hunted. There would be plenty of food for all until it dried up again.

Reaching her fingers out to touch one soft round cloud, she wished it would rain down on top of her. The sound still echoed in her ears, but the sensation of those cold little droplets against her skin was only a rumour in her memory.

A bird soared into view, appearing as a black line against white and blue, her shape becoming more distinct as she circled down down down, gaze no doubt fixed on some unfortunate animal below. At last, she came to a hover, then dropping her magnificent wings she dove instantly out of sight. There came a sharp cry down in the valley, and she fluttered past, much nearer this time, carrying a rather large mouse or small rat.

Sunshine laid like that for hours, watching the clouds float through the sky, and birds and insects as they whizzed past. Then she moved to sit on the edge of the broad, flat cliff, and stared down into the valley. It was rather flat, peppered with copses of stout trees and bushes—all looking very dry and dead under the baking sun. The grass was yellow and brown, but blanketed the low foothills all the way down to the bed of a struggling stream, far smaller than the one that skirted the village. There were things moving down there; more rodents, reptiles and other things that crawled. They hurried from shade to shade, or peeked from their dens, but mostly avoided being exposed to the heat—or things that swooped and snatched—for long.

*

Eventually, the shadows of the western ranges lengthened on the grass, and the temperature showed signs of dropping. Crim stirred from where she had been napping in her nice cool patch, and clapped at Duncan, who jolted awake. The mule bucked at her and she growled back, threatening to turn him into dinner (an empty threat). They ate a late afternoon tea from some of the parcels Miguel had given them, since they did know exactly how long it took for food to go off (Sunshine was quite nervous about the things in the cart, which had been sitting there all day), and did not want to let his careful packaging be for naught. It tasted the same as enchanted fare, surprisingly.

Burdening themselves once more with their packs and satchels, they took a moment to look back on the peaceful mountain village before turning their backs on the squat houses, the streets and squares ringing with gossip and the laughter of children, the rows and groves lovingly tended further down the hill. Crim lingered like this over-long, and Sunshine was loath to move her.

When will she ever come Outside again?

Crim's expression was unreadable, her mind closed. She just stood there, gazing at the lights now beginning to appear in some windows, watching as a group of men made their way lazily back up the road towards the square.

"It's getting late," Sunshine hinted, and with a sigh her friend stepped away from the edge, laced her fingers under Duncan's bridle then led him under the jutting shelter to the other side of the slope. Here the road branched around and down the other side of mountain, with a fork also leading out and across, clinging to the near side of a jagged ridge. This was the way they turned, walking single file with Crim ahead, and Sunshine behind the cart. Most of the time, the narrow track led straight across to the neighbouring foothills, but at this moment exactly, at the halfway point exactly, they were able to turn to the right through a gap just wide enough for the cart to pass.

Here, Crim paused again, and Duncan perked his ears as he ambled past her, wheels rattling over bumps and stones. Sunshine let him lead on; he knew his way now, and was probably dreaming of his nice, cosy stable, his netful of hay and Polly (his pony friend).

This road led up gradually again, rising to high slopes as far as the eye could see. At this point, the mortal world seemed to fade out gradually; dust and scree giving way to tufts of dark green grass, that became a rolling plain, that bordered the edges of a dense forest marching up up up to the slate-grey walls and cliffs of a mountain that pierced the heavens. The sky around faded from cobalt blue to dark navy dotted with stars, and the lower portion of a small moon could be seen peeking through a rounded cleft high on the left-hand face. That cleft was in fact a hole, where in eons past an asteroid struck the mountainside when all was still young and half-formed. That asteroid is said to have barrelled straight through to the Core, creating the deepest and oldest caverns in which the Sidhe came to dwell.

For this was *the* Mountain, and they were *Sidhe*, the ancient folk that dwelt on the edge of the universe. The vessels of the gods.

*

"Can we sit here awhile?" Crim asked, gesturing to the two boulders that guarded the entrance to the gap.

Sunshine bit her lip; they had already lingered too long in this realm. Mentor had given them 'One day, and one day *only*' for the younger Sidhe's first excursion to the mortal world. Thus far, it had been a day and a half, and Mentor was likely already after their hides. "We have just rested, Crim."

"I know. I just…"

Sunshine followed her forlorn gaze back into the valley, knowing it went back beyond the cliffs and hills to that village, and the reminder of who they had been before. This was the most dangerous part of their journey; when she would face the choice of returning or departing into exile. All of them had been given this choice at their graduation from Acolyte to Anointed, and Sunshine knew of no one who had made it lightly.

"Would you go?" She probed.

A long, painfully drawn-out silence. In which fear caught her heart, and she thought that Crim truly might turn aside.

"No. There is no life for me there," Came the hard truth. "I could go back and try to get by but…it would never work. What I am now is not of that world."

"I see." She did. She felt it, too.

"But still I would like to sit. You can go on, if you like—Don't worry, I *will* follow. I just feel something…like remembering something I've forgotten."

"I'll sit with you. But not long."

They perched on the rocks, Crim pursing her lips and squinting at the trees and the rivers, the peaks and the valleys. Sunshine watching her, admiring the concentration on her face rivalling anything brought on by Mentor's lessons. Her own first outing had been ages ago, before Crim was made, but she held it fast in her memory. Mentor had taken her to a little seaside town. The bay full of fishing boats, large and small, and groups of men shouted to one another as they loaded and unloaded their holds. Children played in the icy grey waves that rolled up beaches covered in round pebbles, some picking crabs and shells out of shallow pools. They had bought oysters sold by two smiling sisters and eaten them sitting at the head of a disused jetty staring out to sea. It had rained that day, and though Mentor had grumbled and hidden under a tree, she had let Sunshine stay until it finished and she was done splashing in the puddles. That had been her moment, and this was Crim's.

At length Crim stood and stretched, taking one last deep breath of fresh air (Sidhe had no need to breathe, of course, but many of them found it relaxing), then she turned her back decisively on the Outside and marched up the Mountain.

*

The Mountain was bordered by the Forest on all sides, which did not reach even halfway up its colossal slopes, for after a few kilometres of low foothills it leapt heavenwards in sheer cliffs that could only accommodate the hardiest forms of vegetation. Beyond the Maw (the large hole in its side), nothing grew save icicles, as the Mountain finally began to taper off into its crooked summit. From afar (if one could get far enough away to view it in its entirety), it looked rather like a witch's hat banded and rimmed in shades of green.

It was through this greenery that their path led them, though now there was no obvious path to be found. They knew their way by the location of the Maw (always keeping this on their left), and made for it in a rough diagonal. At these lower levels, the mortal world could still be seen below, though with each passing step it would blur and darken, until they reached the first of many great obelisks that formed three great rings parallel to the borders of the Forest. These marked the hard border between worlds and, stepping beyond one and looking back, Sunshine saw now only a sharp edge sat beside an ocean of stars. Crim did not turn around, but pressed on through the trees.

Their way was made easier by clear lines in the leafy floor, made by the wheels of a cart being dragged up at surprising speed by a stubborn old mule. Sunshine hardly had to think about where they were going before they came to the next stone, and the next, at which point they turned sharply left. So they were spared some time wandering (the Forest could be a trial to navigate even for the oldest denizens), and came upon the Gate while the moon was still high.

Sunshine reached out and touched it, feeling it stir under her hand. Crafted by gardeners and metalworkers back in the time of the Patriarch, the Gate would only open for those welcomed by the Mountain; at their touch, the images of trees, bushes and vines made of shining truesteel shuddered, inset gemstones winking as the entire structure unwound and disappeared into the surrounding rockface.

They entered a long, wide tunnel ascending into the Mountain in broad, shallow steps, each roughly five metres apart to allow for the passage of most of their livestock, and unfathomably high. Carved from solid black marble, it was dark as night in its earlier portions, the only illumination being a meagre orange light ahead. This, of course, came from the Foyer; a vaulted hall with passages leading in six different directions, each passage in turn branched out into smaller tributaries again at various intervals, leading to most of the main areas within the Mountain. At its head was an immense copper-coloured phiale set atop an ornate tripod, where travellers from the Outside—such as they—were expected to give libations.

The orange light itself was a combination of various sources; blazing red lamps, sconces burning blue and mauve over grey dust, the three glowing yellow sunrocks set into the ceiling, and the scattered white starstones. Sunshine looked up into the rafters, and found herself staring into the curious faces of three young acolytes. Sure enough, as with any open space under the Mountain, looking about she found groups of figures—and indeed some lone figures—sitting on beams, above and around doorways, huddled in corners and even spread-eagled in the middle of the floor. Some, like these three, liked to watch those coming in, but most were indifferent, and chattered or played or slept while taking no notice of them.

"Hoi!" Another Anointed shouted, waving. Suri, one of Silver's mentees.

Sunshine waved back. "Oi."

"Laal was here a while ago," she said. "She was waiting for you, I think. Your maid was with her."

"Thanks." *Gods.* Laal had no doubt expected her yesterday or at least first thing in the morning. She was not an irrational person, but she did *not* like being left waiting. Sunshine turned to Crim. "I should go to her. Can you take Duncan?"

"I'm pretty sure he's ready to take himself," Crim remarked. Duncan, like most of the animals they kept, had been trained to wait in the Foyer for his mistresses to make their offerings. He was currently stomping about in front of the phiale, scraping his hoofs and snorting and *hawing* in a most unimpressed manner.

"Oh relax!" Sunshine flicked his ear as he made to bite her. "You weren't here that long!"

In response, he raised his head and let out a resounding *haw-hee-hawww!* For everyone to hear. All of the unfortunates who had until present been napping jerked up to glare at them.

"Shut up! Look!" She had bought a cheap bottle of wine just for the occasion, and prying the cork out with her teeth dumped its sharp-smelling contents out into the bowl. "Crim?"

The food Miguel had given them, well-wrapped as it was, was already starting to look like it had sat out in the sun for a good few hours. Crim peeled off the wax paper and tossed the remaining wedge of cheese and strips of pork in after the wine.

"What do the gods need with this anyway?" She asked.

"Nothing. It's a ritual. It's for us, really. To feel like we're being useful."

"Ah."

"Go to Mentor when you're done. She'll want to hear about everything. And be sure to include that it was *your* idea to stay."

Crim saluted and clapped for Duncan to follow her. He headbutted her and huffed and puffed but went eagerly enough. Sunshine, turning in the opposite direction, weighed the bag of fabrics hanging from her shoulder, and wondered if a nice scarf would be enough to win Laal's affection.

III

Bang-clap-bang!
bang-clap-bang!
bang-bang-clap!

She groaned and rolled, pressing a pillow firmly over her head. It only partially muted the *whump-thump* of a thick belt hitting the hardwood floor. Tried to remember the dream she had been having. It had felt so real in the moment, and now it was trickling away over the edge of her awareness. Something about a meadow full of grass that sang as it swayed, dotted in wildflowers budding with light. The colours were blurring together now, but she did her best to recall some, to fix them to her memory. Until a jewellery box was dropped with a crash, its contents jingling as they rolled away.

"Yuki!" She barked, now thoroughly awake and fit to kill.

"Oh…sorry?" Her neighbour never meant to disturb anyone's sleep, they just moved at a volume that was unnatural for most people.

"Ugh." She closed her eyes again.

"Li-Li?"

"Wh-what!"

"It's almost midday."

She sat straight up. "Crim! I h-h-haven't got her robe out! O-or her paints! Did she s-suh…send for me?"

Yuki attempted to flatten their hair, but the blue spikes just bounced right back. "I don't think she's back yet."

"Huh?"

"Well she didn't send for you, and Princess has been mooching about with Gia all day."

Li-Li looked over the raised walkway between the rows of beds to where Sunshine's maid slept. Colourful dresses and robes were scattered over and under the covers, around and hanging out of the open storage compartments that bordered the recessed feather mattress. Signs of someone meticulously searching for something to wear; someone who had plenty of time to do so and no obligations or chores standing in their way. Princess was not known for being attentive to her duties (which was part of the reason why she had been an acolyte so long), but Sunshine was determined to set her on the right path, and would never let her slack off long enough to cause such a mess. Not on her first day back, at least.

"M-maybe they're r-r-resting?"

"Maybe," Yuki agreed, tying their cincture in a nice flower shape. Li-Li could never work her fingers around the images they made so easily with a single piece of rope or string—they were requested to tie hearts and butterflies for her on a daily basis, and always obliged. "Either way, both of you have another day to yourself. Will you go to the Menagerie again?"

"Hmm…" Li-Li often volunteered in the Menagerie or the Gardens, and had spent three whole cycles of the Sun and Moon bouncing between one and the other in search of work. Any work. Ever since Crim had let her retire early the day before her journey she had been hopelessly bored. "I d-don't think so…I-I duh-didn't get m-much to do yesterday."

"Right. You said that." They thumbed the knot and tugged on the ends of their belt, though it was tight enough already. "Laal gave me the morning, but she asked me to pick up a few things for later. You could keep me company, if you like?"

She grinned, and immediately began to root around for her favourite robe. "Help me w-w-with the sash, will y-you?"

"Whatever the lady needs."

*

The Market occupied the veritable heart of the Mountain; an enormous, bustling hive of stores, trades, artisans and anything in between that sat on the mouthward (that is, the side of the Mountain that sported the Maw) side of an endless chasm known as the Pit. Facing it on the other (fortward, i.e. where the Fortress and the Eyrie sat) side was the Forum, which following the downfall of the Patriarch was seldom used for its official purpose. He and many of his supporters had died on its steps, marking the end of a reign of tyranny and terror.

Some merchants who could not find space in the Market on any given day, or who did not trade enough to warrant their own store, often spilled over to the Forum, despite the scathing remarks and cold looks from more traditional denizens.

On this particular afternoon, the crowds had not yet culminated to their full potential, so that Yuki and Li-Li wound their way through the helter-skelter array of shacks, tents, stalls and stands with relative ease, and Li-Li did not get anxious. Yuki had been given a list of ingredients for dinner, but was also happy to browse, and allowed her to lead them around and around as Li-Li sniffed perfumes, sampled dishes, and ran offcuts of fabric through her fingers. She traded three jars of paint for a beaded necklace from Kata, and one more for two piping hot bowls of braised pork with vegetables and a whole bread roll from Tsai, which they ate hunkered at the feet of a dozing chimaera carved from marble by the brothers Xipe and Totec (who gave them a skin of sweetwine for free).

There were not many visitors, which disappointed her. They passed a group of Ahii all sitting shoulder-to-shoulder at one round table and eating from the one pot, hissing and croaking quietly. Li-Li offered a smile, and one reptilian head jerked up to study her for a long minute before snorting a greeting and returning to its meal. Not the friendliest people they tended to receive, but Ahii minded their own business and never caused any trouble, so they were always welcome under the Mountain.

*

After lunch (or breakfast), they divided Yuki's messages and went in opposite directions. Li-Li's first stop was Honey's tent, where Laal had placed an order for a dozen candles (*multicolours, sweet fragrance*). The two had been friends for centuries, meaning Honey knew exactly what combinations were wanted, but showed them to Li-Li anyway, smiling sweetly.

"She says 'sweet', but she really wants it cut with something. 'Not overly sweet' would be more accurate." Pulling a white-and-gold wax flower from the parcel, she held it up for Li-Li, who hesitated. Honey raised her eyebrows, and Li-Li sniffed obediently.

"V-v-very nice."

"Vanilla and cardamom," Honey declared proudly. Replacing it, she picked a pastel pink-and-green spiral next. Li-Li sniffed.

"Strawberry?"

"And?"

"Um…"

"Elderflower!"

"Of c-course."

It was only after they had gone through the entire assortment that Honey seemed satisfied that her duty had been fulfilled and allowed her to leave. Li-Li, no better informed of the differences in the scents from one plant to the next than she had been before, exited with a pulsing headache.

*

Adik was next, whose clothiers stood on stilts atop a knobby hill close to where the natural cavern wall curved down to meet the frescoed, Sidhe-made wall. The Market, like most spaces in the Mountain, was a mishmash of natural and hand-crafted scenery, and when most of the floors and walls had been tiled and levelled in centuries past, many veterans such as Adik had vehemently refused to have their little knolls or nooks touched, so the paving and frescoes were placed around them. A set of creaky wooden stairs wound around the jagged slopes, which bounced and swayed with every step upon it. Naturally, it had no rail, so Li-Li edged her way to the top, trembling as more confident patrons stomped past. The fall would not kill her—it was not even enough to properly maim her—but still, she had no desire to test it.

Laal had a rather excessive collection of scarves and headwraps, which she rotated through on a daily (if not hourly) basis, and most of them had been made by Adik and her army of apprentices. In fact, Adik was sure to contact her as soon as she came across or came up with a design she thought suited Laal, so the two were more or less constantly doing business. Today, Li-Li arrived to collect a beautiful lavender-coloured piece with gold detailing and small sequins. Tal, one of Adik's acolytes, had also included a set of gorgeous pins. Li-Li gushed over all of these so much that before she knew what was happening, an assortment of fabrics, threads, ornaments and pins had been laid out before her, and both Adik and Tal were handing pieces to her to admire.

"I-I *would* like a n-new s-suh-sash…" She admitted. Most of her own were looking rather threadbare, and she had nothing as fancy as what was being offered. "B-but I d-d-don't know wh-what to offer?"

"What can you do, Sweetheart?" Adik said, watching the way she ran the green silk through her fingers. They had no currency under the Mountain, and exchanges were made purely in goods and favours.

"I c-can m-m-make paint. B-but all acolytes do th-that…" She made to put the fabric down, reluctantly. "And I p-paint pictures. But I d-d-don't thuh-think—"

"I've seen your paints. And your paintings," Tal told her. "I can never make pigments so smooth. Certainly can't draw a garden like the one on your part of the wall."

She blushed. She had thought the girl looked familiar, now she realised she slept just a few rows down from her. Had on some occasions seen her sitting on her bed watching as she painted figures and animals resting and playing in a vibrant garden. "Thanks."

"Master," Tal turned to Adik. "You said you'd like to do something with the back wall. Maybe Li-Li can help?"

Adik clapped her on the shoulder enthusiastically. Tal staggered. "Too right! Of course she can! And she can teach *you* to paint me properly!"

Tal and Li-Li both snorted. Adik was right; though Li-Li had been too polite to say so, the paint on her ears was streaky and uneven; she could see patches of bare skin, particularly in the creases. Her face was well enough because the design she had chosen was simple, but Tal had failed to grind out some of the lumps in her paints, and the colours were inconsistent.

"I w-would be ha-happy to help."

"Right. I'll talk to Crim. See when she can spare you," Adik agreed. "You can come here every few days to work on the wall and give this one some pointers, and we'll stitch something together for you."

Li-Li, having no doubt that Crim would allow her the time, grinned right back. "I'll see you in a few days, then."

*

A few more stops, a few more bits and bobs; a small parcel from Goro the spice merchant, a bag of grain from Raj, smaller packets and tins that she threw into an ever-bulging bag. She was done soon enough, though, and sat by Hol at his flower stand to wait for Yuki. It was not a long wait at all, and they soon appeared from the stream of pedestrians with a whole plucked goose over one shoulder, a rather heavy-looking bag on their back, and a wheel of parmesan tucked into their elbow.

"That's m-more than h-h-half!"

"No. You just got the smaller bits."

Li-Li doubted it, and took the cheese from them, pretending to glare as best she could without laughing.

"To be fair, I'd take all of this over Honey shoving things into my face any day," Yuki said with a wink.

"Y-you knew!"

"I knew!"

"Take y-your cheese b-b-back."

"Can't. Too heavy."

"Hmph!"

She stormed off ahead, Yuki trotting along behind on their short little legs and pleading for forgiveness.

*

They arrived at their mistresses' apartment to find Laal fanning the fire, adding sprinkles of glowsilt as needed to make it burn hotter while remaining a manageable size. She had sliced some yams and onions already—they lay oiled and seasoned in a pan on the low round table in the centre of the living space.

"Yuki—and Li-Li, how are you, Darling—just in time. Give me the bird and finish chopping, will you?" She took the goose and set about puncturing the skin and rubbing it with whatever herbs and spices tickled her fancy, sniffing and tasting pinches from what they had brought, tossing them into a small bowl alongside cuttings from her own shelves of miniature plant to smear over and under the pale flesh.

Yuki and Li-Li sat at the opposite side of the table cutting up the vegetables she tossed to them.

"Is Princess c-c-coming?" Li-Li asked innocently.

"Ugh." Laal slammed her box of salt down on the table, making her jump a mile. "She was with me for a short while in the Foyer. I thought she might be waiting for Sunshine so I sat with her. As soon as those friends of hers turned up, it was off into the Forest, of course."

"Oh."

"We'll take that as a 'no', then." Yuki rolled their eyes. None of them had much patience for Princess and her insolence.

"Are you surprised?"

"No."

*

Sunshine burst through the door just as the goose was beginning to golden, and Laal was snipping a sprig of rosemary over the vegetables. She bore bags of plunder from the Outside, a small bouquet from Hol, and what was undoubtedly another scarf hastily wrapped in coloured paper. She danced into the room in search of her 'beloved', flames from the fire leaping up happily to greet her as she reached to embrace Laal. Her beloved accepted the affection, but remained fixed on her task. The flowers were laid down on the table without much consideration.

Yuki shot Li-Li a glance. Though the fire was more than delighted to see her, Sunshine was clearly receiving a colder-than-usual reception from Laal (though not unexpected, based on the gifts she now pushed into her hands). The air turned gloomy.

"Li-Li, looks like Crim's back," Laal said stiffly. "Why don't you go help her with Duncan?"

"Er—"

"Yuki you go with her."

Yuki did not have to be told twice. They jumped up and hoisted Li-Li along by the arm (not an easy feat when someone towers over you), kicking her chair out from under her at the same time. Li-Li, now seeing the look Laal was giving Sunshine, scrambled after them.

"Will they be alright?" She asked once they were out the door.

"Laal? Yes. She just needs to vent. Sunshine, on the other hand…" Yuki let out a long puff of breath. "Let's hope she doesn't tell her to calm down."

She laughed, but the conversation on the other side of the door was already turning sour.

"Come on," They urged, offering their arm. "Let's go get Crim."

*

Crim was Li-Li's mistress, as Laal was Yuki's. At their induction, every acolyte was assigned to an Anointed to help with their daily duties and hopefully learn a few things in the process. From the beginning, she had thrown herself into her role; preparing and mending clothes, mixing and applying the body paints that were a daily necessity for any remotely fashionable Sidhe, dressing hair, sweeping and dusting floors and shelves, running errands and generally being at the beck and call of her mistress no matter what. She was the perfect servant, and everyone agreed that Crim was lucky to have her.

All, it seemed, except for Crim herself. Despite Li-Li's enthusiasm for her work and eagerness to please the older Sidhe, Crim never seemed to have much time for her. In fact, she often felt like a nuisance.

It was no different this time; Li-Li and Yuki arrived at the Menagerie to find Crim struggling with the catches on Duncan's harness. Li-Li, ever dutiful, rushed to help, taking the opposite side and tugging at where it had twisted.

"Stop it! You're pulling his mane!" Crim scolded. She was right; Duncan stomped in agreement and snapped. Li-Li shrank back. A few more seconds of fumbling, and Crim had the bridle off the animal, who perked his ears and trotted into his stable, where his dinner was waiting for him. Polly the pony whinnied in greeting. Crim, still struggling with the tangled harness, looked up just long enough to say: "I don't need help, Little Mouse. Shouldn't you be with Laal?"

'Little Mouse'—the name Crim had given her the first day they met, when Li-Li failed to muster the courage to say her own name. Two centuries later and she still had not mustered the courage to correct her (or talk to her much at all, for that matter). It was not a bad name, really, and certainly not meant in a derogatory way, but she preferred her own.

She could never quite explain why she was so fearful of her mistress—Crim had never been cruel to her. Dismissive at times, but never in a mean-spirited way; she just preferred to do things on her own. Deep down, Li-Li knew that in her own detached way she was fond of her, but for some reason she still shied away from any form of conversation with her. Perhaps it was the darkness she saw lurking deep beneath the surface, or her temper, which was seldom lost but vividly remembered. Though both Sidhe of fire, and close friends, Sunshine and Crim could not be more different: Sunshine was a glowing ball of light—warm and bright and vibrant. Crim was more like a volcano—stony, cold and prone to violent eruptions.

"Laal is talking to Sunshine," Yuki explained. "She sent us to help you."

"Oh…sorry." Crim, clearly understanding their meaning, winced at the thought of the 'conversation' Sunshine was probably enduring, then pointed into the small wooden cart. "If you can take some of those up, I'd appreciate it."

Yuki grunted their agreement and began sorting through the bags and boxes, stacking some on the ground for Li-Li. They nudged her as they strode out of the stable, but she just stood there wringing her hands.

"Is it too heavy?"

"Huh?"

Crim pointed at her pile. "You don't have to take all of it if it's too heavy. I can manage."

Li-Li shook her head.

"Is that 'No it's not too heavy' or 'No I can't lift it'?"

Li-Li bent down and began to gather her portion of the goods. Naturally, Yuki had given her all the lighter bags, and was probably struggling up to the apartment with the heaviest things they could find.

"Mouse?"

"Unh?"

Crim pulled a small pouch from her pocket and tossed it. Li-Li dropped a bag of apples but still failed to catch it. Untying the string, she found a small soapstone mouse inside. Feigning a small laugh, she retrieved the apples from the ground (Polly had already claimed one) along with the rest of her burden.

As she scurried away, she thought she heard Crim mutter: "You're welcome?"

IV

"Oh! You're home late!" Whisper was passing with an armful of hissing badger as Crim exited the stables, and seemed far more encumbered than the latter, despite all of the baggage she carried.

"We um…got side-tracked," Crim responded, struggling to balance a basket of dried herbs and fresh flowers across her shoulders.

Whisper, turning the irate animal aside, helped to tie the cords more securely around her. "I'm guessing you found it tough? The road back is uphill, after all."

"Yeah. Uphill the whole way and hardly a minute's break."

"Li-Li was looking for you, you know. She came and sat by the stables for hours yesterday evening."

"I didn't know," She said. She struggled to make sense of Li-Li, who followed her around silently one minute, only to retreat as soon as she was spoken to. "I saw her just now, but she ran away as soon as she came."

"Maybe she wouldn't run away if you weren't so mean to her."

"I am *not…!*" Then she saw Whisper's lip quirk. "Shut up."

"Did you get her a present, like we mentioned? Your 'peace offering'?"

"Yes. She took it and ran away."

A soft giggle. "She's just a flighty one, Crim. And you're…not the most charismatic yourself. You'll get there, both of you."

"Hmph." Crim poked the badger in the rear. He snapped his teeth at the offense. "What happened to this one?"

"He got into a fight with another male. See?" Manoeuvring the grouchy mustelid around, she extended his right rear leg, which boasted clear puncture wounds on either side.

Gibber, Whisper's twin took this as her queue to jump around the corner of the stables, mumbling and holding up what seemed at first glance to be a bloodied bundle of rags. Her silver-grey hair was unkempt as always, her robes stained with the day's adventures.

"The loser, I presume?" Crim remarked, and Gibber laughed, swinging the mangled carcass.

Whisper narrowed her eyes at her sister. "Ugh."

Gibber held the remains out to her like a gift and reached to grab her arm with one hand, leaving sticky, blood-scented paw prints on her sleeve. "Crim…come."

"Sorry, I can't. Mentor wants to see me."

Gibber stomped her foot, badger swinging uncomfortably close to Crim's face. "Come!"

"Not now Gibber, sorry."

"Crim come!"

Whisper, sensing her sister's agitation wrapped her free arm around her, and stroked her mussed hair. "Crim's busy. Next time."

"Criiim!"

Crim's heart sank. She would prefer to spend some time with the twins, rather than receive whatever lecture Mentor was sure to give her.

"Next time I swear. I'll help you all day."

"She needs to go see her Mentor now, My Love," urged Whisper, rubbing her back. Only then did she allow herself to be led.

"…next time," Gibber agreed, calming with every stroke, but still eyeing Crim suspiciously until she nodded.

She studied Gibber as they walked away. Watched her toss the dead animal in her hands around and giggle while Whisper tried to shush her. Others pretended not to notice as they passed; everyone knew about Gibber. Most treated her with polite tolerance, others like Crim managed to befriend her, a select few unsavoury types resented her, and her sister spent all her time trying to steer her away from them. When necessary, Whisper could be fiercely protective of Gibber, and could be seen thumbing the hilt of her scimitar if someone looked at them the wrong way.

The process of making a Sidhe was a traumatic experience, one that most of the denizens of the Mountain preferred to forget. The majority of fledglings awoke in a broken state of mind, their memories and instincts wiped by a process that reconstructed them from the inside out, twinning their soul with the spirit of a god for all eternity. Frightened, angry, lost and alone, they were nurtured back to sanity by the love and acceptance of their kin. For a few, such as Gibber, however, the efforts of those around them were not enough. Unable to forget the horrors of the Making, they remained unravelled.

Of the three of them, Gibber had been the first to rise—two centuries before Whisper, and a further three before Crim. She had crawled from her resting place silent and shivering into the arms of her mentor, who fed her and coddled her as best she could. Time passed and she found a voice, but no words, and so her crueller peers named her 'Gibber', after the noises she made when excited. Whisper, coming later, had tried to give her another name, for a long time she called her by anything and everything that came to mind, but by then Gibber only responded to one thing.

Crim had come centuries later, but no less broken. She had been vicious, feral and inconsolable at the very beginning; Laal and Sunshine had been frightened of her, and not without good reason—she had even attacked Mother when she came to welcome her, tearing into her neck with her teeth and clawing marks into her forearms that remained to this day. Somehow, Sunshine and Laal had calmed her, but she remained manic, unpredictable. She spent her earliest days under the Mountain mute and vacant, staring wide-eyed at nothing in particular and responding to no stimuli, only to snap all of a sudden and attack those around her. Mentor, Sunshine and Laal had done their best to coax her out of her shell, and also bore the scars of their efforts, but despite their love she remained unable to live, and only endured. That was until one day, sitting in the Gardens, Whisper had joined them under their shady pear tree, and introduced Crim to Gibber. As Mentor told it:

"I think she saw something in you that she recognised. Perhaps the pain she felt herself. She saw that and somehow knew how to help. She took your hand and led you away under the trees, babbling all the while. I followed, of course, not knowing what she was at. For her sake as well; you were still not cured of your fits of rage, and could turn at any second. Anyway, she brought you over and sat you down on a log, then called a tiny bird down from the branches—you know how those two are with creatures…Well, it was like magic, and maybe it was, but Gibber has never been able to explain it. A little robin redbreast; she put him in your hands and you just seemed to start, like someone shook you from sleep. You looked down and stroked his feathers. You *spoke*, Crim. First to the robin, then to Gibber, and she listened, of course. You told her all about a little robin you had found in a bush just the day before—of course that had happened when you were alive, not the day before at all. You arrived, at last."

So it was that Crim came to truly *be* under the Mountain and began to find her place. So it was that she owed Gibber her life.

*

Crim found Mentor in the Arena. She was sparring with Silver when she arrived, so did not immediately notice her. Knowing better than to disturb them, Crim sat on a bench in the shadows by the wall, where the bright sunrock's light could not reach. The Arena was circular; a large sand pit bordered by arches and further encircled by this darkened walkway. Opposite the entrance she had come through was the door to the Armory, where Silver kept shelves upon shelves of weapons for training. Dull, mortal weapons of course, as juniors were not permitted to train with truesteel. Elders and priestesses who had already finished commissions brought their own weapons; in this case two finely crafted *katar* clanged melodically against Silver's rather plain longsword.

A fully-trained Sidhe in combat is akin in many ways to a dancer. As Mentor and Silver dove and leapt and pirouetted around one another, Crim was once again reminded of this. And reminded also of her own heavy-footed, jerky movements when in possession of any weapon, or her own *draoi* (a Sidhe's ability to manipulate the world around them, which mortals might think magical), for that matter. Arm moving so fast it was barely visible, Silver thrust forward, and in the blink of an eye Mentor darted aside, disappearing for a split second and reappearing a few steps away. Round and round they went, one movement flowing into the next, until Mentor made a daring jump, swinging her katar in a scissoring motion and aiming for Silver neck.

Two well-timed flicks of her blade, and Silver knocked both arms away without even flinching, the point hovering before Mentor's throat.

"Do you see what I did, Crim?"

"Um…" Springing up, Crim replayed those last few seconds in her head.

"I'll give you a hint; you're going to unlearn it if it kills you."

"…You got impatient."

"And?"

"Ran in without thinking."

"And?"

39

"Gave yourself no chance to disengage."

"Good. Now, go pick something out. Don't take forever. One for you and one for me."

Crim obediently jogged into the Armory, where as usual she was immediately overwhelmed by the sheer number of items stacked on shelves, thrown into crates and chests, hanging from hooks fixed to the walls and ceiling. There were aisles and aisles for her to get lost in, to get distracted by the glistening steel and carved wood—

"Crim!"

"Right!" Grabbing the two closest to her, she hurried back out.

"Really?" Mentor eyed the two spears she had chosen. "You *do* remember last time, don't you?"

"Yes." Last time she had tried to show off and nearly impaled herself. "...should I get something else?"

"No! ...No. I really just want a word. Silver, do you mind?"

Silver bowed and took her leave. A word. Crim's stomach churned. She wondered how much trouble she was in for staying Outside longer than permitted. She edged into the middle of the Arena, spear gripped tightly in her hands, not at all ready when Mentor came at her.

"Hands like this, remember? Move your feet, Crim, your *feet!*"

With one quick sweep, Mentor knocked her legs out from under her, hard wood of the pole cracking against her shins. Crim hit the dirt and lay there for a bit. She hated combat training.

"I thought we were going to talk?"

"We will." Mentor raised her spear and struck her between the shoulders with the haft just as Crim tried to pick herself up. "*Move*, Girl! Dart if you have to!"

Crim rolled away instead. 'Darting', in Sidhe-terms, was the action of momentarily shedding one's physical form in order to move quickly from one position to another, like she had just seen Mentor do. A horrifying process of pulling oneself apart and shoving oneself back together again before disintegrating. No longer mortals, they were not strictly bound to their physical forms, so performing such feats was simply a matter of learning them, and also learning not to fear them. Crim had not quite mastered the latter.

She stood up slowly instead, vainly trying to knock some of the sand from her skirts. Clearly annoyed, Mentor increased her speed, launching across the circle in an instant and assailing her with a barrage of quick jabs and thrusts. Crim tried to knock her attacks aside, tried to step around them, then, unable to match her, backed away instead, and eventually managed to get one of the pillars between them.

"Coward!" Came the irritated shout, and a spear clashed threateningly against the stone, one end flashing into Crim's view where she hid. Perhaps if she kept this up Mentor would leave her alone.

Yes. That's most likely to happen.

Clicking her tongue, Mentor chose this moment to dart herself. She appeared at Crim's side faster than she could react, spear opening a great gash from wrist to elbow. With a yelp, Crim dropped her weapon to press against the gush of blood that spilled forth.

"Ignore it!" Mentor barked. "It is nothing!"

She was right; to their kind, wounds inflicted by mortal weapons healed almost as soon as they appeared. Crim removed her hand to see that while it still looked unpleasant, her arm had already stopped bleeding. Still hurt, though.

"Ignore it!"

Retrieving her spear from the ground, Crim moved back into position opposite Mentor. Her opponent wasted not a second, but jabbed at her. With the blade now turned towards her and the haft away, the threat of imminent injury became ever more real, and she broke into a sweat struggling to dodge and weave and parry.

"Move!"

Crim skipped away.

"Faster!"

Bouncing off the wall, she managed to get her foot up against the masonry and made a leap right over Mentor's head and behind her. Anyone else might have been impressed, but Mentor only caught her in the stomach with the broad side of the handle. Knocking her clean out of the air.

"Ooof!"

"Faster, come on!"

She would have to do it, she realised. Or Mentor would beat her black and blue. There would be no hesitation to open her up, either, if she continued to disobey. She saw the glint of bloodlust in Mentor's glare. Grasping her weapon firmly and closing her eyes, Crim listened for the next thrust.

There.

As it whistled through the air, she turned her attention in, feeling for every single tiny little atom of her being and carefully began to pick herself apart. Once this was done, she only had to grope around the physical plain for where she wanted to go, and choose to be there. All of this happened in seconds; first, she was standing waiting for Mentor's blow, then she turned to a dark red dust, a cloud that burst apart and travelled through the air in ribbons of mist, and finally she reappeared at Mentor's side, and caught hold of her shaft in one hand. Mentor, pleasantly surprised, let out a loud "Aha!" and knocked her flat on her rear.

"That's it!"

Crim groaned, rubbing her bruised cheeks. "I still lost."

"Yes. But I left you in one piece."

"Thanks?"

"Now put these back. We'll talk on the way."

"Yes, Mentor."

-

"You found the Outside so alluring?"

They were edging their way up the Winding Stair, stopping on occasion to stare out at the large Moon that peeked through and was magnified tenfold by the glass of regular slit windows that pierced the Mountain walls. In some places, the inner panes had been covered with stained glass, spilling coloured imagery across the flagstone and rock within. Mentor moved with deliberate sluggishness; the Stair was quiet, giving them the time and space to discuss Crim's experience openly.

"Yes…no…That is to say…" Her pupil stammered. "At first, it was. It seemed so much more vibrant, for some reason. But as the hours went on—and I spent most of the night concerned with it—I began to feel more and more like an outsider."

"And now?"

"Now? Well, I think I could go back, but only for a short time again. I think if I stayed any longer it would weigh me down."

"The lack of 'belonging'?" Mentor absently moved her hands across a pillar of moonlight, summoning shadow puppets on the wall opposite. "Was it so bad?"

"I think it could eat away, if you let it." Crim jabbed a finger at one of the figures, and he crumpled into a ball.

"Hmm…did you remember anything?"

"Yes. Pieces. I saw a woman light a fire to make the food, for example, and I remembered making one from sticks."

"From sticks?"

"Yep."

"A fire?"

"Yes. Sometimes rocks."

Mentor cocked a brow. "Anything more?"

"Nothing I'm certain of. It's there, just not clear."

"I was the same, the first time."

"Did you remember it all, in time?"

"No, no. Not all. But enough."

"I'm not sure how much I want back."

"Fair." Her teacher pursed her thin lips into nothing. "But you could benefit in a lot of ways, as well."

"How?"

"Sunshine named you."

"Yes, I know." She did not remember—this had happened in the dark days before she met Gibber.

"I think perhaps you might come up with something more personal."

Crim mulled this over. There was nothing wrong with her name, really—it served its purpose—but from time to time she *did* find herself considering others. "My name…"

"I think you could benefit from going Outside a few more times. Not immediately; whenever you're ready," Mentor assured her. "Mother will want to speak with you, in her own time. You can make your decision then."

"M-Mother!" She exclaimed, wheeling to face her Mentor. What had she done? Mother rarely summoned her underlings, and when she did…

"She has expressed an interest in you."

"An…interest?" Crim had a most unsettling vision of her head on a platter.

V

Most inhabitants of the Mountain understood the concept of time. That is to say; they were aware of its existence, but also understood that it was irrelevant to their kind. Any notion of *'action' should be done at 'time'* was generally believed to be a vestigial instinct—one gradually unlearned, though not entirely quashed. Things such as meals, hobbies, chores and sleep were done more or less whenever one wanted, with very little schedule.

The above applied to all denizens, except those under the teachings of Mentor. Sunshine had often remarked—usually out of earshot—that her superior upon her Making had 'constructed a sort of time unto herself'. Her mentees, by extension, were all expected to observe the movements of the Sun and Moon, and plan their lives 'properly'. That meant rising in the 'morning', when the sun rocks turned from orange to yellow, channelling the light of their miniscule star as it climbed the fortward slopes, and retiring when the moon was halfway down the mouthward side. The younger Sidhe complained loudly and regularly about all this, but agreed it was probably in their best interests to do as they were told. Mentor was not unreasonable or cruel, but her scorn was cold and biting.

So they had dwelt peacefully together for an age, until Princess arose.

*

Princess, by all accounts had been created with the express purpose of testing Mentor and, by extension, Sunshine. Whenever she misbehaved (which was often), her mistress was forced to endure another rant from their teacher about the 'proper way of things', manners, and 'basic decency'. The two of them had been working on ways to correct their young ward's behaviour for what seemed like their entire existences (though in fact it had only been around five centuries), to no avail. She remained as trying as ever.

On the eve of Sunshine and Crim's return from the Outside, it was customary for their servants to greet them as Li-Li and Yuki had done. Though not obligatory, it was a matter of pure respect, a way for the younger to let their elder know they were at their service. By Laal's account, Princess had disappeared at the start of the day, and been found causing a ruckus with her friends outside the Forum. Laal had immediately summoned her back to their chambers, and insisted she come along to wait in the Foyer, at much objection. She had gone under threat of a thrashing, and managed to disappear while Laal was talking to some of the other loiterers.

It was only well after dinner was done, and the entire goose picked clean (and even beyond this point; Crim and Yuki both had the habit of munching on bones, and continued to return to the carcass throughout the night), that Princess finally appeared at the door. She sauntered right across the room without so much as a 'hello' and reached for the jug at Sunshine's elbow.

"Ow! Mentor!"

Sunshine turned, not having noticed her underling before, and found Princess struggling helplessly in Mentor's iron grasp, her fingers just brushing the handle. Mentor sniggered. "You have some gall, girl."

"I just—"

"Don't you dare!" Mentor said flatly, shoving the girl's slender arm aside. "You've been gone all day, and now you walk in here and try to take your mistress's wine. Don't you *dare.*"

Princess had a doll-like face, with round rosy cheeks, bright blue eyes, and a crown of bouncy golden curls that fell about her shoulders. When she pouted, her cherub's mouth quivering and lashes glittering with tears, it was hard to remember just how old she was, just how vicious she could be. Hard to resist giving her anything she wanted. They all presumed this was why they had been so easy on her in the beginning, had all spoiled her rotten. And now they were certainly paying the price.

"But I'm *thirsty*, Mentor!" She whined, snatching at the jug again, attempting to twist her arm out of her grasp. "I just wanted *one cup.*"

"You did not ask."

Still pouting, she turned to Sunshine. "I'm sorry, Mistress. May I have some?"

"No."

That little mouth dropped open, then tried in vain to form words. Eventually she sat back, defeated and glaring at the table. Mentor back glared a moment longer, then let it go.

Sunshine, moving her wine out of reach, (she knew Princess was not beyond swiping it) spared her a glance, only to be pinched by Laal.

"Pay her no mind," her lover whispered. "She has to learn."

"Maybe she really is thirsty. She just wants a drop of wine."

Another pinch. "Don't *you* dare."

She turned her attention back to her cards, though there was not much point; Crim had already matched three sets, and only needed her forth to win. She had not asked for any cards last turn. Sunshine, on the other hand, had a full hand and no matches. She was still wondering why she had agreed to play cards, of all things; Crim always won.

The round went on, then another. Crim won on the third, by which time even Li-Li was asking to play something else. A rare show of defiance against her own mistress.

"You'll be trying to take the wine from in front of *me* soon enough," Crim joked, winking at Sunshine who was still guarding her jug.

Li-Li sat up straight, aghast. "N-no. I would n-n-never—"

Crim reached over and topped up her goblet, causing poor Li-Li even more confusion (underlings were always expected to fill their elders' cups). The young one did not understand her teasing at all, and often reacted rather dramatically. Sunshine pitied the poor child sometimes; she was so fearful of Crim, yet wanted her approval so very much, concerned herself with impressing her mistress to the point where she could not see that Crim already adored her, in her own detached way.

Presently, Princess moved from her side and went to sit with the other younglings, not acknowledging the way Yuki watched her. Sunshine had almost forgotten she was there; had blocked out her sulking and her huffing and her puffing as she watched them play. She observed as the little nuisance settled next to Li-Li and offered a suspiciously innocent smile which Li-Li nervously returned. Yuki barred their teeth at her, jagged molars coming together in a sharp *snap*. They had no time for Princess and they were also fiercely protective of Li-Li. One false move and Sunshine imagined herself having to pry those gnashers away from Princess' throat.

They changed games in favour of one Sunshine rather liked; a simple matter of moving four pieces around a board to reach their objective. For this, they split into teams; Crim and Yuki, Laal and Mentor, and Sunshine with Li-Li. Princess, still in a huff, refused to even read the question cards. She just sat there criticising every move poor Li-Li made.

"Move it that way."

"No th-this is better." Li-Li pushed their piece in a rather risky move counter-clockwise.

"*That way!*" Out of the corner of her eye, Sunshine saw Princess reach for it.

Li-Li lifted the wooden animal out of reach. "You d-d-didn't even want to play!"

"And you're being *stupid*."

"Princess," said Sunshine, a note of warning in her voice. "If you want to play, you can just ask."

Princess ignored her, but went for the piece again. "Stupid."

"Princess!" Li-Li was turning red now. Across the table, both Crim and Yuki looked ready to leap at her tormentor.

Still determined, Princess moved more quickly this time, and snapped the piece right out of the other girl's fingers. She had no chance to move it, however; in a flash, Crim was across the table, and had her by the wrist (the same one Mentor had caught, incidentally).

"Li-Li said *no.*"

Princess snarled, that angelic mask falling away to reveal her true form. She moved her head as if to bite Crim's hand. Before she even turned, however, there came a loud *crack!* And a shriek, and Crim threw her to the floor. Sunshine was surprised to see that Princess came crawling around the table, sobbing and holding her broken, bloodied forearm out to *her,* of all people. Behind her, Li-Li wordlessly placed her piece back on the board. Visibly shaken by the whole thing, she quietly started to shuffle through the cards, hands trembling and unable to look at the injury.

"I don't know what you expected," said Sunshine, with a sigh. Still her heart felt heavy with pity. Part of her wanted to scorn Crim for being so aggressive— Princess hadn't meant any real harm, but she had only been defending Li-Li.

"B-b-but…I…" Princess blubbered. She tried to straighten her arm herself, wincing and whimpering as she could not find the will to set it fully. "Please, Mistress."

"Go to your dormitory, Princess."

Princess sat back on her haunches, looking like she had not quite understood what she was being told. She held her arm out further. "Mistress, I can't—"

"*Go,* Princess," she ordered. "You've disturbed our evening quite enough."

Those perfect little lips twisted all the way down. Those big blue eyes sparkled with tears. "I just wanted to play."

"No, you didn't. Now go."

Sniff. Princess stood, hugging her twisted limb to her chest. She tried to look around one last time for support, but found none. Those that met her gaze met it with anger. *Sniff.* She nodded, curls falling in front of her face. The floorboards creaked loudly as she tiptoed over to the door. *Sniff.* The hinges squeaked quietly. Princess cast Sunshine one last, pleading glance.

Go. Her mistress demanded.

*

"Was I too hard on her?"

The sunrock overhead was already burning bright. It was well past midmorning and hurrying towards noon. Mentor had given them the hours before the sun was highest to do with as they pleased, and she had spent all of those hours in bed. Laal was bustling around the room, laying her robes out on the bed and picking paints out of the vanity by the wall. Clad only in a thin chemise, her hair still in disarray, she looked almost too good to resist. Sunshine eyed her voluptuous brown thighs as she moved, watched the sway of her broad hips and the slight bounce of her generous breasts. Even her plump tummy was gorgeous. And that face—that square jaw and high cheekbones, turquoise eyes and chin-length platinum waves. Succulent lips that she now tinted with vibrant pink. Laal the beauty. Most beautiful being under the Mountain. Sunshine couldn't imagine anything better than waking up next to her, drinking in all of her grace every day. Wanted no-one else to share her worries with.

"No, you weren't."

"Maybe if I just talked to her—"

"You've tried that, remember?" Laal reclined next to her. "Several times. Mentor too. That's just how she is."

"Yes, but if I could just make her *understand...*"

"Sunny. You know me. So you know I do not say this lightly: she is a lost cause."

Sunshine toyed with her baby hairs, and allowed Laal to wrap around her, soft and warm and smelling of vanilla and spice. She kissed her neck as Sunshine lay in thought. Laal was her more sensible side, the one who knew what her limits were and how to set up limits, too. The one who would tell her she was being naïve or rash or a downright idiot without hesitation. Sunshine's heart was often too soft, especially when it came to Princess, and she spent much time worrying about her, making up excuses for her behaviour and trying to hide some of her transgressions from Mentor. She knew she shouldn't—Laal reminded her of this every day—but deep in her soul she knew Princess was lost, hurt, angry. Perhaps with just a bit of kindness she could be great?

"Perhaps if I—" Sunshine sat up, displacing her lover, who made no effort to conceal her offense. The idea struck her so hard she was compelled to move, crossing the room in just three strides of her long legs. She pulled a robe from the closet, hanger and all. "I will train her."

"No," Laal groaned, attempting to pull her back down.

"She has not been trained since she was a fledgling."

"There is a reason," her lover sighed. "And also untrue. Mentor has tried. I have tried. *You* have tried yourself. And not very long ago."

"So perhaps some of this stems from boredom—"

"She is simply volatile. Defiant. Unteachable. She refuses to listen and she refuses to learn."

"And if I can just teach her to use her powers."

"Please do not. She already tries to torment poor Li-Li with what little she commands."

"She will be able to channel her feelings through her *draoi*."

"That is what I would be concerned about."

"Don't be!" Sunshine pounced rather suddenly, pecking Laal on the lips, and leapt away just as quick.

"Sunny..."

"Don't worry I'll be fine!"

The Servants' dorms occupied the levels immediately below the Lake; the damp, cold levels that none of the Anointed wanted to live in. Accessed by a few dark, steep servants' stairs, it was divided into eight long halls that housed roughly fifty younglings and fledglings each. Princess, as well as Li-Li and Yuki, was assigned to the sourceward-most dormitory, overseen by Bull.

The old matron looked up as Sunshine approached, and hopped down from his bench outside the little guardhouse by the dormitory entrance (due to past younglings' misbehaviour, none of these bed chambers had a door any more). Tossing his crochet work aside (it may have been a hat), he took her by both hands, grinning ear to ear.

"Sunshine! Always a pleasure, Darling. Come here, into the light. Let me look at you!"

She obliged, smiling back and bending down to offer a kiss on each cheek; Bull had been her matron once upon a time. "You look the same as always."

"And *you* are well on your way to becoming an elder, I can see!"

She guffawed. "I think Laal might be ahead of me there."

"Oh yes, Laal!" He clapped his hands. "Ever the diligent student I expect?"

"Diligent, yes."

"Still keeping you on your toes, is she?"

"Yes indeed."

He chuckled back. "To what do I owe the pleasure, Dear?"

"I'm looking for Princess."

"Princess! What has that little miscreant done now!"

"Nothing…Nothing today, that is."

"Not here to give her a hiding?"

"That remains to be seen. She is my maid, you see."

Bull gave her a look that conveyed both pity and amusement. "Rather you than me."

"Thanks, Bull."

He pointed down the rows. "On the left. She's still asleep, of course."

-

There were two lines of beds on either side, and Princess was curled up on one seven rows down, immediately across the aisle from Yuki and Li-Li. The other two, ever the model of good servants, were already dressed, and busy painting each other's ears, hands and feet. They waved as she approached.

"Did Laal send for me?" Yuki asked, carefully evening out the line of lavender-coloured paste stretching from Li-Li's ear to her temple.

"No, she's hardly up. She'll want to eat first, so take your time."

They nodded.

"And Crim hasn't even surfaced, Li-Li."

"Sh-She rarely c-c-calls in the morning, a-anyway," Li-Li remarked, somewhat bitterly.

"As for this one," Sunshine jumped down off the walkway and gave Princess a kick in the leg. "Good morning!"

Princess grumbled and batted groggily at nothing.

"*Good morning!*" Sunshine shouted this time, jostling her. "Get up and get dressed. I am summoning you."

Princess, not thoroughly awake, shoved her away and pulled her blanket over her head. Sunshine ripped it away once more, only for it to be replaced in the next instant. Then, with a click of her fingers, she set it on fire. Princess yelped and jumped into the air, slapping at the hem of her nightgown, which was also smoking.

"Bitch!" She spat.

"Oh good, you're up." Behind Sunshine, Yuki and Li-Li were choking on muffled laughter. "Get dressed, *now.*"

"What? Why?"

"Because I told you to."

"But I don't want—" Princess gasped again as flames licked at the hem of her gown.

"Don't worry, they're not hot," Sunshine assured her. "Not yet. Better take that off and get dressed before they get worse."

Spewing profanities, Princess threw off the gown, and dug through the contents of her cubby stark naked while the others watched. Finally picking out a robe, she sprinted into Bull's guardhouse, slamming and locking the door from the inside before he could even react.

Sunshine sighed. "How long will it take her?"

"Hours," Yuki replied, standing. "Hope you're not in a hurry."

With that, they trotted off, trailing deep blue footprints as their paint had not yet fully dried. Sunshine looked at her own feet, brown and bare and now covered in dirt from walking through the Mountain. She sighed again.

Li-Li cleared her throat. "W-wuh-would you like…I-I mean…I c-c-could do that for you?"

"Hm?" She looked down to find the girl already picking colours out and laying them on the floor between her bed and Yuki's. "Oh…you don't mind?"

"I like it." Li-Li gave a shy smile, already making for the water fountain. "C-Crim doesn't bother m-much with her p-p-paints so I rarely get t-to do it."

So Sunshine sat on the boards between their beds, and Li-Li washed her feet, hands and face. She chose a pearly white and vibrant magenta from among the pots laid out, and the maid set to work, first coating her palms, soles and ears generously with the white, then using both colours on smaller brushes to draw basic patterns across her feet and hands, up her legs and arms, and over her face. She was quick and attentive; the work was done with plenty of time to spare before Princess emerged.

"D-do you want anything done wi-with your h-h-hair?"

Sunshine touched her tight curls, which she had secured away from her forehead with a blue headband. "No, that's fine, Sweetheart. Thank you."

"Right." Averting her eyes, Li-Li began to replace the paints back into her cubby. They had a certain order, Sunshine noticed, arranged by colour and intensity.

"Li-Li?"

"Unh?"

"Why are you afraid of Crim?"

"I'm n-not!" The poor girl nearly dropped her magenta.

"You are. I know. She knows too, as a matter of fact."

"She does?"

"Yep."

Li-Li's ears flushed, and she lowered her head. "Well…"

"Does it have anything to do with what she said? That first day?"

"…Sh-she said she didn't w-w-want me."

Sunshine brushed the girl's blush-coloured hair out of her face, and lifted her chin to look into those forest-green eyes. "You know that has nothing to do with *you*?"

Li-Li squirmed away. "How so?"

"Crim is—well, Mentor calls it 'nostalgic'. Laal calls it 'angst-ridden'," she tried to explain. "It happens sometimes to our kind; even though they can't remember any of it, Sidhe can sometimes become mournful for their past lives, become angry that they were taken from them and brought under the Mountain. They act out by resisting our norms. There's no harm in it, really, at least there's none meant. They're just…a little lost."

Li-Li lifted her head. "So what she said…"

"I think she meant she didn't want a maid. Not *you*, specifically."

"Oh."

"Crim's not bad, but she can be a little crude in the way she talks. I doubt she even realised how it might make *you* feel."

"Oh."

"Do you understand?"

A nod. "I think so."

Sunshine patted her on the head. "Good."

"Sunshine?"

"Uh-huh?"

"Is th-that why P-P-Princess is the way she is, t-too?"

She blinked. "You know, I never thought of that."

"Do you think you can help her?"

Sunshine pulled the girl into an embrace, entirely without warning. Li-Li yelped but passively endured the sudden display of affection. "You go talk to Crim. I'll see what I can do with Princess."

VI

Li-Li was not the bravest of souls. In fact, her nervous and flighty nature had inspired Crim to nickname her 'Little Mouse' when she was newly-arisen, and, since she had never formally introduced herself, or uttered more than a few words to her mistress in their time together under the Mountain, that was what she continued to call her. Yuki often urged her to 'speak up for herself', but it had never seemed important enough, so she held her tongue.

Today was different. She told herself this as she marched up the servants' stairs to her mistress' chamber. Today she would voice her grievances. All of them. She would not quail.

Yuki and Laal were seated at the table when she arrived, the former twisting the latter's hair into thick braids that would easily tuck under her headscarf. Laal was simultaneously applying a fresh coat of paint to her trimmed nails and humming tunelessly. She smiled and blew a kiss to Li-Li.

"She's not up yet, Sweetheart."

"O-oh." Li-Li wrung her hands.

"Her first trip Outside; she's probably still dreaming about it," Laal went on. "Still processing, at least. You'll understand when it's your turn."

"I'm sh-sh-sure."

"Sit. Have something to eat. There's congee on the fire."

Li-Li's stomach grumbled at the sight of the thick rice porridge. Laal had also prepared some boiled eggs, crisp bacon and sliced scallion to go on top, as well as a pot of tea. All were kept warm by obedient flames, who had been trained by Sunshine not to overcook food. She helped herself to a bowl.

"Wh-when will she be up?"

"I've not been brave enough to disturb her," Laal answered. "Yuki and I were planning to go picking, if you would like to join us?"

She took her head, mouth full of rich, soft egg. Laal and Sunshine had always been very good to her, and treated her as their second maid of sorts, but today was the day she would connect with her own mistress. Perhaps they could go to the Library together. She always wondered what Crim did there. Or even the Menagerie...

"Did you see Sunshine?"

"Yes sh-she came to get P-P-Princess."

"And was Princess feeling...cooperative today?"

Li-Li prodded at her breakfast. "She...d-did what she was told. M-more or l-less."

Laal inspected her nails and began to fold her scarf. "She's going to wear Sunshine out, that girl."

"Princess isn't suh-so bad."

Yuki snorted.

"She isn't!"

"Tell me that next time she steals your paints," They retorted.

"She c-c-can't ma-make her own."

"Can't be bothered to more like."

"Please tell me she didn't paint Sunshine," Laal said, clearly imagining the potential outcome.

"No, I did."

Relief. "Good. Thank you."

The fall of feet from behind Crim's door. A bang and a curse. Li-Li shot up. Yuki gave her a questioning look but did not comment. Laal did not notice; she was busy pinning her scarf into place.

"Now!" She clapped her hands and adjusted her robe. "Sound like your mistress is up, Li-Li. We'll leave you to it."

She pecked leaned over and Li-Li on the cheek as she stood. "And don't worry if she's grouchy."

*

Li-Li tapped lightly on the door, listening to the sounds of Crim moving about inside. She thought she heard the tinkle of broken glass.

"Come."

The door slid back to reveal Crim crouched by her dressing table, holding up the pieces of a fallen vase. She held them up as Li-Li entered, looking agitated.

"I bumped into the table and...well...you see."

56

Nodding, Li-Li went on her knees and began to gather the shards into her skirt. It was mortal glass, so there was no need to be careful. At least, she saw no need until one of the edges bit into her skin. She hissed and sucked her finger.

Crim laughed. "Careful. It still hurts."

She felt herself turning red, and quickly stood up, looking for somewhere to dump the glass.

"Drop them into the fire," Crim instructed.

Still with one finger in her mouth, she held her skirt up, edged awkwardly over to the hearth and shook the pieces out. With a snap of her mistress' fingers, the flames leapt up around them, heating enough to reduce them to glowing blobs. When she then inspected her hand, she found the cut already scabbed over.

"You'll get used to it," The older Sidhe informed her. "Soon enough you'll barely notice mortal wounds. Well…most of them. Larger ones are still a problem, and harder to ignore."

Li-Li nodded again and tiptoed past her to the dressing table. Opening the drawers, she found the small pots of paint she had made many moons ago still there, though completely out of order—Crim had clearly been using them, but treated them in the same way as the rest of the things in her room. She eyed the unmade bed and open wardrobe. Not important. Pulling her gaze away from the disarray, she picked out three colours and set them on the table, then, without making eye contact, gestured for Crim to sit. Her mistress, clearly amused, settled into the chair and tied her tangle of red hair out of her face with a piece of (surprisingly sturdy) string. Li-Li diligently set about preparing her as she had for Sunshine, all the while searching for the correct words.

"How long have you been here, Little Mouse?"

The question came suddenly and unexpectedly. Li-Li stared up at Crim, brain lagging behind her ears.

"Must be a couple of centuries now."

Nod.

"Though I'm not sure I know what a century *is* anymore."

Nod.

"Do you want to go Outside? Are you looking forward to it, when you are eventually anointed?"

Li-Li shook her head. Crim frowned, then let out a light laugh.

"You've foiled yourself there, Mouse."

Blink.

"Now you have to tell me why."

She was turning scarlet again. Li-Li opened her mouth, but it snapped shut of its own accord. *Go on.*

"When I was like you it was all I could think about."

Nod.

"Oh *come on!*"

This was said with so much frustration that Li-Li physically recoiled, and felt all the more foolish for it.

Crim's expression softened. "No, I'm not angry. I just want to know."

Taking a deep breath, Li-Li forced her tongue to form the words. "I-i-i-it's g-gone."

"What?"

"Guh...gone."

"Gone?"

Nod.

"What's gone?"

Shaking, Li-Li blurted, a little too loud. "Home!"

Crim nodded this time. "Yes. I suppose it is. For both of us."

This was not so difficult. Her hands still trembled, but Li-Li felt her nerves settle a little. "D-d-do y-you ruh...r-r-ruh..."

"Relax, Little Mouse."

"Do y-y-you um...remember?"

"Remember?"

"Before?"

"Oh," Crim tucked a wayward strand of hair behind her ear. "No. At least, I don't think so. I talked about this with Sunshine and Mentor, as well. There are times when I feel like I've *almost* unearthed some memory or image and then it just—" She waved her hand. "Drifts away."

She took a larger breath this time. "I do."

Her mistress pulled away from the brush to stare at her. "What?"

"I do," Li-Li announced. "I r-remember."

Gently, Crim took the brush from her hand and set it on the table, brow furrowed. "Tell me."

Having never confided in any one, not even Yuki, Li-Li hesitated. Sidhe hardly ever spoke of their lives before the Mountain, and she had always assumed that this was some sort of unwritten rule. Being asked to describe those times felt surprisingly intimate, and she was not certain she wanted to share with Crim.

The older Sidhe relaxed back in her chair. "Of course, you don't have to."

But this might be her only chance to connect with her mistress. "Umm…I-I…I had four sisters."

"Four?"

"Yes. A-at least I'm fairly certain. There m-m-may have been wuh-one more…o-or maybe a b-b-brother. I think someone d-d-died. An infant. Some-sometimes I see a b-bundle on a p-puh-pyre." She measured its length out with her hands. "I hear my mother crying."

"Your Mother?"

"She c-cries, and my fa-father puts his a-a-arm around her."

"Father…" Crim's face was an unreadable mask, but her voice cracked.

"And c-c-cats!" Li-Li quickly changed the subject. "So m-m-many cats! I u-used to chase them around the v-v-village!"

Crim forced a smile.

"I used to p-p-play in the r-river when it was hot…It w-was shallow around th-th-the reeds. A-and there were b-big fuh-frogs!"

A sigh, weighted. "It's rare to recall so much. You're very lucky."

Suddenly, a wave of emotion crashed into her. An insurmountable sorrow that made her stagger. It did not come from inside her—it was flowing out of her mistress in a cold, cold torrent. At least, Li-Li now understood why their kind rarely spoke of *before*; Crim's entire demeanour had changed, and there was an unmistakable gloom in the air. Her voice was also tainted by a bitter tone—something akin to envy. They had all been stolen from their lives to serve the gods, and only now did Li-Li realise how heavily this might weigh on one's soul.

"I-I'm sorry."

"Don't be—I asked."

"I sho-shouldn't have—"

"It's fine. You've done nothing wrong. Just …"

"Y-yes?"

"These memories you have. They're precious, Little Mouse. Hold them close to your heart."

*

Crim took her to the Library. A huge, three-floored maze of shelves, cabinets, trunks and free-standing totems of all the literature the Sidhe had collected since their inception. There were twelve different entrances across the various floors, but in order to work on the scrolls and tomes and manuscripts one had to enter at the parlour, and be scrutinised by Bart.

Bart, a hunch-backed and unfathomably ancient minotaur, was the guardian of the Library, after having been brought back to the Mountain from unknown regions by Lykourgos the Wanderer. Following the death of his dear friend just a few centuries later, the old beast retreated to the quiet company of words and ideas. He never left this place, and never interfered with the ways of the Sidhe. He was happy just to exist alongside them.

To Li-Li's astonishment, he and Crim seemed almost *fond* of one another— an uncharacteristic feeling for either of them—and embraced with warm words as they stepped into the light of Bart's little round parlour. A fire blazed merrily in a hearth large enough for Li-Li to walk into without so much as stooping, illuminating a haggard, bull-like face. Swathed in shapeless brown robes, he was covered in coarse black hair peppered with grey. Below two bushy brows, two tiny eyes stared blindly from behind a seemingly useless pair of glasses, a pale light emanating from their milky surface. One of his horns was broken roughly in half. He reached out to her as Crim introduced Li-Li, the charms on his bracelets and a large gold medallion jangling as he moved. He took her hand, which did not even fill the palm of his, and placed the two stout fingers to her cheek and forehead.

"Hmm," Bart rumbled, face twitching as he searched her. "Fearful, this one. Jumpy. But good, nonetheless. You will vouch for her?"

"I will," Crim said.

"Now, now, don't be so shocked, Little Mouse. Crim brought you here and she knows the rules. She knows that she must speak for you, but she also knows not to bring you if you are not trustworthy." Bart lowered his massive head, and Li-Li imagined he looked straight into her eyes. "Still, you'll forgive me that I must double-check."

With a pat on the head that nearly buckled her knees, he released her, but did not move away.

"Now," he continued. "Three Rules. Number one: Don't touch anything you're told not to (for your own good). Number two: Stay close to your mistress (for your own good). Number three: Nothing is to leave this Library, and don't damage anything! (Also for your own good)"

"That's four, Bart," Crim cut in, smirking.

"Don't be smart."

"Is that the fifth?"

Bart growled. "At least, promise me you have better manners than her?"

"I-I…" Li-Li glanced nervously at her mistress. "Yes, I d-do."

Crim laughed. "She's honest."

"Yes. I like her." Limping slightly on his right leg, Bart made his way over to an armchair large enough to seat three people and settled back, humming as he picked up a cup of steaming tea and slurped it noisily. "Go on about your business then, girls. And take a cake; there's raisins in them."

They took their leave and their cakes (though Li-Li had to give hers to Crim; she quite forgot that she didn't like raisins). Crim lead her out of the parlour and along a twisting, turning, zig-zagging path through the shelves. Up a slender, almost vertical stair and past more bookcases. Across the great study hall on the second floor; rows and rows of long tables dotted here and there with the more academic denizens of the Mountain. Up the grand staircase in the middle to the third floor and through another tunnel of tottering tomes.

At last, they reached a door, which Crim opened with a slender brass key. Inside was a cramped room complete with a writing desk, chair, small sofa and a single bookcase bursting with contents.

"Welcome to my study."

VII

Months passed like hours, but also like years. For a Sidhe time moved both too fast and too slowly. For a Sidhe like Crim this became a maddening cycle of monotony—trying to fill each hour with hobbies and chores until she was tired enough to sleep, only to wake up again and again and again in the same place with no end in sight. She had read about ones that would hibernate for centuries just to escape this endless loop, and had thought about doing the same herself more than once. There were other, more permanent ways to end it, too, which more than a few had also been reduced to, but she was not yet ready to take such decisive action against her own existence.

So she took it one day at a time, finding things to do in the Library or the Menagerie or the Kitchens. If she could not find anything, she would start asking—a helping hand was always welcome, and a new face to talk to even more so.

At this very moment, she was rearranging a pile of worn scrolls in a dark corner of the library, organising them into smaller stacks by date, author and topic, which she would then tuck into the satchel slung across her and carry up the rickety ladder that she was currently leaning against. Most of the shelves behind her were empty, all of their contents having been deposited onto the floor, giving her plenty of space to rehome the documents.

Bart, just a few aisles away, was meant to be helping her with the cleaning, but was currently distracted by an atlas of the Bevechian homeworld, Bagnoee. The book itself was far too large for Crim to handle, measuring at least five feet wide when opened, so she had asked him to put it away.

"Onto the shelf," she called.

Bart snorted and stood upright—or as upright as he could. "I…What?"

"I meant for you to put it on the shelf."

A chortle. "It is meant for the shelf. But all this knowledge is meant for inside one's head, Child."

"I have plenty of time to get around to that one," she replied, then, looking up into the dizzying heights of the cases and stacks, she sighed. "Perhaps I'll get through all of them, one day."

"Plenty of time. Until there's none left. And then the coastlines of East Brei'ai will be forgotten."

"Huh?"

He held the atlas up to show her the map he had been admiring. "The Bevechi are thriving now, but that will not last forever. One day they will be gone, and probably their world too. As immortals, it is up to us to ensure their legacy lives on."

"Do you have to ensure it at this very moment?" She rubbed her numb rear as she stood, then, trying to ignore the one wheel that squeaked and jittered, clambered up rung by rung to the correct shelf and rolled across to the next empty space.

"This moment is as fine as any other," Bart mumbled, something on another page catching his eye.

Crim shook her head and focused on her own work. There was no point in talking to the old minotaur when he was engrossed in words. Best to leave him until he either finished the book or lost interest.

*

It was early afternoon by the time she finished, leaping from the middle shelves of the mezzanine to land on the lacquered boards of the walkway below in a brief fit of joy. An Elder seated at one of the many narrow writing desks turned her head to glare disapprovingly at the noise. Bart did not scold her; he was too occupied learning about ancient tart recipes.

Crim ambled back to her study to fetch her robe (she preferred to do any sort of work in just her blouse and breeches), only to find Li-Li sitting on the collapsed sofa reading. Her maid jumped up as she entered.

"I didn't know you were here, Little Mouse."

"I f-finished weeding the o-o-orchards," Li-Li said, fumbling with her sash. "C-c-came h-here to see if…if I could huh-help. B-but I c-couldn't find you or B-b-Bart."

"So you came here."

"Only be-because I d-d-didn't want to wander!" The younger Sidhe explained. "I'm n-not being l-luh-lazy!"

Crim blinked. "I didn't think you were, Little Mouse. You're welcome to use my study."

Li-Li hung her head. She spoke more now, but her fear was very much like a wall between them. Crim tried her best to put the girl at ease, but had to admit to herself that at times she was short and impatient. She also knew that Li-Li had seen her temper and very much dreaded it, though she had never been on the receiving end. "Are you d-d-done now?"

"Yes. Bart still hasn't finished his end, but that will take him a week at least."

"I can help!"

"Don't worry about it. He enjoys taking his time, and probably enjoys cataloguing even more than that. Leave him to it."

"Oh." Li-Li met her eyes now, a hopeful smile twitching at her little mouth. Such a sweet creature, really. She was such a precious girl. "Could…could I help you, m-Mistress?"

Crim's first instinct was to tell her no, she did not need any help, to send her away to find Yuki or some of the other Acolytes. But Li-Li would not want that, and she was determined to coax the Little Mouse out of her hole. "Um…actually. I *could* use some assistance."

Li-Li perked up, grinning now. "Yes! Anything!"

"I have nothing else to do for the rest of the afternoon, you see. Do you know any odd jobs we could help with?"

Her maid touched a finger to her lips, thinking. "I…well…I know *one* th-thing."

"Oh? Well good. I'll be bored out of my mind if I don't find some chores." Crim shrugged on her robe and belted it tightly round her waist.

"Adik. I'm he-helping Adik re-p-paint her shop."

"Not much of an artist, I'm afraid. But I can paint a wall, I'm sure. Lead the way, Little Mouse."

*

She had not lied—she wasn't an artist at all. When Adik's pupil handed her a paint brush, Crim eyed it nervously and sighed with relief when she was asked to simply go over the beams and posts holding the shop together. Shaped like a

64

longhouse of old, it sported plenty of these—vertical posts were royal blue and horizontal beams yellow. Anything in between was stark white, so her task was easy enough. Crim found a slender ladder outside and set to work almost at once, working from bottom to top and back to front.

Li-Li, on the other hand, hunkered by the rear wall, surrounded by dozens of open paint pots all spread out on a sheet. She and Tal (Adik's acolyte) whispered and giggled to one another as they painted life into the mural before them; a lush garden full of dancing fauns and frowning satyrs, flowers at their hooves and in their hair, a pond with two laughing naiads, surrounded by trees from which curious dryads peeked. She could never have even imagined such a scene, and told her maid as much.

"It's n-nuh-nothing," Li-Li responded, blushing. "I-I j-just like to p-p-paint."

"Maybe I can help?" Crim reached for an unsupervised brush slathered in violet pigment.

"No!" The younger Sidhe made to grab it out of her hand, a brief panic in her eyes. "I mean it-it's fine. We c-c-can—"

"Little Mouse."

"Huh?"

"I wouldn't dream of ruining your work."

"Th-that's not what I meant!"

Crim laughed, secretly pleased at Li-Li's reaction. She was getting bolder, more confident. Of course Crim had never meant to touch the mural, but it was good to know that Li-Li would stand up to her if needed. "Yes it is. It's fine, Little Mouse. I couldn't possibly match what you've done here."

*

Turning a deeper shade of crimson, her underling thanked her. When she looked up, however, her gaze drifted past Crim, and she shrank.

The woman standing in the doorway was not as tall nor as sturdy as her mother—in fact she was rather skinny and fragile-looking. Somehow, though softer and slimmer, she had the same face. Those same high cheekbones and square jaw. Her nose was smaller and her eyes larger, her entire expression less stern and fierce, but there was no mistaking her as one of Mother's trueborn children. She swept her pale orange braids back over her shoulder as she approached, maroon eyes fixed on Crim, who shrank next to Li-Li.

"You are Crim?" Onaldi demanded, her voice far softer and higher than expected.

"Y-yes," she managed.

"Mother has summoned you. Will you come?"

There was no choice in the question; no-one with any sense defied Mother. Crim swallowed, nodding. With a jerk of her head, Onaldi wheeled around and strode out of the shop, not even acknowledging anyone else. Trembling, Crim followed.

*

Mother's chambers were located at the very top of the High Stair—a daunting set of steps on the sourcemost side of the Mountain that overlapped backwards and forwards for an age. Walled in by white marble and floored in dark slate, their footsteps rang loudly as they climbed, the torches lining the walls spat and shuddered with Crim's agitation, turning from bright orange to a moody red the closer they got to their destination. To her credit, Onaldi turned to check on her a few times, brow raised. Concern? Or amusement? Crim could not tell. She forced a smile each time.

At its peak, the stairwell suddenly opened out into a lofty hallway. The white marble that made up the walls and ceiling here was untouched and rough, supported at its centre by slender columns and adorned here and there with tapestries. Facing them was a pair of glistening ebony doors with no obvious handle or other decoration.

Crim paused, feigning interest in her surroundings. Onaldi, a few paces ahead, stopped to watch her, not pressing or judging. Only watching.

A short laugh startled her, and Crim spun to find two guards stationed on either side of the stairs. Tall as their sister, and only slightly broader, their faces betrayed very different characters. Seti, the youngest of the three, looked nervously at her, smiled and averted his gaze when she turned to him, fidgeting with the strap of his belt. His features were soft, eyes a warm caramel and hair falling about his head in loose white twists. He did not look like he could harm a fly. In sharp contrast, his elder brother, Yamanu flashed her his usual cocky grin. Unfathomably handsome and lithe, all he had to do was smile and Crim would find herself staring at him, helpless. His blue locks fell forward over as he bent towards her, grey eyes flashing with mischief.

"Oh no. What have you done now?"

"Uh…what?" Crim managed, mouth dry."

"I haven't seen her pace like this in centuries."

A cold, heavy dread settled in her stomach. Crim's hands went cold as she began to tremble again. "I-I…"

Onaldi hissed behind her. "Leave her be, brother."

"I'm just saying." Yamanu lowered his head more till his lips were next to Crim's ear. She froze. "It's been nice knowing you."

He laughed again then, and even Seti glared at him. Crim rolled her eyes back in makeshift nonchalance. "Yes, you too Dear Prince."

He scoffed. "Least I know she would never skin *me*. Her own flesh and blood."

"Wouldn't be so sure of that," Onaldi shot back dryly. Now she finally beckoned to Crim, taking her arm as she approached. "He's just being an ass, you know. I'm sure it's nothing."

"Mother doesn't summon us for nothing." They were at the doors now, and Crim touched her palm to one side, asking it politely to open. With a click, the latch turned and it whispered open. "But if she wanted me dead I think I would be dead already."

Onaldi shut her mouth, offering a thin smile. There was no arguing with that.

*

Mother's chambers were grand, but far smaller than Crim had imagined. She stepped past the entryway into a well-lit living room. Here, the marble of the walls was flat black and bare, the warm blue light of burning sconces gleaming off the smooth stone. Underfoot, the slate was now covered by an eclectic collection of rugs in various colours and patterns. The floor fell away in front of her, with three short steps leading into a recessed seating area lined with an equally random array of cushions. There were dressers and bookcases all around, lined with neat arrangements of figures and vessels and trinkets. On the far side of the seating area, a large statue of Isis spread her wings across most of the wall.

Knees like jelly, she sat and busied herself with carefully arranging some pillows behind her back. Crim assumed Mother was still in her bedchamber on one side of the apartment, though the scent of warm water and lavender drifted in from behind her, where she assumed Mother had a private bath. Neither of the other rooms had doors, but she dared not peek into them for fear of death.

A stirring to her right caused her to leap up off the couch, knocking some cushions to the floor. She was not sure exactly what she expected to appear out from the folds of the seat, but breathed a sigh of relief when she found a scaly little head gazing curiously up at her. Apep, Mother's gargantuan albino boa constrictor, flicked his tongue in greeting.

"H-hello," she said. "I'm Crim."

Beady pink eyes surveyed her with an intelligence far surpassing that of a mere snake. She felt inclined to sit, and did so obediently. Inch by inch, with cushions shifting and sliding where his body moved, the serpent wound himself around her, squeezing her waist slightly as he went, before coiling his upper body into a knot in her lap. His nose peeped out from between two loops, and Crim imagined he was smiling.

"You are warm." The voice nearly made her launch poor Apep to the ceiling. A low, smooth voice devoid of expression. "You command the flame?"

Crim, feeling no heat at all in her quivering body, nodded. "Y-yes M-Mother."

The shadows in the doorway seemed to shift and move backwards like a veil, and the ruler of the Mountain stepped forth. Swathed in white, banded in gold and studded with turquoise and carnelian, Mother more closely resembled a deity than any Sidhe Crim had ever seen. Taller than most of her subjects, broad-shouldered and strong, Crim sat transfixed by her golden eyes as she strode unhurriedly across the room to sit opposite her. Apep curled around himself to look at this master, then tucked his head away and slept, leaving Crim utterly alone with the most powerful of her kind.

She gulped.

Mother looked her up and down critically, face set and unreadable. Quiet filled the room and pressed on Crim's shoulders.

Should she speak?

"Your Mentor speaks highly of you."

Crim, assuming there was some mistake but daring not to say so, merely responded: "She does?"

"Yes. She says you are intelligent. That you show great potential." Mothers gaze locked with her, petrifying Crim in place. "But that you fail to *learn*. Why is that?"

"I d-don't—"

"Do not lie to me."

"Um."

Mother tilted her head. Only the slightest hint of annoyance. Crim, fear reaching fever-pitch, struggled to form words.

"I suppose…I suppose I do not see the point. That is….I do not see the need. Um. I. Um…Well, we have our *draoi*, and I suppose it makes sense to learn to use it but—er—it—um—we have no enemies. Why do we learn to fight? We-we sometimes go through the Portals to other realms, but—um—that seems so far away to me that I don't see the point. Or I suppose I don't see the *hurry*…in…uh in learning—"

"You do not need to see its purpose," Mother intervened. "Those of us with foresight are tasked with seeing. All you must do is follow."

Chest heaving with frantic breaths, she nodded. So Mentor had spoken to Mother about her laziness. Crim had not thought it so bad. But then, Mentor did not suffer defiance gladly. "Yes, Mother."

"You went Outside?"

"Yes."

"And I am told you wield your *draoi* well enough when you want to."

"Yes."

"But you fail to become the Sidhe that you *could* be. Your studies are behind. Your combat skills are lacking. Have you even commissioned a weapon?"

"No, Mother."

Her superior stood, and seemed to grow taller. "Then that will be first. Go now. Onaldi will accompany you. You will be one of us, or you will be banished. Understood?"

"Yes, Mother."

"Apep, come."

Crim liked to think the look the serpent gave her was one of empathy, as he unravelled and flopped to the floor to follow his master. Though it might have just been amusement.

VIII

"Will you *stop* dragging your heels." Sunshine had made the gross mistake of bringing Princess out into the Gardens to work. Located just outside the Temple at the midmost point of the Mountain, what the Sidhe referred to as 'gardens' was actually a small strip of land fronted by the great, dark Lake. What little earth they could cultivate was covered in orchards and crops, with the rest home to dense clusters of trees and bushes. A single worn path led from the Courtyard situated just at the doors of the Temple down to a stony beach punctuated by four short, squat piers. The boats were still now; a small collection of handmade currachs and rafts that carried the Reavers out into the mortal world in search of Vessels, but Princess was utterly distracted by them, the Lake and the gaping Maw overhead. It did not take much to distract her, truly; the girl would do anything but work.

"How do they know when to go?" She asked, scattering seeds in the furrow she had just dug as well as outside and all around. Hand raised to fend off blinding sunlight, she jerked her chin at two Reavers that were busy inspecting and repairing the boats. One looked up from painting the prow and winked at her.

"You were here last Making," her mistress answered, carefully folding soil over her own seeds. Usually she did not care much for sowing, and only pretended to listen to the instructions Mentor and Laal gave her. Now she was silently apologising to both of them for dragging out such a simple task well into the evenings.

"I didn't attend."

"Yes. We noticed. Mentor sent me out to look for you afterwards, remember?"

Princess tilted her head and batted her long golden eyelashes. "No I don't."

"Do you remember what you were *taught* about the Making?"

"Bits and pieces." Another handful of seeds thrown carelessly across the rows. Sunshine swore she felt her eyebrow starting to twitch.

"Well. How does it start?"

The younger Sidhe pointed up into the Maw. "Something appears there."

"One of the *gods,* yes."

"And then *they*—" Princess waved at the flirtatious Reaver now eyeing her hungrily. "Go to kidnap some children."

Sunshine sighed. She was not wrong. "They fetch mortals. Vessels for the gods."

"What does a god need with a Vessel?"

"Crim!" She threw her hands in the air at the sight of her friend. Delighted both to see her alive and to be done with this conversation. "Did you come to help me? Please say yes, my love!"

Crim curled her lip at Princess and scowled. The action was probably meant to scare her off, but the ever-insolent acolyte just stuck her tongue out and skipped away. She was just as happy to be dismissed as Sunshine was to see her dismissed.

"How goes it?" Asked Crim, scanning the seed-littered ground critically.

"She's worse than you."

Crim made a face, then laughed. "So Mentor told you? That Mother summoned me?"

"She implied as much. Laal and I inferred the rest." Sunshine kissed her cheek and hugged her. "You have been spared; I see."

"Not without an ultimatum."

"Which is?"

"Move my arse or get out."

"Mother's words?"

"Every syllable."

"Can I say it?"

"Go on."

"Laal and I *told you*. How many times have we told you?"

"Oh about once every few days."

"They don't want any more like Princess."

"Hmmm." They both looked to the shore now, where the prissy little cherub was already sitting prettily on one of the rafts and being rowed out onto the water by two rather attractive Reavers.

"So what will you do, Crim?"

"What I'm told, for once," Came the surprisingly confident response. "I have been Outside now, and I see no home for me there. It is time for me to accept my fate and be a Sidhe."

"Hmph." Sunshine adjusted some of her crimson locks, pinning them back from where they had come loose. "That's a rather mature decision. I'm proud."

"Alright Mentor." They both giggled. "But I need to commission a weapon."

"What? Now?"

"Onaldi was meant to take me to the Forge. The only reason she let me out of her sight was because I said *you* promised to help with this."

Sunshine's mind wandered back through the centuries, to a day when she and Laal had brought Crim out here on their own. One of the first times Mentor had let her out of her sight. They had tried to get her to speak then. To move. React. Anything. All manner of bribes and promises had been made. She had whispered so very many things into that Fledgling's seemingly-deaf ears. Now, hearing Crim's words, her heart soared. "You remember that?"

"I remember most of it, if I try hard enough. Nothing from before, but those days…I don't think I was as catatonic as I made myself appear."

"No." Laal had said as much not long after Crim finally awoke. Sunshine would have to tell her she had been right. "But I'm glad you recall it. Come. I have something for you."

*

Back across the Courtyard past the whirring brass astrolabe. Through the Temple full of whispering and giggling from the alcoves. Circumventing the dais and passing between the Steel Stair and the rickety pulpit where the doors to the Last Stair stood wide open revealing the long way down to the Tomb. Here there was a different kind of murmuring, a different sort of noise that tickled inside their heads, so much so that Crim pressed her palms to her ears in a foolish attempt to block it out.

Scraping. Tossing. Thumping. Scratching. Somewhere in the dark depths of the Tomb, beyond one of the dozen stone archways, there rose a wail. Closer at hand was a weeping. Side to side, above and below the slumbering Vessels sensed them coming, and stirred.

The sounds that rode on the air were bad enough; by the time they reached the foot of the steps and were about to turn off into one of the Spiral Stairs Sunshine's head was full of such a clamour that she could hardly think for herself.

Help me. Someone pleaded, the message coming with a vision of the inside of a coffin lid. She shook it away.

Let me out. Another, weaker. Bloodied and broken nails raking helplessly against the walls of their sarcophagus.

Mama? Is that you? A dream. A hopeless dream.

Sunny. A familiar presence. Crim was swaying next to her. Hands on either side of her head, balling to fists as she tried to knock the ruckus out.

She took her in her arms. "Shhhh. No. Do not listen. Come on."

Sunny! Crim rarely cried, but two trips to the Tomb in one day was enough to drive anyone to the brink. Sunshine pressed both of their hands over her burning ears and pushed her to one of the riveted wooden doors. It was quieter once they descended a few steps down into the Spiral Stair, but Crim collapsed backwards and tucked her head behind her knees, elbows wrapped around it as one expecting a blow. "They're so loud!" She gasped.

Sunshine, now seeing the blood trickling from her ears and smeared over her palms, pulled her up. "Keep going."

"Can we not…Just one. Just one, Sunny!"

"No Crim. No my love. We cannot help them."

*

Further down and Crim collected herself, sniffing and rubbing at her temples. They reached the apartment without many people noticing them, and Sunshine ushered the younger Sidhe into her and Laal's bedchamber.

"Sit. Let's clean you up first."

Crim sat, clenching and unclenching her fists, extending her fingers as far as they would go in slow, soothing motions. Sunshine fetched a brush, cloth and filled a shallow bowl with water from Laal's jug. She carefully combed her friends deep red hair away from her face and ears, restyling and pinning it back in a neater version of its usual shape. The paint on her ears was all but rubbed off and much of the hair matted down with dried blood, so she washed everything off and fixed the tight braids that lined the sides of Crim's head. The top of her hair was well enough, and she brushed the loose waves as neatly as they would allow.

"I think I dropped a pin or two," Crim said hoarsely.

"You did." Sunshine had already replaced them, and added some of her own hair beads (she seldom used them, anyway). "There. Beautiful."

Crim scoffed. "A mess."

"A beautiful mess then." She kissed her crinkled nose and returned the jug and brush to the dresser. Then, crouching, she turned the dial on a large wooden trunk. Upon striking the correct combination, the latch moved by itself, and the lid sprang upwards. "I have been meaning to give this to you for…oh forever. I knew that whenever you chose to make your weapon, you should see it first. It might give you some inspiration."

"Inspiration?" Repeated Crim, eyeing her curiously. When her gaze fell on the axe in Sunshine's hands, she sat up as one struck by lightning. "Where did you get that?"

There was nothing special about it, really: just a relic of a weapon slowly ravaged by the centuries, yet still amazingly sturdy. Time flowed differently under the Mountain, and affected all manner of things in unpredictable ways— this was no exception. Its short bronze head had tarnished beyond use, and the ash handle looked ready to snap at any moment, but as Crim took the axe and weighed it in her hand, eyes wide and mouth set in a hard line, it held together. She turned it, thumbed the dull blade, swung it experimentally.

"It was on you when they brought you in," Sunshine explained. "I don't know why the Reavers didn't take it, but it seemed precious. Mentor suggested I keep it until…Until today." Crim's eyes were shining, staring both at the weapon and far away. "Crim?"

"Hm?"

"Do you remember it?"

"Yes." Her voice was distant. Part of her was away, striding through the halls of memory, turning handles on doors that had previously been locked. "Yes and no. Oh, Sunny, it's so close!"

"Focus. Keep going."

"I think…" Crim stood, searching the floor for what, Sunshine could not tell. Suddenly, she leapt forward and brought it down, stopping just inches from the surface of Laal's favourite rug. "There was a deer. A hind. I killed it."

"Hunting?" Sunshine wished she could see the vision surrounding her friend. Wished she could share in this moment. She probably could, if she pressed, but somehow that seemed intrusive.

"Yes," Crim chortled. "My brother helped. He brought it down, really. I just finished it."

"Brother? I don't think you ever mentioned him before?"

Nudged down another corridor, Crim wandered away from her kill, turning here and there. She giggled. An innocent, girlish sound. "Three of them! They're tall. As tall as Mother, and one even bigger. Even my father—"

She stopped short. Sunshine edged close, reluctant to disturb her. "Your father?"

Crim shook her head, chasing the memory away. "No. No I'm not ready for that just yet."

"Right." Sunshine rubbed her arm. "There's no rush."

"Uh-huh." The axe turned again. The blade made a dull sound as it was flicked. "So what do I do with this?"

IX

Bart pushed a tray of biscuits towards her, scraggly beard peppered with crumbs. "Take some more, Child."

She turned the Grimoire of the Parach-ma over on the couch next to her and placed her quill down into the oblong box it had come in. Bart loved to bake, she had learned, and spent what little time he was not patrolling the library in his humble quarters below the main level busying himself with buns and pastries and cakes and all manner of treats for his visitors. He was fond of knitting as well, and had already presented her with a rather cosy striped blanket, which she currently had folded over her lap. Li-Li carefully picked three without raisins and sat back against the soft cushions, munching merrily. The biscuits were Minotaur-sized, and she had to break them up to eat them with any sort of delicacy.

"Are th-the Parach-ma still around, B-B-Bart?"

"Huh? Oh yes, still allies too," he replied, pouring her another veritable bowlful of red tea.

"I've nuh-never seen one."

"That you know. Fond of illusions, that lot. They like to disguise themselves as Sidhe when they come here. I received a pair just last week."

"Wh-what do they u-usually look l-l-like?"

"Rather charming creatures, actually. Something like a large meerkat, though far slimmer. Colourful too, for the most part, and they dye their fur with patterns…" He sat up. "Li-Li? Are you well?"

She had dropped a biscuit. It bounced off her lap and hit the floor, breaking apart. Her head hurt suddenly. *Gods,* how it hurt. Li-Li hissed in pain and pressed her hands against her eyes. "I-I'm f-f-fine…"

"You are *not.*" He was saying something else, but it faded into the background. Another noise was filling her head. A cacophony. Scraping.

Tossing. Thumping. Scratching. Wailing. Weeping. Clawing at the insides of a stone box.

"Let me out," she gasped.

"What? Little Mouse?"

"Please let me go."

She was using her fists now. Pounding at the lid until she scraped the skin from her knuckles. Her right pinkie was immobile—probably broken. She couldn't breathe. Could hardly summon the strength to scream. It was warm suddenly. Unpleasantly so. She was floating in liquid, then drowning in it. Her mouth and nose filled up with blood.

"I want to go home!"

"Li-Li!" Bart was shaking her now, and placed a hand to her cheek. "Oh I see. No, Little Mouse. Those are not your memories. You do not belong there. Come."

The Minotaur snapped his fingers, and she started. Then sprang from the couch tossing the rest of her biscuits to the floor. "Crim!"

"There is no need. She is in no danger now."

"I h-have to—I n-n-need to see her!"

"It is *past*, Little Mouse. What you saw happened a long time ago."

"I know." She was already jogging towards the door. "I know."

*

Li-Li caught Crim and Sunshine coming down the stairs from their apartment, arms linked. The former carrying an old axe, a look of determination on her pale face. She did not seem to be in any sort of distress.

"Li-Li!" Sunshine kissed her cheeks and took her with her free arm. "There you are, my lovely. Where have you been today?"

"Th-the Library," she answered, looking across her at Crim, who was fixated on the relic in her hand.

"Aha! That old beast fattening you up with sweets as usual?"

"Hehe, yes. I…um…I c-c-came as suh-soon as y-you called?"

Crim finally looked up, cocking an eyebrow at her. "I did not summon you."

"Y-you d-didn't?"

"No," Crim grunted as Sunshine elbowed her in the ribs. The two shared a look. "But you may come with us, if you wish."

Li-Li fell back. If her mistress had not sent for her, what had she seen? "I think—"

"Oh come, come!" Sunshine urged, squeezing her to her side. "This is a big moment for your dear mistress! A big day! She would *love* for you to be there! Right, Crim?"

Crim's head jerked back up. "Um. Yes. Who knows—you might get to do this soon enough, too."

*

She had never been to the Forge. Had never been this far under the Mountain—in the cramped maze of passages and caverns untended and unchiselled by Sidhe hands. It was hot down here, under the Maw and the Market and the Forum in the depths that hugged the uppermost walls of the Pit. Years ago Mentor had told Li-Li that the Mountain had a Core, much like thriving planets of the universe, and now she wondered just how close to it they were as she wiped the sweat from her brow and tugged at her robes in desperate hopes of cooling down. Concentrating, she was able to churn up a slight breeze around herself, but even that was little help.

Crim and Sunshine seemed unaffected; the latter more than her mistress who, despite wielding fire, did not endure heat very well. Glancing sideways, Li-Li caught her fanning herself more than once.

There were signs of life, all the same. They passed Sidhe moving to and fro in the dim, most of them also beaded with perspiration and concentrating on keeping themselves cool. No-one said much, and the only sound that met her ears with any regularity was a constant *tink tink tink* that grew louder the further they went.

Sunshine brought them round one last corner, and all of a sudden the walls were bathed in an orange glow emanating from a doorway on their right. It was sweltering now, and Li-Li puffed audibly, frantically trying to transform her breaths into some sort of wind as they were absorbed by the oppressive wall of heat. Soon enough she saw why: beyond the door was a room with a slender trench of gushing lava against one wall, and an immense metal furnace facing them. A grindstone set on the counter at the other side of the room was spinning so fast it was little more than a white blur at the corner of Li-Li's vision. A burly woman with arms wide as tree trunks held a sword to the wheel, completely unfazed by the shower of sparks flying at her eyes. Behind her a tall black-clad Sidhe pounded a red-hot blade between hammer and anvil.

"Aha!" Smith erupted, making Li-Li jump. "It's our Sunny! And Crim! Why hello. HAMMER! Say hello."

The one with the hammer lowered their hammer to nod at the trio, then promptly resumed hammering their hammer at the same unbroken tempo.

"Good to see you Smith," replied Crim, smiling. "Been a while."

"Not a while since I saw you, you grumpy little gremlin. But I can't for the life of me recall the last time you were down here." Smith chuckled, leaning over the counter on two boulders of fists and winking.

"I've bought knives, remember? The ones with the rubies?"

"Yeah, probably about a century ago that was."

"Really?"

"*Really.*"

Sunshine, looking ready to burst, bounced on her heels as she added: "Then you'll be glad to know she's here with a *commission*, no less!"

"*Sunny!*" Crim grumbled. Li-Li assumed she had wanted to announce this herself.

"HAH!" The large woman boomed. "Well I'll be, our little Crimson Flame here to get her very own weapon! I thought you were going to snub me forever!"

Crim's mouth fell open, aghast. "Snub you? I would never—"

"Deny me the absolute *pleasure* of creating for you—the Crimsonest of Flames—something that both encapsulates and enhances who you are as a Sidhe? Deny me that *unspeakable bond* that exists between commissioner and commissionee? Deny me the degree of friendship and trust *entrusted* in the moment you show me exactly who you are, and who you have the potential to be when you finally place your heartstone into my hand?"

"I-I-I…Uh?"

Chuckling, Sunshine stepped in: "Mother made her."

Smith burst out laughing. Hammer ceased their hammering. "Oh so it took *Mother* to finally light the fire under your arse?"

"…Yes," Crim conceded, clutching the time-ravaged axe to her chest.

Hammer resumed their hammering. Smith reached out a hand to touch the splintered handle in Crim's grasp. "Something like this? Seems about right."

"Something like it, yes. Please. Maybe a little more—"

"Ah-ah!" Smith snatched the weapon from her and walked over to one corner of the room and came back with something enclosed in her massive hand. "Your heartstone."

"It will see what you desire," Sunshine explained both to Crim and Li-Li. "And also what you need."

Crim extended her palm, and scowled when the black, dull rock plopped down into it. "This is *coal!*"

Smith batted her upside the head, and Li-Li thought her mistress might actually fall to the floor, but she steadied herself against the counter. "It's not a heartstone until the connection is made, fool! Doesn't your Mentor teach you anything?"

"She doesn't listen," Sunshine tittered.

Li-Li watched as her mistress weighed the lump in her hand, then retreated over to where the glowing orange rivulet bubbled and boiled between two openings in the wall. Face fixed in concentration, she then cupped the coal tightly between her hands and plunged them into the lava. Li-Li shrieked, moved to intervene, but Sunshine grabbed her, shaking her head.

This is how it's done, Lovey. Observe.

After a few seconds, Crim pulled her hands out of the molten rivulet and turned, crumbs of dark ash falling from her skin. She returned the stone to Smith, only now it was glowing white, a sleeping power thrumming at its core, which was full of swirling coloured smoke. Smith took in a long, sharp breath as she caressed its glassy exterior.

"Yes. I see."

"You will do it?" Asked Crim, now eager.

"I will. It will take time of course. Perfection cannot be rushed."

X

"Again!" Mentor demanded, wiping some of the blood from her brow. The gash across her scalp had scabbed over in an instant, and if it hurt her at all she did not show it. "I said *again!*"

"But—"

"Now!"

Crim circled to one side, then the other. Mentor favoured her right side, so she darted left. A broad-bladed scimitar hissed towards her and she brought up her spiked metal vambrace to knock it away. Mentor was pleased with her for once. She was no longer afraid of being injured, no longer stumbled and ducked her way through their encounters. She ran head-first into attacks and batted counters aside instinctively. When her foe was open, say, after a failed attack, she did not hesitate to strike.

This time her blade found Mentor's groin as Crim pretended to buckle under the force of the assault. It sliced through the soft flesh, and a fresh spurt of blood coated her face. Mentor collapsed sideways with a gasp—that one had *definitely* stung.

"Are you—"

"I'm fine!" Her elder barked back. Crim waited fervently as she watched her struggle to stand. As much as she knew she could never truly harm Mentor, she did not like injuring her.

"Right." She tried to clean her face in the elbow of her robe, but that was already drenched in her own blood from a strike that nearly took her whole arm off.

"It wouldn't have taken your arm," Came the correction. "And even if it did we'll just put it back."

"I rather like my parts where they are."

"Can't blame you for that. Watch your footing this time. I could have easily knocked you over. Try to use your *draoi*, too. Remember it is a weapon as well as a tool."

Draoi. To Crim that meant fire. She was slowly learning to manipulate other aspects of the world around her with her power, but for now fire was the only thing she could control enough to fight with. When she fought with it, however, it was still difficult to hold back. She forgot about maintaining volumes and temperatures and simply…unleashed.

The one weapon in her arsenal that could truly end Mentor, and she could not restrain it.

"I still don't know how to stop," she said. "Mentor, I do not want to—"

"I said use it. So you will use it. Do not think you can rid yourself of me so easily," Mentor smirked, standing.

Crim retreated a few steps. Mentor would not hesitate to use her own draoi, now that the option was on the table. Of course she had enough training and restraint not to kill her pupil, but her pupil had seen enough to fear her power.

The slightest movement. A jerk of the fingers in Mentor's free hand, and Crim cartwheeled aside. The ground burst open where she had just been standing, thick green tendrils snapping up to catch her. Where she landed, the earth was already rumbling, and she raised her foot too late—a vine lashed round her ankle and began to tighten, angry red thorns biting.

"Argh!" She hacked at it and jumped forward, aiming for Mentor. The elder Sidhe did not move, only smiled, and Crim knew she was in trouble. A tangle of writhing, wringing greenery exploded upwards, ensnaring her arms and legs. Squeezing, squeezing and pulling so much she feared she would be torn asunder, Crim howled in pain.

"Use it!"

The demand rang in her head but she hardly heard it. The harder she thrashed the tighter the tendrils that had her wound themselves, one thick creeper now looping about her waist, her ribs crunching.

"I have you. So easily, too!"

Something about the tone of her voice. The sneer on her face. The way she planted her hands on her hips like she was disappointed. It crept deep under her skin and slithered around, striking nerves in places she tried to keep quiet. Suddenly, unreasonably, she was angry. Perhaps it was all the frustration, all the months and fruitless months of trying to impress her and Mother. The nights mentally flogging herself for not living up to their standards. Her anger boiled up to rage in an instant, and spilled over in the form of fire.

She swiped at her restraints, blazing blades slicing them and singing the ends. They recoiled and writhed like serpents before hitting the ground. Her insides roiled to an inferno, and with a roar she unleashed a wave of fire that crashed out in all directions. The Arena would not burn; she knew that much, though the paint on some of the columns began to peel. Mentor's eyes went wide, and she summoned a water bubble around herself just in time. Crim was vaguely aware of her floating there, struggling to maintain the temperature of the water around herself so she did not boil alive. That awareness was slipping away, however, along with her proprioception. It started at her extremities, then ebbed upwards through her torso, grasped her neck like choking hands and pushed at the inside of her skull. Then she was experiencing something much like what happened when she darted—that sense of being outside one's body. Only this was not for an instant—rather they were moving further and further apart. She wanted to scream, to cry out to Mentor for help, but her mouth and lungs were no longer under her command. This was it. She would drift away into the void. Be lost forever in the great cosmos, just a wandering soul evicted from its vessel—

"Crim! *Crim!* Crimson Flame come back here!" Mentor was shaking her violently, slapping her across the face. Her hair was scorched, one side of her face raw and bloody and blistered. Her hands had lost most of the top layers of flesh. Still, she had struggled through the fire to her pupil. Still, she had the courage to take hold of her—both parts of her—and draw her to herself. Still, she cared enough to open one of her wrists and press it to Crim's parted lips. "Drink. Drink, girl. There. You will be fine."

She drank, letting the thick, rich fluid fill her. Invigorate her. She felt it coursing through her veins like liquid light. With Mentor's help, she sat up, blinking about at the peeled murals, the burnt sand, some of it turned to glass near them. The two mortal swords lay warped and smouldering where they had been tossed and forgotten.

Mentor was the worst; blistered and bleeding, her clothes smoked and had been seared right through in places. Her green hair was in disarray and her violet eyes…her eyes were the worst. For the first time in her existence, Crim saw her teacher's eyes filled with fear.

"I'm fine," she croaked, struggling to her feet. Tottering, she adjusted her sash and began to dust herself off. "I'm sorry, Mentor. I don't know what happened."

"I think we should finish for today." Mentor was still on her knees, still eyeing Crim like she was scared of her.

"I can do better. I can control it, you've seen me."

"Yes, I know. But that's enough."

It was then that Crim saw her legs; blackened and cooked beyond all recognition. Her stomach churned at the sight of them, and she reached down to help. "Mentor!"

"No!" Her elder crawled away from her, useless legs dragging through the dirt. "No. Go Crim. Send Silver in as you're leaving."

She was welling up. How could she have hurt Mentor like this? What had she done? "I-I didn't mean to…"

"I know. I *know* Crim. I will be fine."

Crim backed away. Should she really leave her like this? Would anyone be able to heal her? What had she *done?*

Monster. She told herself. *You're a monster.*

*

Crim retreated to the apartment, locked her door, and threw herself down on her bed. With her mind racing, she struggled to piece together what had happened in the Arena. At some point between accessing her *draoi* and releasing it, something in her had just *snapped.* Not her temper—that had been strained for some time. Rather, the link between her thoughts and actions had broken. No longer in control, she had felt like a stranger watching her body in action.

Now calm, lying atop her soft mattress, she searched inward, feeling for that link and the mechanism that had released it. Was this something she could achieve at will? She had heard tales of Sidhe who managed to ascend to incorporeal states—they were the stuff of myth: The Martyr, Achellion and Yazma. Sidhe who could leave their bodies at will in order to attain impossible power, or even as a means of escape. Achellion had apparently occupied five different vessels before finally disappearing. As much as she abhorred what she had just done, she was also intrigued.

A knock at the door. "Crim? Are you home?"

"Yes." Had Laal heard about it already? What would she say?

"We're going to the Lake, if you want to join us. Some of the others will be there."

Crim exhaled in relief. "Others?"

"Smith, Hammer. Some of the Reavers. Probably Whisper and Gibber, too."

She examined the soot-stained arms of her robe. "Yeah I'll…I just need to get changed. I'll meet you there."

*

The Lake was black; barely a ripple disturbed the satin surface that silently reflected the sky above, which watched over them as always through the Maw. The sparkling stars and the gibbous moon shone silver and white and palest gold, their light skimming the surface of the stony shore.

The bonfires were already lit by the time Crim arrived, with groups of Sidhe standing or sitting around, most meandering from halo to halo of pulsing light in search of friends. She spotted Sunshine near Cara's pale blue fire, beaming as she joked with the crowd around her. As always, she drew people like a magnet, but made room in her circle for Crim to stand. A whole pig was placed on a spit by the flames, and soon enough the smell of it slowly roasting became too much, and she left Sunny to investigate.

"Here. That robe is too nice to let grease drip all over it." As she helped herself to two ribs, Hyeong appeared at her side offering a handkerchief. He grinned, revealing overlapping rows of pointed white fangs. Not a perfect smile, but a warm one.

"Thanks," Crim replied, wrapping her food in the white cloth. Sure enough, some of the oils seeped through almost immediately.

"You found the others then. I saw you walking around. I guess it's hard to spot them in the crowd." He nibbled on a morsel of tender pork. "Apart from Sunny, of course."

Crim cast a glance back to where her friend was still entertaining. "Of course."

Hyeong cleared his throat loudly. "If you're not in the mood for people, we're down by the water. I mean. If you want to join us. You don't have to. It's quiet there."

She was rarely in the mood for people, particularly large clusters of people she did not know. She came for the food, and to spend time with the few individuals she enjoyed. "Lead the way."

*

Hyeong brought her down to where silent waves kissed the rounded pebbles. To the right, the boats bumped rhythmically against their posts. There was already a blanket here laden with food and jugs of wine. Nashoba, another Reaver, looked up as they approached and grunted something like a greeting. Crim grunted back and settled down between the two.

Hyeong talked. He always talked a lot, filling up every silent space with meaningless chatter. But he also made sure she had plenty of food, and that her cup was never empty, so she listened and tried to get a word in where she could. Nashoba was silent at her side for the most part, only responding in noises and short answers. He liked to throw stones into the lake, and soon Crim joined him as she and Hyeong chatted.

Eventually, the conversation died down, and the only noise was the odd *plunk plonk* of larger and larger rocks hitting the water.

At length, Hyeong ventured: "I saw Mentor today."

Crim became acutely interested in the stone in her hand. It was coloured granite, larger than the span of her fingers, and shaped like a smooth disc. She turned it, letting moonlight glint off flecks in its surface. Nashoba could make these ones bounce almost to the other side of the lake, but as much as he tried to show her, she could never get the hang of it. "You did?"

"Uh-huh. She was in a bad way. Injured."

"Hm."

"It looked like she had been burned."

She felt Nashoba pause next to her. Felt him turn. Even sitting down he towered over her—he was one of the few Sidhe actually *taller* than Mother, and broad. He felt like a barricade blocking all escape. "I know."

"Did something happen?"

The larger man made a noise, not quite a growl. A sharp rumble in his massive chest. Crim was not sure if it was directed at her or his friend. "…Yes."

"Oh." Hyeong seemed to understand suddenly, and his expression changed. He put a hand on her shoulder. "I'm sorry. I'm sure it was an accident."

"It was." Nashoba's voice was quiet, but deep and firm. He rarely spoke, but when he did people listened. Even Hyeong.

"These things happen, you know. Nashoba, remember when we were training together for the first time? You almost sent Caius through the wall!"

"I crushed his arm."

Crim looked up at the big brute. Only he was not really a *brute*—of the two he was quieter, gentler, calmer. He was certainly not as handsome as Hyeong, who had almost feminine good looks—but there was a certain pleasantness in his sharp features. Even his pale gold eyes, though striking, always seemed warm to her. He didn't really smile, but the hard line of his mouth softened, corners relaxing slightly upward.

"Did it take him long to…to…?"

"To recover?" He combed his fingers through jet black hair. "A few days, at most. The blood heals."

"It does," Hyeong agreed, putting an arm around her. "And Mentor is one of the strongest of us. She won't take long to recover."

XI

Sunshine propped herself against the warm brick wall of the Armory, watching as Yuki perused the high shelves, meticulously examining weapon after weapon with feigned understanding. They always did this, religiously, before every training. In her younger days, she had pushed swords into their hand and grumbled about keeping Mentor waiting, but the years had made her soft, to where she now viewed Yuki and the others as younger siblings rather than a burden. She knew how impatient Mentor could be with them—with all of them, and despite the fact that they clearly respected their teacher, they were now more trusting with her, so she couldn't help feeling proud of herself, despite the fact that Yuki was actually Laal's servant.

Come to think of it, she had not seen Princess in weeks—not after she had tried to drag her away from her friends by the ear. For the first time since her making Princess had actually *swung* and *snapped* at her, which had caught her by surprise just enough for the little gremlin to run away. Some other Anointed had told her that her servant and her friends spent most of their time lurking around the Temple, but she had not bothered to look for her. Sometimes she made progress with Princess, and others she felt they were back to square one. She was unpredictable. Occasionally it crossed her mind (and passed Laal's lips) Princess was a lost cause. After all, even Mentor had loudly announced that the angel-faced demon was part of their clan by name only. For the most part, she refused to give up on her, however.

As for Crim…

Crim, who until recently had hardly been better than Princess.

Crim, whom they all now knew was responsible for the scars all over Mentor's body.

Perhaps it was better sometimes to let things be. If Princess learned to use her power better, could she do so much harm?

"This one?" Yuki asked, turning a short one-handed sickle in their hands. They gave it an experimental swing. "Feels nice."

Sunshine watched them wave it about, turning it this way and that in their hands and shifting through different stances. A smile tugged at her lips. Yuki would make a great fighter one day. They moved like flowing water and learned quickly, though they were still being far too aggressive for their tiny frame to allow, but Mentor was gradually beating this out of them. They were even beginning to control their *draoi*.

She picked a slender disarming knife off a rack and handed it to them. "If you're not going to use a shield, at least keep that in your other hand."

"I'm not really good at duel-wielding, though."

"It's just a backup. C'mon, Mentor's waiting."

The others were already in the Arena, stretching and moving through their forms under Mentor's scrutiny. Every now and then one of them would get a bark, or even a smack, and have to start whatever they were doing over again. Sunshine dragged Yuki into line by the elbow, picking her sword up along the way from where it had been discarded by a pillar and immediately starting her movements. Yuki frowned at the disarming knife before deciding to tuck it in to their side and focusing on the sickle.

In a flash, Mentor's foot kicked up and swept their back leg out from under them. Yuki yowled, tried to catch themself in a half-split and then fell backwards. Li-Li giggled.

"Watch your footing," Mentor commented, moving on to Laal, who was seamlessly moving through each exercise with her staff.

"Did you huh-hear?" Sunshine heard Li-Li whisper as she helped a red-faced Yuki up off the floor. "W-w-we're going through a p-portal today!"

"Oof. I hope you haven't eaten," Sunshine cut in.

"Huh?"

"Mentor didn't warn you?"

"Eh?"

"Oh nooo…"

Yuki looked up from brushing dirt off their sleeve. "What?"

Laal, remaining silent, side-eyed her. *Don't you dare.* Crim nodded.

"If you go through on a full stomach, the portal will turn your insides out."

Li-Li turned grey. Even Yuki, brave as they tried to seem, patted their stomach worriedly.

"Sunny!" Laal barked. "Stop scaring them!"

Crim sniggered.

"I'm warning them."

The two acolytes turned to Laal, wide eyed. Li-Li looked as though the contents of her stomach might soon be expelled.

"No you're—*ugh!*—She's teasing you. Both of you." Laal's posture deteriorated as she reassured them. "You are *not* going to turn inside out!"

"Not all of you at least."

A snort from Crim.

"Sunny, I swear—"

"Laal! Watch your arms!" Mentor ducked as the tail of a whip arced far too close to her face.

"Right!"

"And you two, get back to your forms!"

Li-Li and Yuki, still looking shaky, resumed their practice. Sunshine chuckled to herself, ignoring Laal's glare. What was the point of having underlings, if you could not toy with them once in a while.

*

Portals were created using Orbs; swirling dark spheres imbued with the Elders' combined magic. When fitted into a Doorway, these stones created a rift that allowed denizens of the Mountain to traverse space (and possibly even time, though this has yet to be accomplished) in a manner of seconds. From the days of the Founder right until the days of the Mother, such Portals were used to visit new civilisations, to gather new knowledge and resources. Elders were regularly sent through these to converse with allies, and hopefully obtain new ones. Friendly nations were presented with Orbs of their own and, if they had the power, taught to make their own. For the younger Sidhe, they were used to access new training grounds on wild, untamed worlds where they might learn to fight and fend for themselves under their mentors' supervision, in hopes that one day they might be ready to go out into the great dark universe alone.

Orbs were held in a large stone basin in the middle of a long, narrow chamber referred to as the Crossroads, which was lined on either side with narrow doorways, with two larger entrances leading to opposite sides of the Mountain on either end. Some of these doorways were broken, crumbling, with whole sections wholly collapsed and unusable since Mother's Rising, but twelve remained intact.

Sunshine watched carefully as Mentor picked an Orb up and rubbed it gently with her palm, whispering with her lips almost touching the smooth stone. At her attentions, its inky blackness shifted, and a single swirl of purple light awoke within. Giving it an encouraging pat, she passed the stone to Laal.

"Go on."

Laal, clearly giddy at being picked, shot Sunshine a sideways smirk as she passed. She stepped up to one of the doorways and held the stone up in offering, arms shaking and lips pursed. She bowed her head. Seconds passed, and nothing happened.

"Please." She heard Laal whimper, raising it higher.

"It doesn't like you," Sunshine teased.

"Sunny I swear by the *gods*—"

"Oh!" Li-Li yelped, jumping back as the Orb flashed. Crackling with unseen energy, it leapt out of Laal's hands and into the centre of the doorway, where it stuck. Held by an invisible force, its purple light began to seep out, followed by an inky black cloud, creating a shimmering curtain from corner to corner, both colours leaked from the stone faster and faster, until the Orb completely disappeared, and the doorway was completely filled.

"Go on then!" Sunshine said, giving Yuki a little push. They wobbled forward a step, clutching the handle of their little sickle to tightly that their knuckles turned white.

"Um," They managed.

"Sunny stop bullying them," Laal scolded. "I'll go first, ok? Then Yuki, then Li-Li, Crim. Sunshine you can come behind them, but *don't scare them!*"

Mentor cleared her throat. Loudly. "Just get a move on!"

Falling. Twisting. Turning. Her stomach doing somersaults as she was jolted first one way, then the other. The stars streaked by so fast they appeared as straight lines of brilliant light. And the noise. She had forgotten the noise. That otherworldly screeching. So loud it filled her entire head. After only a second, she felt herself drifting away from her body. Or was her body falling apart? She could not tell the difference.

With a force that felt like she was crashing through the Mountainside, the pull of the portal ceased, and as the world corrected itself she was flung to the ground. Luckily, it was muddy, and carpeted with soft leaves—or things that resembled leaves, and she did not hit her head this time.

Someone was moaning. Someone else was heaving. Sunshine rolled to one side and found Yuki lying flat on their back, staring blankly up at the sky, one hand pressed against their forehead. At her feet, Li-Li had managed to raise herself to all fours, and was loudly spewing her lunch all over an unfortunate shrub. Crim was tottering about, using the trees (or things that resembled trees) as props and trying to regain control of her form.

"Told you," Sunshine laughed, though she should not have. Laughing hurt.

Li-Li could only moan back.

A jingle just a few feet away. Sunshine rolled again, shielding her eyes from the sun. Of course. Laal, looking unphased by their journey, was busy fixing her robes, bracelets ringing clearly with every movement. Sunshine reached out to her.

"Help me."

"You're fine."

"I think I left my insides in the void."

"Get up."

"Everything hurts."

"No it doesn't."

"Does."

Laal produced a small mirror from the folds of her skirt and proceeded to check her hair.

"Laal...please..."

Strong hands grabbed her by the wrist and hefted her up. Sunshine's legs found their place under her, through reluctantly. Yuki was lifted by Mentor next, and stumbled against her.

"What was that?" They wheezed.

"*That* was being flung through space far faster than any physical being is meant to go."

"I hate it."

"Yep."

"Sunshine, pick Li-Li up," Ordered Mentor, taking one look at the vomit coating the glossy foliage and blue buds of what must have been a rather pretty little bush and walking away.

"Yuki you heard—" But of course Yuki was already at Li-Li's side, taking her round the shoulders and brushing away the hairs that stuck to her foul-smelling lips. Crim, her back to one of the boles and eyes squeezed shut, forced herself forward.

*

Mentor split them into groups: Yuki and Li-Li versus Laal, Crim and Sunshine. Their objective was simple; survive their time in the dark, unknown landscape, find food and water, construct a shelter, fend off any threats that came their way.

Li-Li's hand shot up. "I-I-I don't understand the p-purpose of this, Mentor? We a-a-are immortal. Of cuh...course we can survive."

"Don't be so sure, Li-Li," said Mentor. "Laal, would you care to explain the exercise?"

Laal cleared her throat. "The mortal dangers in this jungle will not kill you, that is correct. But they can still weaken you if taken for granted, especially as an Acolyte. If you are not careful, you may be injured or even poisoned for a time. A time in which *more notable threats* may present themselves."

"Th-threats?"

"Beasts. Natural phenomena. Accidents. Not the mention all the *unknowns* that exist out there. *We* are not the only things that lurk on the edges of life," Sunshine added. Laal opened her mouth to silence her but she went on: "There are plenty of things that are *not* mortal. Plenty of things that might consider you nothing more than a snack."

"Such as?" Yuki pressed, trying to sound tough, though their voice wavered.

"You'll have to wait and see." Laal jabbed Sunshine in the arm, and she shut her mouth, but her work was done. Li-Li clung to Yuki's arm, both of them trembling.

"Keep your weapons on you, and your wits about you. And no conferring! That goes for you as well, Laal! No babying them!"

Sunshine snorted. Laal jabbed her again. "I wouldn't—"

"You would and you do."

"How are we supposed to know what to do without them? Without you?" Yuki asked, their brave face slowly fading away.

"Instinct, intellect, common sense."

"They're doomed," Sunshine scoffed. A proper punch this time. Her arm throbbed. Crim laughed weakly.

"Wh-wuh…where will you be, M-Mentor?"

"Right here." Mentor folded her legs under her and sat right down in the damp brush eyes closed. "Meditating. Projecting. Watching all of you."

"So if we cheat you'll know?" Yuki deduced.

"I'll know."

Sunshine gave the younger Sidhe a wink and a wave. Crim was already moving away, still looking disoriented and slightly ill. Laal, always the softer one, favoured them with a look of pity.

"Don't—"

"Laal! No advice!"

"Yes, Mentor."

Choosing the left path after Crim, the one that led downhill and into the darker depths of thick sinewy trunks and hanging vines, Sunshine led a reluctant Laal away from their wards. Not without a look back—for she was not entirely heartless. She caught a glimpse of them arm in arm, shuffling off in the opposite direction where the trees were sparser and eventually were halted by the sheer walls of a long grass-topped plateau. Sunshine smirked at their mistake. It would be easier for her to find them up there.

XII

The squelching. That was the worst part. The grotesque *squelch squelch squelch* of the carcass as Yuki struggled to skin and gut it for cooking over their modest fire. They had taken the animal down themself, and enthusiastically recounted the whole ordeal for Li-Li as they worked.

"I knew it would get tired. Would run itself to exhaustion after the fright I gave it. So all I had to do was sit up there and wait. Because where else would it rest, besides its own den? Not where something else might catch it. From up there I could hear all around, and of course I picked up on those fat trotters coming back. And the snorting. I suppose it's some sort of pig, don't you? I hope it tastes like one…"

Li-Li winced as Yuki finished cutting, and a wet pile of, well, *everything* slopped onto the ground. It stank.

"D-d-don't you think y-you should have done that a-a-way from camp?"

"What?"

"I just m-m-mean…the smell…"

Yuki laughed. "Afraid it'll attract predators? Monsters, like the ones Mentor tried to scare us with?"

"N-no, I meant…" Li-Li paused. "Well y-y-yes, that too. Bu-b-but can't you s-s-smell that?"

They shrugged. "Yes. I guess I'm used to it."

She tilted her head. "How?"

Yuki bit their lip. "I don't really know."

"Oh." Li-Li had never told them how much she remembered. Crim had been the only one she had ever told. For Yuki, just like everyone else, it just seemed to painful a topic to bring up. She regretted asking, but silently Li-Li began to wonder who had taught them to hunt. Who had taught them to skin and prepare a kill for cooking? They clearly had not taught them properly, if the animal's guts were currently stinking up their camp.

A branch popped, sending sparks into the air. The orange and yellow flames immediately moved to lick at its exposed innards. Li-Li watched them move to and fro for a long while, lost in thought. She and Yuki had worked together to summon it, and even with their combined efforts the flames had sputtered out of their hands. How was it so easy for the others? Both Crim and Sunshine favoured fire; their *draoi* commanded it with ease, but in completely different ways. She had observed them for a long time before finally understanding just how dissimilar they were. Sunshine's fire was warm, steady and merry. It was the one they most often used for their candles and lamps. The one they most trusted by their bedsides at night. Crim's, on the other hand, was volatile, unpredictable, burning red-hot one moment and dying away to a cool, heatless glow the next. She usually lit their hearth and cooked their food, though they always kept a watchful eye on it when she was away lest it be burned to a blackened husk. Li-Li guessed that the way their *draoi* behaved depended on the emotions of the Sidhe that commanded it; Sunshine was always warm, reliable, trustworthy and Crim was…

Crim was Crim. Li-Li poked the fire with her staff, then blew on it with a gentle breeze. It flared and roared at the indignation.

*

"Looks about hot enough now," Yuki said. "Give me a hand, will you?"

She stood up and rubbed her sleeping legs, stepping over their bedrolls to help Yuki mount the carcass over the fire. It was going dark now, and a greenish-yellow tint lined the grey clouds overhead.

"Wh-where do you think w-w-we are?" She pondered. She had never seen a sky this colour, or a sun so pink. Everything around them was familiar enough—things that resembled trees, flowers, bushes and grass, yet entirely unknown. Even they dry branches and foliage that they now fed into the fire were strange; round at the base but splitting into two pointed fingers. They had not seen many creatures besides a few insects and what they had decided was a 'pig' (for lack of a better word), but they were clearly on a different world.

"Far away," Was all Yuki could say. "I once heard Silver telling her pupils that the portals can take you anywhere in the universe, if you ask them properly. The places that are chosen for training are given to the mentors as a list of least lethal locations. Bad as Mentor might be, I doubt she would be willing to take us anywhere with any real danger."

"But sh-she said…about n-n-notable threats?"

"Notable, yes, nothing that would *really* kill us. But I don't doubt that they're out there." Yuki jerked a thumb up to the stars. "You've seen the people that come to visit, and the weapons they bring. Some of them could kill us, I'm sure. Just that they're allies so they won't. There are things out there that wouldn't hesitate, though, and if we're ever to be Anointed—if we ever see the day that we're sent out alone—we'll need to know how to fend for ourselves."

"Hm" Li-Li looked into the fire. They had gotten it going rather despite its slow start; she had fanned with her wind a few times and it seemed to like that. She wondered how she could have managed if left alone. Could she have made her own flame? "Can you t-t-teach me? To m-muh…Make lightning l-like you?"

"I'm not even sure how I do it," They remarked, flicking a few sparks at the fire for added effect. The flames rose up over the branches, pale blue and yellow. "It used to be they only came out when I was angry but now it's like any other movement."

"Yeah." The wind was the same, but she still needed her breath to get it going. "I wonder h-how lo-long it t-t-takes. To get p-proper c-c-control."

"Seems to come easy enough to Laal."

Li-Li scoffed. Everyone knew Laal was a prodigy. She could command both water and wind, lightning and earth came slowly to her but showed great potential (in Mentor's words), and was quickly learning the intricacies of fire from Sunshine. Her *draoi* was powerful. "She's the exception."

*

The remnants of the pig hung over the smoking fire, its rich, gamey aroma hanging over their camp. Li-Li lay stretched out on her back, stomach bloated and feeling sluggish from the meal; the two of them had eaten most of the animal between them. Beside her, Yuki was snoring, sprawled on their side with their blanket tangled around his legs.

Overhead, stars studded the greenish-black sky, twinkling from the harsh line of the plateau all the way to where the horizon met the treetops. With hardly a cloud in sight now, Li-Li was able to get a better look at them, and had quickly concluded that they were entirely foreign. She had spent hours trying to puzzle familiar shapes and constellations out of the heavenly dots, with no success. This was not her sky. She had been replaying a conversation in her head. A lesson, rather, something her father had told her about the stars and fate. They foretold one's destiny...Or did they determine it? Something about the dead, too? Perhaps they lived up there? She wondered if he was there now, did he see her? Was her mother with him? Her sisters? She fell asleep painting pictures of them in her mind.

*

A twig snapped in the forest. Not far from where they were. At first, she paid it no notice, assuming perhaps a deer was foraging about past its bedtime, but then she started. There were no deer here, and this sounded too big anyway. Another *crack,* the hushed rustling of branches moving slowly aside. The largest creature they had seen they had just eaten. Perhaps its mate? She thought of the tusks on the 'pig', wondered how might this one's might be, and moved her hand to wake Yuki.

That's no pig. A chill travelled up her spine, and Li-Li froze. If it was an animal, she should be able to sense it. They had tracked the 'pig' halfway across the forest just by sensing its base thoughts and desires, which all animals transmitted loudly and frequently. Sidhe spent most of their time tuning this chatter out, but now that Li-Li really *listened* she could sense nothing from this newcomer.

She closed her eyes. Perhaps it would not come near them. Perhaps it was just something foraging. Perhaps it was nothing. Perhaps she had fallen asleep and was dreaming some horrible—

Crack!

Closer now. Much closer. Li-Li went still, pretending to be asleep. Something was creeping through the undergrowth. Something large, moving without stealth. It did not care if they heard. The leaves rattled again on the far side of the fire. Something had stepped out into the clearing.

She opened her eyes a crack, peering past her feet to where the carcass was propped. At first she saw nothing, or at least thought it was nothing, just the darkness of the forest. Then she shuddered as the realisation settled in her stomach, cold and heavy. This darkness stood in front of the trees. A great shadow, swaying slightly. Something like a head lowered and sniffed what was left of their kill. Then there was a wet sound, like some monstrous mouth smacking its lips.

It was at precisely at this moment that Yuki stirred, then moaned. The shape moved, and Li-Li found herself staring into a pair of glowing violet eyes. It snarled.

"What the fuck is that!" The sound brought Yuki fully out of their doze, and they shot up. Li-Li, pinned in place, could not stop them as they freed themself from the blanket and lunged at the beast.

"Don't!" Was all she could squeak.

Yuki swung at it. Struck it with a dull thump. It did not hurt it, of course, and only aggravated it. The monster swung one arm and knocked him aside. Yuki tumbled through the remnants of their fire, flames springing up in their wake. Li-Li gasped, the blue fire giving detail to the formless hulk that now advanced towards them.

A guardian of the woods? It must be, for it was nothing more than a walking pile of branches and vines, all tangled together to give it something like a humanoid shape, with long, dragging arms and shining eyes.

It bellowed.

She shrieked.

Yuki hauled them up off the ground and rummaged under their bedroll. They pulled out their sickle, continued to rummage, then seemed to give up on the knife and turned to face their foe once more. Once again, it raised an arm as soon as they made eye contact, vines swinging like whips lashed out as it brought it down, hitting Yuki in the legs with a painful *smack*. They grunted, but stayed up this time and slashed at the vines. A few flew off and the monster roared in anger, its body turning as it swung its other arm. Yuki, braver now that they had wounded it, took their chance to thrust at its skirts (it had nothing quite resembling legs). Their sickle cut through wood and tendril alike, opening up a hole in its lower half. It roared again as it attacked, only for Yuki to leap out of the way. Flames leapt up with him and the creature recoiled at their heat.

Li-Li's arms and legs, still leaden with fear, began to move as its attention turned aside. Before she knew what she was doing, she was out of bed and picking her staff up off the ground. Yuki could not face this thing alone. But what could she do? She struck out, whacking it in the back as it turned on Yuki.

It did not seem to notice, or her attack did not hurt, and it lashed at Yuki again. She tried jabbing it, but that only got her staff stuck between its knotted exterior. She tried to yank her staff back and broke a few twigs in the way, but even this did not hinder it. Only when Yuki managed to hack a few pieces away did it give any sort of reaction. It moved with both arms this time, swinging horizontally with one has it slammed the other down to the ground. Yuki jumped away from the former only to be pummelled to the ground by the latter with a cry.

The beast stood up straight, backing away from the dented spot where Yuki lay, groaning and bruised. This time, with limbs balled up into something like a fist, it hammered at them. Again, again, again. Yuki did not cry out again, but lay broken and bloodied where they had fallen.

Panic welled up in Li-Li's stomach. Could it kill Yuki? It was definitely a *notable threat*. She had to help, but it would not face her, and she hadn't the courage to leap in front of it like they had done. On the ground, Yuki twitched and coughed up dark mouthfuls of blood.

"Leave them alone!" She screamed, throwing the staff aside. With her hands and claws and fangs, she pounced on it, tearing and snapping at its side. She ripped out a huge gash where she attacked and found that the thing was completely hollow inside. This finally got its attention, and the monster wheeled around as fast as its lumbering bulk would allow, arms flailing. With speed that surprised even herself, Li-Li darted away, and it struck at thin air. It growled, eyes flaring enough to remind her of her fear. But she could not cower. She had to help Yuki.

"Go away!" It seemed foolish to demand anything of such a monster, but demand she did, stamping her foot for good measure. "Just go away!"

It roared back. A terrifying, ear-shattering roar that shook all of the forest. But Li-Li did not back down. Instead, the fear that pooled in her stomach turned to warmth. A pulse that raced through her. She raised her hands, and the wind rose up to greet her. A breeze at first, then a gale. The monster seemed to hesitate as the embers of the fire were picked up and flung at it, scorching where they landed.

"I said GO AWAY!" A tornado. Then a hurricane, as she reached up and pulled clouds out of the sky. It assaulted the beast, shoving it from side to side. Leaves and twigs were ripped from its body as the wind wailed past. Curled up in the dirt, Yuki moaned, raising one crushed hand, and lightning flashed from

their fingertips. Pale and thin though it was, it joined the storm eagerly striking and stabbing at the monster, until the whole thing burst into flames.

XIII

A gust picked up, sweeping the salty tang of a nearby ocean towards her. Crim sniffed thoughtfully. Oceans meant fish, probably. But she was not in the mood for seafood. She would explore that later. Inhaling more deeply this time, she picked up something more gamey. A bird, perhaps?

Her consciousness crept out, crawling through the twisted bushels and pale trunks. She stalked the trail carefully, not wandering too far. After the incident with Mentor, she still felt untethered—like she might slip from her body at any moment. Their journey through the portal had not helped this, and now her arms and legs felt like they belonged to someone else. She had volunteered to go hunting in hopes that Laal and Sunny would not notice, though they had been eyeing her cautiously lately. Maybe they thought she was losing her mind.

The idea had occurred to her as well.

The leaves that were not quite leaves jumped just a few meters away. Something was peeking out. Watching her fearfully. Did it hear the rumble in her belly?

That did not matter. Her knife took it neatly by the neck, and it flopped lifelessly to the ground. She had been right, and wrong. It was like a bird, but with teeth and jaws of a lizard, and the hindquarters of a snake. Smelled good enough. Crim strung it to her waist and crouched again, staying perfectly still and hoping for signs of more. Perhaps they flocked or roosted in groups?

It turned out they did, and she had three more dangling from her belt when she found the others. Laal had built a shelter and a fire pit, whilst Sunshine already had a flame crackling yellow and hot. They sat peeling a pile of slender purple-skinned roots, which they then sliced and placed on a hot stone to bake. Crim set to work bleeding and plucking the 'birds', swearing at the fact that they had coarse hair rather than feathers, eventually losing her temper and singing them off with a quick burst of sparks.

"Don't cook them just yet." Sunshine laughed. "I have some onions to stuff them with."

The 'onions' were small yellow bulbs. Though fragrant, they smelled more similar to ginger or garlic than onions, and were rather mushy on the inside. Crim hesitantly nibbled on one as she helped, then pulled a face.

"That's bitter."

"They're fine once you get them hot," Laal said, spearing one on her small knife and holding it to the flame. It sizzled, juices dripping down onto the roots and quickly caramelised at the edges. "Much sweeter."

"Hah. So you've been tasting all this without me." Crim poked at the anaemic-looking meat. "Maybe I should've done the same."

"I'm too hungry to care how any of this tastes, Loves," remarked Sunshine, already trussing her second carcass to her spit and balancing it over the fire. "Come on, the sooner they are cooked, the sooner we can eat."

Laal screwed her eyebrows at the milky fat now trickling down onto the hot stones, adding even more marinade to the smoking roots. "Not sure I should be excited about that."

*

One 'bird' each was enough for both Laal and Sunshine, though the latter tried to pick at their fourth catch stubbornly even as Crim took it from its resting place by the fire. The meat when cooked was dark, rich and oily. Much like duck or goose though with a slightly zestier bite, possibly from the small yellow 'onions'. The roots were flavourless and benefitted greatly from the grease of the other foods, in fact she found it hard to eat them without an accompanying handful of meat. She ate with her fingers, much to Laal's distain, only occasionally wiping her greasy fingers on the napkin she had been given.

Once they were done eating, they all washed from the water jugs, which Crim and Sunshine heated. The other two touched up the paint on their faces, feet and hands, but Crim was happy enough to leave it, cracked and smudged though it was by now. Laal studied her critically as she cleaned her knives and fitted them back into their narrow sheaths. When Crim went to step, and rolled her ankle like an idiot mortal, she took note.

"You're wobbling."

"I'm fine."

Sunshine raised her head slightly and frowned. "You *do* seem a little…Unsteady."

"It's just the portal," Crim insisted. "Still a bit travel sick, I guess."

"Doesn't usually last this long."

"No," Laal mused pursing her plump lips. "It's not just the portal, either. You've been off for a while now."

"Off?"

Sunshine rolled onto her side and propped herself up on her elbow. "She's right. It's like you're…clumsy."

"I'm always clumsy."

"*Clumsier*. Like those little mortals with the big heads."

"Toddlers," Laal corrected.

"Yes. Those."

"I don't know what you mean." Crim pulled the strap across her chest. Somehow, it didn't feel right. She fingered the closure, found it at its usual hole, *tutted* loudly and tugged again.

"It's caught in your robe," Sunshine offered, pointing at her back. "See?"

She felt for the crumpled fabric, pulling it down. "Thanks."

"There!" Laal said, gesturing to her. "You saw that, too?"

"I did. You stumbled. Like you're off balance," Agreed Sunshine.

"She *is* off balance. Ever since what happened with Mentor—"

"I'm FINE!" Crim said. Crim *roared*. Her voice echoed through the sparse trees. Somewhere in the dark an animal barked back. Her friends just stared, silent. The concern on their faces said enough, and she hung her head, ashamed. "I'm fine, I just…um…I'm going for a walk."

Laal seemed ready to protest, but Sunshine held out a hand to silence her. They both nodded. Crim, not able to bear their worry any longer, spun on her heel and stormed off into the night.

*

She walked. And walked and walked. Past the swaying plants and chirping wildlife. Tiptoeing along the edge of a muddy, motionless riverbed, until the sky opened up ahead, and she was staring past the peaks that guarded the entrance to a circular cove. The unfamiliar sky was now jet, with the edges emanating a ghostly green glow. Some trick of the atmosphere, she suspected. Water lapped sluggishly at the smooth sand of the crescent grey beech. No notable waves disturbed it, however, and as Crim approached she understood why. Even more so when she let her toes past the hard line of dry sand—the water was thick, heavy and almost gelatinous. It left behind an oily purple residue on her skin. Crim shuddered and stepped back, looking up and down the silver shore for any sign of life. She found it in the form of stone-shelled crustaceans and something shiny and black that slithered under the surface, leaving wavy lines where it passed. These resembled leeches far too much for her liking, so she perched atop a large round boulder under the treeline and gazed out at the horizon.

Surrounded by silence, she struggled to focus on herself. Searched for the connection between her body and soul, testing. It gave easily, and her vision doubled, head bobbing as she struggled to remain conscious. She would not lose control, would not lose her grasp on her physical form.

Suddenly, she sensed something else moving. Wriggling about in her mind like those enormous leeches. It touched the connection and then she was floating up up up, twisting, trying desperately to find that tether. The other presence did not seem to fight her, or push her further away. Rather, it simply demanded her attention. Without eyes and ears the world seemed strange, but as she hovered there it gradually began to take form. A blackness punctuated by vibrant colours and lights. The things slithering under glittering sand moved in waves of purple and blue. The crustaceans that marched towards the flashing sea were little balls of yellow luminescence. And the figure perched atop a smoky rock was a wash of deep red and burnt orange.

The other was in control now, and Crim had the disorienting experience of watching her body move without her. She looked down, inspecting the surface of the boulder. Looking for something. One hand felt along the surface until it found the smallest thread of a crack which shimmered a faint white. Forming a fist, she struck here and the stone split apart, a large sliver sliding to the ground to reveal more spectral light.

Someone had a hold of the other end of the tether. They pulled, hauling her back into her body at frightening speed. Crim was suddenly aware of her eyes and how awkwardly they rolled around in their sockets. They hurt slightly, swimming with bright spots as she tried to adjust her vision. Her hand was still on the broken section of rock, which was glossy and smooth under the surface, but her fingers touched a strange rough pattern and then a larger section much the same. It felt warm.

Once her sight was back she looked down and started at the object under her hand. The image of a skull fossilised into the boulder. A skull not much smaller than her own. Was the rest of the animal attached, hidden away in the heart of the soft stone?

For some reason thinking of it as an 'animal' felt disrespectful. Something about the visage looking up at her betrayed intelligence, culture, sentience. This was no mere beast, but a *person*. The Other looming that the back of her head stirred.

Yes.

How long had they been here? How had they come to be encased in a stone on the shores of this moonlit sea? Had they been carried here by the currents from afar?

Her attention turned to the water. The deep, dark ancient ocean. The water turned purple and thick with pollution, now home to strange creatures that thrived in the most adverse of conditions. The plants around it that bore a strange resemblance to fungi. The mangy animals that scrounged to survive.

What had happened here, to make it so inhospitable?

*

A scream much further up. Past their camp and nearer the plateau. Fear. Anger.

Something had found Li-Li and Yuki.

Crim sprang up, patting the outline of a skull goodbye as she went. How long would it be before he had company again? Would another soul ever visit his lonely beach? She tucked his memory away in the archives of her mind. He would find this place in the vast Library of the Sidhe and be welcomed into the annals of time.

XIV

The ground sloped up steeply beyond the portal. Sparse, slender trees rising straight and tall from dry, clumpy soil. Sunshine kicked up large lumps as she stumbled upward, bent low with the effort of running. She had already stumbled a dozen times, but picked herself up again and again as the shouts and screams from Yuki and Li-Li's camp became more and more frenzied. Another roar shook the ground, and she jumped up the few low banks that now reared up to block her path.

Crim had caught up to them somehow, moving at a speed she had never witnessed before, leaping over obstacles and clambering up trees, bent almost to all fours at times in a posture that left Sunshine's stomach unsettled. Laal, panting and huffing behind, now moved farther away—she could not jump as high as Sunshine, so the embankments proved more of a struggle. Sunshine paid her no heed. She would catch up. Right now she needed to help…

"Li-Li!" She burst into the clearing, arms in front of her face to shield her from the mounting storm. "Stop!"

The youngling stood opposite, hands outstretched and eyes shining. Whether or not she heard her, she did not stop or move. The flames engulfing her opponent grew larger and hotter.

"*Stop!*" Sunshine yelled again. Heedless, she charged headlong into the hurricane. Buffeted and staggering every which way, she half-crawled to its heart, where a pile of sticks was blazing. A painted foot could be seen poking out from under the kindling. Crim was there too, trying to tame the growing flames, lulling and cooling them to prevent further injury. Laal appeared a few feet away, though obscured by the wall of wind. She waved her away. "Get Li-Li!"

Laal stared down worriedly at she pulled Mentor out. Burnt but still conscious, the elder Sidhe cursed quietly as Sunshine propped her up. Sunshine shushed the fire and it quailed, turning dim and cool at her feet. There was nothing she could do about the rest of the storm, however.

"I-I…what? M-M-Mentor?" Li-Li's voice, amplified by the wind, echoed around her. "What?"

At first, a gap appeared in the grey, swirling wall. Then the whole thing faded and slowed to a stop. A few straggling zaps of electricity set both Sunshine and Mentor's hair on end. In a hole in the ground, Yuki groaned and rolled into a reclining position, clutching his head. Laal, too busy calming Storm Li-Li, did not notice them. Crim to her credit knelt and petted their bloodied blue bristles, inspecting their broken limbs. Sunshine eased Mentor down beside them and she turned back and forth checking them both; Mentor's burns were mostly healed already—Li-Li could not summon flames nearly as strong as either of them, and she had a few minor cuts and bruises, including some claw marks on her calf, but she was mostly just in a bad mood. Yuki was battered and blue from head to toe, and was currently trying to set their own nose. She clicked it back into place for them and patted his shoulder, which only elicited a painted grunt.

"B-b-but I d-don't…" Li-Li was still babbling. "The monster—"

"Was just Mentor," Crim said.

"But…but wh-why would she? Sh-sh-she hurt him! She at-t-tacked us!"

"It's a test," Sunshine replied, smiling. "She wanted to see how the two of you would react. If you could defend yourselves."

"You knew?" Said Yuki hoarsely.

"I had an inkling."

"She did more or less the same with us," Added Crim.

"More or less," Laal chimed in.

"We still have to take tests. Though I haven't had one in a while," Sunshine told them.

"I haven't had one in longer," Laal bragged.

"Yes well we all can't be as gifted as Laal."

"True."

"But she…she n-n-nearly killed…nearly…"

"I'm fine, actually," Yuki cut in. "I mean I hurt everywhere but definitely not nearly dead."

"Oh." Li-Li, deflated, slumped down onto her upended bedding. "Mentor. I'm so sorry."

Mentor, looking less and less cooked by the second, accepted a handful of cool water from Laal and cocked an eyebrow. "I'm impressed more than anything."

*

They spent another day in the foreign forest. Mostly training and hunting, but they climbed to the top of the plateau after the midday sun cooled. It baked the pale trees, and brought with it fine clouds of vapour that drifted languidly around as they stood on the flat, rocky top. From here, Sunshine could see that where she and Laal had camped had actually been just a few miles in from the coast, where a pink, still sea stretched out as far as the eye could see. On either side, spaced at fairly regular intervals, other plateaus and pillars of rock stood in a line across the land. Opposite the forest and the ocean, a sweeping plain of tall white grass was interrupted only by two perpendicular silver rivers.

"Mentor, where are we?" Yuki asked, watching a herd of long-legged animals canter away from the water. Only their backs and heads could be seen as they reached the deepest parts of the grass.

"Hsei," Mentor answered. "It was discovered in the time of the Matriarch. Though we did not visit it again until sometime later."

"Why not?"

"Some worlds are inhospitable when we first come to them. We still keep them in our archives, of course, and the elders may study them if the urge takes them. But in general it is better to wait until they are ready."

Li-Li pointed to a dark spot to their right where, at the furthest visible edge of the plain, a pile of strangely regular-shaped stones occupied a great clearing. "That l-looks like it was c-c-constructed."

"It was. A while before we first came."

"Wh-what happened t-to them?"

"Time."

*

After that Mentor brought them home, and placed the now-transparent Orb into Sunshine's hands.

"Take it to Viper and Isme in the Archives," she instructed. "They will teach you how to fix it."

"Why not Laal?" Sunshine, knowing her lover was prone to envy, wondered what she would think of Mentor trusting this to her.

"Laal is good at many things. She understands her *draoi* and our lore better than all of you. She works hard." Mentor patted her arm. "But wit is not the same as talent."

"I'm talented?"

"Only if you never mention that I said this again."

"Right."

Sunshine, cupping the Orb carefully in both hands all the way, made her way down to the Archives—a branch of the Library overseen by Viper and Isme, located under the three main floors and accessed via a narrow door to which only they and Bart had keys. Afraid to unhand the fragile-looking stone, she kicked the bottom firmly, knowing that Isme was missing an ear and therefore partially deaf. Viper answered.

"Who are you?" She asked coolly.

"I uh…" She held out the Orb.

"Yes, I saw that. I asked who you are."

"I'm Sunshine?"

"Are you sure?"

"I am."

"And who teaches you?"

"Mentor."

"Yes, Child. Everyone has a mentor. What's their name?"

"Um." Did Mentor have a name?

"Jeepers the child is simple," Viper muttered, then turning she shouted down the stairs: "Do you know who owns Sunshine?"

A muffled voice yelled back up.

"No. *Sunshine!*"

Another muffled yell. A name? Mentor's name? Sunshine didn't catch it.

"Right. Come on down then."

-

Viper took the Orb from Sunshine, and set it into a smaller basin, similar to the one at the Crossroads. It made a feeble *tink* as it hit the bottom, and Sunshine wondered if she should be more careful with it.

A titter from behind. "It would take more than that to break it, Dearie."

Sunshine leapt out of her skin and promptly stuffed herself back in. Esme had silently appeared out of the shadows of one of the narrow doors that led to the other, cramped chambers of the Archives and was now standing hunched behind her. Esme, one of the few Elders known to be older than even Mother, had suffered greatly under the rule of the Patriarch, mostly due to her refusal to create more and better weapons to combat the unknown enemy he constantly raved about. The one that would destroy the skies. The one never to be seen, that spurred the siring of thousands of fledglings (most of whom did not survive the process) as well as hundreds of experiments and excursions out into the void.

Esme had volunteered for some of these experiments, believing at first that the Patriarch would lead them to greatness and not depravity, at the first sign of insolence they had gotten worse, and she had been locked away in the Dungeons, thought destroyed. Whatever had been done to her—most of which was rumoured but not openly affirmed—had left her scarred, bent like an old crone with twisted limbs and skin like withered scales. After the revolt, when she had finally been released from her cell, she had refused to re-join society, instead hiding herself away down here and dedicating herself to her work. Viper, her long-time partner, followed suit, though she could sometimes be seen in the Market or Forum in the company of Silver and Ashara and Hammer.

"It…um," Sunshine said. "It just looks so fragile."

"Oh, I startled you. So sorry," Esme rasped, shrinking.

"Yes. I didn't hear you. I should be the one to apologise."

"Sorry. But the Orbs cannot be destroyed but by great force, or powerful magic. We made them this way."

"I see." She nodded, prodding it so that it rolled around in the basin with a pleasant ringing. "So then why do they lose power so easily?"

"Easily?" A scabbed brow raised. "How much power do you suppose it takes to tunnel through the stars?"

Sunshine paused. She had never considered that this was how the portals worked.

"How else would they work?"

"…Magic?"

"Even magic has rules. And while it exists in this realm, it is hindered by the constraints of this realm. It is not limitless."

"I see."

"Your mentor sent you here to imbue it?"

Sunshine blinked. "No she sent me to...I mean you and Viper should probably do that. I can't—"

"Nonsense. If she trusts you to do this then you must be ready." A sharp laugh. "No, don't worry we won't leave you alone. We shall both help."

*

"Grasp it firmly now."

"Um."

"Relax your shoulders."

"Uh."

"Focus on it. Close your eyes if you need to."

"Er."

"It might feel like glass, but it's so much more. Reach through the physical. Feel it."

"Eh?"

"You understand how it works, right? How to feel beyond the physical?"

Had Mentor taught her this? She knew how to dart, and the basics of projection. Maybe it was like that? Maybe if she disengaged from...

"No, no. Be careful, Dearie, don't project. You might get stuck inside it."

"Stuck?"

"Yes. It's not like projecting. You must remain anchored."

"Oh."

"Try from your fingertips out. Imagine them melting into the glass. Like part of you is leaking into it."

"But *don't* project into it, Dearie. I don't want to have to go digging you out."

"Yes." Melt her fingertips into it? What the hell did that mean? She gripped it tighter, so tight she feared it might smash in her hands. The Orb was cold, smooth. Surprisingly strong. Nothing happened.

"It's hard the first few times. Don't worry."

"Maybe try to use your *draoi*?"

Her *draoi*. That made more sense. She reached down into that well and pulled out a morsel of fire. It travelled up, out of her core and over her shoulders. Down her arms and through her fingertips. The Orb began to warm.

"Yes, Dearie. That's it! Push it through!"

"*Ugh.*" She felt queasy. Her *draoi* was streaming out of her and into the stone. Fast. Much too fast.

"Easy. Easy." Another pair of hands covered her own. Warm, strong hands. The stone continued to heat up, but now did not drain her. "Esme."

Dry, shrivelled fingertips gripped her shoulders. Her fire flowed now without end. "There we go, Dearie. Just a little more…*there!*"

Esme pulled her back just as Viper tore the Orb from her hands. The sudden disengagement sent a shockwave through her, and Sunshine immediately broke out in a cold sweat. Viper dropped the Orb back into its basin and helped Esme to ease her down onto a creaky sofa. She promptly vomited over the arm onto the floor.

"Sorry."

They both laughed.

"Everyone gets a shock the first time," Viper stated plainly. "Be grateful there was no seizure."

"Seizure?"

"Your mentor had one her first time. Took her days to recover," Esme put in. "Looks like you're tougher than her."

She might have felt proud if she had the energy. "You two do that all the time?"

"Yes. You get used to it," Viper replied. "Soon you'll be doing Espers and Carbuncles."

XV

Yuki was strangely quiet, and even more poker-faced than usual as they made their way back to their dormitory. They did not speak for the entire walk, and only grunted when Bull greeted them back with a cheery smile. Inside, Yuki made straight for their bed. Li-Li watched as they eased I down with a loud groan. Unlike Mentor, they still bore a lot of the marks from their scrap, so she supposed their spirits were mostly low due to the incessant ache in their side. Mostly.

Princess and her friends, lounging around in the corner, giggled as they approached. Yuki snarled back.

"Yuki?"

Yuki let out a loud huff and closed their eyes. Li-Li sat cross-legged between their beds, fussing with the hem of her skirt. Were they angry at her? Upset? Or simply in pain? She gently probed their thoughts. Just enough to sense their emotions. Going any further without express permission or dire need was considered extremely rude.

"What a-are you s-s-so frustrated ah…about?"

Another puff of air escaped their lips. They stretched, resting an arm across their eyes to shelter them from the sun rock blazing above. The movement seemed to hurt their ribs, and they grimaced.

"I-is it m-m-me?"

A long silence. "No, it's not you."

It's also not not *me.* Li-Li, catching the hesitation, pulled at a loose thread in her hem. Rearranging her skirt over her legs, she let Yuki simmer a while longer, hoping they might open up on their own. When they did not, and that while began to stale, she pressed: "Yuki, what's w-wr-wrong?"

"Nothing."

"Liar."

"Leave me, Li-Li."

"N-nope."

With a loud *tut*, they turned their back to her.

"Yuki."

Sigh.

"I'm n-n-not leaving un-until you tell me."

Grunt.

In their corner, Princess and her cohorts were not oblivious to their conversation. Rather, their own hooting and squawking had died down incrementally as Li-Li tried to coax an answer out of Yuki. Now, in the quiet, a series of giggles broke out, punctuated by sharp whispers and giddy *shushing*. Yuki stirred.

"I-if you would j-j-just *tell me*—"

"Shut up, Li-Li!"

She started. Yuki had never raised their voice to her. Had certainly never told her to shut up so aggressively. It worked. Her mouth snapped shut. She glared at their back long enough for them to feel the heat of it, then stood up.

"I'm g-g-going to the Market."

Another titter from behind as she made for the doors. Louder, more deliberate. Another snarl from Yuki. Footsteps and a shout. Lilith—Princess' right-hand—let out a sharp cry. Li-Li spun to find Yuki holding Princess up by the neck, teeth barred and nails jabbing into her smooth flesh. She kicked at them and scratched, but they only squeezed harder.

"Yuki!" She made to intervene, to pull them away or at least calm them down, too late. With a smirk, Princess gripped Yuki's arm tightly in both hands. Sheets of ice spread out from under her palms, encasing them from wrist to shoulder. Yuki yelped at the cold and tried to yank their arm away, but she was quicker. With a mere twitch, she hammered both of her fists into Yuki's face, then kicked them away. Howling in pain, Yuki struck the doors hard enough to bend the hinges, hugging themself with tears streaming down their cheeks. She could hear the grinding and crunching of their obliterated ribcage as they moved, as they struggled to stand. They looked up at Li-Li, eyes welling pitifully, leaning back against the wall for support, but all she could do was shake her head. Princess had only defended herself, and Yuki had been out of line. She would not fight for them this time.

Princess, dabbing daintily at the welts in her neck with a handkerchief, shouldered Li-Li out of the way as she strode out, the rest of her group trailing behind. Only Lilith stopped to say anything.

"Keep your pet in line, will you?"

*

"Hah!" How comedic; Princess' lapdog calling Yuki her 'pet'. She watched Lilith as she stepped past a bleary-eyed Yuki. Not without a complimentary sneer.

"Li-Li…" They groaned.

"Wh-why did…you d-d-do that?"

"I…"

"What duh…did you e-e-expect? She wu-would just let you thr-throttle her?"

"I…"

"A-and y-you *know* better that t-t-to rise to th-them! It o-o-only encourages th-th-them!"

"Please," They implored. "I can't dress these myself."

"I should l-l-leave you," she remarked. "O-or let you g-guh…go to Mentor. Try to ex-explain how *stupid* you j-j-just were."

"Please?"

"They o-only *just* g-got bored of t-t-tormenting me! I've h-h-had five *centuries* of-of it!"

Yuki slumped back against the door. "Right."

She unfolded her arms. "I'll ask Bull for some bandages."

Their matron had plenty of bandages to spare in one of their countless cupboards. He even had an assortment of splints propped under a shelf of ointments and elixirs.

"It's not unusual for fights to break out," he told her with a wink. "What with so many of you sharing quarters."

"D-did you hear…?"

"I heard a kerfuffle. I don't intervene until it becomes a ruckus, though. Most times it's best to just let you younglings knock the sense into each other for me."

"Y-Yuki got it s-s-sn-snapped into them."

"Haha! They'll live. And they'll learn to choose their battles more wisely, too. Or at least ensure that they have an ally at their back."

"Do you th-thing I sh-sh-should have—"

"No. They needed a slap."

"Snap."

"Pffft! *A snap.*"

They both chuckled at Yuki's expense, though Li-Li could not help feeling a pang of guilt. She accepted a splint, a wet cloth, a roll of bandages and a small bottle of elixir ('to see them through the night') from Bull and I to Yuki, who had dragged themself back into their bed. A trail of smudged blood ran from them to the door, staining their sheets a dark brownish-red.

"You c-couldn't w-w-wait for me to g-get b-b-back?" She grumbled.

"I'll change the sheets tomorrow." They said dismissively. "…Yours, too."

Li-Li followed their line of sight to the smear on her own blanket, temper flaring. She had half a mind to throw the bandages at them and leave. "*How* did y-yo-you…!"

Yuki, looking ever greyer by the second, only shrugged weakly. "Sorry."

She took a deep breath. Let it out as she told herself to calm, then knelt beside them. Wincing, they let her wash and cover the worst lacerations on their arms and face. Li-Li wiped each one clean with the cloth, which had been drenched in a clear concoction that looked like water but smelled strongly of aniseed. Setting their ribs turned her stomach, and the crackle of their bones being forced back into place rang in her ears for days after, not to mention the deep, guttural roar of pain Yuki let out. Thankfully, a sip of the elixir took effect almost immediately, and they became almost giddy as they watched her wrap them up.

"I'm sorry, Li-Li." They mumbled through a stiff jaw and numb lips.

"It's f-f-fine. You c-can wah-wash everything t-t-tomorrow."

"Wha…? No, no. I mean. I'm so grumpy."

"Just today? O-or always?"

"Always. But I'm mostly sorry for today."

"A-are you g-going to tell me wh-wh-why?"

An awkward smile. "I lost."

"Lost what?"

"Against Mentor. I got slapped around like a ragdoll."

Li-Li burst out laughing. "B-by the *gods*, Yuki! Tha…that's why y-you-you're in such a *mood!*"

A sheepish smile this time. "I wanted to impress…um…to impress everyone."

She shook her head. "S-so you threw yourself I-into the fight. L-l-lost. Then g-got into a h-hu-huff?"

"Uh-huh." They laughed now, too. "Don't forget you saved me, too."

She blushed. "Oh I d-didn't. I-I'm sure Mentor let me w-w-win."

"You flattened her!"

"Just a-a-a little! I d-didn't mean to!"

Yuki flopped down onto their bed, grinning stupidly thanks to whatever Bull put into his elixirs. "But you *did*. You saved this idiot. And here you are having to patch me up after I made a fool of myself *again*."

"You di-didn't m-make a fool of your-yourself."

"Yes, I did."

Li-Li hid behind her hair before admitting: "Yeah. Maybe you did."

When they woke the next day Yuki's memory was hazy. They remembered returning to their dormitory, and had a vague sense of what had happened with Princess, but not much else. After their last few drops of elixir, they returned to being cantankerous and snappy thanks to the pain that had now migrated from their ribs to their arm. Li-Li was sick and tired of their attitude at this stage, and did not help them to get dressed, but set out for their mistresses' chambers alone, leaving them to struggle with their robe in a flurry of growls and curses.

She arrived surprisingly quickly without them dragging their heels, and found Sunshine, Crim, Laal and Mentor already seated round the table, staring into their bowls and not passing a word. The room was chilly, the air icy and tense. She tiptoed across eggshells to the fire and made herself a small bowl of cold noodles in a fragrant, spiced broth. Even the flames had gone into hiding under the coals. When she turned, she wondered if she could go and eat in the hallway, not wanting to face whatever had happened on an empty stomach. Unfortunately, Mentor caught her eye and gestured for her to sit.

"Where is Yuki?"

"G-g-getting ready."

"We'll wait for them, then."

"Or you could just not—"

"What was that, Crim?"

The younger Sidhe crossed her arms and turned away. "Nothing."

Laal patted her shoulder and sipped her tea.

Yuki burst through the door as Li-Li was halfway through the worst breakfast of her existence. Sunshine would not so much as look at anyone, Crim was still staring into the fire, and Laal only stared into her tea with tears in her eyes. Mentor, unbothered by their sorrows, had been sharpening her *katars* the whole time. At a look from Li-Li, Yuki forwent their breakfast and immediately sat down between Laal and Mentor. Not the best place to sit, and they soon realised this, but before they could move Mentor declared:

"I'm leaving."

*

Neither Sunshine nor Laal even flinched, clearly having heard this news already. Crim's eyes narrowed and red flames peeked their heads out from among the coals. Afterwards, Li-Li wondered if their initial reactions had been the same as hers and Yuki's. Cold soup slopped over her lap as she slammed her hand down on the table, overturning her bowl. Yuki leapt up from their chair and backed away, then looped back to Mentor.

"Wh-wh-WHAT!"

"Leaving?"

"Wh-where!"

"You're joking?"

"Why!"

"But who will…what about…"

"Is it b-b-because I suh-set you on f-fuh…fire?"

Mentor chortled. "No, Li-Li. Though that *did* confirm my assessment of both you and Yuki. It showed me that you are almost ready to be Anointed, and I can leave you for a while with your mistresses without worry. If anything should happen in my absence, the five of you must be there for one another."

"Five?" Yuki tried to correct.

"Princess cannot be counted on. We all know this."

Yuki asked, wide-eyed: "Where are you going?"

"A world known as Epim. Mother received a vision of them some time ago, and called the council to decide who should go. Only three candidates were chosen, and I was lucky enough to be…"

Another mutter.

"Sunshine?"

"Nothing."

"Good. I have the honour of being our ambassador to a new race."

"How long will you be gone for?"

"I cannot say."

Laal, chewing her lip, said: "Five hundred years, seven months, two days and fifteen hours."

"What?" Mentor responded.

"That's how long Cassius has been gone. The longest any ambassador has been away."

"Yes, well he's not coming back."

"And you?"

"We shall see."

XVI

Crim fell into the Library. She was not well today, not at all. Her visit to Hsei had weakened her hold on her body, and now the thought of Mentor leaving, of being left to cope with this with no guidance, was distracting her from—quite literally—holding herself together. She bumped roughly against a wooden chair, hip singing where the arm dug in. It did not matter, the sensation was for her physical form, and that was being shared with another.

Collapsing onto her usual sofa, she closed her eyes and fought of the vertigo-like sensation humming through her. Whenever this got worse, as it was now, she felt herself running cold, like her body was a cocoon keeping her insulated. She shoved back against the other force trying to commandeer, and it backed off as usual; unwanted guest as it was, it was rarely forceful.

A stack fell over, and she heard the heavy *clump clump clump* of Bart hurrying towards her. Gnarled fingers touched her forehead, and the Minotaur rumbled gravely.

"What has happened to you, child?"

"I was hoping you could tell me."

He took her hand and squeezed it. Somehow, she felt this through all of her being—body and soul—and all of a sudden she was firmly in the present, staring perplexedly up at his worried old face.

"Oh, but you are all wrong, Dear One," he said. "All wrong. Fading. But how?"

"I will sound insane."

"All the more reason to tell me."

She gulped. What would happen to her if everyone knew? What would Mother do?

Bart, clearly reading her thoughts, lowered his head and whispered: "Nothing leaves this Library. I swear it. Not even *she* can read me."

"There's someone else. Someone...um...in here."

His brow furrowed, and he caressed her forehead again, searching gently. She felt him opening and closing door in her mind. Surprisingly, her guest moved towards him, and made itself known. Bart started, lids fluttering shut. His lips moved as though speaking to someone. Then he laughed.

"But they have always been there, Child. At least as long as you have been a Sidhe."

"They have?" Crim sat up, understanding. "They can do this?"

"They can do anything," he replied. "Well, almost anything."

"So why now? And why like this?"

"Perhaps they need you to do what they cannot."

*

His words echoed in her head, but he could not determine exactly what her visitor wanted. For once, Bart seemed to have encountered a puzzle that was beyond him. All he did was assure her that the other meant no harm, and then distract her with work. So much sweeping and polishing and stacking that she forgot about the other presence lingering at the back of her mind. That ghost of a thought crouched in the dark and knocking at her skull.

He did keep an eye on her, to his credit. Wherever she went, she could hear and sense him nearby, jewellery clinking and clacking as he occupied himself with dusting the shelves. This inevitably led to him getting distracted by the titles he was meant to be cleaning. Eventually, he went quiet for so long that she dropped her broom and wandered up and down the aisles searching, only to find him sitting on an ottoman, flipping through a volume of Nichebian fairy tales.

Not wishing to disturb him, she tiptoed up and peered over his arm to see the page he was on, and immediately regretted it. The pictures, made of simple shapes and block colours, were hard to discern, but as Crim studied them she was able to discern something like a floating city in a starlit sky, and a town below it in ruins. As though roused by the image, she felt the Other stir, and foolishly fought for command of her mind.

No use. She was not strong enough to fight it and was quickly overpowered, sent reeling outward where, much like before, she observed the world around her on a new spectrum of shimmering colours. The books in their ghostly shelves glittered mesmerizingly. She was aware of a couple of Sidhe on the floor above—saw them *through* the floor, in fact. They were not reading, at least not at present, and the vigour of their movements seemed to shower sparks into the air.

Then there was Bart—ancient, unfathomable Bart. In this realm, he appeared young, strong and even larger than before. A shining beacon of light in the terrifying dark. Crim swam towards him. Anchored herself to him like a planet caught in the pull of a vibrant star.

The Other stood in front of him, and they seemed to converse. She pointed Crim's finger at the book, urgency in her face, though Crim could not hear her voice. The old Minotaur was nodding grimly as he responded. The exchange was short, but heated, and when it was done they both turned to face her. Unphased and apparently able to see through the planes that separated them, Bart reached out one giant hand and Crim took it. With a jerk, he brought her forward, and suddenly she was looking at him through her eyes again, gaping stupidly into his wizened face.

"I-I…what? Where was I?"

"Somewhere between this world and the spirit," he stated matter-of-factly. "Are you all right?"

She patted her body, her limbs. Ran her hands over her face to ensure everything was still there—still in the right place. "I think so?"

"They—that is to say, the Other You. I had a word with them. Explained that pushing you out of your body like this can't be good for you."

"And?"

"They seemed to understand. But I believe it is the only way they know to communicate."

Crim touched the corner of the page, ran it through her fingers. There was still some residue on it from her Other Self. She felt her power tingling down her arm. "What did she say? Something about these pictures disturbed her."

Bart huffed. "I can't say I understand it very well myself, but the message was for you, so perhaps you will know…"

"Tell me."

"She said: '*The angels of death fly through the heavens*'."

"Huh?"

He clapped his knees and stood. "Her kind are purely of the spirit world, My Dear. They have little to no concept of time or the physical limitations of our kind. My best guess would be she is trying to warn us of something yet to pass."

"She couldn't stick around to clarify?"

"Commanding your body is just as disorienting for her as being out of it is for *you*," Bart explained. "Her speech was slurred and child-like and I would say it took a lot of energy just for her to do that much. She may improve over time, if you let her."

*

They strolled back to Bart's parlour, where he made for Crim a pot of sour-smelling tea. It was bright yellow and tasted foul, so he encouraged her to drink it between bites of confectionaries.

"I cannot improve the flavour, I'm afraid," he said apologetically. "But it will soothe your soul."

To his credit, once she had finished the whole cup Crim began to feel more grounded and lively. The Other was still there—she was very much aware of their presence, but they had backed off considerably to the point where she no longer staggered around like a drunkard, or felt ready to faint.

When she stood to leave, Bart also raised himself ungracefully from his chair to check her. Once he was confident that she would not fall apart, he surprised her with a crushing embrace. With her arms pinned firmly to her sides, Crim could not quite return the gesture, but pressed her face into his thinning mane, tears pricking the corners of her eyes for some reason.

"Do not oust her, Crim," he whispered in her ear. "For everyone's sakes, leave her be."

XVII

In a matter of weeks following the announcement of her departure, Mentor was ready to leave. Sunshine and Laal, though not pleased, had more or less resigned themselves to the situation, but the effect on Li-Li and Yuki was undeniable. Rather than progressing, the two of them seemed to have reverted several decades. Li-Li fell silent, fearful and powerless. Yuki became angrier and angrier with each passing day, but failed to summon much more than a spark. Their clashes with Princess and company became more frequent, with even Li-Li attempting to trade blows on one occasion, though she had quickly retreated back to their quarters for reinforcements when the other group proved far more capable and bloodthirsty.

Sunshine wondered if all of this behaviour was not deliberate—an attempt to demonstrate to Mentor that they were *not* ready to be left alone, that they still needed her guidance and support. If this was the case, it was done very cleverly and convincingly. So much so that she and Laal began to actively pull them aside for extra training.

*

"By the gods Yuki—*hit her!*" Her voice was ragged from repeating the same commands again and again, her forehead sore from the slap of her palm. "And Li-Li *put your damn guard up!*"

Sighing louder than she was inclined to speak, Li-Li lowered her stance and held up her staff the way she had been shown a dozen times already. Yuki, sickle high and knife low just the way they had been shown, still skirted around her despite their target making no attempt to turn with them or defend herself. A quick upward flick of the lower end of the staff could have sent them flying, but Li-Li stood more or less stationary.

Crim had stopped training with them. Had stopped listening to Mentor or even trying to feign interest in her own development. She now spent almost every waking hour in the Library, burying herself in stories of other worlds and civilisations past.

"Someone hit someone." Princess groaned in that perfectly melodic voice of hers. Sunshine had managed to get a hold of her as they were making their way down to the Arena. Now she just sat on the side-lines passing unwanted commentary.

"Why is she here?" Yuki complained, feigning a swipe at Li-Li. She stepped back and nearly tripped over her own staff.

Sunshine gritted her teeth to keep her voice low and calm: "Moral support."

"She's not supporting either of us."

"For me."

"Is she helping you somehow?"

"I can't murder the two of you if there are witnesses."

Princess inspected her nails. "I won't tell."

"For once we are allied." She felt like pulling her headband down over her eyes as Yuki continued to circle. Around and around without end. Li-Li had dropped her arms again.

"Can I help?"

She started, and all three of them turned to gawk at Princess. "I'm sorry?"

Her impudent underling stood and adjusted her sleeves. "I'm bored. And I know you won't let me leave until these two morons have learned something."

Yuki wheeled on her. "You little—"

"Go ahead."

Li-Li whirled this time as well. It was the most she had moved since beginning her training. "S-S-Sunshine!"

"If that's what it takes to get these two to put in some effort, be my guest, Princess," said Sunshine, ignoring their protests. "Go pick something out of the Armory."

With a wink and a wave, Princess trotted off. She returned shortly with a glaive that was slightly too long for her, but carried it with such confidence that Sunshine made no remark. She stood at the edge of the circle and squared herself. Properly, unlike Li-Li, and ready to strike, unlike Yuki. When no-one made a move, she looked imploringly at her mistress. Sunshine, still slightly unsettled by her uncharacteristic display of helpfulness, raised her eyebrows at her, then clapped at the other two.

Yuki of course took their place in front of Li-Li, ready to defend her if necessary. Li-Li fumbled with the staff at first, but then took a deep breath and actually began to rotate around of the ring, looking nearly ready for Princess to strike. Princess giggled.

"A mouse and her lapdog. How *endearing*." The glaive made a wide arc around her, and Yuki hunkered, ready to whack it away as it came towards them. Instead, it slashed the air just in front of their face and they just tilted their head in confusion, oblivious to Princess' right hand which raised with palm towards Li-Li. A jet of snow shot forth, coating the sand at her feet with black ice. Li-Li's cry barely made it out of her mouth before her rear hit the ground. Princess giggled.

"*Bitch!*" Yuki spat, leaping at her, both arms thrust forward. Not what Sunshine had taught them, and a mistake. Princess ducked under them and used the haft of her weapon to vault them right up to the ceiling. They hit the rough natural stone to the left of the sun rock and bounced right back down to the floor.

"Sunny?" Li-Li whined, struggling to stand up on an ever-growing patch of ice. Princess, clearly having a little too much fun at her expense, was currently skating slowly over, blade glinting at her shoulder.

Sunshine only shrugged. "If you defeated Mentor, you can take down another acolyte."

Too cold? Maybe, but as the glaive made the slow line through the air towards her, something seemed to possess Li-Li, and she stood, straight and tall with her staff held firmly in one hand. The other moved, mirroring Princess's previous technique, and blasted her with a gust of howling wind. Princess hurtled past Sunshine and crashed into a bench somewhere behind. She only laughed louder.

"Mouse fights back!"

Sunshine ducked as this time the remains of the bench flew over her head, then slid well out of harm's way after seeing what followed. Li-Li, unfortunately, only saw the chunks of timber, and easily deflected them with a wall of wind. This Princess's darts of glass-sharp ice easily tore through, and though Li-Li then danced away, she moved too late, and two struck her; one in the hip and the second slicing clean through her leg and taking her down with a sob. Those doe eyes looked pitifully up at Sunshine as she clutched her thigh.

127

"Enough!" Moving in front of Li-Li, Sunshine drew her sword and raised her shield. Princess stopped, though surprisingly she did not seem to be moving in for the final blow—her weapon was lowered.

Her servant. Her insubordinate and mean little servant, who disobeyed every order Mentor had ever given her, threw the glaive down and raised her hands in surrender. "Can I go now?"

"Yes. Go on."

Wiping her bloody nose on her pristine sleeve, Princess glid past over the swathe of mirror-perfect ice.

"Princess?"

"What?"

"You did well today." Sunshine forced a smile. "Thank you."

Princess blinked up at her, then seemed to shake herself. Donning her usual aloof expression, she disappeared out the door.

*

Laal had the dinner on the table when they returned; a platterful of marinated venison with seared berries, roast vegetables and a giggly milk pudding. Mentor was nowhere to be seen—recently she spent most of her days with Mother and the other Elders, preparing for her excursion into the unknown. When she did join them, it was only to inspect the younglings, and ensure that Sunshine and Laal still kept things more or less in order. She also provided plenty of feedback.

Laal watched Yuki and Li-Li sit down with two dark, surly faces and immediately turned to inspect Sunshine. Seeing no battle scars on her, she questioned:

"Did they actually fight *each other* this time?"

"Nope."

"Then who?"

"Princess helped."

Laal reeled, and had to find herself a seat before she fell down. "Princess? Helped? *Princess helped?*"

"I know. Volunteered, would you believe, and not for any price, either." Sunshine jabbed a meat-laden knife at her students. "Though I suspect getting to hand these two their arses was payment enough for her."

"And you let her," Yuki grumbled.

"Considering I was on the verge of doing so myself before she offered her services, you're damned right I let her. That's the most I've seen either of you move in ages."

Laal scooped some vegetables onto her and Li-Li's plates, though Li-Li was still busy mashing the portion she already had into a formless pulp. "Oh, stop sulking, both of you! You need to learn!"

"Not from Princess," said Yuki.

"If it takes Princess to teach you, then yes: from Princess," Laal corrected firmly. Then to Sunshine: "How was she?"

"Proper form. Good use of her *draoi*. She could be anointed, too, if she would only attend the Trials." No one was more shocked than Sunshine by her assessment. Laal's brows shot up. Li-Li and Yuki looked betrayed. "It's true. She's a pain, but from what I saw today she's more than capable."

Laal huffed. "A waste. And she only has time for wandering about with her friends."

"Wh…why don't you t-t-train *her?*"

Li-Li probably meant it as a jab, but Sunshine did not respond. She had been thinking the same thing herself. In that moment, when she thanked Princess, something had passed between them. Something like respect. Perhaps her obedience could be earned, if Sunshine only put in the effort to help her? Could she become trustworthy? Loyal?

*

The younglings returned to their dormitory after dinner, and Laal kissed Sunshine goodnight before hurrying out to meet Suleyman and Rakhib. She sat at the table well into the smallest hours, thinking about how best to win Princess over. She had responded to praise, and to the prospect of fighting her peers, which told Sunshine she was competitive. She also held back after injuring both Yuki and Li-Li, which showed that she only wanted to win. If Sunshine taught her how to fight better, how to hone her *draoi* and even harness other elements…perhaps that promise would be enough to entice her.

Then when Mentor came home, she could show her….

At once, another voice spoke in her head, undoubtedly hers but harsh and foreign: *Forget Mentor.* She stared at the few pieces of venison sitting cold on the platter, then picked one up and nibbled it.

Princess. Mentor had tried to bully Princess into line. Had belittled and beaten and abused her in a desperate attempt to make her submit. To make her unquestioning and compliant. The more Princess had spoken out, the worse her punishments became, until one day she seemed to snap and, cursing Mentor, cursing her peers and their mistresses, cursing Mother herself, she had taken her leave. Sunshine had seen it happen—they all had—but never dared speak out. After all, had obedience not made her existence *so much easier?* She recalled her own musings at the time: *Why was Princess always so difficult?*

But had she really been difficult? Would it really have been so unreasonable for Mentor to accept her?

Crim and Princess had only ever said no to their Elders' cruelty. Had only ever wished to exist in their own way. Away from the rituals, away from the training, away from duty, away from the gods. For this one had been ostracised and the other was close to being driven away.

I will get them back. Sunshine promised herself. *Both of them. I will make it right.*

XVIII

Mentor left after a feast in the unused Banquet Hall. A rather quaint feast attended only by a few Elders, her underlings, and Mother herself. Li-Li did not eat much; her stomach ached and was full of knots. Beside her, Yuki did not seem to have any interest in their food, but sat glaring about at the other guests, and would only grant a few words to anyone who tried to talk to them. Li-Li smiled and tried to keep up the conversation, but inevitably found her gaze drifting back down to her plate.

She allowed herself another glance along the table at Mentor, who occupied the seat of honour, Mother at her right hand. Li-Li guessed the Elders at her left were Bjorn and Erco, the two other candidates for this journey. Though they spoke to Mentor with great interest, and even laughed from time to time (Had Mentor told a joke? Or Mother?), their smiles did not reach their eyes.

Mentor looked up, and caught Li-Li before she could turn away. Li-Li, not knowing what else to do, only nodded. Mentor nodded back, an unfamiliar expression on her face. Something like regret? Guilt? When she turned to say something to Mother it was gone, but that sickening feeling in Li-Li's gut grew. She found herself wondering if she would ever see Mentor again. Would she disappear beyond the border, never to be seen again? Would she become another lost soul, like so many before her?

"Hey." Yuki's hand, warm on her shoulder. "You're shivering."

"Is n-nothing."

They glanced at Mentor. "Did she say something to you?"

"Nuh…no, Yuki. I'm f-f-fine."

They squeezed her shoulder. "You don't need her. You know that?"

"Huh?"

"I know it's not right. I'm not happy about this, either. But the more I think, the more I realise we don't need Mentor. If Princess learned what she can do on her own—"

"Yuki!"

"—then we can do the same. You *definitely* can. You're ten times smarter than that brat!"

Li-Li blushed in spite of herself. "Don't t-t-talk like that."

"Like what?"

"Y-you don't n-n-know what might hap-happen. What if w-w-we n-never see her again?"

"What do you mean?"

"N-nothing."

"You're *certain* she didn't say anything to you?"

Laal appeared behind them to save Li-Li from having to explain herself. She clapped them both on the back with forced cheer.

"Come on you two, Mentor wants us!"

Grudgingly, they stood, and Laal led them over to a quiet corner where Crim, Sunshine and Princess sat waiting. Yuki glared at the other youngling.

"What are *you* doing here?"

"The same thing you are."

"But why?"

"Because Mentor is leaving."

Yuki scoffed. "Like you care."

"On the contrary. I want to make sure she's really gone."

"*Princess!*" Laal scolded, and Sunshine rapped her on the arm (not without a small smile playing on her lips). Crim snorted. "Do the three of you understand what we're to do?"

"No," Yuki replied.

Li-Li shook her head.

"Maybe if you told us," Princess sneered. At her side, her mistress laughed. The two had become surprisingly close in just a few short weeks and it was unsettling.

Laal remained stern-faced. "Sunshine, if you would?"

"Right." Sunshine opened her satchel and produced a small, oblong wooden box. Its surface, scratched and chipped, with whole patches of lacquer rubbed away, was decorated in gold leaf and studded with small crystals. She unclipped the tiny latch and eased it open quietly. Inside were six stones of varying shapes; amethyst, emerald, pink tourmaline, ruby, citrine and light blue topaz. Though clear, polished and shining, they simply lay at the bottom of the box, silent and lifeless. Much like the heartstone Crim had created for her weapon. "You remember what these are, I hope?"

"Espers" Yuki answered.

Princess rolled her big, blue eyes. "*New* Espers."

"That's what I meant."

"You don't even *know* what that means."

Yuki glanced at Li-Li, who shrugged. Neither of them had ever seen new Espers before.

"So why don't you *tell them*, Princess?" Laal pressed, not nearly as tolerant of the youngling's attitude as her lover.

"New Espers have no power. They have been harvested from the depths under the Mountain and are kept in the Archives until they are imbued. I assume that is why we are all hiding back here, Mistress? We're going to imbue them?"

Li-Li almost gagged. Yuki audibly choked. Had she really heard Princess call Sunshine that?

Mistress?

Sunshine did not seem to know how to react, herself, so instead simply answered: "Yes."

Laal, also staring at Princess, elaborated: "To be precise—*Sunshine and I* are going to do so. With your help."

"That's right. Laal and I were taught by Viper and Esme, *you three* were not. Strictly speaking, you're all too young to be doing this but…but…"

"But we need to give Mentor every chance."

"Yes. Thank you, Laal." Sunshine took a deep breath, relaxed, and went on: "We think three younglings should be more than enough help."

"More like one of *me* and two of *them*."

"*Princess.*"

"H-how do we…" Li-Li said. "Um…how I-is it d-d-done?"

Sunshine pursed her lips and considered the boxful of colourful stones for a while. "I reckon we could do two each. Laal? Crim?"

Laal nodded back. "Two shouldn't be too much. They're small."

"I can do two," Agreed Crim, her voice low and devoid of emotion.

"Alright, so. Here's yours," Sunshine placed a stone in each of Crim and Laal's open palms. "and I'll take mine. Now—one of you to each of our hands, form a circle and be ready to push apart if we start to get too drained."

Yuki, first to move, stopped short of whatever they were about to do and looked up at Sunshine. "…what?"

Laal sighed. "Yuki and Princess take one of my hands. Li-Li, to Crim and Sunshine. Yuki, Crim's not diseased. Crim, neither is Yuki." Once they were thoroughly entangled, the three younglings looked from one Anointed the other. Yuki opened their mouth to ask another question, but Princess kicked them. Laal growled, and the two of them settled, following their mistress' lead and closing their eyes in concentration. Only Li-Li remained, looking about and feeling utterly lost.

Then she felt it; a tingling current of power enveloping Sunshine's hand and bleeding out into hers. She gasped as it pulled, pulled forth from deep in her core. Seeping through and then into the stone, taking her energy second by second. Li-Li imagined her limbs softening, her mind blurring. She blinked her eyes back open slowly, fighting sleep. Beside her, Yuki was breathing heavily, trying to remain calm. She wondered if she should help them. Perhaps they needed her to intervene. Opposite, Princess opened one eye and shook her head. *They're fine.*

She tried to relax, tried to close her eyes again and be good like the others, but she started to tremble, hand gripping Sunshine's tightly as that warm sensation turned to burning, and a chill settled in her knotted stomach. She broke out in a cold sweat. Was she being leeched? She tried to remove her hand, but it held fast to Sunshine—or rather, could not pull away from the draw of the Esper. Was held down by a magnetic force. She wheezed.

A fist struck her in the chest, sending a jolt out from her core. Li-Li's limbs, suddenly free, spasmed, and she fell back against the hard floor. Unconscious before she struck the tiles, she was unaware of the *crack* her head made, or the cries of the others. Instead, the world cut to black, and she found herself floating. Floating alone in an endless night. She bobbed slightly, and found that she was underwater. Looking up, she found the surface rippling miles overhead, the light of a million stars scattered and lengthened by languid waves, utterly dwarfed by another swirling ring of light, which scattered a full spectrum of colours in all directions as it entered this bottomless ocean.

Suddenly, that light was broken, lost in a flurry of white foam as something broke the surface at unrelenting speed. It tumbled down, down towards her. A body condemned to the depths. Where had it fallen from? And why? As the initial shock subsided, the newcomer righted themselves and, taking a minute to consider each direction, turned their head down towards her, and began to swim.

"Li-Li! Li-Li!" Laal's call brought her back, and she breached the surface of reality with a gasp, sitting bolt upright and spluttering as one saved from drowning. She reached out frantically and was caught by four other sets of arms all seeking to both steady and calm her.

"W-w-w-whuh…what?"

"You fainted. That's all." Laal hugged her, rubbed the warmth back into her limbs with her bare hands. Sunshine patted her head. "Oh! But I thought you'd trapped yourself!"

"T-t-trapped?"

"You didn't, that's all that matters," said Sunshine, stroking her cheek. "How do you feel?"

"I….I…" She thought a moment. "I d-don't think I've e-e-ever felt wo-worse."

"Sounds about right." Sunshine laughed.

Sunshine gave her a generous draught of blood, which worked far faster than all the food on the banquet table combined. Li-Li stood, feeling far more awake and *tingly* than usual. None of the others seemed to notice their absence from the feast, or at least did not care enough to remark.

Laal pushed the box into her hands. "You're the youngest. You should have the honour."

"I…but—"

"I don't want it," Yuki interjected. "So don't even think about suggesting me."

Princess turned up her nose.

"W-wh-what d-do I say?"

Laal patted her shoulder. "I can't tell I. Just say what you feel."

"Which is why I *definitely* don't want it," Yuki remarked, earning themself a clip on the ear from their mistress.

"We're all trying to be nice. You should too."

Pinching the feeling back into the point of their ear, Yuki fell into step next to Li-Li as they emerged back into the orange-red glow of a thousand flickering candles. Conversation round the table seemed to fizzle out, and heads turned to watch. Apparently the attendees had politely been talking over their preparations so as not to ruin the surprise.

It was not *much* of a surprise, however, as it was customary for a Sidhe's underlings or pupils to present them with a gift of Espers before embarking on an expedition. Mentor stood, grinning with delight as they approached. The others halted, shoving Li-Li forward. She hesitated, staring around at the dozens of faces now fixed on her.

Her gaze fell to Mother, and she jolted. Those gold eyes were fixed on her, unblinking. At once a hum took over her mind, coupled with another sensation—like something groping, touching the edges of her thoughts and pulling away. Was Mother testing her? Checking the strength of her barriers? Or was she searching for something? Li-Li tried to push back, and Mother finally blinked and smiled. She got the distinct impression that whatever test she had just been given, she had passed.

"What've you for there, Li-Li?" Mentor prompted, jerking her chin at the box.

"Oh...I... um—" She snapped back to the task at hand. "W-w-w-we... uhh—"

"Thank you." Mentor took it from her outstretched hands and gave a slight bow. She opened the box carefully and stared down at the six vivid, shining Espers that lay against the plush velvet cushion.

"What's she doing?" Yuki whispered behind as Mentor gradually pressed her fingers against them, one after another. Each touch was prompted by a sigh.

"Checking them," Laal hissed back. "Now *stand still.*"

Seemingly pleased with her gifts, Mentor unsheathed both of her katars and laid them on the table, then picked three stones for each and pressed them into the blade. The stones already embedded—those imbued by her own mentor and peers when she had made her weapons—flared in welcome for an instant, until the newcomers were safely fixed, and throbbed in rhythm with the rest.

"Thank you, girls," said Mentor, and Li-Li thought she heard a catch in her voice. "It's nice to know you'll be with me."

"Um..." Li-Li breathed, a lump now growing in her own throat. "Mentor, I...I hope we can see each other again."

Mentor frowned, then looked to Mother. Something seemed to pass between the two of them, and when she turned back her expression was unreadable. "Yes, Li-Li. I hope so, too."

XIX

It appeared on the Mountainside, roughly two centuries after her first experience of the Outside. A spindly, multi-limbed monster with a glowing head. Laal and Sunshine took her to the Gardens to see it, its featureless dangling through the Maw to look upon its subjects. At the very sight of it, the strength left her body, and she fell to the ground.

"What i-i-is it?" She heard Li-Li whine. Past the spots in her vision, she saw the girl clinging fearfully to Sunshine, entirely fixated on the horror above.

"Here. Careful." Laal helped Crim to sit up, and drew some water from the nearby Lake for her to drink. It was cold and crisp, and electrified her limbs. Yet her heart remained heavy.

"So soon?" She managed.

"Li-Li and Yuki are close to being Anointed, Crim. It is just in time."

"I'm not ready."

"Mother warned you, remember? She said you would be chosen soon."

"I remember but…" She braved another look at the thing as it peered down at them. Its bulbous head shone with a white light, and swayed back and forth across the Maw. It had no eyes, yet she felt it studying them. "I can't, Laal."

"You can. You will."

"To take another's life…"

"Is to grant them eternity."

Eternity? At what cost?

*

When the gods called, the Sidhe answered. When they came to the Mountain in search of a vessel, they knew one would be delivered. After all, didn't the denizens owe them?

In the days of the Patriarch, they had supplied more vessels than could ever be demanded, so that no god ever wanted, but could pick and choose at their leisure. Many rotted away in the walls and floors of the Tomb, waiting for an eternity that would never came. Then Mother slew the Patriarch, and rallied against their masters, and to everyone's surprise the gods did not destroy her or her followers, but agreed to their terms; a new batch of vessels every generation. Not many, four or five would do, but they would be offered promptly.

On the eve that their visitor arrived, the Reavers were sent out into the mortal world. The Anointed gathered in the centre of the Temple to see them out, Acolytes huddling in the alcoves and hanging from the columns. Mother blessed them as the Elders chanted, and spilled her own blood from her wrist into a goblet for them to drink. Crim stood between Laal and Sunshine, cupping a bright red flame in her hands, watching how its light shifted and changed against the rippling surface of Laal's ball of water. Mother, her voice deep and clear, called:

"And they shall be delivered into the hands of the Sires!"

That was her queue. She looked up, frozen. Sunshine gave her a shove forward. Laal, ever gentle, whispered: "Chin up, Love."

Straightening her back, Crim held her expression neutral as she spared a glance around at the other Sires. There were four of them in total—one to every Vessel—to her relief, none of them looked especially happy.

A cry went up around them, raised to fever pitch by the Reavers, who stamped their feet and brandished their weapons. In contrast to the Sires, their expressions were ravenous. They lived for this. It was to them that Crim offered her flame; it floated up, high above the altar, where it was joined by the *draoi* from her counterparts and reeled in a waltz of colourful orbs. The rest of the gathering whispered blessings as the *draoi* melded together, and showered the Reavers in a rain of sparks. With a shout and much stamping, the Reavers accepted their blessing, and stepping away from the altar marched through the rows of Anointed, receiving a few cheers and claps on their backs as they passed. Past the Gardens and to the Lake they would go, from a narrow jetty paddle their little boats out to the River, which would take them to their destinations.

*

As soon as they were out of sight, the din died down. Those that were not Sires joined hands in silent prayer. Crim, with all eyes closed around her, let her expression slip just a little, feeling the strain in the muscles of her face. One of the others shared the same horrified look with her across the way, his forehead creased for a minute with deep lines. Then Mother stirred, and from her place on the dais turned to look at her. As always, Crim's insides turned cold. She forced a slim smile.

This is your duty. Mother reminded her silently, gold eyes flashing. *You will not shun it.*

Crim began to tremble, fearing what might happen if she refused. Remembering the stories of what had happened to the Patriarch. Mentor had said that Mother had taken an interest in her, but for what purpose Crim never found out. Mother had called on her twice in the past few years, only to remind her of her duty to the gods, and her place under the Mountain. Crim dared not question her reasons.

With the Reavers sent, the congregation disassembled. One of the Elders whose name she did not know congratulated Crim with a jarring whack on the back, and Sunshine and Laal each treated her to a crushing hug. Li-Li and Yuki hung back, unsure of what they were supposed to do. Princess, of course, was nowhere to be seen. Crim mussed Li-Li's blush-coloured hair, and the Acolyte complained as she brushed it meticulously back down. Yuki was satisfied with a handshake.

"So may we see it now?" Yuki asked for the millionth time, tugging on Laal's sleeve.

"It is a god, not a beast on display in the Menagerie," Laal scolded, brushing an invisible crease out of the fabric.

"But can we?" Sunshine pressed. "You said after the Sending."

"Not *immediately after.*"

"Why not?"

"Because I said so."

"*Please!*" Yuki implored, looking strangely sweet. "They might come back sooner than expected—"

"And then we'd have to wait another generation to see one!" Sunshine chimed in, half laughing at the irritation on Laal's face. "And it won't even be the same!"

"It w-won't?" Li-Li piped up, only daring to glance at Mentor out of the corner of her eye. "Th-They're not a-a-all the suh-same?"

"Nope! Mentor didn't tell you? They choose their forms. The next one could look like a house cat for all we know!"

Li-Li's eyes widened, and she forgot her fear. "Please m-m-may we see it L-L-Laal?"

Laal foolishly looked into those big, dark doe eyes as they turned to her, staring down pleadingly. She tried to look away, but the spell was cast. She *tutted* loudly in defeat. "Not for long!"

Sunshine whooped with joy, and taking Yuki by the waist pulled them to the front door of the Temple. The others followed, with Crim trailing a good distance behind; intrigued, but still horrified. Denizens who had already gone out to see the beast reported that it was best seen from the Eyrie, so Sunshine led all of them along one of the winding paths past the Gardens and through the Groves, until they came to the inner rockface. Here, just where the stony lakeshore met coarse tufts of dark green grass, was a narrow gate that opened onto the Narrow Stair; a steep, uneven set of steps that led straight up to a trapdoor in the ruins of the Fortress.

This place had once been the dwelling of the Patriarch. Set high above the forest on the snow-clad slopes near the summit, it had long since been torn down and burned by Mother and her rebels. All that was left now were a few battered buildings, tottering sections of the outer walls, and the Eyrie; a tall, slender tower left mostly untouched, where he had once retired to sleep and read and observe the stars. It was to this that Sunshine led them, hurriedly explaining its story to Li-Li and Yuki in a hushed voice as they ascended the littered steps. Crim, still keeping her distance, took her time here also, toeing and inspecting some of the bric-a-brac underfoot—cups, pages, ornaments and the like. Near the top they came across the door to his bedchamber where, waiting until Laal had climbed out of sight, she let her curiosity take hold, and stepped into the stagnant gloom.

A rather large four-poster occupied the wall to her left, with nightstands to either side. Directly facing her was a high window, a few fragments of coloured glass still clinging to the metal frame, the rest blown across the floor where they glistened in the moonlight. To her right was a wall of shelves, with a small desk and broken chair tucked into the far corner. To her dismay, Crim found these shelves mostly empty, their contents shredded or burned by the opposing side, but not all. Two scrolls and a small diary were already tucked into her robe before Laal found her.

"Crim!" The bark made her leap back against the desk. Laal looked more annoyed than usual—almost *angry*.

"I…um…"

"You shouldn't be in here. You know that."

"I know that, but…"

"But?"

"Um."

Laal rolled her eyes, expression softening. "Come on."

But she made the mistake of turning her back again, giving Crim the chance to stuff another small book up her sleeve. She grinned to herself.

"What's so funny?"

"Nothing." Crim now followed Laal closely up the stairs. "Just didn't think his room would be so *normal*."

"And what were you expecting?"

"An iron maiden? Breaking wheel?"

"No. He kept them elsewhere."

*

Laal walked her to the zenith of the tower, where there was a wide walkway hemmed by small parapets. The monster was up the mountain to their right, or at least part of its slim grey body was, held up by spider-like legs that dug into dirt and rock alike. It was covered in a shaggy, hair-like substance that glowed faintly with starlight and tapered into a rounded tail at this end.

"What's its name?" Yuki asked, mouth hanging open as they stared at the beast.

"We don't know. They rarely tell us their names," Laal replied.

"Only a few of our kind know the names of their gods. They aren't really interested in speaking to us," Sunshine elaborated. "Though Kash the Bold is famous for his close friendship with his goddess Mara. But she only showed interest in him after he projected."

"P-p-projected?"

"Some Sidhe are able to separate themselves from their bodies for extended periods of time."

"Only a select few," Laal corrected. "And they train themselves in the art of projection for centuries before ever achieving it."

"It's dangerous," Sunshine added. "If you can't put yourself back…well…*poof!*"

"You disappear?" Yuki said, clearly amazed.

"Well…there's not many accounts of it happening," Laal responded. "Mostly due to the fact that the people it happened to are *gone*. Accounts of Myram the Fool's last moments say his body *disintegrated*."

"And his presence disappeared from the air," Sunshine added spookily, jostling Yuki playfully. "So don't you try it 'til you're at least an Anointed."

They paled. "I promise I won't."

Suddenly Li-Li gasped, and grabbed hold of Mentor. With a trembling arm, she pointed into the air. "L-look!"

They followed her gaze, and found that she was not just pointing into the air. She was pointing up into the face of a god. Whether roused by their presence or their talk none of them could tell, but it had turned itself bodily away from the Maw and was now looking down at them with its eyeless face. Crim staggered back against the wall, feeling suddenly cold, and willed herself not to faint again.

"What do we do?" Yuki whispered to Sunshine, looking like they wanted to duck behind her. Li-Li was already making her way behind Laal. Even the elder Sidhe, confident and learned as she was, stood frozen.

"Sunny," Laal hissed. "It's not *angry*, is it? Have we disturbed it?"

"I don't think so, no. Perhaps it's just as curious as we are."

One of the limbs lifted from among the trees and planted itself into the cliff to their left. Another rested itself against part of the broken wall. The monster lowered its head. For a long minute, Crim knew that it was aware of her. She felt it feeling, examining, searching about within her mind. It brought with it a searing pain, a white-hot light so intense that she pressed the heels of her palms firmly against her eyes, moaning. The rock wall behind her turned to nothing, and she was standing alone in a vast bright nothingness. She cried out.

Warm hands took her by the elbows, drawing her forward out of that void and hugging her.

"It's over," Laal cooed, stroking her hair. "It hurt but it's over."

Crim opened her eyes, which still stung and watered down her cheeks. Laal's face was wet too, but she smiled reassuringly. "What did it do?"

"I'm not sure. I feel like it was assessing us. Maybe even saying 'hello'."

"Didn't feel like a 'hello'," Yuki grumbled, clutching their head.

"I doubt it meant any harm," Laal continued. "It probably doesn't even understand the concept of pain, or it didn't know that it would hurt us with its greeting."

"Yeah I..." Sunshine agreed. "The more I think about it the more it felt like a greeting of sorts."

"I-it's going a-a-away now," said Li-Li, waving as the beast twisted itself back out of view, presumably to peer through the Maw once again. "Bye bye!"

XX

Did you see Crim?" Sunshine mused, floating idly past on the placid black water of the Lake. "She's petrified of that thing."

Laal surfaced right next to her and bobbed thoughtfully for a moment. "I'm not sure it's more so a fear of the god than a fear of what she knows she must do."

"Well they're one and the same aren't they?"

"We all have to do it, Sunny. Every single Anointed becomes a Sire at least once in their existence."

"I know. I'm not saying it's not her duty but, well, sometimes our duty is *unpleasant.*"

"And I'm not saying don't empathise with her. But when the time comes if she falters—"

"Yes. It's *our* duty to ensure she does *her* duty."

Laal turned to face the dock, where Crim sat paddling her feet in the water (they had long since discovered her fear of the depths and stopped trying to get her to swim). "I'd rather not force her to do anything. But we can't risk angering the god."

"For their wrath is swift and devastating."

"Don't do that."

"What?"

"Quote Him."

"Why not?"

"You know Mother and Mentor…"

"They're not here, and He's part of our history. Besides, it's true."

Laal disappeared back beneath the surface, leaving Sunshine to stare up into the face of the god. Over the past few days, seeing Crim's strife, she had found herself sympathising more and more with the writings of the Heretic. The first of their kind to speak against the Patriarch and the gods. The first to speak to the

144

questions that secretly plagued each Sidhe's mind: Why were they here? Why did the gods need them? What right did the gods have to take their lives from them? What if they just *stopped* serving them? The loyal had tried to silence him, of course, and he had disappeared into the Forest to escape persecution with a small following, but they were soon betrayed and put to death before all of the Forum.

Sunshine both felt and feared for Crim; her angst was not uncalled for, but what if she followed the path of the Heretic? What would happen to her if she did? What would happen to all of them?

"Would you kill us all?" She asked the faceless god.

It did not respond.

*

A clamour rose up from the shore, and Sunshine righted herself. Laal paddled forward, eyes on the narrow opening from which the River flowed.

"Aha!" She exclaimed.

Four boats drifted into view, carried up the Mountain by the current, which obediently delivered the Reavers wherever they willed. Hardly causing a ripple, they edged slowly across the Lake towards them. Laal and Sunshine splashed out of the way, eliciting a cackle from Hyeong, who patted the prow and thus stopped his blue-hulled currach next to them.

"Pull them up," he ordered, laughter still in his voice.

Nashoba, who sat to stern, extended a hand to each of them and lifted them easily into the boat.

"Thanks," Sunshine offered.

Grunt.

"Just don't step on her," Ayo ordered, blocking them with an arm. Luckily enough, too, for Sunshine had nearly stepped on the body curled up at the bottom of the boat.

The poor girl was playing dead, lying on her side and silently praying for mercy to her local deity. Sunshine sat on the bench next to her and listened to her thoughts as she repeated the same name over and over again. She swore to be better, to help her mother, to marry the boy her father had selected, if only she could go back home. Her pleas went unheard, for the only god present watched silently through the Eye as its Vessel was delivered.

"Four of them," she muttered to Laal, glancing at the other boats. Three boys and this girl. All battered and bloodied. All starved. All terrified.

"The Tomb is empty. One will serve this god, and the others will sleep," Laal said. "This way we needn't send the Reavers out for another age."

Sighing with pity, Sunshine looked back to the dock. Crim had seen the boats, and was now standing with a blank expression, mutely watching as they moved into the moor, bumping gently against the piles. Hyeong hopped out first, winking at Crim as he passed, who deliberately ignored him. She was fixated on his prisoner, whom Ayo slung bodily over his shoulder before disembarking somewhat more carefully. The thump of his feet on the boards, however, seemed to rouse the girl, and she let out a blood-curdling scream. Following this, all of her prayers spilled from her lips, this time directed at the Sidhe, who were slowly gathering around.

"Let me go!" She begged raspingly. "Please! I want to go home! I don't want to…to…I'm only sixteen! *Please!*"

Sixteen. Sunshine's breath left her in a loud *whoosh!* Had they all been that young? The boys were being unloaded now so she took a good look at them. They were each around the same age, the youngest not even man-high. Her heart ached, and she thought back to her singular experience as a Sire, to the boy she had offered to the gods. How old had he been?

Led by her example, they also began to cry and plead, scratching and slapping at their captors as they were carried towards the Temple. Fighting in vain against the fate the gods had dealt them. They would be caged in the upper floors of the Temple to await the Making.

*

"The pink one," Laal concluded, finally pointing to the patterned sash in her left hand. Sunshine held it up against her yellow gown. Li-Li had painted her limbs fuchsia right up to the knees and elbows for the occasion, and this tied around her waist would balance the colours perfectly. At least, that's what Laal told her.

Laal herself dressed in her favoured blues, greens and purples, glittering and jingling with baubles from head to toe. She wore one of the dozens of scarves

Sunshine had gotten her, loosely draped over her head so that some of her cream-coloured hair fell about her face. Yuki, following Li-Li's guidance, had painted her limbs and face with dots and lines of aquamarine to match her eyes.

"Can you help me?" Sunshine offered Laal her brush and knelt by the bed. She had already oiled and tied her hair back in a puffy bun but could not see the back. Dutifully, Laal brushed down the short, sparse hairs that grew there, and fitted the gold comb Sunshine handed her into the ribbon.

"Beautiful," Laal declared, kissing her neck. Sunshine fell back into her embrace, grinning stupidly.

"*U-ummm…*" Li-Li, having appeared at the open door, inspected her nails.

Yuki, having none of her bashfulness, stuck their head around the frame. "Crim's ready, but she won't come out."

"Your turn," said Laal.

"*Ugh.*" Crim had become increasingly difficult in the past while, and after the delivery of the Vessels had more or less locked herself away in her room. She refused all food and drink, and would not answer any of their summons.

Sunshine strode across the parlour and rapped on her door. She heard rustling inside, but no footsteps. On the third attempt, she thrust the door open.

"Crim come on—everyone's waiting."

The younger Sidhe sat by the dressing table, eyes fixed on her hands. As Sunshine approached she clenched them into fists.

"I can't."

"You can. You will."

"I—"

"*No*, Crim," she said firmly. "I don't want to hear it. Whatever reasons you've come up with, none of them outweigh our obligation to the gods."

"What obligation?"

Sunshine sighed. "Don't do this."

"Do what?"

"If you don't…" She bit her lip. "If you refuse to take part in the Making, I can't say what they'll do to you."

"Mother?"

"Mother…the Elders, the gods. Even *Mentor*. If she ever gets back."

"Would they destroy me?"

She fell silent. None of them had ever heard of a Sidhe who had refused Sirehood. She could not say for sure that Crim would be destroyed, but the outcome would not be pleasant.

"*Please*, Crim. I'll be right there with you. We all will."

"And who will be there for *her?*" Crim snapped. "What about *her*, Sunny?"

"She is dead already, Crim. She cannot go back. And she cannot stay here as a mortal."

Crim buried her face in her hands. Sunshine knew this guilt; they had all felt it. She felt a shadow of it even now. Guilt for what she had done then, what she would witness now.

It has to be done.

"Crim. Please." Kneeling in front of her, Sunshine coaxed her out from behind her hands. "You'll ruin your paint."

A laugh. Cut short. Tinged with hysteria. But a laugh, nonetheless. "I really have no choice, do I?"

For a second, Sunshine was silenced. She chewed her lip. "No."

Her friend—her sister—looked at her reflection in the mirror. "I did it myself today. Li-Li didn't want me to but…but it's the only thing I remember from back then. It seemed right to do it like this."

Sunshine looked to the mirror as well; Crim had painted her face in thick streaks of blue and red over a greyish base. The effect was striking against her emerald-coloured eyes. With her hair braided and her fur-lined cowl she looked almost savage.

"Come on," Sunshine repeated. "Let's go."

*

"We're late! So sorry! So, so sorry!" Whisper scooted into line behind them, dragging Gibber by the hand. Her sister, oblivious to the goings on around her, was trying to make a break for the door.

"Crim!" She shouted, and Whisper shushed her.

"Crim's there, look. Right there with Mother."

"Crim there!" Gibber insisted, pointing out into the Gardens and trying to shake her off. "Crim there!"

Whisper fished around in her pockets, producing a large, plump peach. "Yes. Okay. We'll go see her in a minute. Can you sit for now?"

Gibber took the fruit with a giggle and skipped over to one of the alcoves, where she hunched down and proceeded to nibble at it daintily.

Whisper caught Sunshine's eye. "Sorry."

"Just glad you could make it," she responded, turning back to the altar.

A Making was a communal affair. The Sires and all those closest to them gathered in the Temple, where Mother blessed them, and bade them drink from her as she had the Reavers. This time, however, rather than offer a sip, she held out her bare wrists, and the Sires, one by one, all stepped forward to receive their communion. Unlike the Reavers, they needed all the strength they could get, and she let them drink their fill, seemingly unaffected. Each hesitated, naturally, but took it greedily enough. Crim lingered the longest, turning her face aside at the hungry, feral sounds the others made as they drank. Sunshine got her by the shoulders and steered her forward.

"You'll need it."

Crim dug her heels in at the last step. This time Sunshine gave her a shove. She tripped and fell at Mother's feet, jostling one of the drinkers aside. They hardly seemed to notice, but latched back on to the ragged, gushing puncture marks, lapping at the spilled blood with their tongue. Crim's face contorted, and she glanced back at Sunshine.

You'll need it. Believe me. Hurry.

Stone-facedly, the younger Sidhe turned back to Mother, and finding an open space below the elbow of her right arm, hesitantly pressed her mouth to it. She seemed to probe the stone-hard flesh carefully before finally sinking her fangs in.

Mother sighed. The noise drew Sunshine's eyes away from Crim, who was drinking slowly but obediently. She met her gaze; saw the golden light flare in her narrow eyes. Mother's otherwise immobile lips quirked at the edges, like she wanted to smile but had quite forgotten how. There was something in that gaze that…

No. Sunshine backed away, and brushed the thought from her mind. Mother was far more powerful—far more perceptive than any of them could imagine. Best to leave such ideas till she was out of her presence. She stepped back into line.

Mother smiled.

XXI

Not quite sure what she had expected, Li-Li nonetheless admitted to herself that it had not been this. For an Acolyte, the Making was a ritual shrouded in mystery and spoken about in whispers and rumours. Those that had witnessed it were loath to tell of their experiences as they, as Princess had once said in a rare moment of sincerity, "did not want to scare anyone." Now, finally, she understood this sentiment. As she watched Crim bite into Mother's outstretched arm, she considered if she would tell all to her peers and decided against it. This was a brutal, deeply private affair.

With the Sires fed, Mother shook them off with a flick of her arms. Two fell backwards off the dais, but Crim and another moved away in time to avoid being thrown. Crim swayed, bracing herself against the altar and shaking her head.

"Can you imagine what it's like to drink from Mother?" Yuki whispered. "All that power—"

"Shhhh!" Laal hissed.

A whimper from the Steel Stair, which was tucked away into the far corner. The youngest Vessel stumbled forward, pushed by one of the Reavers. Blindfolded and bound, he moved gingerly in the direction he was steered, shaking and hesitating every few steps. The Reaver slapped him and he sobbed, tripping over his own feet till he made it to the dais, where he threw himself down and grovelled.

"Please...please..."

He patted the floor, searching until he touched Mother's feet. She gazed blankly down at him. Li-Li wondered if she was at all moved by his prayers. The other boys followed more or less quietly, thoroughly broken by their few days in captivity, but the girl turned on Ayo as she was brought out and hit him a ferocious blow. A loud *crunch* and she wailed, clutching her broken hand. Ayo tried to turn her around but she struggled and continued to slap at him. Finally, he simply grabbed her round the waist and lifted her over to Mother.

"Open the Tomb," Mother commanded, looking at each of the mortals in turn. "Bear them down."

Each of them was picked up, and whether complacent or struggling, they were brought towards the huge stone doors that stood open at the back of the Temple. The procession followed, down broad, smooth steps and into the grey-and-black dim of the Tomb. Once upon a time, Li-Li had heard, this place had been full to the brim with Vessels, some of whom were claimed by the gods, others were not chosen, and perished here. Now it was only used when the gods demanded a sacrifice, so it was deathly quiet, its few condemned souls hushed as they listened in horror.

At the bottom of the stairs, archways on either side led into dozens of burial chambers, each with four sarcophagi fixed to the floor. Smaller metal coffins—usually meant for the more long-term occupants, who would be encased behind the walls—lined each of these chambers, bearing silent witness to what they were about to do.

*

Each group broke off here, choosing one of the rooms as Mother lingered at the base of the stairs, humming and chanting in her own ancient tongue. Ayo led them to the third archway on the right, with Crim just behind him, eyes fixed on the screaming girl in his arms. Stepping inside, Li-Li found a sarcophagus already open and ready to receive its occupant. It was into this that Ayo dumped the child.

Whether or not she knew where she was, she touched the sides and shrieked. Li-Li wondered if she could sense them; the other lost souls that had been brought here. They had met their mortal ends in a box just like this one. Surely some echo of them still lingered.

Tears brimming in her eyes, she reached out and took Yuki's hand. They did not turn, or seem to notice her distress, but squeezed anyway.

The Reavery stepped up to the sarcophagus beside the girl, and gestured for Crim to follow. Crim, face stricken, slowly followed. He held out a hand and cordially helped her to step over the lip. The girl hugged her legs.

"Hold her," he instructed, reaching in and sweeping her long black hair away from the girl's neck. "They tend to thrash."

With that he bared his fangs, and backed into the corner. Reluctantly, Crim grabbed the poor child by the back of her neck and hauled her up. Her victim looked terribly hopeful for a second, seeing the pity in Crim's gaze. Then the Sidhe licked her lips, fangs protruding. She let out a choked, horrified moan and immediately began to thrash, as Ayo had said, smacking, punching and kicking at Crim.

Li-Li shook her head, still blinking back tears. Had Crim known it would come to this? Now all of her protesting made sense. With a cold feeling growing in the pit of her stomach, she realised that she, too, would be called upon to do this one day.

"Crim!" Mother barked from outside. How had she known she was hesitating?

Crim gaped at the door, at all of them, utterly helpless. Li-Li met her glance and only bit her lip, too afraid to intervene.

After all, what could she do?

Grimacing, Crim turned her attentions back to the girl, who had now gone back to pleading for her life. She took her hands as she batted at her. The godforsaken child, in one last-moment effort at mercy, laid her head gently against Crim's breast and whispered: "Please."

Crim considered her for a long moment, chin resting on her dishevelled hair. A moment in which Li-Li imagined she heard her debating with herself, wondering if there was any way to end this and let this girl live. Then her expression hardened, and with a sigh, she leaned down and bit into the other side of the Vessel's neck. The girl sobbed and went limp, finally defeated. Li-Li squeezed Yuki's hand again, disgusted but unable to turn away from the snarling, slurping Sire as she drained this Vessel to a mere husk. Crim stroked and caressed her as she died, feeding pleasant dreams and illusions into her mortal mind. Humming quietly against her mangled neck. It seemed to go on forever, beyond the point when the girl must surely have passed on. She drained every last drop.

Ayo waited patiently in his darkened nook for Crim to finish, the drawn, pale corpse hanging chillingly from her hands. With a smack of her lips, Crim looked at him, and he smiled, then she looked back down at their victim and dropped her with a cry. The Vessel fell back into the sarcophagus with a dull *whump*. She staggered away, own legs reduced to sticks, and he moved to steady her, this time lifting her bodily out of the stone box. It was the spectators' turn to take part in this ritual, and Yuki pulled Li-Li forward by the hand. Laal and Sunshine led them, opening their wrists and letting their thick, hot blood spurt over the prone Vessel. Yuki followed suit and Li-Li…She snivelled, wiping her eyes in her sleeve, chin quivering. It was so cruel. So very, very cruel. She did not want to take part in this, but she felt Mother like a force pressing down on the back of her skull, waiting for her to do her duty. Sobbing, she cut her own arm and watched it drip, drip, drip over the girl's arm. Crim, supported by Ayo, joined them last, blood flowing out of her in a dark font. They would not stop until she was fully submerged.

On and on they stood, watching the red pool rise up to drown the girl, who, teetering on the edge of death, was beyond all begging. Beyond all hope. Yuki squeezed Li-Li's hand, hissing as Crim's face became as drawn as her victim's, her eyes bulging in bruised hollows as she fought to remain upright. Li-Li almost sighed with relief when she finally dropped her arm, but gasped instead when Crim collapsed against the Reaver, eyes blank and staring.

"Crim!" She shrieked, and Yuki held her back from rushing to her mistress' aid.

"It's fine, Li-Li," said Laal. "It has taken a lot out of her, but her strength will return."

Ayo delivered Crim into Sunshine's arms, who kissed her and muttered praise. At a nod from Laal, he hoisted the lid up, sliding it securely over the Vessel with a bang. Bowing, he dismissed himself.

"Crim." Laal edged over to her worried lover, and gently took Crim's hand. Li-Li imagined she was feeling for a pulse; imagined, because surely nothing could stop their immortal hearts? Not even this?

"C-C-Crim…" She managed again. Yuki put their arm around her.

"She's fine." They assured her.

"Hmm," Laal concurred, then, with her hand against Sunshine's back, urged her to the door. The latter cradled her friend protectively against her chest. Crim's head lolled backwards at a sickening angle, but Laal carefully righted this, and folded her arms across her stomach. "The feast should be ready. Let's get her out to the Gardens."

The other Sires and their companions had already made it out to the Gardens, where most of the other Anointed and Elders awaited them. There were several fires burning in the courtyard before the Temple, and the rich aroma of sizzling meats, charred vegetables, and stewed fruits, rose up to meet them. Li-Li's mouth immediately began to water, and she remembered that she had not yet eaten.

"Not yet," Laal instructed her, taking her by the arm as she gazed longingly at a dripping rack of lamb. "We must find somewhere to put Crim, and then she will have to be fed. She needs her strength."

"Right." Reluctantly, Li-Li allowed herself to be pulled away. Into a corner that had already been fitted with rugs and cushions for them to sit on, and a whole pile of pillows in which Sunshine delicately laid Crim, propping her head up against the wall. Her mistress stared blankly at Li-Li, mouth hanging partially open, and Li-Li shuddered. She appeared more deceased than the girl they had just murdered.

"Li-Li, come. You too, Yuki," Laal commanded, and they scurried after her. "Crim needs sustenance if you don't want her to fade away."

"*Fade a-a-a-way?*" Li-Li squeaked. "I th-thought she was fuh…fine!"

"She is. For now. And all the more because we are here to help her," she replied. "But with all the strength she has given to the Vessel, she is fast losing her hold on her body."

"What does that mean?" Even Yuki sounded concerned.

"It is not unheard of for Sires to….fall apart after the Making."

Li-Li choked. Yuki put a hand on her shoulder, steadying her.

"But that's not going to happen, is it Mentor?" They insisted. "If we feed her she will regain her strength?"

"If we feed her enough and in time, yes."

*

They bore back platters and bowls and jugs all brimming with grilled meats, bubbling stews, sizzling vegetables, steaming fruit and spiced wines. At Laal's instructions, these were placed on the rug around Crim, who was beginning to turn rather grey. It took several trips, but soon enough there was hardly space for them to sit down.

Laal and Sunshine, knowing exactly what to do, wetted Crim's lips with wine before carefully pouring some into her open mouth. To Li-Li's surprise, she finally moved, mouth and throat working to send the dark, fragrant drink down. She even licked her lips. Stewed fruit followed, and boiled vegetables followed; anything soft enough for her to ingest without chewing. As the light slowly ebbed back into her eyes, Laal told Li-Li and Yuki to carve off small pieces of meat, cheese and bread, slowly urging her to work her jaw and masticate. Bit by bit, Crim began to move more, and even laughed at an offhand remark from Whisper, who was now braiding her hair. Hearing this roused Gibber, who had been crouched quietly by her sister's side, watching Crim with obvious worry. She came and knelt next to her, gingerly stroking her forehead.

It took a while, but eventually Crim was sitting up on her own, joking with them and shovelling whole platefuls of food into her mouth, washed down with jugs of wine. She hugged Gibber tightly, who still refused to leave her side, and was now pushing more and more portions into her hands.

"Crim…there…"

"No, I'm here, Sweetheart."

"Here. And there."

Crim smiled. "Yes, of course. I see what you mean."

Gibber giggled and wandered off to find more fruit. After a while, she returned with a whole mango (one of Crim's favourite foods), and dropped it onto her plate. Crim sang her praises, and she blushed.

*

"Your first making," said Sunshine, coming to sit between Li-Li and Yuki. "And not the last, I assure you."

"Hm," Yuki grunted, poking at their pickled radish.

"What did you think? Li-Li?"

Li-Li jolted. She had been busy studying the contents of her stew, scooping up spoonfuls and letting them drip back down into the broth. She had been hungry when she asked Uta for it, but it tasted like dirt in her mouth. "I d-don't know, Sunny."

"Yuki?"

They put their plate down and shifted uncomfortably. "It…was not what I expected."

Sunshine gave a wry smile. "You expected something more grand? Chanting and singing? Vessels bathed in white light as the gods enter them?"

"I suppose."

"H-how do we know…" Li-Li tilted her head. "Was it a s-s-success? Is the god ap-p-peased now?"

"Well—it's gone, isn't it?" Sunshine rightly pointed out, nodding up towards the Maw. The beast no longer peered through. Li-Li had heard some of the others saying it was nowhere to be seen anywhere on the Mountain.

"S-Sunny?"

"Yeah?"

"Th-there were f-f-four of them."

"Yes. Correct." Standing, she brushed crumbs off her skirt. "One will be taken immediately by our most recent visitor. Assuming one is to its liking."

"And the o-others?"

"The gods tend to appear in waves. Or at least that's what Mentor says. Crim, Whisper and Gibber were all made around the same time, though if I recall only Whisper's god actually appeared. The others will be kept for the next ones."

"And if there is only one in this wave?" Yuki pressed.

Sunshine shrugged.

"They die," Li-Li concluded. "D-don't they?"

"I would assume so, yes," Sunshine agreed.

Li-Li shook her head. Setting her dish next to Yuki's, she turned for the millionth time to study Crim's tormented expression. All she found this time, however, was a half-eaten mango in a pile of pillows.

"Shit!" Sunshine exclaimed behind her. "Where did she go?"

XXII

Gibber set her down awkwardly propped against a trunk. Mumbling and hissing, she raked her hands through her hair and tipped Crim's face up to her own. From her pockets, she produced a few morsels taken from their picnic—small cakes, biscuits and even some braised meats. These she carefully raised to Crim's lips, who reluctantly nibbled. She had a flask of ale, too, and though Crim was not fond of ale, her parched mouth urged her to drink deeply.

When all was eaten and drunk, Gibber stood. Crim moved to join her, not wanting to be left alone in the silent orchard.

"Crim here."

"…Yeah. I'm here," she replied. "But where are you going?"

"Here."

"What for? Why are you leaving me alone?"

"Here."

"But I can't—*oof*!" She had tried to stand, but crumpled immediately back against the hard trunk. "I can't move by myself, Pet. I need you to—"

"Crim here!" Gibber exclaimed, tugging at her silver-grey hair.

"Alright. I will. But stay with me, please?"

"Crim." Gibber pointed at her, like a dog commanded to stay.

"Please…" A haze was creeping into her eyes, and shadows drifted over Gibber. Over the trees. She was much too weak for this.

"Crim wait. Crim here."

"Yes, I am. But you must have a reason for leaving me here?"

Gibber shook her head and released her. "Wait."

She strode away, still muttering and biting her nails. Crim turned, but only succeeded in sliding down the tree bole onto her side. She tried to crawl, but her legs lacked any strength. Her arms, not much better, were full of pins and needles. She could only haul herself back up against the hard bark. Once she was sitting back up, a swoon took her, and her eyes fluttered shut.

A hand on her knee brought her crashing back to consciousness, though her lids resisted the bright orange of the evening light, and struggled to focus. Someone was kneeling in front of her, silhouetted by a large, low-burning sunrock just behind. They touched her forehead and she shuddered for some reason.

Crim stirred. Tried to sit forward. Failed. "…Who?"

They swam out of focus, but squeezed her leg in a way she supposed was meant to be comforting. Their fingers seemed to pierce her very skin, sending another cold shiver up her spine. Crim squirmed, trying to shake that hand off, and willed herself to make sense of their lines and features. They seemed to understand this, and, removing their touch, also moved out of the beams of the fading sun rock to her side, so that the light hit their face. A familiar face, though she could not recall where she had seen it. Had they accompanied one of the other Sires?

"Do I know you?"

They tiled their head, a small smile on their thin, chapped lips.

"I don't know you…" But the doubt rang through her voice.

She took a closer look. Watery grey eyes stared back, full of a deeper light that made them unfamiliar. A pale face peppered with small freckles. Top lip marked where a ringed fist had struck them, the right brow too. Brown hair combed back and secured with plaits and metal rings. Crim's recollection stirred, and she lowered her gaze to their neck. Long, jagged lines trailed from her jaw and disappeared under the collar of a stained green cloak. No doubt her arm was marked as well; the flesh of the shoulder dimpled and pink where the beast had sunk its teeth.

"Who are you?"

They grinned. Crooked teeth, though clean and near-perfect white.

Crim managed a laugh. "Who?"

They laughed. That is to say, their face screwed up, and their mouth opened in the shape of a laugh, though the sound was absent. They realised this quickly, and snapped it shut. Their image seemed to wane for a second, for the blink of an eye the branches behind them showed in silhouette, but they collected themselves and became opaque just as quick.

They gestured all the way down to their feet and then back up to their face, smiling once more. Crim followed the gesture, still confused. At first, it did not help, but then the ground under her seemed to tilt, and her surroundings morphed. The trees, now so close, floated away and grew up up up—far beyond the frames of regular fruit trees. They now wore the guises of towering ashes and splayed oaks. Bent-backed willows dipped their long arms down into dark, icy water as bushy hazel huddled further away from the banks.

She lurched again as a breeze stirred up the glassy blackness of the lake, and their boat bobbed gently. Hands gripping the carven edge, she looked down as they settled, and found that very face looking back up at her. They scowled back, tilted their head to one side, then the other, and opened their mouth wide to inspect her teeth and tongue.

A gruff chuckle from the prow, and a deep, soothing voice mumbled something in a language that rose up from the depths of time to stir her heart. At once, her whole being pained her, and she was catapulted back to the orchard.

*

"Why are you wearing my face?" She croaked, for some reason a lump stuck in her throat.

They blinked.

Only it was not her face. Not any more at least. When had she ceased to be this girl and…

Two millennia ago. She reminded herself, aching neck creaking as she frowned down at herself. At the flawless skin and hardened frame. Sharp lines and harsh features. Had she been happier then, too?

Her eyes stung. She blinked it away. The creature wearing her past smiled patiently through all of this. "Who are you? Really?"

At this they nodded, and stood upright. Several inches shorter than she was now; the lowest branches of the apple tree barely grazed the top of their head. They shuffled back a few steps, then considered her as she struggled to get her legs under herself. Pursing their lips, they waved for her to follow, and Crim growled back indignantly.

"If I couldn't follow Gibber how do you expect me to follow—to follow…you…?"

Her limbs no longer pained her. Rather, a pulse of energy suddenly surged through her body. Crim pushed against the apple tree and leapt up, all notions of helplessness gone. She stamped her feet and shook her arms for good measure, tingling with electrifying energy, then laughed.

"How?"

They giggled silently back, and waved again. Her legs moved eagerly, if not slightly mechanically, carrying her forward. She struck a root with her toe and caught herself against a pear tree before falling flat on her face. This did not make sense, as she had seen the root sticking out of the ground and meant to step over it, so why had she not?

Am I not in control?

She was answered immediately; her arms braced and pushed her away from the tree of their own accord, and she staggered after her other self, who waited partway down the path. They turned and continued, ignoring the growing horror on her face as she fought to regain control of herself. They brought her through the groves of fruit and laden bushels, through a clearing of waist-high grass and into a denser copse that led to the lake. Hanging branches grabbed at her shoulders and hair, and the fading light of the sunrocks only touched the upper limbs, so that she tripped and staggered through a blackness only broken by blacker shapes. Ahead, her other self glowed with a faint white luminescence; her only beacon in this nightmare.

Something far firmer than leaves struck her head, and she cried out. Her other self stopped to watch as Crim tried to push it away, but whatever it was came swinging back at her. She blocked it with her arms and reached up, groping without recognition. Something wrapped in a blanket? Crim formed a small flame in her hand and held it up; faded blue cloth wrapped around two white branches. The twigs were round, stunted.

A foot? She reached out and gasped at the coldness of the flesh, then with foreboding creeping up her limbs raised her flame. Blank eyes mirrored the light, already starting to rot in the drawn face of the hanging woman. Crim shrieked and fell back, fire drifting out of her grasp only to hover before the corpse. But how did a mortal woman enter the Mountain? And why had she chosen to die here?

Crim turned to her other self for answers, but they were already walking away, unphased. When she looked back up, the body was gone.

"Who was that!" She demanded, already unwillingly scrambling to her feet. She managed to grab the bobbing ball of red fire before being steered away. "Answer me!"

They did not.

"Hey! You better—"

A strangled cry fell from her mouth as her light, as well as the light of her other self, fell on more bodies. Not in the branches this time but on the ground, or propped against the trees. Some sporting the wounds that killed them, others ravaged by disease or hunger. A woman bloated and drowned. A man burned beyond recognition. She counted over three dozen in total.

"Why are you showing me this?"

Her other self finally stopped and looked around. Crim, following their gaze, saw only trees.

"You saw them! I know you did! Who are they?"

Her other self shook their head and walked on, dragging her with them. Had they truly not seen? Had she summoned the corpses herself, out of some deep recess of memory or imagination?

"Who are they?" She whispered, peering into the dark, but they appeared no more.

Her flame melded with a white glow, and Crim found herself standing just behind her other self at the end of the path. The trees rustled behind, no longer full of ghosts, and the Lake lapped lethargically along the stony shore. Perfect circle of the moon stretched lazily across the mirror-black water.

*

A deep rumble brought her gaze upward, and immediately staggered back under the eaves of the copse. She gasped, then moaned, as she found herself staring up into the face of a great dragon. It lowered its head, seeming to acknowledge her, fiery eyes unblinking, flames lapping at spikes of ebony protruding from its enormous jaws. Wreathed in phantom fire and bright embers, its dark scales hard as the stone of the Mountain itself, it hung from the roof of the Maw by claws as long as swords. So big was it that only its shoulders and neck fit through; the rest of its body no doubt gripped the Mountainside, as the other god's had.

So soon? Crim despaired. *But we have only just—no, no. It will take one of the boys. No doubt. There will not be another Making.*

She turned to look at her other self, and found them also staring up at the dragon, smiling more broadly than before. And also more vacantly. Their eyes were as glassy as the hanging woman's. Beyond them, the reflection of the moon still shone on the Lake.

"But how…?" Crim looked at the beast blocking the Maw, and back to the reflection, head swimming. "How…?"

Her other self laughed silently.

From the dragon, to the moon, to the dragon, then the girl. Until finally: "Is it you?"

Her other self turned, and the dragon faded enough for some of the moon to show. They prodded Crim sharply in the chest, sending another cold shock through her. Her limbs spasmed and she collapsed onto the ground like a ragdoll.

"I am your vessel."

Of course. It was the only explanation. The girl nodded as the dragon snorted. One and the same.

"But I did not summon you. I haven't even mastered meditation, or my chants. I can hardly dart, let alone *project—*"

A louder snort. The girl faded.

"You summoned me?" Sidhe were not prone to headaches, but one now assaulted her. "With Gibber's help…She saw you, didn't she?"

Snort.

"But I don't understand why—"

The girl *shushed* her, placing a cloudy finger to invisible lips.

"You need something."

The dragon, more solid than before, lowered its head. At once a gust of wind swept up, whistling through the Maw with chilling intent. Both it and the girl were assailed, and like clouds of dust they were both swept apart.

Crim, powerless, could only watch from where she lay amid the sand and stones, voice raised in wordless protest.

Her strength was gone, but still she pulled herself up the Narrow Stair, panting and puffing all the way, moving on hands and knees nearer the top. The trapdoor up here hung open and shuddered noisily in the wind, forgotten by some reckless admirers of the light-faced god. Falling out into the Fortress grounds, she took one last up at the Eyrie and the sheer cliffs beyond. Satisfied that the enormous monster was now gone, she turned aside.

Turned down the Mountain. With her last drops of strength, she willed her legs to move, forced them to carry her first at a jog, then a sprint. Down, down, down she ran. Tripping. Falling. Tumbling. Her robe caught on a branch and ripped but she kept going. She rolled down a bank and into some brambles, and there she wished to give up, but no. She picked herself up and barrelled on as fast as her liquified limbs would carry her. Over the River. Past the trees. Out of the Forest and across the ribbon of grass that skirted the entire microcosm.

She would leave the Mountain, leave the sight of the cosmic horrors that the Sidhe called gods.

She would leave and never turn back.

XXIII

Their chambers were silent, cold and desolate when they finally returned. Sunshine—well heated by the vats of wine and liqueur that had been uncovered as the doors to the Forum were thrown open, and the majority of the Mountain joined their small party to drink and revel and raise their glasses in farewell to Mentor—shivered as she closed the door, and shuffled over to wake the fire from its slumber. A handful of glowsilt and some kind words brought it roaring back, but did not dissipate the chill that had settled into her bones. She rubbed her arms and hunkered by the hearth.

Laal had gone into their room and slid the door fast behind her, leaving each of them alone to converse with their misery. Flames licked at Sunshine's feet, the paint on her soles cracked and flaking as it always was. Her palms, rubbed nearly bare, waved over their pointed heads, giving shape and features to them; tiny figures that danced and twirled in the ashes. She quickly grew bored of playing with them, however, and they reverted back to pointed tongues that continued to tickle her.

"What did Crim teach you?"

Crim had been notorious for playing with her *draoi*, rather than hone it for combat as Mentor so plainly wished. This stubborn determination to craft sculptures and images had led most of the Elders to underestimate her ability, but Sunshine, after trying this herself under Crim's gentle guidance, guessed that her creations were a sign of a deeper, more innate power than any of them gave her credit for. Taming fire was hard enough; it was unpredictable and prone to acting out, but she has also shown a talent for moving and moulding earth and solid rock—heavy, stubborn substances that took far more concentration and skill than she would ever let Mentor suspect.

Sunshine stroked the flames and asked politely: "Show me what she taught you, please?"

The fire retreated and seemed to die out, flickering tongues disappearing under a blanket of soot and broken coals. The whole pile at the bottom of the hearth seemed to stir, then ripple and grow. Mounds of ash formed into limbs, and the heap nearest her began to resemble a head. Before Sunshine could make sense of each particular change, there was a pup sitting in the fireplace, staring up at her with fiery eyes and wagging its dusty little tail. Then, almost as soon as it formed, it fell apart.

Tears started in her eyes, and she thrust her hands into the remnants, only to pull out two handfuls of warm grey ash. She let it float down through her parted fingers. "Where are you?"

*

Leaving the flames to doze, Sunshine stood and wiped her hands on her skirt. Crim's room, nearest the fireplace, had not been touched in their search. They knew she would not disappear back to their apartment; knew she was nowhere to be found in all the Mountain. Still, they had spent much of the hours after the Making running helplessly about screaming her name. Only traces remained. Shadows of her beloved companion.

The wooden door stuck a little as she slid it back, but she knew to lift it over the bump in the frame and, creating a light with her fingers, stepped into the cold, lifeless shadows. The bed, unmade as always, was strewn with robes, trousers, tunics, skirts, shirts, belts, sashes, scarves…everything she had considered on the morning of the Making, and hastily discarded. Set into a mahogany dais in the same fashion as hers and Laal's, two short steps leading up from a moth-eaten rug that lay slightly skewed and wrinkled over the cold grey flagstones. A large, packed bookcase spilled its contents into piles and stacks on one side, while an open wardrobe and a dressing table occupied the other wall.

Sunshine sat at the table and began to slowly sort the mess of paints, inks, brushes, quills, ointments, powders, perfumes and candles that took over its surface. She assorted the paints and inks back into the open drawers, placed the quills and brushes in the proper holders, and lined the bottles and jars in front of the mirror. In doing so, her knuckles grazed the glass, and she started as the image reflected no longer mimicked her.

No, it did not even look like her. Nor did it look like Crim. At least, not entirely. Though the girl that now blinked out at her was pretty enough in a

166

simple, mortal way, she was both softer and rougher than her Sidhe counterpart; plump cheeks and a weak round jawline, a low, broad nose and a high forehead, all coated in a light dusting of dirt. Skin scratched and bruised in places, hair combed and styled but ultimately dishevelled by whatever hardships had taken up her day. Her eyes, though sharp and clever, did not glow, and her teeth though white were dull and slightly crooked, her ears rounded. The right side of her face and neck was marred by jagged scars.

Crim. And yet it was not. This girl knew nothing of the Mountain or the Sidhe, and smiled back at Sunshine with an innocence that had been stolen from her friend—from her sister. Why had Crim left this image here, in the mirror; for herself to look at, or for Sunshine to find? Was it a message, or a reminder?

Sunshine took a brush up and, dipping it in the reddest paint, wrote a message on the mirror. The girl tilted her head at the streaky letters, then blinked at Sunshine. Perplexed, she stared right back. Crim could read better than any of them—save perhaps Laal the Perfect—but this imperfect doppelganger did not even seem to recognise that she was looking at letters. Sunshine observed her for a while as one pale, gritty finger traced the reflection of her scrawl with intrigue, but no comprehension. After a while, the girl caught her eye again, giggled and disappeared.

It was all too much. Mentor was gone. Lost. Now Crim had run away. Disappeared without a trace. How would they go on without them? Did she even want to? For the first time in her timeless unlife, Sunshine found herself doubting her purpose as a Sidhe. Found herself cursing the nameless gods and this godforsaken place. Wondered if perhaps she should follow Crim, wherever she had run to.

But where are you? There it was, the panic. The suffocating loneliness and loss that had threatened to overcome her when she first realised Crim was gone. She had fought the urge to shake answers from Gibber. Fought the need to wail and rave. Instead, she had listened to Laal—good, unshakable Laal—and gone out to look for her. Had sent Yuki and Li-Li into the forest to search and brought Princess up to the Keep and the Tarn as Laal and Whisper made for the swamps. All for naught. So much for naught. Crim was already gone.

Crim is gone. She wiped at her face, letting her makeup smear and smudge the wetter it became. *Gone.* Tried to breathe an air of calm into her shaking frame. *Crim.* She slid from the chair to the hard, cold floor and curled up clutching a discarded robe. It still smelled of her—of roses and vanilla. She breathed her in, sighing. *Crim.*

*

Laal was quiet. She was quiet. Li-Li and Yuki were quiet. The only one who seemed unphased by Crim's departure was Princess, but that was to be expected. She was only concerned with her lessons recently—ironic, considering Mentor's absence, and the day immediately following the Making did something she had not done since she was a fledgling: arrived at Sunshine's door, dressed and ready to go to the Arena. She still did not do chores, or help her mistress to dress, and Sunshine suspected that she never would, but still her offer to help Princess use her draoi had worked better than she could have imagined.

Still, on this particular day, Sunshine herself was not overly enthused at the prospect of training. She met her underling still in her dressing gown.

"It's well past dawn," Princess remarked, ever blunt.

"I know, Princess. I was thinking we could all rest today."

"We rested yesterday."

"Yes, I know, but considering the circumstances…"

"I want to train."

"Tomorrow."

"I already dismissed my friends!"

She was flushed, and looked ready to throw one of her tantrums. Sunshine, not in the mood for any sort of ruckus, tugged at her untamed coils. "Alright, alright. I need to get dressed. Just—"

"I want breakfast."

Still our Princess. "There's food on the table. Help yourself. I'll get ready."

Victorious, Princess strode right in and picked a plate out of the cabinet before piling it with scones and fruit. Laal, equally as unready as her partner, glared at the disruption. It sat down opposite her to eat noisily.

-

Hair wrapped hastily, hands and feet painted roughly, face perfect as always, Sunshine led Princess down to the Armory, where she picked out her favourite glaive. When they walked back out into the Arena, however, Princess fell out of step.

"I heard Li-Li and Yuki talking about the portals. About that time, Mentor brought them through."

"Oh? What did they say?"

"I didn't hear everything. Something about another world. And a test." Princess stuck the end of her weapon into the sand. "I want to try."

Sunshine nodded. "I'll let Mentor know when she—"

"No. I want to try *soon*, preferably *now.*"

"Princess, you're not ready."

A loud scoff. "And *those two* are. I saw them when they came back. Mentor pummelled them. Or at least I think that's what happened. Yuki could hardly walk."

"And *you* didn't exactly help them, did you?" Sunshine laughed at her expression. "Yes, I heard. Bull told Mentor and Mentor gave *me* a talking to. You know I have to answer every time you get up to your mischief?"

"Every day?"

"Not every day."

"Then it's not *every time* is it?"

She snorted. The girl was sharp, she had to give her that. "Apparently not."

Princess looked at the ground. "I'm sorry, though."

"I don't think I caught that?"

She met her eyes this time. "I'm sorry that you get into trouble for the things I do. It's not fair."

No, it's not. "Don't worry about it."

"I really think I can do it, Sunny."

She stopped short of her usual mark. Princess never used her name. She never used to train with them either, but something in her had clearly changed since Mentor left—probably *because* Mentor had left. She was more personable, less impudent. Better. Sunshine looked her up and down carefully. She had seen the things Princess could do—she was quick, powerful, *smart*—Sunshine knew the youngling was not bluffing.

"I've never given a test, Princess," she said. "I don't even know where to begin."

"Make one up."

"I don't know how to use the portal."

"You just put the Orb in the door and *whoosh!*" Princess clapped her hands together. "Please?"

"We might end up somewhere dangerous."

"Like *where?*"

"Fúren."

"We'll just come back!"

"If the kyedhen catch us…"

"They'll have earned their supper!"

"What a lovely sentiment."

"*Please?*"

"No."

"Please!"

"No!"

"I won't let you down!"

"That's not what I—" Sunshine rubbed her temples. "Are you listening?"

"Yes. Danger. I heard." Princess stamped her foot. "But I can hold my own. You know I can! Against your test, against another world, even against cannibals!"

"Princess, they're not cannibals if we're not the same species."

"Predators?"

"More accurate."

She was waning. Princess knew this, too. The truth was, she could really see no reason why she should not test her, especially with Mentor gone indefinitely. In fact, she was rather intrigued. Princess seemed easily more capable than both Li-Li and Yuki, and was far beyond the level that Crim had been at when she had her first test. Perhaps it was finally time for her to ascend.

"Please."

"I can't—"

Princess shook her. Sunshine supposed she meant it playfully, but it rather disoriented her. "If we end up on Fúren, we can come right back, and I will not speak of the test for another age!"

"A whole *age?*"

-

They arrived at the Crossroads unchecked by anyone on their way. A pity for Sunshine, as she half-hoped someone would interrupt their plans. On one hand, she was reluctant to lead Princess into danger, reluctant to administer her half-baked idea of a test—one that might result in grievous injury, reluctant to become someone else's meal. On the other, she was eager to see how Princess would fare, eager to become a mentor to her—one that might actually help her to become the Sidhe she had the potential to be, eager to take her mind off Crim and Mentor and the empty spaces around the table.

Princess, tittering with excitement, insisted on picking the 'right' orb from the basin (though they were all identical), and handed it eagerly over to her mistress. She then trotted over to a door on their right.

"This one!"

Sunshine looked down at the orb, then to the door. "I'm not quite sure how Mentor does this."

"She never told you?"

"I don't recall if she did."

"Try thinking of somewhere?"

"I don't know anywhere to think of."

"How many times have you done this?"

"A few."

"Pick one of those."

"I don't know where they are."

"You must remember some names! At least one!"

She remembered all of them, actually, but chose the most recent. "Hsei. That's where we went with Yuki and Li-Li."

"Perfect!"

Hesitantly, Sunshine lifted the orb towards the door and thought of Hsei. Imagined the rose-coloured ocean and the grass that looked like rippling snow. The steep slopes and sparse forests The grazing herds and glimmering rivers. The flat-topped hills and mountains and the remnants of a doomed civilisation.

The portal opened. Princess started towards the threshold. Sunshine grabbed her at once, and took her hand. Her underling almost jerked away, but caught herself, only asking:

"What, afraid I'll run away?"

"Afraid you'll get lost, actually," Sunshine retorted. "I have no way of knowing if this actually goes where I want it to, if it forks or could lead each of us in a different direction. Bad as you are, Mentor would have my head if I misplaced you."

Princess laughed a genuine laugh, and edged closer to her. "Very well, Mistress. Lead the way."

XXIV

With Mentor gone, their duties were lessened, and apart from the occasional summons from Laal or Sunshine, both Li-Li and Yuki were left mostly to their own devices. Tasks and odd jobs around the Mountain were infinite, thankfully, as both Anointed and Elders approached the matrons daily for help with their own personal projects. Bull, well aware of their free time, was sure to volunteer the two of them whenever something came up.

Today they were painting the Temple alongside a dozen other Acolytes, including two of Princess' group; Ola and Bim. Fearful that they would try to aggravate Yuki again, Li-Li picked the far side of one of the wooden walkways well away from where they were half-heartedly slapping their brushes against the courtyard walls.

She sat cross-legged in the grass, dabbing bright orange into the cracks in the skirting boards. She had already finished the better part of the panelling, and Yuki had climbed up onto the roof to adjust some tiles. With that done, they were currently hanging half-off the edge to reach the support beams. They wanted to move up towards the minaret, were the colour was clearly flaking but Li-Li vehemently refused; the top of the slender tower reached the cavern roof several tens of meters above, and despite her immortality she had no desire to risk breaking all of her bones should she fall. She was not a climber like Yuki, and preferred to exist with both her feet firmly on the ground.

"Y-you're d-dr-dripping yellow all over the f-floor."

"Put a blanket or something down."

"You're the wuh-one dripping!"

"And you're the one complaining." They smirked, flicking their brush. Droplets flew at Li-Li, bright yellow against the white of her robe. She scowled back.

"You're m-missing spots t-too."

"So?"

"So…so it l-l-looks—"

"They'll have another group out here painting it in another moon," said Yuki. "No need to break your back."

"Ha-have you ever c-c-considered that *we* might be p-painting this in another moon?"

They paused. Then shrugged. "At least, I'll know who to blame for this shoddy work."

Li-Li rolled her eyes. When they were not training, Yuki did not have much attention for anything. All they wanted to do involved having a weapon in hand, and no other task seemed worth their time. There was no point in talking to them when they were in this state of mind, so she just turned back to her own work. The Temple had been built in the time of the Matriarch, when most of the Sidhe's building and advances had occurred. A time of exploration and creation, it showed the labour of many different hands working together; each wall a different fresco, each panel gleaming with bright paints and gilded borders, the floors smooth, dark wood, the skirtings and ceiling sprinkled with various images and carvings. Inside the pillars spiralled up into clusters of leaves and staring creatures, tapestries hung in every direction, and bright lanterns hung from patterned rafters.

When the Patriarch came into power, many things that were built in the oldest days were neglected, and the Temple, though used for Making after Making, fell into disrepair. The two upper levels and the minaret saw the worst of this, and even now, despite all of Mother's efforts to restore them, they were discoloured, the wood chipped and warped, the balconies and railings sagging or broken.

*

"Wonder what's up there," Yuki mused loudly.

"Nothing."

"You don't know that."

"C-Crim told me."

A scoff. Louder. "Did she tell you what *used* to be up there?"

"Sires yuh-used to have to st-stay there. B-b-before and after the muh…Making. Vessels too, o-of c-course. Th-they s-s-still do. The s-Sires were meant t-t-to keep watch over their fuh-Fledgelings for the first th-th-thousand suns after the cer-ceremony."

"Crim didn't even wait one sun."

Li-Li nearly dropped her brush. *"What?"*

Yuki, looking startled as one who had not meant to say something aloud, floundered and struggled to pull themself back up onto the roof. "I just meant….um…"

"What d-did you m-m-mean?"

They sighed and dropped down. "It was a bad joke. I'm sorry."

She turned her back on them. "You can w-wipe up the p-p-paint now."

"I don't have a—"

"Go f-find r-r-rag or suh-something!"

They jumped and scampered away, almost tripping down the temple steps as they left. Li-Li bit her lip and tried to focus on her brush, on the paint, on the rasp of the bristles on the boards. *Don't think about Crim.* She told herself. *She's gone and she left you. Don't think about her.*

Crim had promised to take her up the minaret. Years ago, before the Making that broke her, she had caught Li-Li staring at it and promised to show her all of the upper levels of the Temple. She had promised to show her all the secrets of the Library as well, or at least those that she herself knew; the forbidden zones and haunted, forgotten corners. *The only one that truly knows every inch of this place is Bart.* She had said. *And I have no desire to dig up that which he has hidden.*

Crim…And Mentor. Gone. Lost. With them went all semblance of normalcy, that feeling that everything under the Mountain always was and always would be. In their absence there was only a mounting foreboding. A sense that clung to the back of Li-Li's mind that they were now falling towards some uncertain doom.

"Oh, don't c-cry," she scolded herself, wiping at her eyes with her sleeve. "S-s-stop crying."

*

She laid back in the grass of the low hill, breathing in its fresh green fragrance. Her face was puffy and she had a headache, so she flung an arm across her sticky eyes and listened to the sounds around her. To the acolytes pitter-pattering back and forth. To the ruckus of paint pots and brushes being flung about carelessly. To the laughter of the trio down the garden from her who were painting their section in handprints.

The more she listened the more the sounds merged. The more she found herself drifting off into a fuzzy, warm doze. Then the world seemed to flip, and she was thrown into darkness. Laughter faded and dispersed. The Sun went out high above and the heat ran away from her. She heard screaming. Crying. Someone begging. Acrid smell of blood. Thick smoke invading her lungs. The halls empty. Chambers sacked. Deathly silence. The Mountain desolate, its slopes aflame.

*

Footsteps coming round the corner. Painted feet on the varnished deck. Li-Li was catapulted back to the present, sat bolt upright. Shuddering while coated in a cold sheen of sweat. She wanted to throw up but forced it down. She knew she shouldn't show them weakness.

Ola and Bim had come up behind her, each of them splashed and smudged with paint. So much so that she wondered how much they had gotten on the wall. Li-Li stared at them, waiting for someone to speak.

Ola clicked his tongue loudly. "It's just you."

"And y-y-you," she responded. "A-are you l-l-looking for someone?"

"We were looking for the others. They're meant to be by the Lake."

"Princess is w-with S-S-Sunshine."

Click. "Again?"

"Again."

"Lilith?"

"D-didn't see huh…her." Li-Li sighed. "Finished your w-w-wall?"

The two of them laughed.

"You could say that," answered Bim. "We're bored."

"Well if y-you w-want to he-help here—"

Another laugh. "No. We're going *up.*" Bim pointed to the domed top of the tower. To the spike that pierced the belly of the Mountain.

Li-Li considered chastising them. Considered telling them to go back to their work. Considered reminding them that the upper floors of the Temple were forbidden.

But they're not forbidden. She told herself. She could not recall ever being told *not* to go up there. People just didn't.

She reminded herself of her fear, and sure enough as she stared up, she began to feel somewhat heady. Then another sensation took over her. A sort of determination. While it did not eliminate her sense of vertigo, she somehow found herself dismissing it. Instead, she stood and brushed herself off.

"C-can I c-c-come?"

Bim blinked at Ola. Ola shrugged back. "Not sure your Mentor would approve?"

"She's n-not h-here."

"What about your pet?" Ola jerked his chin behind her. Yuki had found a rag and was returning with increasing speed. They appeared concerned.

"Li-Li. What?" Yuki shot each of the two an accusatory glance. "Are you alright? Why are they here?"

Ola and Bim shared another look, and made to walk away. When Li-Li made to follow them, Yuki caught her elbow.

"I'm g-going with them," she said, shaking them off.

"With *them?* Where?"

Li-Li pointed upwards. "Up there."

Yuki cocked an eyebrow. "*You?* Going up there? I thought you were scared?"

"A l-l-little."

"Something about making a *splat*?"

"B-but I also w-want to s-s-see." Li-Li had them by the arm now. "Come on!"

*

At the furthest, darkest corner of the temple was the minaret stair, set behind an iron gate and twisting tightly up up up out of sight. The four of them half-crept (meaning that Li-Li and Bim crept while Yuki and Ola strode) through the scattered groups of loiterers and people passing through. No-one seemed to notice them, not even when Ola shook the latch to test if it was locked. It released with a slight rattle, and he led the way up the short, tight steps to the next floor.

This was the most used; though they rarely brought in Vessels since the fall of the Patriarch, the gods still demanded some sacrifices, and this was where they were kept. This is where Crim's fledgling had spent her last days, along with those poor boys. Scared and starved, she would have had little distraction save the view out of the metal lattice covering a narrow window. The stair led to a short passage with three small rooms on either side. Within each cell was nothing but a stripped bed. Or at least this was all Li-Li saw at first.

"Why do they need to chain them?" Bim asked, pointing to the manacles hanging from the ceiling of one cell. "Surely they don't expect them to escape? If the doors are sealed, no mortal should be able to pass them. And no-one could squeeze through these windows."

Li-Li shuddered. Somewhere in the recesses of her mind, she knew she had seen them before. She rubbed her wrists where the cuffs had chafed, and felt a growl in her stomach, ran her tongue over cracked and bloodied lips. She pushed those memories down, back where they belonged.

Ola, clearly as disturbed as she was and slowly turning pale, returned to the stairs. "Come on."

The second level was far nicer than the first; a spacious, simple chamber with windows and doors that overlooked the Gardens, Orchards and Lake. A narrow veranda surrounded it, and the four of them took a moment to gaze down on the fields and the copses, the stony shores and the still water. The room itself was divided, with the four corners raised and inset with soft, white bedding. Each of these little nooks had a desk, a window, and a tall screen that could be drawn around it for privacy. In the very centre was a low stone oven surrounded by cushions, individual trays for all occupants, and squat bookcases completely filled with reading materials, games and puzzles.

"This was where the Sires stayed?" Yuki asked, and she nodded.

Bim, turning in the spot, thought aloud: "If we stayed here maybe no-one would make us paint the temple."

Ola punched him in the arm for this, but Yuki just snorted.

"It's no secret to anyone that you lot don't sleep in your beds all the time."

"If you rat on us—"

"W-we won't r-r-rat," Li-Li interjected. "R-right, Yuki?"

They held Ola's glare. "Right."

Bim leaned over and whispered to Li-Li: "They won't so long as you ask them not to."

Li-Li blushed, but did not respond.

The third floor was unremarkable; gleaming wooden floorboards spread wall-to-wall and another, even smaller walkway that Li-Li refused to set foot on. After a quick inspection, they hurried onward and upward.

Round and round they went, till the stairs became almost vertical, and Li-Li wondered how ridiculous she would look if she resorted to crawling. The spiral turned tighter and tighter till she felt rather dizzy and had to prop herself against the wall.

"What's wrong?" Bim moved to steady her, but Yuki was there already, guiding her up the next few steps.

"She's fine," They snapped.

"I was just—"

"I know. And she's fine."

"Yuki, he's j-just trying to h-h-help."

"Right."

"You know," said Ola, coming back down a few stairs to face them. "Maybe if you weren't so *prickly* more people would like you."

Yuki moved so face him. "And what exactly do you mean by that?"

"Sorry I didn't realise I was being cryptic—"

"I want you to say it again."

"Yuki, s-stop it!"

Ola rolled his eyes and marched on. "You're ridiculous."

With a growl, Yuki made to grab him, but Li-Li caught a hold of them first.

"I s-s-said *st-stop it*!"

"But—"

"He's j-just trying to r-r-rile you," she said. "D-don't let him."

They growled again, but backed down. Bim, caught behind Li-Li received the full force of their glare.

"I really *was* just trying to help," he added.

-

They reached the top after what seemed like hours of climbing, and Li-Li threw herself out of the stairwell onto the solid floor of a round balcony, just big enough for the four of them to stand. Bim stepped over her to the wall. Yuki and Ola moved to opposite sides, the former still simmering.

"Oh! You can look right out the Maw from here," Bim announced, pointing.

Li-Li fussed with her hair. "Y-yes. I th-think I read that Vessels used to be in-introduced to their g-g-gods from huh-here."

"Introduced?" He cocked an eyebrow. "I don't remember anything like that."

"Probably because it happened before you were made?" Ola suggested.

"No…I remember some of it…."

His friend's mouth snapped shut mid-laugh. "Oh…what am I saying…I shouldn't have…"

Li-Li sat up straight, scooted right back against the wall so that she could not see the Maw or the stars beyond. "You remember your Making?"

Bim nodded. "I remember a lot. Not my home. Or my family. Being taken. Being made. Lying in that box."

"I remember the rest," she told him. "Not the Making. Or the Reavers. Everything before that."

"I would prefer it that way."

"Hmmm."

"We all remember," Ola elaborated. "All of us. Me, Bim, Princess, Lilith, Star…we all remember something from before. Bim remembers the Making. I remember my sister. We all carry something."

"Is that wh-why. Um…"

"Why we don't cooperate?" Bim offered. "Yes. Mostly. There are other reasons, of course. But when I think about how they treated me before—why should I obey them?"

"I re-remember a lot."

"You do? What?"

"M-my family. Our h-h-house. My s-sisters." She searched further. "I th-think I remember b-being t-t-taken, too."

"But you obey?"

She nodded. Behind Ola, Yuki was shaking their head.

"Why?"

"O-our mistresses a-aren't so b-b-bad. They muh…make it easier."

"But your mentor is a bitch."

Li-Li laughed. "She's n-n-not always l-like that."

179

Bim sat, Ola followed suit. Standing apart from the three of them, Yuki looked lost.

"Do any of the others remember? Are there more?" Ola asked.

"Yes," she answered. "Crim did. She told me once. Or at least she thought she was remembering more of it before…before she…"

"Before she left?"

"Uh-huh."

"Where did she go?"

"I don't know. Outside."

"Will she ever—um. Do you think she…"

"No. She's never coming back."

XXV

Is this the right place?" Princess turned, looking around them at the tumbled columns, the collapsed walls and broken streets, all sprouting green and white where nature slowly worked on reclaiming this place.

"I'll know once we get up there." Something like a flight of steps led up a strangely regular-shaped hill. Sunshine started up them, leaving Princess to inspect the ruins below. The stairs opened up onto a flat shelf that hemmed the very summit, and on this side stones had fallen into an opening that looked very much like a doorway in the rockface. Looking out from here, she saw the grasslands stretching out below, and the long line of what she supposed was one of the rivers. A line of flat mountains blocked the forest and the ocean from view. Hsei was just as beautiful as they had left it. And just as eerie. Though life persevered in every inch of it, it was punctuated by deep shadows. A world haunted by what had happened to it.

"This is it," she called back down. Surely the Elders knew how to open the portals in exact locations, and Mentor would have been able to deposit them in the exact same place as before, but she was proud of herself for having made it even to the same planet. And there was no-one but Princess to share in her success.

"Princess?" Sunshine turned and looked down the steps to where she had left her. "Princess!"

Gone. Of course, she was gone. She had probably run off. This had probably all been a ploy to escape from the Mountain. To escape from her and Mentor and the life—or un-life—she loathed so much. Sunshine wondered if she should even search for her. In the past few years, she had come to understand Princess and her plight more and more. She even empathised at times—

A shriek from below made her jump.

"*Princess!*"

181

Beyond the path that led down the hill and around onto a shady part of the plane sat a squat pyramid. Sunshine skirted this as she ran towards the sounds of Princess' mounting distress. On the opposite side of this heaps of overgrown rubble sprang up, and tottering towers drew closer together to follow the line of an upheaved road paved in large yellow stones. Another scream. Now sprinting, she vaulted a shell of a building and pulled herself up onto one unsound wall to look about. Perched there like a cat ready to pounce, she reached out for her pupil. Princess had gone silent. Though she called and called, there came no response. Her stomach lurched.

Captured? Or killed? Those were the only options. Nothing else could silence Princess. But who or what had overpowered her? There was no one left living in this place.

"Sunny?" The call came from her right, weak and frightened, resounding off the empty homes. Sunshine leapt from her vantage point down to the ground, upsetting some loose tiles and broken earthenware as she went. She hoped whatever beast had found them was hard of hearing.

She found Princess just a few blocks away, turning about in a frantic circle. Her blotchy cheeks were stained with tears, and she was babbling, babbling at apparent nothingness. Sunshine crept closer, passing under an archway and out into the broad street. Touching the youngling's arm did not bring her to her senses, and in her head was a jumble of frightened pleas.

What had happened? What had she found, or what had found her? Sunshine glanced up and down the narrow side street. It was lined with arches on either side, with short steps leading into what must have once been homes and businesses, little more than outlines and memories now.

There was something *off* here. More so than the chill she felt on the main road. Somehow, the walls and stones around her looked less substantial, their shapes rippling slightly as though the whole space was a mirage. The more she looked the worse it got, the more she tried to make sense of what she was seeing the more it shifted and distorted. Finally, she relaxed, and allowed her eyes to see what they were trying to see. This place clearly had something to show her. A blink, a turn of her head in the right direction, and the sagging walls righted themselves, the dented road smoothed, all signs of decay faded. Flowers bloomed in pots that huddled around doorways and hung from pillars. Vibrant flags fluttered against walls in the afternoon breeze. Canopies and awnings sheltered most of the way from the harsh sun, and were also hung with samples of wares—cloths and jewels, pots and plates, smoked meats and garlands of fragrant herbs.

Mentor had taught her about these phenomena: Echoes. Places or times where the fabric of reality was torn, and eras and realities leaked into one another. There were plenty of these around the Mountain; some popping up unexpectedly and disappearing before one could even react, some—like the ones in the Dungeons—clung to certain places stubbornly, haunting all trespassers. Most of them were small, dripping images and sounds into the minds of passers-by. This one was exceptionally large—large enough for two Sidhe to walk around in.

Restored streets and buildings were not all that this particular Echo had to offer, though that was impressive enough. A few righted walls were not enough to frighten Princess to such wordless hysteria, nor were they enough to stop Sunshine's very heart. No, it was the people that had her quaking. People bustling all around, going about their daily business like their world was not obliterated around them. They passed both around the two travellers and through them, and Sunshine tingled wherever they touched.

"Hseians," Sunshine stated. Turning in a far calmer circle than her companion. They were small, slim creatures with a distinctly marsupial appearance—most of them were covered with smooth brown or sandy fur, though three or four that passed were coated in black, and she even spotted a single albino eating fruit sitting in the doorway of one building. They moved silently; Echoes were rarely strong enough to convey sound, but Sunshine imagined a lively chattering surrounded her. The music of a city still alive. The voices of a people lost for millennia. Though the sight of them made her heart ache, she smiled.

"Ghosts?" Princess managed, still wide-eyed with fear.

"I suppose. Relax. They can't hurt you." Sunshine put an arm around her.

"But why are they here."

"This is their home."

"Why are they *still* here?"

"This is their home," Sunshine repeated. "It always will be. Even if most of them have moved on, some fragment will always remain here. It's like…existential residue."

"What?"

"You really never listened to anything Mentor tried to teach you, did you?"

"She never taught me about *ghosts!*"

"Fine. Do you at least know what the world is made of?"

"…stuff?"

Sunshine put a hand to her forehead. "Stuff. Yes. Of course. But there's two kinds of *stuff.* The stuff we're made of and the stuff we are."

Princess blinked.

"Look at this." She held out an arm. "This is part of my body. Part of my physical self. But that's not what's talking to you, or what you find when you reach out to me. That's my spiritual self."

"Uh-huh…"

"And what would happen if I died?"

"Your physical self would be destroyed?"

"Destroyed? Not quite. Nothing in this world is ever truly *destroyed.* My body would still exist."

"But…oh." Princess snapped her fingers. "It would separate from your spiritual self."

"Mostly, yes," Sunshine concurred. "Like my body would eventually be broken up and re-absorbed into the cosmos, most of my spirit would also be split, and drift into other lives and other places beyond the physical."

Blink.

"But some part of my body, and some part of me, would still remain where I died."

Princess nodded. "Residue."

"Right."

"So the spirit leaves something there, too?"

"Yes."

"And that's what they are?"

"Yes. The greater parts of themselves have moved on—have been re-distributed throughout the universe. Only these Echoes remain."

"Why this street?"

Sunshine smirked. "This street was only the weak spot in the physical realm. Our entry-point. Come."

*

184

Princess took her arm and, still nervously glancing this way and that, allowed herself to be led through the streets and alleyways. Sunshine, having never properly experienced Echoes herself, was just as perplexed by them, though delightfully so. She found that tilting her head a certain way, or closing one eye, changed her perception, and parts of the vision would fade to reveal the ruins underneath. After a while, she was able to wilfully look through the ghosts of the city to see the reality. Beside her, Princess was also beginning to move her head strangely, blinking and squinting comically at the same time as she struggled to control what she saw.

Suddenly, she stopped short, pulling Sunshine to a halt with her. She pointed through the crowd to one of the houses. "There!"

A man stood in the doorway, waving his arms and pointing. Sunshine took a moment to register that he was pointing at *them*. Then to the sky. Waving his arms. Pointing at them. At the sky. His mouth was moving the whole time and she was certain he was yelling something, but his voice had been lost long ago. In the darkness within the house, two pairs of eyes peered fearfully out.

"He can see us?"

"It would appear so."

"How?"

"Some mortals are more sensitive than others. Like us, they can see through rifts in time and dimension, though they can seldom make sense of what they see. He clearly thinks we were there in his time."

"But were *here?"*

"Yes."

"In…in the *now?"*

"Yep."

"And he's *there*…he's *then!"*

"I know it's confusing."

Princess sighed, watching as the Hseian gesticulated wildly. "What's he doing?"

"He's asking for help."

"But we can't, right?" Now she sounded distraught.

"And it is much too late for us," Sunshine replied, sorrowfully observing. Would they see it? Or was this poor man forever trapped in his last desperate act?

"What's he pointing at?"

"Doom."

Sunshine looked to the sky this time when he gestured, hand squeezing Princess's shoulder. It rippled and blurred for a moment as she forced her eyes to adjust, forced them to peek through the ages. She shook the youngling's arm.

"Look there. Concentrate. Look through what *is* and search for what *was.*"

"I don't see anything."

"Focus."

Princess' eyes narrowed as she pushed her awareness beyond the swirling clouds and into what once was there, then she started, and cried out: "What is that!"

Sunshine could not answer. It was difficult to make out any shape through the haze, but the light blazed through all awareness. A sizzling orange beam that now drove towards the ground like a column of lightning. The man's calls turned to screams, and in one last moment of desperation he pushed his children back inside, diving after them. The bolt moved slowly, yet all too fast, and struck the street in a flash, a plume of smoke and a cloud of flying debris. Princess braced as a chunk of wood hurled towards them, braced in vain as it passed through them and rent a wide gash in the earth. Then as suddenly as it had struck, it faded from existence, leaving only a smoking crater in its wake.

"Sunshine!" She yelped. "Sunshine, what's happening!"

"We're witnessing it."

"Witnessing *what?*"

"The end of their world," she answered, standing transfixed, unable to tear her eyes away from where that terrible light had fallen from. "This is how they die. How they *died.*"

Crouching, curling into a ball beside her, Princess began to sob. Despite the destruction all around them, it was the only sound either of them could hear. A dense, black cloud grew and grew, blocking the street and sky alike from view. A thick, blinding force full of the flotsam and jetsam of a civilisation annihilated in seconds, pierced only by a single orange beam.

*

At length the light died away, the darkness dispersed. Everything turned dim as dust hung in the air, dense and black and choking. The sun went out, and Sunshine imagined the acrid reek of fire, the stench of burning bodies, the profound, jarring silence. Time seemed to leap forward, and light began to peer through the clouds, grass began to sprout underfoot. It rained, and the last of the dust was washed from the sky, becoming ashes on the ground that begat more grass and trees and vines and flowers. Nature crept over the bones of the dead city, and life thrived anew. Still there remained the fallen bricks and toppled columns, and a dark, bottomless pit yawned in front of them as Sunshine and Princess found themselves at the bottom of a great bowl in the earth.

Princess, face red and puffy from crying, looked up at her. "What *was* that?"

"I don't know. Lightning, maybe? A great storm?"

"The sky was clear!"

"Natural phenomenon," Sunshine guessed. "Or something from outside?"

"Outside?"

"Solar flare?"

Princess sniffed. "That was nothing natural and you know it! Who could do all this?"

"I don't know." Sunshine turned. The crater was lumpy with overgrown mounds—no doubt the houses they had just seen, and probably whatever was left of the people. "It was a swift end, at least."

Her underling gaped up, appalled. "They didn't deserve this!"

"No, they didn't. But all things must end. It's tragic, but this was their fate." Sunshine shrugged. She was coming off far more nonchalant than she felt, ignoring the ache in her chest, and the urge to throw herself down on the ground next to Princess. They had just been people. Simple, innocent mortals going about their daily life. And that light—hairs rose on the back of her neck—there had been something very *wrong* about it.

Wiping her eyes, Princess stood up. Then, with newfound determination, she made for the deep, dark hole.

"Where are you going?"

"There must be something left. A book or a totem; some record of who they were, what they believed.*"* Princess toed the edge of the pit. "I'm not leaving here without something to remember them. They've been forgotten for so long. It's the least I can do for them."

"You could do more," Sunshine told her. "You could be their Scribe."

She blinked. "I'm only an Acolyte."

"It's unusual, but you discovered them. And you have clearly connected with them." Sunshine joined her, staring down into the abyss. Water dripped somewhere far below. "Write their story. They would want you to."

"I don't know how?"

"Go to the Library. Bart will help you. And Li-Li too, if you ask nicely."

XXVI

It kept coming back to her. That dream. The charred slopes and blackened trees. The Swamps turned to tarpits and the River, the Tarn as well as all the little ponds scattered around the lowlands—all choked and discoloured, the fish floating to rot on top with no scavengers left to eat them. The echoing tunnels and ransacked rooms of a Mountain left standing but utterly destroyed. She wished for someone to wake her.

"Hey!"

Anyone but *her*.

"Oi!"

Princess' toe connected her side. Li-Li growled. It was much too early for this. "Let m-me sleep."

"You're having a nightmare anyway."

"What m-m-makes you suh-say that?"

The other acolyte bent down and tugged the corner of her blanket. Sure enough, Li-Li felt the cocoon she had wrapped around herself tighten. Her legs in particular were firmly stuck together.

"I want to go to the Library."

"Go ah-huh-head."

"You need to come with me."

"Why?"

"Sunshine said so."

Li-Li wormed away from her and shut her eyes again. "Sure she d-did."

A stronger yank on the covers. Li-Li found herself hanging over the edge of the bed, the frame digging into her hip.

"I have a project."

"A project?"

"Yes. I'm going to be a Scribe."

Li-Li did not know whether to laugh or gasp, so did both and ended up choking on her own spit. She sat up. *"You?"*

Princess flicked her hair. "Yes. Me. I will write the story of an ancient race. But I need *you* to introduce me to Bart. You know he won't let anyone work on the Annals without an introduction."

It was true. Crim had shown the Annals to Li-Li, or some of them at least. All Sidhe were allowed to read them, of course. But to *write* in them…

"Y-you'll need to i-i-impress him."

"I will."

"You'll n-need to b-b-be *polite*."

"I can be polite!"

Li-Li unravelled herself and opened the cubby nearest her, picking out a pale blue robe with red detailing and a yellow sash. "Huh-help me get d-dresses at least."

"Ugh. Your little pet can do that."

"Well, if y-y-you d-don't want to me-meet Bart—"

Princess snatched the garment from her and held it out. "See? Polite!"

*

Yuki wasn't talking to her. They still followed her, of course, trailing behind like a disgruntled shadow as she let her newfound friend to the Library. Princess, on her left, linked arms with Li-Li and leaned in to whisper:

"Why are they here?"

She sighed. "I d-don't know. T-told them the-they didn't have to."

"They haven't said a word since they woke up."

"I know." She glanced back. They walked with their eyes to the ground, not meeting her gaze.

"You don't have to…you know. If it's going to drive a wedge between you, I'm sure I can figure this out on my own."

"N-no. It's f-f-fine," she spoke loudly, her word echoing off the corridor walls. Yuki did not blink. They met her gaze momentarily, something like an accusation that went unspoken.

What is your problem?

Yuki scowled and looked away again.

"Still…" Princess began. Li-Li was not used to her being so nice. All because she wanted something. She did not trust it to last, but for the moment it was pleasant.

"I want t-to h-help."

Princess had told her about the Hseians. About the ruins and the ghost and the apocalypse she had witnessed. She had shown her the relics she had pulled out of the bowels of the forgotten city; a statuette carved out of marbled blue stone, a chain studded with jewels, and five slate tablets covered in strange carvings. Writing, probably, though none of them could make sense of it. Most likely, no one under the Mountain had ever seen such a language. But there was one person who seemed to recognise everything ever written—Bart. Li-Li had seen him at work, had watched Crim approach him with books and scrolls and tablets just like the ones now tucked into Princess' bag; he understood them all, whether by recognition or some sort of natural affinity for language. He was always able to make sense of the senseless.

Bart only received people brought to him by ones he trusted, so Princess would have no chance if she approached him alone. Li-Li, on the other hand, he had come to know in the absence of Crim, as she tried to visit the Library often to carry on her work restoring and transcribing older pieces. She liked to think he was quite fond of her. If he was not fond of Princess…they would know quickly enough.

*

The old beast was sleeping (as usual) when they arrived, sat in his favourite chair by the fire, with his feet up. The last few sips of tea sat forgotten in their cup at his elbow, alongside a tray of half-eaten biscuits. Li-Li put her hand on one massive hoof and shook.

A snort that became a roar, then ebbed away into a growl. The old minotaur sat bolt upright, planting both of his hooves on the floor with a loud thump, blinking and squinting about in confusion. He smacked his lips groggily.

"Aha! There you are Little Mouse," he rumbled. "It's been ten days!"

"Yes. I w-was painting the Temple," said Li-Li. "B-b-but I'm here to help n-n-now. And I've b-brought friends!"

She gestured to Yuki and Princess, both of whom were standing behind her—*cowering* behind her. They knew Bart's reputation for being a cantankerous old

191

goat, and were unwilling to approach. Bart frowned down at them, not making any effort to ease their anxieties. In fact, he towered over them rather ominously.

"Who are these ones?" He demanded.

"Th-this is Princess." Li-Li gestured for her to step forward. "A-a-and Yuki."

Yuki shrank back more, which did not go unnoticed by the old minotaur. His frown deepened, but he offered his hand to Princess all the same. At a nod from Li-Li, she took it and allowed herself to be examined.

"Hah!" Barked the beast, and Princess near jumped out of her skin. "Hot-headed wee thing! Full of fight! Bull-headed; like me—haha!"

"I'm sorry." Princess bowed her head. "I'll behave myself."

"Oh I'm sure you will. Full of mischief, but not ill-meaning. Just don't lose your temper. Mind your breath, count to ten. Be kind."

She flushed and looked at Li-Li. "I'll try."

He ruffled her perfect curls and she grimaced, stepping aside to straighten them in a small hand-mirror. Bart reached two great arms out to Yuki, who had retreated all the way back into a dark corner.

"Come now. There is no entering this place but by my approval."

"I can wait outside."

"Yuki!" Li-Li snapped. "Y-you will greet Bart…o-o-or you will l-leave! No waiting out-outside or s-suh-skulking about!"

They stared at her, aghast.

"Why d-d-did you even c-come!"

"Easy, Little Mouse," Bart cooed. "They only want to be near you. Am I right, Yuki?"

Yuki muttered something and nudged the corner of one rug with their toe, then edged forward. Bart patiently waited for them to offer their hand.

"A little storm," he remarked. "The other one was short-tempered but you are *angry*, Child. Raging, roiling. You want to fight everyone but at the same time you are afraid of everything. Li-Li—you vouch for them?"

"I d-do." Bart seemed undecided, relying on her opinion. He huffed at her response.

"Do *not* betray her, Little Princess."

*

Bart invited them to sit, so they sat, legs swinging off the edge of a worn settee that faced his chair at an angle. They watched as he bumbled about, pulling a coffee table as big as a dining table right up to them and setting upon it a teapot, coffeepot, a steaming jug of hot chocolate, along with several plates and bowls laden with cakes, tarts and biscuits. He hummed tunelessly the whole time he worked, and would not answer a single question until they were served.

"Alright now, Little Princess," he said at last. "You mentioned something about a…um…"

"Stone tablets," Princess told him, reaching into her bag. "Five of them, actually. Li-Li told me you had a way with writings, so I was hoping you could make sense of these."

"I *do* enjoy a puzzle." Bart leaned over eagerly as Princess pulled the cloth-wrapped bundle out, the end of his beard grazing a platter of scones. Yuki made a noise of disgust at Li-Li's elbow and received a jab and a *shush*. He took the whole stack of slates in one hand and lumbered over to his chair to unwrap it. The slates were slim, made out of a darker blue stone than the statuette, and dappled with spots of reflective mica. He let out a pleased "*Hummm*" as he sifted through them. "Fascinating. Most fascinating."

"Can you read it?"

"Not yet. Give an old coot a moment, Child. I need to take it in first." Bart traced the strange characters with one long fingernail, tapping here and there where they seemed to be more difficult. "It's similar to Kyedhen, I think. Hseian?"

"How did you know?"

"Similar to Kyedhen, like I said. Their systems are near—or rather they *were*. They've drifted further apart, I'm sure." He pursed his lips, concentrating. "It's quite a simple language, I must say…phonetic. I can make out words but by the gods there's a lot of fluff. Like the Kyedhen, indeed."

The three of them waited, Princess on the edge of her seat as she daintily sipped at a veritable bowl full of fragrant tea and picked at an iced fairy cake. Yuki, now leaning all the way back with their feet stretched out, was loudly slurping on a mug of black coffee, biscuit crumbs cascading down their tunic and onto the plush brown cushion under them. Li-Li crossed her legs and rested her chin on her hand, staring into the fire as a cup of hot chocolate went cold in her lap. The only sound for a long while was Bart's excited monologue as he deduced more and more of the alien writing.

Presently, he stood up, triumphantly striking the mantelpiece with his fist and laughing gruffly. Princess jumped down and hopped over to him, trying to peer up at the slates as though they made sense to her now, too. Bart, to his credit, hunkered down (knees creaking audibly) and let her look.

"On the fourth day of the fifth moon Ji'Kara and I collected more of the harvest. It has been greater this year than last, but the stars foretell a bleak horizon...I will put it away. The spot behind the clouds grows larger. We watch it."

Princess blinked up at him. "What?"

"It's a journal. Someone's journal. A farmer, by the sound of it." Bart sorted through to the last slate. "It records the last...ten days before the calamity."

"How did you know about that? Li-Li, I suppose you—"

"It appeared in the sky yesterday evening. A great, shimmering shape bigger than the moon. We prayed to it at first, lit fires in the streets and sent up coloured smoke, but it only lingers there menacingly. Ji'Kara and some of the others fired in hopes of scaring it, and now the noise, the noise. The sky trembles."

Princess' excitement turned to sobriety. "Yes. Something in the air high above. That's what we saw. The sky lit up, and some sort of beam...some sort of power hit them. Like a massive entity using its *draoi*."

"Something or someone wanted to get rid of them." Bart nodded sombrely. "It is not unheard of."

"But they were primitive, simple...*peaceful*!" Princess cried. "Who could possibly mean them harm?"

"Think of the world you were taken from, Child. Are the peaceful always left alone? Do the powerful never seek to wipe out the primitive? Have whole civilisations not been levelled in an instant?"

She struck the table with her fist. Hard. "It's not *fair.*"

Bart patted her head with a hand big enough to crush it like a grape. "Not fair. But they were probably in the way."

"D-do..." Li-Li began. "Do we h-h-have anyway of no-knowing who did it? Wh-who k-k-killed them?"

"There are many possibilities. Too many to tell from such a description," responded the minotaur sadly. "However..."

"Yes?"

"In the few months before she left, Crim had been working on something new…an encyclopaedia of sorts. A list of all of the peoples the Sidhe have come into contact with, or heard of so far. With my help, of course. My mind struggles to go very far back of late, but if I ever recalled something, I would tell her and she would write it down."

"Really?" Li-Li had helped Crim with plenty of her projects prior to her disappearance, and discovered even more in her absence. She had never come across such an encyclopaedia.

"Indeed. As far as I could tell it was quite close to her heart, as a matter of fact." Bart adjusted his spectacles. "She kept it in her study, I believe."

"Sh-she did*?*"

*

As it turned out, Crim had not shown Li-Li all of her work. Bart, stomping through the aisles on tired old legs, made sure to emphasise this as he led the way past shelves and stacks and up two flights of stairs to the highest level of the Library. When Li-Li was not with her, she apparently locked herself in her study for days on end and produced reams of research that she happily presented to the old librarian for approval. Some of these even made their way onto the shelves.

"This one…this one she could never quite get around to finishing," he explained. "I only caught glimpses of it in passing, and heard her ranting about it when she would eventually get frustrated—she would never want me to read anything that wasn't finished. Though once or twice she *did* have to let me take a look. Writing a record of all known peoples is no small feat, you know. I expect it would have taken her eternity. Now you three go on."

He crouched at the door and ushered them in (he was too large to enter himself). "There's bits of it in the bottom drawer on the left. More in a box under the sofa. I think she stuffed some into that cover by your head, Little Mouse."

Li-Li opened a black leather cover and found it full of loose pages and sketches. A few fell to the floor; a pencil drawing of a Rowghel and a page on the anatomy of a Zugu's ear. Both covered in her mistress' wonky scribblings.

"Incredible."

"A mess, you mean." Bart chuckled. "There should be an index there, somewhere. That folder is finished as far as I'm aware. I'd check that first before trying to tackle the rest."

"Thank you, Sir," Princess said, causing Yuki to spin around like they had just heard something offensive.

"Oh, no *sirs*, please Child. I'm just Bart."

XXVII

She was never going back. As she hurtled down the Mountainside, Crim came to this decision rather easily. She would never return to that life in hiding, that life outside the realms of life, that life spent fighting and serving and frightened, that life that demanded she take life from others. Sunshine, Laal, Li-Li…they would understand. It hurt her to leave them behind, hurt her to go without saying goodbye. As much as she loved all of them, she could not stay in that place. That immortal prison.

The edge of the forest came rushing towards her, rays from the departing sun shining through the trunks and leaves. Her last look at that miniature star that so many eons ago had become enamoured with the Mountain, who had pulled in a wayward moon as company to dance around this floating island at the edge of space. So meagre was its light that other stars shone through it, blurry dots in a navy-blue sky, and the moon still peered down, white and hazy.

Goodbye. She did not pause, but bid them all farewell as the burst forth from among the trees and sped down the grassy slopes towards the final circle of standing stones and the Edge.

*

A blink. And the Edge became nothing but another downward step. A blink, and the lush green foothill became another forest, quite similar to the one she had just left, though dark and foggy and damp. Crim slowed, drawing her cowl up higher around her neck and pulling the hood over her head. Within seconds, droplets had already gathered on the soft grey wolf's hide. She let out a puff of air and watched the tiny white cloud disappear into the mist. It was cold; far colder than under the Mountain, so much so the mist turned to frost where it settled on the ground, and crunched underfoot. Crim found it invigorating.

Taking her time now, she picked her way through the dense forest, moving down a far easier slope, though not without its fair share of steps and drops. Before long, she discovered a narrow path, which made things easier. This she followed in a rather straight line to a steep embankment, over a meter high, which broke the forest. She found herself looking down into a narrow ditch, and past this a wide patch of flattened earth. At least, it had probably been flattened once upon a time; now it was rutted and trampled and full of puddles.

Crim jumped over the ditch onto the road, splashing mud all over her robes. The mud was soft and cool under her feet, and she laughed, stamping about for a while for good measure.

She thought it best to follow the road, as she most wanted to find a town. Preferably one like that hilltop village Sunshine had brought her to. One full of mortals going about their simple lives. She would visit for a while and watch them, and then move on to the next town, and the next, until she had visited all the towns of the world, and then she would visit them all again. The road was much easier to follow, anyway, as the woods seemed seldom used apart from that old path.

She stopped, listening, not one hundred yards from where she had struck the road. A familiar sound. Two familiar sounds. Three. Horses, snorting and huffing, their hooves muffled by the muck. A man, whistling and humming to himself, wondering when he might get in away from this winter's night. The creak of wheels carrying a heavy load. Crim turned around and sure enough there was a light, the swaying orange light of a candle set in a lantern and hung from the cart's side. A rather large cart, by the outline, and as it drew nearer Crim saw that it was roofed, its dark brown bulk gleaming wetly. For some reason, the driver had chosen to sit on a bench on the front, rather than inside where it was warmer, and was steering the horses with one hand while trying to warm the other in the folds of his coat, a tall hat tipped down over his eyes and a woollen scarf wrapped tightly around his face.

The lamp sang as it swung, louder, louder. The horses, smelling her, pricked up their ears. So intent was the man on staying warm that he did not see her until the cart was nearly on top of her.

"*Christ!*" He yelped, pulling the horses to a dead stop. "What on earth are you doing out in the middle of the road, girl!"

Crim looked from him, to the Mountain looming behind, back to him. "I...I'm lost."

The man looked her up and down. Crim willed him not to see her strange attire, so he did not. All he saw was a lost girl shivering in the middle of the road. He took off his hat and smoothed back his hair. He was not old; maybe fifty or so, his dark hair turned grey over his ears, tall and slowly turning soft with age, as all mortals do. When he smiled, Crim knew he was no harm. "Well, you're lucky the village is on our way. Hop up, Love. I can't leave you out here on your own at night."

He offered his hand, and she allowed him to pull her up onto the bench beside him. Once she was seated, he took off his scarf and draped it over her shoulders. A knock from inside the cart startled her, and he laughed, but put a finger to his lips as he turned to look over the side. A door opened and he exchanged hurried words with someone inside. Someone else was snoring.

"Who is that?" She asked, trying to peer through the curtains on her side.

"The lady of the house," he answered. "Wondering why we've stopped. Best get moving before she gives me a *real* talking to."

His name was James. A strange, foreign name for someone born and reared not twenty miles away from where he had picked her up. He did not ask her name; she did not let him. Instead, he told her about his masters, his life, his family. He was father to four girls (now women) and two boys (now men), and his whole family lived on his masters' land.

"You are a slave?"

He laughed. "They call us 'servants' now. They don't own us."

"So you are free to leave?"

"Ahhh…" James took a swig from a metal flask and offered it to her; the liquid inside was sharp, warm and fragrant. She took two swigs. "Hah! Easy, Love. Too much'll blow your head clean off."

She handed it back immediately.

"No, we're not quite free leave but…well…things are better than they used to be."

"What did they used to be?"

"Ah. In the days of my father…well. You know I'm sure."

She did not know, but did not press the topic. The carriage (apparently 'cart' was not an apt way to describe it) trundled on through the mud and the mist, pulling her downhill and further and further away from the massive shadow of the Mountain. The banks on either side of the road shrank down to meet it, and the trees, now sparse, were hemmed in on either side by fences and walls.

They turned a sharp bend, and the slope rolled down steeply. On their left, wide fields of grass, wheat and barley stretched out for miles. On the right, the final lines of the forest marched down to...

To...

Crim's heart stopped. A vast, round lake set in a half-circle of hills. Trees bordered it on most sides, though far fewer than before. Where once there was nothing but green there now stood scattered houses, fields full of crops, grazing animals. Even a lone, round tower. Gone was the island. Gone were the fences and the squat buildings. Gone was the little boat dragged and tethered ashore. Gone was everything she knew. And yet she knew this place.

"Home."

James looked at her. "I should hope so. It's where I'm bringing you!"

They wrapped around the lake, Crim transfixed by the glimmering water. The white moon rippling in the waves. The scattered stars reflected perfectly. The grey haze that hung just above the surface. What once had seemed so mundane to her, she now looked at with agonising familiarity.

They passed the tower, now abandoned and dark where it stood on a knoll overlooking the water. Crim stared at it. Just past this on the opposite side was a small house reached by a worn path leading up from a lopsided gate. Lights in the window and people talking inside. The farm's wall curved gradually inward until eventually the road forked. James hardly had the horses reined in when she jumped down.

"Well. This is where I'll be leaving you," he said. "Go straight home, Love. No more wandering about."

"Thank you." Crim handed his scarf back. "Thank you for bringing me home."

"Not at all. If any of my daughters were caught out on a night like this...well. Damn me to hell if I'd left you."

"Thank you."

"Good night, then. God bless."

"God bless?"

He whistled to the horses, and with a grunt they marched on. He waved back as Crim waved. For just a second, a face appeared at the window below, scowling at her.

*

She started away from the lake, towards the warm lights and shadowed buildings less than one mile in the distance. Crim knew she could have covered the distance in less than a minute, but kept a mortal pace. With each step forward she felt heavier, her heart thundering in her chest as she wondered how long it had been since she had been so close to home. What had this road been before? Had she walked this very way all those centuries ago? Who lived here now, and where had they come from? It was very possible that some were descended from her brothers and sisters. Would she know them? Would they know her?

Cobblestones underfoot now. Stone buildings all around. The road opened into a small square, where it wrapped around the plinth of a bronze statue; a man with one hand on the hilt of his sword, staring out into nowhere. She approached him. There were words carved into the marble base. Probably his name. Numbers too, though the date made no sense.

Behind him was a building that dwarfed all around it, set behind a high wall and dark iron gates. She crossed the road to peer through the bars. The lawn that surrounded it was covered in stone markers and reeked of decay. Graves. But what kind of people collected the dead like this? She frowned up at its pointed turret and stained-glass windows.

A temple of sorts. She concluded. There were many gods of the dead, she knew. This was probably built for one of them.

*

Opposite the temple was another building, not as large but clearly important. Crim could hear several people inside, talking and laughing. Pipe smoke drifted out the door in plumes. Two men standing outside were watching her.

"You alright, Pet?" The elder of the two called.

"I came from the road," she replied. Not really an answer.

"Where from?" The other—his son—asked.

"Um…the estate?" James had mentioned it, and it seemed the best excuse.

"They didn't send you on an errand this late!" The father, offended by the notion, put his pipe back in his pocket.

"No. No they didn't. I um…I left?"

The two shared a look.

"Why would you—"

The son received a clap on the head that knocked the remainder of his sentence out.

"Not that that's our business!"

"Right!"

"You ran away, Girl?"

"Yes."

"Here. At night?"

"Yes."

The father looked her up and down, then nodded. That was enough for him. "Have you eaten?"

"No."

XXVIII

Seamus' family lived outside of the village on a farm that faced the main road. They were not rich by any means; but their house had four rooms (plenty of space for his nine children), a good plot of land for their crops, and a field and barn for their livestock. He explained all of this in elaborate detail as he and his eldest son (Diarmuid) walked her home. Crim, still new to this world, listened in rapt silence, but also carefully probed his rather open mind for further detail.

He had been a boy when the Hunger came. When the crops failed and people began to starve. His parents had died when he was just seven, and he and his elder brother left their home the day they buried them. Whether they left by choice or were evicted, Crim could not discern. They walked for days before coming to the village, passing many more unfortunate souls on the road. Some of the less fortunate they left behind on the road. When they arrived, they were nothing but skin and bones, and tried begging for food from the locals, who had nothing to spare themselves. An elderly woman took their hands where she found them on the street and led them to the church, where the priest and several well-dressed, well-meaning strangers were giving out food.

He lived on odd jobs, both from the townspeople and the Lord that lived in the big house up the hill. With the little money they earned, he and his brother managed to rent a room where they lived for three years until his brother died of cholera at the age of eighteen, and the loss of his income meant Seamus found himself on the street again. Not for long, this time, not like before. Mickey Flaherty had opened a public house in the town, and took him on as a barman. The same pub that the Meaghers had then bought after none of aul Mickey's children wanted to take it—sons gone to the city and daughters married off to run houses of their own.

*

"I met the missus in that pub back there," he boasted. "Life's all been uphill from there."

It had not. Crim saw a flash of painful memories at his words, but left them alone. To her right Diarmuid gave a "hmph."

"Anyways, here we are!"

A good-sized house. Plenty of rooms. Big enough for a family of eleven. All these things it was not. Staring at the white walls and thatched roof of the cottage, Crim could tell it was smaller even than the round building of wattle and daub her father had built countless centuries before. And that had only housed eight. Seamus clapped his hand on the wall proudly, smiling as though it were a palace. Diarmuid lifted the latch on a battered wooden door and gestured for her to step inside.

Eight pairs of eyes, all clustered around a table meant for four, turned to stare at Crim. None more intense than those of the woman prodding the fire, infant sleeping at her breast. Sharp, grey eyes that bored through her. Crim felt a cold weight settle at the bottom of her gut, and backed away.

"Who's this?" Said Eileen, without even a greeting. Steel eyes narrowed. Piercing.

"She's from up the hill, Love," her husband explained. "Wandered into town with naught but the clothes on her back."

Clothes. Crim willed herself to focus on her disguise. Had it slipped? No. According to mortal eyes she was not wearing the coloured robes and jewels of a Sidhe, no. Just a simple girl in a simple dress and worn shoes. Nothing more. Eileen continued to glare at her. Unconvinced.

Seamus turned and patted her shoulder. "You go on and sit by the fire, Pet. Get yourself warm. Eileen is there anything left in the pot? Some bread, even?"

The woman nodded, eyeing Crim relentlessly. She hesitated, not wanting to move closer. She felt Eileen could see *through* her, sweat beating at her temples as she struggled to hold onto her illusion. Seamus invited her again, laughing, steering her into a seat. At once, the questions came.

"What's your name, girl?"

She picked one out of the air. It had been common in her time, but no longer, judging by the way the woman's features narrowed at the sound of it.

"You local?"

Yes. She knew it was the wrong answer, but panicked. Eileen knew she was not from anywhere nearby, had grown up here.

"Where from?"

"Up…up the hill…"

"You were born there?"

"Yes…"

"Oh, I know some of the servants up there."

Crim shrank.

"You Peggy's girl?"

"Y-yes!"

"Funny. I was sure she had all boys."

She glanced into the fire, frantically searching her brain for the right lies. The flames rose up encouragingly. Eileen prodded them back down.

"Now, Love." Seamus came to her rescue. "The girl's probably scared out of her mind. Only a matter of time before that old bat up the hill has the men after her. Let's save the questions for later, yeah?"

Eileen nodded, her gaze finally turning aside. Yet Crim still felt as though she were pinned down; a mouse caught under the cat's paw. The fire crackling in the hearth, warm though it was, was no comfort. One of the older girls passed her a bowl and a heel of hard brown bread, smiling but mirroring her mother's wariness.

Crim ate slowly. The stew was bland; full of fatty lumps of lamb and questionable vegetables and thickened with milk. The bread was better by far; fresh-baked and soft in the middle, with a good crunch to the crust. She dipped it in the broth and nibbled piece-by-piece. Seamus' family resumed their normal table-side chatter, but the air in the room had changed, and every now and again someone would turn to study her, or do a double take, like something had just caught their eye. Only Seamus himself remained oblivious.

*

The night grew dark, the mists rolling in from the nearby lake to caress the fields and the barn and the tiny white house. Eileen used logs from the fire in the kitchen to start the piles of coals in each of the three adjacent rooms. One by one the boys trickled through their door, the girls through the other, and the woman of the house herself beckoned her husband to join her in the smallest room, where the bed stood right up against either wall, a bassinet perched on an old chair in the corner for the baby.

Crim was invited to sleep with the girls. Four of them were already bundled head-to-toe in the one large bed, the eldest one sitting up and frowning at her. She tried to decline, but Seamus ordered his daughters to make room, and they moved aside without complaint. She hesitantly lowered herself down onto the sliver of mattress left over.

She did not sleep, but lay there and listened. Listened as the breathing of the four girls slowed to the rhythm of slumber, and their minds quietened. Listened to the boys crammed up against the wall of the next room, snoring and tossing. Listened to Eileen and Seamus—their hushed argument. The baby was fussing, sensing his mother's agitation. Eileen did not want her here, and Seamus was trying to calm his wife.

Her eyes would not close. The knee currently lodged against her back did not help the matter. Crim inched her way off the bed, gently tucking the blanked around the smallest girl. The eldest, no longer pretending to doze, sat up. She was sixteen or seventeen, with silver eyes no less acute than her mother's.

"Where are you going?"

"I need some air," Crim told her honestly.

"You can't!" Manoeuvring her sister with far less care than Crim, she hopped out of bed. The child grumbled but did not wake. "You should never go out there in the fog!"

Crim cocked an eyebrow. "Why not?"

"It's dangerous!"

"Fog is just clouds, girl."

"Girl?" She got a scathing look for that. "We're the same age."

Crim nearly laughed. Of course. This little mortal thought she was talking to her contemporary. "Aoife, wasn't it?"

"Yes. Not *girl.*"

"Right. What's so dangerous about some fog?"

"It's not the *fog* that's dangerous. It's the M*an.* "

*"*The Man?"

"The Man in the Fog!"

"Nonsense." Crim turned and strode out the door, Aoife on her heels.

"Listen!" Aoife covered her mouth, realising it was the dead of night and her whole family was asleep. She checked each door in turn before continuing: "The Man—he comes with the fog. I don't know if he brings it—"

"Probably does. Considering you're telling me a folk tale," Crim mocked, her hand already on the front door. She turned to find Aoife shrugging on her coat. "What are you doing?"

"If you're going out, at the very least you shouldn't go out alone!" Aoife put up her hood and grabbed Crim's hand. Surprisingly strong for a mortal.

"Aren't you scared of the Man?"

"Yes."

"Then go back to bed."

"Only if you come too! And wear a coat!"

Rolling her eyes, Crim allowed herself to be shoved into one of the boys' patched coats, ignoring the frightened gasping behind her as she flipped the latch. Outside was damp, cold. The blackened sky shrouded in a grey veil. Aoife closed the door behind them, already shivering. Breath coming out in short round puffs.

"I'm fine on my own."

"I'm not leaving you," Came the stubborn retort. "So be done with your walk and let's get back inside."

With her hand still firmly clasped in the mortal's, Crim followed the narrow path that led towards the road, turning right before the gate and stepping over a stile and into a frosted field trampled and disturbed by cattle. She could not see her hand in front of her fence, but marched on, leading Aoife blindly into the gloom. The girl at her side trembled with both cold and fear, but did not falter.

"Have you ever actually seen this man?" She asked at length.

"Yes. We all have."

"Where?"

Aoife pointed. "He walks down the road into town. Never walks back."

"You're sure it's not just someone who lives nearby?"

A shudder. "Dad thought that, at first. Tried to approach him. He said the Man turned and...well...he wasn't one of the living was all he would tell us."

Crim eyed the road. No-one there. Ahead, the fog broke and crawled up the dark walls of an old barn. Smell of the animals inside. Huffing and stomping of the ones still awake. She paused, Aoife drawing closer as the fear took over.

*

She knew something was amiss before the horse began to kick his stable door. Before Aoife's fingers dug into her arm and she buried her face against her shoulder. Before the night air grew colder, thicker, full of static. Crim tensed, feeling the hairs rise on the back of her neck, roused by the same current that raced down her spine. The noises from the barn became distorted, then muffled. Aoife tried to stifle her sobs in Crim's sleeve.

"The Man!" She whimpered.

Crim turned to the road to find a dark figure now moving through the mist. His gait was uneven, probably from an old injury, and he was hunched as one broken down by the torments of life. She could make out no more than his shape, for when she reached for his thoughts she found nothing.

"Stay here," she commanded, shaking Aoife off. Ignoring the girl's shrill protests, Crim made her way to the wall, vaulting it easily and placing herself not three yards behind the black figure. He walked on, not hearing her or her companion.

Strange. Crim knew there were things that walked the line between the physical and the spiritual. Knew it was possible for such things to be seen by mortals. Knew that such apparitions were often just shadows, remnants of what once was, with little to no thoughts or will of their own. They were rarely so bold as this, however.

Nonetheless she felt the urge to call out: "*Hey!*"

She was not surprised when he stopped short.

"I'm here."

He turned, slowly, his right leg dragging stiffly. A bad knee, wounded in his youth, the memory of which hindered even his ghost. When he faced her, Crim's immortal heart stopped in her chest. Clarity struck her like a blow, driving the fog from her mind. She knew this place, these hills, this lake, *this man*.

And with such clarity came the question: "Why are you still here?"

A blink. Just a blink. The mist shifted, wrapping around him. Crim, frozen in place, could only stare into her father's pale eyes as he disappeared. Could only ponder at the forlorn expression in his haunted face. Then he was gone.

It came up from deep within her, that scream. That hysterical roar that split the night. In a tongue, she had all but forgotten, she cried to him. Aoife found her there, crumpled in the middle of the road, reaching out into the nothingness and wailing in the Old Language.

"Shhhhh." She pulled her up. Held her against her. "Sshhhh you're safe now. He's gone."

No comfort. Not at all. Crim bawled and clawed at the air where he had stood. "Athair."

XXIX

It appeared in the sky, roughly five moons after Mentor's departure. A glowing white oval, easily as big as their minuscule sun. Its hull glittered with winking white light—whether windows or just the pattern of the outer shell, they did not know. Still and silent, it hovered over them. A whole horde of Sidhe now stood on the Mountainside, chores and pastimes forgotten as soon as they sensed it. Whisper and Gibber stood nearby, wrapped in each other's arms. Silver clambered up onto an outcrop and held a slender black spyglass to her good eye.

Sunshine felt it before anything else, and she was clearly not the only one. The sudden arrival of all those souls ejected her from her sleep. Noise. So much noise in her head. Minds buzzing, incoherent. Louder now that they were right under it. Laal was further ahead, rubbing her head and scowling at the sky. She did not hear Sunshine approach, and jolted at the feeling of a hand on her shoulder.

"What is that?"

"I....don't know." Laal's eyes narrowed as one suppressing pain. She pressed her fingers into them, hissing.

As they stood there, Sunshine felt it more, blazing white-hot through her mind. She thought she might be sick, and swayed in place. Laal groaned.

Her sword and shield, already strapped to her, felt heavier and heavier. Her vision doubled and tripled erratically. Would she need her weapons? "An attack?"

Groaning, Laal shook her head. "Who could attack us? Here, under the Mountain?"

"That's what it feels like."

"Don't be absurd."

"Get your whip."

"I don't think—"

"Then it won't hurt. I'll send for the younglings." She tried to sound stern, but her voice cracked. "Come on. Back inside."

*

You won't need it. She told herself, finishing the final knot to steady her pauldron and shrugging her shoulders. This armour had been crafted by Smith before Crim was Anointed, and had not been worn since the ceremony. Like all things made of truemetal, it gleamed as though it had not spent centuries at the bottom of a trunk, the snow-white leather still supple and fragrant, the gold plate gleaming out from patterns cut into the hide. Her helm, also bright gold and plumed with horsetail, fit snugly over her halo of orange curls. Staring into the mirror, she hardly knew herself.

"Valkyries. Is that what they are called?" Said Laal, plump hands reaching round her waist, head resting against her back.

"Hmmm?"

"The ones…the North People once sang about."

"Oh." Sunshine laughed. "Let's hope I won't have to carry any fallen. Let's hope we're getting dressed up for nothing."

"Can you help?" Laal invited. "With the straps?"

Her armour was far simpler; pale plates over a turquoise tunic and beige breeches. Her whip hung loosely from her belt, and her helm was pointed. Still, she was a vision. Sunshine helped her secure her breastplate tightly. They paused to look at each other, and she opened her mouth to say something, but words failed her, so she went to sit by the table instead.

*

Li-Li and Yuki arrived not much later, looking disoriented and rightfully frightened, though the latter tried to mask it as usual. They huddled close to their elders, rubbing at their ears and nagging them with questions. Li-Li, red-eyed, tucked herself up against Sunshine.

"Buh-but what is that *n-n-noise?"*

*"*We don't know."

"I ha-h-heard there's another m-moon."

"Is that so?"

"C-c-c…can you sense them? Up th-there?"

"The same as you."

"How…how many a-are they?"

"Can't tell."

"Sunshine?"

"Yes?"

"Wh-what…what do Y-Yuki and I do? I-I-if they at-attack?"

Sunshine met Laal's eye, and saw the same fear there. What would happen to these two if there was a fight?

"You take this," Laal commanded, unbuckling her knife belt and fastening it around Yuki, who grasped it white-knuckled. "They're truesteel. Small, but will kill anything that gets in your path. The two of you…if anything happens to us…"

"Mistress!" Yuki protested feebly.

"If this day takes a bad turn, you run for the border. You hear me, Yuki?" Laal grabbed them by the shoulders. Forced them to meet her eye. "You take Li-Li. Find Princess and the others, if you can. You *run* to the Outside."

Li-Li looked ready to cry; her breath came in short bursts. Sunshine unclipped her own slim dagger and pushed it into her hand. The Youngling, usually fearful, bit her lip and nodded, a strange determination coming across her delicate features. Her hand slipped under her sash and she brandished another blade. Its edge curved wickedly and it was studded with red stones—garnets and rubies and opals. When had Crim given it to her?

A knock on the door. Firm. One of the other Anointed called in: "The Forum. All of you. Mother has summoned us."

*

A dreadful hush had fallen throughout the passages and halls, the tunnels and the caverns of the Mountain. Their group, hurrying together in a tight-packed cluster, ran into Whisper and Gibber on their way down one of the lesser stairs, the twins with arms still wrapped around each other, Gibber strangely quiet, Whisper panting with adrenaline and eyes wide.

"Sunny!" She called. "What's happening?"

"We don't know."

"What thing in the sky. And now Mother calls us to the Forum. Why?"

She shrugged.

"What does it mean?" Whisper hugged Gibber close, her sister let out a soft mewl. "And we can't find the others."

Lilith and Gia, two of Princess' cronies, were rarely if ever seen in the presence of their mistresses. So much so that most people forgot they were even affiliated. Sunshine took a moment to realise who she meant.

"I'm sure they're fine," she said. "Probably off with the others as usual."

"Yes but what if something happens. They won't know. They could be caught—*or worse!*" Gibber made a noise. "Oh…oh I'm *sorry*. I'm not trying to upset you—"

"Why don't you come with us, Whisper?" Laal offered, extending her hand. "We're missing two, as well."

Whisper, looking near tears with joy, stepped into their tight circle. For an instant, Gibber looked directly at Sunshine.

"Crim?"

"No…no she's not here."

*

The six of them arrived at the Forum, arrived to the resounding hiss of thousands of frantic Sidhe echoing off the walls and floors and in the depths of the great black Pit. Some were asking those around them what they knew, others were spreading rumours and theories, a certain few were weaving this way and that through the growing crowd, searching for those that were missing.

Sunshine dragged Laal all the way to the right, where there was still a corner unclaimed right by the wall. Li-Li cowered away from the edge and sat down heavily on one of the stone benches, accompanied as ever by a concerned Yuki. Though dubbed the 'Forum', this place really resembled more of an auditorium in truth; broad tiers lined with benches sloped down to a half-circle, from which three short steps led up to a round stage that hung precariously over the dark abyss below. It was to this that all eyes were inevitably drawn, for this was where Mother stood.

Regal, powerful, and commanding. One could not help but be both enraptured and terrified of Mother. Like a statue she stood; tall and sculpted, her onyx skin swathed in layers of cream-coloured silk and finest cotton, dripping from her shaven scalp to her painted toes in gold and precious stones. A true vision of a goddess turned flesh, she stared out, orange-gold eyes gazing through time and space, no doubt seeing the ship far above as well as her babbling subjects.

One turquoise palm raised, and all chatter cut short. Those that still stood made themselves seated. Every face turned to the stage.

"Children," her voice boomed, smooth and steady, seeming to fill both the bottomless void and the lofty cavern. Sunshine broke out in goosebumps. "I summon you here to bear witness to a key moment in the history of our kind. Not since the days of the Patriarch have the Sidhe come across a new species. One worth noting in the annals of eternity. And never—*never!*"

That word, echoing back and forth from wall to wall far longer than should have been allowed, sent a shudder through all of them. Laal scooted closer to Sunshine.

"...Never have we discovered such an *ally*. A people equal to us in knowledge and power. A society capable of accompanying us through the eons for the betterment of all."

"What is she talking about?"

"We have allies."

"But they are still strangers? How can we already be allied?"

Silence. Mother's gaze snapped to Laal, who had spoken out of turn last. Laal choked in fear. Now Mother seemed to speak directly to her: "If you do not believe me in this matter. Perhaps you will believe *her.*"

A figure seated near the stage rose, and removing their hood turned to face them. Sunshine gasped, felt Laal start at her shoulder. Heard Li-Li's excited cry. Behind her, Whisper blurted *"What?"*

She should have been relieved, should have joined Li-Li, now bouncing down the stairs and into her embrace, should have been able to offer more of a greeting than her puzzled gaping, but she could not. She felt no joy, no ease at the sight of her. Struggled to understand why, only Laal, still seated at her side, was able to tell her:

"Her eyes. Do you see it? There's something wrong with Mentor's eyes."

It was plain enough, once someone pointed it out to her: Mentor's eyes, though still their usual pale green, were wrong. Gone was the immortal glow, that shining lustre that all Sidhe were blessed with from the moment of their awakening. These eyes were cold, dull and dead. Sunshine's stomach lurched and, looking up from Mentor's haunting stare, she realised that Mother had also lost her glow.

"What's happened to them?" She asked Laal.

"I don't know." Her lover's arm coiled around hers, seeking comfort, perhaps even protection. "I don't like this."

"What in all of creation," Whisper chimed in. "What could do this to *both* of them? Two of the most powerful Sidhe to ever exist?"

*

A cry, rattling down the rows towards them. Another, closer at hand, exclaimed: "What is *that?*" People began to turn. Mother and Mentor both smiled. Thin smiles, lacking any joy. Several creatures were now making their way down the steps towards them. Creatures Sunshine struggled to comprehend; she had studied most of the folk the Sidhe had connected with (though perhaps not in as much detail as Laal or Crim), and never seen so much as a picture of anything so obscure.

Four legs, thin and pointed as stilts, *tap-tap-tapped* on the smooth marble. They supported a slim, tapering trunk that branched into two neck-like stalks supporting a massive ovular head. The whole thing was covered in a slick white fabric; a suit that was more like a second skin, with the head enclosed in a seamless, eyeless, mouthless helm. Of arms they had four, as well, though only two seemed made for grasping with their three long fingers. The other two hung to the front and clearly had a more sinister purpose—they curved downward from the second joint in long, broad blades which had been plated in sharp steel for added effect. Onwards they scuttled, past the speechless crowds and down to Mother. A whole cluster of them taking up the stage and the lower circle.

"They call themselves the Ifram," Mentor announced, sounding eerily like herself. "And today we welcome them to the Mountain as friends."

Laal leaned closer, pressing herself against Sunshine. Whisper and Gibber too, scooted over to huddle with them, Gibber covering her mouth to muffle a sob. The air in the entire chamber had changed—cold yet stifling, still yet humming with something unknown and unsaid. Sunshine looked to Li-Li and Yuki, each holding one of Mentor's hands, so overcome by their joy at seeing her that they apparently sensed nothing. Knew nothing of the danger that their elders were so very acutely aware of.

Come here. She willed them; eyes boring into the backs of their heads. *Get away. Come here.*

Li-Li seemed to start, and turned. Her eyes were clear, Sunshine was relieved to see, and as they locked on hers she blinked and shook herself once more. Letting go of Mentor's hand, she took Yuki's instead, pulling them away and back up the steps. Sunshine did not relax until they were back with them, seated in the centre of their little huddle. Safe for now.

XXX

Mentor was not herself. She could not put her finger on it, but something about Mentor was just *wrong*. Perhaps it was the warmth of her embrace, the loving squeeze, the kiss on her cheek and the quiet "Oh, I missed you.". All very uncharacteristic behaviour. Perhaps it was the way, when Mentor pulled away and looked at her and Yuki, she seemed to stare *through* them, her eyes never quite focusing on one or the other. It could have even been the stiff, upright way she stood, straighter and more rigid even than Silver.

Whatever the case, when she finally felt Sunshine summoning her, felt the warning in that voice, and saw the warning in her eyes when she turned, she grabbed Yuki and hurried back up to the others. Did Mentor notice? She made no sign? Did Mother? Did those *things*?

Yuki was hard to move, when they didn't want to, and took a good deal of manoeuvring to pull away.

But Mentor! They protested silently, digging their heels against the marble floor.

Please. Li-Li urged, now unable to ignore the chill seething through her bones. *Please just trust me in this.*

*

There were times when she understood Yuki's stubborn attitude. Times when she did not blame them for being difficult, as much as she disliked it, such as when she wanted to go with Princess, but this was not such an occasion. She could not deny that creeping feeling of danger running down her spine, nor could she leave them with Mentor when Mentor felt so very *wrong*. To her relief after a few steps they gave in, and came with her almost willingly.

"Wh-what is it?" She whispered, back in the safety of their group. "M-M-Mentor…"

"I don't know," Laal replied. "I can't tell."

Sunshine and Whisper both shook their heads. Yuki eyed the four anointed questioningly.

"What do you mean?" They asked.

"Something's off. Mentor. Mother. I can't sense anything from either of them," Laal elaborated, squinting with the effort.

"They're Elders. They can shield themselves."

"They've never blocked us off like this," said Sunshine. "Usually I can get some sense of their feeling…of their presence. How did Mentor return to the Mountain without us knowing? Why would she do that?"

"Even Mother," Whisper added. "She's like a fortress, but if you reach out she will reach back. There's always *something*."

"They're like shadows," Laal went on.

"Like echoes," Sunshine concurred. "You can see them, but it's as though they're not really *there*."

Li-Li, recalling how Princess described the ghosts of Hsei, concentrated. Tried to touch Mentor's mind, then Mother's. Nothing. But her senses were not honed yet; she had trouble reading even Laal in their training sessions. Yuki, she knew, was even less adept than herself and was barely aware of their own thoughts at times. What Sunshine said resonated with her, however; she could usually sense when Mentor was nearby. It was like recognising a certain scent or footfall: instinctive.

Curious, she turned her attention to the new arrivals. Wished she had not almost immediately. At once, her brain was filled with *noise*. So much noise. A relentless chattering. Clicking. Cluck cluck cluck. Something like nails on a blackboard. All projected over a ceaseless pinging that hovered just at the edge of her hearing. Her head was bursting with it, she pressed her palms to her skull as one trying to hold it together, her flesh warm to the touch, a haze like so much steam gathering behind her eyes and burning. She tottered against Yuki.

"*Ugh.*"

They were saying something. Warm hands reaching to steady her.

"Ugh."

Her name? A cry.

"Ughh…"

Someone touching her face. She looked through the fog that had enveloped her sight. Laal was worried. Why?

"Oh." She sighed. Laal moving towards her, pushing through the haze in her head. Clear thoughts like rays of sunshine through the roiling mists. The sting retreated. "Oh…" She was lying on the bench, Laal with her forehead pressed to hers. Sunshine had one hand. A panicked Yuki being comforted by Whisper. Gibber staring.

"You're back," Sunshine said. "No. Don't sit up. Don't say anything. You gave us a real fright there."

Something was tickling her ears. She reached up with one hand and touched something sticky. Dark blood coating her fingertips. Blood in her throat, too. Tacky lines of it running past her jaw. Was she crying? She reached up to wipe the tears. Gasped. Red, too.

"What h-h-happened?"

"You fainted," Yuki told her, their voice gruff as ever but their eyes wide. "Again."

"Why?"

"We don't know, Sweetheart," replied Laal. "You'll have to explain it."

"I duh-don't n-n-know." Words were harder even than usual. Her tongue leaden and coated with blood. Had she bitten it, too? "I-I thought I w-would t-try like you were. Try to se-s-sense Mother and Mentor. I c-couldn't. But *them*. I heard th-th-them. Oh. It w-was so much. S-so ma-many voices s-sc-screaming in my ears. I t-tried to shu-shut them o-out." She closed her eyes, images imprinted on the back of her lids. "I saw…"Laal leaned forward. "You saw something?"

"Uh-huh."

"What?"

"F-f-f-fire. The Mountain in chaos. The s-sun, the moon, th-the stars gone. The sky dark. Empty halls. Sacked chambers. The Pit. It grew and grew like it was trying to swallow everything. Mother wept."

Sunshine and Laal exchanged glances. For a moment, her voice carried on beyond what she had meant to say. Li-Li sighed.

"Wh-what does it m-m-mean?"

"Death. Destruction. Doom."

Yuki jumped. "What did you say?"

"Death. Destruction. Doom."

Gibber looked to her sister. Looked to each of them in turn. Her eyes clear and bright.

"We should leave this place."

*

"Li-Li!" Mentor's voice behind. The same footfall. The same voice. Scent of sandalwood and fresh lilies. Yet somehow *wrong.*

She groaned. Tried to sit up. Her limbs were heavy. Weighed flat against the cold stone of the bench. Laal, Whisper and Sunshine stood shoulder to shoulder, forming a wall blocking her from view.

"She's recovering," said Laal, her voice stern. Masked tones of fear and anger.

"She fainted? What happened?"

"That's none of your concern."

Even Li-Li winced at that. She had never heard Laal disrespect Mentor like this. Nearer at hand, Yuki scowled at their mistress. Gibber edged closer, standing over her, and pressed a palm to her forehead. She smiled down at Li-Li, and at once she felt a strange surge of energy washing over her limbs. She stood.

Mentor and Laal were practically nose to nose, glaring unwavering into each other's eyes. Li-Li, knowing Laal had not the strength to challenge Mentor for very long, swiftly moved between them.

"I'm f-fine, Mentor," she lied. "Really I j-j-just g-got a bit…got a b-bit dizzy."

"Oh dear." Mentor touched her forehead now. Did not seem to notice how she shuddered. Her fingers felt normal—rough, slightly cold as always—yet there was something *slimy* about her touch. Li-Li fought the urge to move away. "You've been pushing yourself too hard."

"N-n-not too hard," Li-Li said. "Sunny and L-Laal have t-t-taught us a-a l-lot."

"Hmm." Shooting Laal another scowl, Mentor doctored her features into a dead-eyed grin, and this time Li-Li really *did* edge away. Not far enough, however; one long arm snaked around her waist, and suddenly Mentor was pulling her away from the safety of her friends, petting her hair and murmuring in her ear: "Do you want to see something *wonderful?"*

*

Li-Li supposed 'no' was not an option. Was ever more sure of this as Mentor took her forearm and clamped it tightly in her elbow, fingers brushing the curtains of her hair away from her face. Laal moved almost as though to intervene, but was stopped by Sunshine. Eyes dark with suspicion, they followed as Mentor escorted her out of the Forum. Most of the gathered Sidhe followed, too, urged on by Mother, who stayed behind to ensure everyone went. A few brave souls scattered when they reached the entrance, sparing a frightened glance around as they melted into the shadows of the adjacent tunnels. The main host turned right, following the paths and stairs that led them gradually up to the level of the Temple and the Gardens. A few mutterings, a giggle here and there, but overall resounded the irregular *tap tap tap* of pointed feet on the hard floors. The incomprehensible *click click click* of their visitors.

That relentless clicking turned into an irritated chatter that danced around the walls of the Tomb. Li-Li did not need to risk another headache to know that they were repulsed, that they somehow sensed the sins that took place in the cold, cold dark. Could they hear their victims, the ones they had just buried? Could they feel the deep magic slowly working on them, ripping them from their lives and deaths and placing them in limbo?

The Temple was no better. Though their chatter died down, Li-Li felt the Ifram judging them. Did they even have eyes? If they did not she could feel them boring into her, stripping the images of their countless deities from the walls and tearing them apart in their minds. She realised she was ashamed of it; ashamed of all she had witnessed and all she knew her kind had done. And so she should be.

"What's that?" Laal exclaimed suddenly, stopping in her tracks. She made to back away, but Sunshine placed a hand on her shoulder and nudged her forward, saying something in her ear. But this time Laal would not be moved. "I said *what is that?"*

The doors to the Temple stood open as always, showing the courtyard and the Gardens beyond, all of which was awash in a brilliant white light. A light so strong Li-Li shielded her eyes against it.

"You'll get used to it," Mentor said to her, and this time she really did recoil. "You've spent so long in the dark that the light pains you."

This was more than light—it was an assault. Where the shafts struck the walls and greenery of everything they had built and grown steamed and smoked ever so slightly, so much so that Li-Li wondered if they might slice through everything. Mentor patted her captured hand and pulled her into it, Li-Li digging her heels down in fear.

"I-I d-d-don't want to—"

"You're afraid. That's alright."

Her skin. She could feel it sizzling. Li-Li writhed in Mentor's grasp, trying to retreat back into the safety of the Temple. Laal and Sunshine were shouting now, demanding her release from where they stood huddled in the shadows. One or two braver Sidhe followed, ignoring the heat and the blinding rays.

"M-Mentor p-p-please—"

Mentor tilted her chin upwards. Now her hands were clamped on either side of her head, forcing Li-Li to look up. Li-Li closed her eyes, feeling the light jabbing at her lids. Surely it would blind her? "Look, Li-Li. Trust me. Just look."

"I don't want to!"

"*Look!*" Mentor yelled. Mentor never yelled. Not like that. She got frustrated with them, scolded them, but never yelled.

Li-Li's eyes snapped open, stinging. Searing. She whimpered. A wall of white. Seamless and flawless. Blinking, the light somehow became less offensive. Blinking, less painful. Blinking, the rough rock walls swam into view, broken only by the wide oval of the Maw. It was from here that the glare shone forth. From the figure bathed in luminescence. Pale robes flowed from his shoulders, betraying nothing of his form. No discernible limbs or skin to be seen. A hood covered his head, and his face was shielded by a golden disc glimmering and rayed as the brightest of suns. She quailed, stumbling and cowering behind Mentor, who only placed a hand on her head.

"Th-the Vessels," she managed. "W-w-will they be en-enough?"

Mentor laughed. Too lightly. "There will be no more Vessels. No more Makings. It is time for us to heal this world instead of taking from it."

"What d-d-do you m-mean? Our p-purpose is—"

"To serve the gods? What gods, Li-Li. What sort of god would steal your life from you? What sort of god needs a *Vessel?*"

She clutched her leg. Had Crim not asked the same? They were not supposed to ask such things.

"Some things deserve to be destroyed, Li-Li," said Mentor. "To make the world a better place. Even gods."

XXXI

Aoife set the plate down on the floor by the bed. Stared at her a long while before sitting herself down, too. They had wrapped Crim in blankets and given her a glass of whiskey to 'warm her from the inside', but still she barely moved. Hardly even blinked. Aoife adjusted the covers over her again.

"Mammy's cooking isn't the best," she said, words drifting through the dim. "But it's warm, and she makes it with love. You should eat."

Crim scowled down at the food, doubtful of how much 'love' Eileen had to spare for her. A few slices of beef and vegetables slathered in gravy. She should have devoured it. Instead she just sighed.

The knife scraped as Aoife cut the meat. Spearing a smaller piece with the fork, she moved it around in the gravy before raising it. Crim turned away as it neared her face, warm droplets running over her lips and onto the pillow. Still Aoife pressed it to mouth. Like a fussy child.

"You haven't eaten in days." The girl sighed. "You can't go on like this."

"Hmph." How wrong she was. Crim would go on. And on, and on, and on.

"Please. Just one bite."

Crim took a bite. Chewed. Ashes in her mouth. She nearly choked but forced it down. A chunk of potato followed.

"They say one of the Reilly's saw him too. Just the other night. He's…he's not right either. Shivering and jumpy. People are staying in now, too afraid, you know. The Pub's been closed for two days and all so Daddy's livid—"

"Where?"

"Huh?"

"Where did they see him?"

"Well they live in town, right? One of the girls—the sister of this lad—was talking. She's been watching out the window ever since. Don't know if she's brave or daft. She says he was mooching about the churchyard. Can't go past the gates, of course. He just stands there till the sun comes up."

"Why?"

"What?"

"Why does he go there?"

"God knows why the Devil does what he does?" Aoife paused in her cutting. "Though I suppose he's dead, isn't he. Probably buried there or something."

"No. He's not buried there."

"Now how would you know that?"

"He wouldn't have it."

Aoife studied her, that fear that had been growing in her pushing her away. She set the cutlery down on the plate with a sharp clink and stood. Made to say something but closed her mouth just as soon. Then she was gone. Crim rolled onto her side. Stared at the wall. Out the tiny, cracked window and into the dense clouds above. The churchyard. Why would he go to the house of the new gods?

Hours passed as she lay there, watching the white light of the hidden sun darken to hues of rose and tangerine. It had rained for an hour or so, breaking the clouds, so for the most part the night was dry and clear. Aoife brought her supper in silence. She did not touch it. She waited for the darkest hour.

The air, cold and crisp, coaxed up the hairs on her arms and neck as she pulled the front door softly to. Like the first night, there was something else in it. Something like electricity that energised her and pulled her entirely out of her haze. She struck the road with a spring in her step, smiling inanely across the shimmering lake (ignoring the looming Mountain) before turning into town.

*

The pub, though only reopened that evening, was lively as always. The air inside was different, however. More careful, more watchful. A group of middle-aged men turned as she entered, before one of them gestured for the others to listen closely. A servant from the House, he would tell his friends—the one old Seamus had taken in. One of them looked up and nodded at her politely.

The eldest of the Meagher sons was sorting some glasses behind the bar, and grinned broadly as she approached. Crim placed a plain silver coin on the sticky counter and convinced him it was just enough. He slid her a tumbler of whiskey and invited her to sit by the table on the other side of the curved bar where it was quieter.

"How's the farm?" He asked cheerily as he worked.

"There's plenty of work to go around," she replied. "A fox got at some of the hens the other night."

"I'm sure Seamus' language was choice."

Crim laughed. "He sat up all the next evening. Shot the thing before it could even get under the fence. I fixed it for them."

"You're handy."

"It's not hard."

"Eileen still giving you grief?"

"She's less vocal if that's what you mean."

He topped up her glass. "You know we've a room here if you want it. Plenty of work about too."

"I'm not really a people person."

"Jaysus I didn't mean you at the bar. I'd like to keep my customers, thanks."

She swirled the golden-brown liquid around, letting the firelight catch it.

"Think about it, right?"

"I will."

*

The door screeched open. Banged on the glass panelling. The barman boomed something about paying for any cracks he might find next time he cleaned it, but was not heard by the frenzied old man that fell up to the counter. A few laughed, thinking he had drunk his fill, but Crim knew he had only just arrived; he smelled fresh and his mind, though agitated, was lucid. He managed to lift himself up onto a stool, eyes wide as he took the cap from his head.

"He's there again."

Conversation seemed to die around him, and he looked about the room. No one met his glance, but everyone was now acutely aware of everything he said.

"By the gates. I wouldn't go out there, any of you." And he started to shiver. The barman pushed a glass towards him and he drained it in one gulp, cupping it in both hands as it was filled again.

By the expressions of the barman and his patrons, Crim knew none of them had any intentions of passing the door until first light at the very earliest, when the phantom would surely be gone back to his resting place. Nor would they let a single living soul out. Luckily for her she was not living, so the rules did not apply to her. She stood and crept around them all with ease, willing their eyes and awareness away as she slipped out into the night.

*

The man on the horse stared down at her, face stern and imposing, his mount's nostrils flared and one hoof raised as though to crush her. She scowled back up at him, then at the church beyond, its single tower jutting up into the tranquil night sky. The man at the gates took no notice of her, but peered unblinkingly through the iron bars. Crim swallowed the lump in her throat, willed her feet to move. She drew as close as she could without stepping through his opaque frame, eyes wide and fixed on the back of his head, which was caved by the blow that had killed him. Though he had passed his best years, he remained as tall and strong as she remembered, his face stern and unreadable as always.

"You're here," she breathed. "Still here, after all this time."

He straightened, moved with a stiffness she had never witnessed. Pale grey eyes pinning her there. Looking through her façade, through her immortal mask to the girl underneath. She felt them burrowing, opening a well in her heart full of memories. Faces, so many faces. Visions of the forests and the hills and the lake where he had built their home. Her brothers and sisters. Her mother.

You know me. She realised, relieved.

Reluctantly, he tore his eyes away, looking across the churchyard at what she could not tell. His hand raised as though to touch the bars, fading to nothing right up to the wrist.

Though her heart thundered and her soul ached, Crim willed herself to engage her mind. "You cannot enter this place."

He pushed his arm through the gap and she watched it vanish inch by inch.

"Why are you here, Father?"

A flash. A face. Green eyes and black hair. Humming as she worked.

"Mother?" She followed his gaze, still unable to pinpoint where they fixed. "Mother in *there?*"

Two fists raised to strike the gate. That immovable expression broke into a yell. When he looked at her again, his eyes were no longer cold. Crim moved at once, turning the latch, she shoved the gate open on its oiled hinges, its quiet whine ringing across the square. If anyone heard in the pub, they dared not look out the windows. Her father's mouth opened in protest, and he made to grab her. But he stopped short, gaping. She had passed the threshold and yet here she still stood.

"I am not dead, Father. I am not alive. I am lost."

He shook his head. Puzzled.

"I will help you find your peace," Crim told him. "But I cannot join you."

He shook his head. No.

"Wait here."

He reached for her again, hand disappearing in the hallowed air. *No.*

*

With all of her immortal strength, stepping away from that gate almost took the knees out from under her. She had only just found him, but would lose him again this night, if she did things right. As much as she wished, she could not keep him here. He deserved his rest.

Screwing her will into place, she turned off the steps that led into the church, following the narrow path that passed under a line of dark fir trees before hugging the rows of graves.

O'SHEA. A list of names had been stamped into the stone, faded at the bottom and crisp nearer the top. Crim assumed it was a whole family, or most of them at least, and the others she passed followed the same suit. A noise stopped her, and she peeked across the rows. Nearer to the church wall, a woman knelt in the dirt in front of one marker, weeping softly. Whenever she tried to touch the stone, her hands passed through it, so she just sighed instead. Crim left her to her business.

Others she passed as the path curved behind the commanding edifice; a man leaning on his own headstone with a pipe in his mouth. He puffed and tipped his hat at her. Crim bowed back. His neighbour, a rotund old farmer, laughed at that. Some were less attached to their resting places, and walked about freely, with one girl roughly her own age keeping her company for thirty paces before she could go no further. She stopped and waved, tilting her head as Crim paused. She was now at the back of the building, the gate and her father completely blocked from view, and with no better clue as to what she was supposed to do here.

A whistle, sharp and clear. Crim looked up at the girl she had just been walking with, who pointed past her at a young man with dark hair now stepping around a large cross. He was tall, with a cheerful expression, and whipped off a silk top hat at the sight of her. He mirrored her bow, and Crim was struck by his resemblance to James. They were undoubtedly related. He grinned down at her and jerked his head to the side.

"Excuse me?"

He threw up his arms, laughing and gesturing around his mouth.

"Yes, I know you can't speak."

Still laughing, he trotted backwards, ushering her further away from the dark rear of the church. Crim could not help but laugh back, and followed at a jog. This path led towards the wall, where the smaller graves stopped, and she was faced with a tall line of tombs. There were three rows of these, in fact, and her guide hurried around them, clapping soundlessly. Crim expected the path to stop, but it turned where it struck the wall, hugging the backs of the hunkered houses of the dead. The ghost stopped, and made as though to rap on a narrow metal door in the centre of the wall.

"What's this?"

He pointed at the tombs, then at the door, then gestured walking down stairs with his fingers.

"A catacomb?"

Nod.

"Past the wall of the church?"

Nod.

"Who for?"

He pointed at her.

"Huh."

Shrug.

"I suppose I'm here to find out."

Nod.

XXXII

"What are you doing here?" Princess demanded, hands on her hips as she watched Sunshine shove robes, paints, hairpins, anything she could find into a bag.

"Packing some of your things," she replied, shoving it into the youngling's arms. "If there's anything important in this mess, dig it up now. You're coming with me."

"Why?"

"I'll explain later."

Princess threw the bag down and pressed louder: "*Why!*"

A few of the other Acolytes, some of whom were also being collected by their elders, turned. They were not surprised by Princess' antics, of course, but they were clearly hoping for an explanation of their own. Sunshine shared a glance with another Anointed, who mirrored her anxiety.

"Please, Princess," she half-whispered. "I need you to just listen to me. Just for now. I'll tell you everything once we're somewhere safe."

"'Safe'?" Thankfully, bratty as her youngling could be, she was not stupid. Princess' voice was now lower, more cautious.

"I can't say anything here. I can't. Just pack your things, ok?"

Eyeing her nervously, the younger Sidhe finally did as she was told. All around, Acolytes were quietly filling satchels and trunks and pockets with valuables. The Anointed that had come to retrieve them were all armed, all on edge, all stroking or inspecting their weapons as they stood watch. Laal and Whisper had already ensured Li-Li and Yuki got safely back to the apartment, while Sunshine had spent half the afternoon searching for Princess. She had been near hysterics when she finally found her sitting with her friends around a fire in the Forest, and commanded the rest of the group to return to their clans as she dragged the little vagrant away.

She still was not sure why she was doing this; why any of them felt the deep-seated urge to retreat to their rooms with their loved ones. Did they all feel it—that clawing panic, that lingering fear, that unease?

"I'm done," Princess announced. Her voice was chirpy, light. A lie.

Sunshine took her by the hand and Princess allowed herself to be led out of the dormitory. Two other elders were also leaving with their younglings, only to stop short when Bull appeared in front of them.

"Don't. Not just now," he said, then, seeing Sunshine's hand on her sword, he raised his hands. "No! No! I'm not trying to stop you. Well…I *am*, but well—Oh! They're coming! Get inside!"

He pushed her by the hip and gestured for the others to follow. Soon all seven of them were crammed into his hut, which was built for him and certainly not anyone as tall as Sunshine. She nearly hit her head on one of the rafters as she shuffled inside.

"What's coming?" One of the other younglings asked, looking around at them. His friend, who clearly had some idea, shook his head. "Mentor, what—"

"*Shhhh!*" His mentor clapped their hand over his mouth.

Sunshine pulled Princess closer. The wall in front of them boasted one large, one-sided window which Bull used to watch the hallway beyond, which opened out away from the Dormitory entrance before splitting into different passages. It was from the leftmost opening that they came, escorted by Reavers. Two of the creatures scuttling along on their stiff, narrow legs, *tapping* and chattering as they went. The farther one seemed to like dragging this blade-like forearm along the tiles, adding to the skin-crawling noise of them.

Princess backed right up against her, gasping. Sunshine reached out and felt her fear—pure, unfiltered fear. She did not make a sound, only watched them wide-eyed as they traversed the hall and disappeared down one of the other paths.

"What are they?" She finally whispered, turning into Sunshine's embrace. "What are *they?*"

"Mother said they were friends." One of the boys said shakily. "Right? They're friends?"

Sunshine and the other elders exchanged glances once more. *Friends?*

*

Princess was still holding on to her when they arrived at the apartment, plump little hand squeezing her arm. They had not passed any more of the visitors, but sensed them now moving around the Mountain. The Sidhe they passed for the most part were apprehensive, but a select few spoke excitedly about the newcomers. Some of the guests that were currently with them—several Nari, O'othoy and a family of Bishnak—Sunshine observed hurrying towards the Portals laden with luggage and looking more frightened than she had ever seen. She wondered if perhaps they should start evacuating the rest.

"Where's Whisper?" She asked Laal, who was busily making a sponge cake with Li-Li and Yuki.

"Gone back with her sister," her spouse responded, trying to brush hair out of her eyes and only succeeding in smearing greasy flour over her forehead. She caught Princess' eye. "They sent for their younglings, too."

Sunshine thought she heard the little brat breathe a sigh of relief. Tying her curls back at the nape of her neck, Princess pulled out a chair and settled down opposite Li-Li and Yuki. Without a word and seemingly oblivious to everyone staring, she picked up a knife and busied herself with slicing strawberries into a large bowl.

The cake did not turn out right. The sponge itself was fine, if a little dry, but the jam and icing both were far too sweet and lumpy. Sunshine pushed the remainder of her slice aside and instead began to pick at the few berries left in the bowl. Yuki, with their notorious sweet tooth, eyed the leftovers covetously until she told them they could take it, at which point they blushed and shoved the slice into their mouth, spreading even more crumbs and filling over their face.

Princess was helping Laal. Had been helping her all evening. First with the cake, then with dinner. Now she was scrubbing pots and laughing as the older Sidhe told her about their first time ice skating. Li-Li sat in the corner quietly reading.

The door rattled, and they all started. Sunshine quickly counted heads. They were all here, so who could be coming in? Whisper perhaps? But she was busy with her own clan. Sunshine stood, sword half-drawn, and placed herself between the door and the table.

"Oh. Have I missed dinner?" Mentor laughed, spotting the table full of plates and cups. She stepped past Sunshine, seeming not to notice the weapon in her hand, towards Laal and Princess, sitting with the basin of steaming water on a stool between them. "I hope you left a few morsels, Laal dear."

"Uh. There…there's some pieces of chicken left in the bowl there. Vegetables." Laal's hand shook as she pointed. "Help yourself to some cake, too."

Mentor sat down at the table. Yuki immediately left their seat and went to guard Li-Li. She grinned at them as they passed. "Is the cake good?"

They rubbed their mouth with their sleeve. "Good? Yeah. Good. Excuse me."

Laal touched Princess' shoulder. Something went unspoken between them, and the youngling was moving over to the corner, too. At a single gesture, Yuki and Li-Li followed her into Crim's room. The door slammed behind them.

"Are they sleeping in there now?" Asked Mentor, calmly cutting chunks of chicken off the bone and nibbling at them. "Mother told me about Crim. I can't say I'm surprised, but it is a pity."

"A *pity*?" Sunshine started. Laal shook her head. They had plenty to say to Mentor about Crim, but this was not Mentor. At least not as far as they knew. "You knew she would leave?"

"I knew she might break. The Making was too much to ask of her. Too much to ask any of us. I can't say I blame her. Still, I would have liked the chance to say goodbye."

Something in Mentor's voice. Laal heard it too.

Is she…upset?
About Crim?
I thought she would be angry, if anything.
Maybe we misjudged her?

"There will really be no Making this time, Mentor?" Laal questioned, clearly watching to see if their elder had detected their exchange.

"Not now. Not ever." Mentor dabbed at her mouth with a napkin. "We are free from that, girls. Our new friends will protect us, and their god."

"How?"

"By destroying the other deities. Purging them from the world. And all we need to do is help."

Sunshine tasted that sickly sweet cake again, stomach gurgling. "Purging them?"

"Yes."

"And what if we fail to do that?"

"We cannot fail."

*

Mentor finished her food, cleaned up after herself, all while Sunshine and Laal stood watching. The younglings were silent in the next room. Would she want to see them? Could they deny her? Would she want to stay? She stretched, joints cracking, and looked them up and down.

"I'll be with Mother if you need me. We need to make sure our new guests get settled," she said. "Sunny?"

She jerked upright. "Y-yes, Mentor?"

"I'd like you to meet with them tomorrow. At first light. Laal, I know I don't need to tell you."

No words passed between her and Laal, just a wave of pure disgust tinged with fear. She swallowed it. "Of course, Mentor. First light."

To their relief she left, hugging them both as they saw her to the door. Sunshine's skin crawled where she touched.

"Is she gone?" Two silver points of light appeared in the dark as Crim's door edged aside. Yuki's little hand was white at the knuckles where it gripped the edge. Movement behind them let her know Li-Li and Princess were also still awake.

"She's gone, Darling," Laal replied, patting their mess of blue hair. "You can come out."

Li-Li appeared at their side, eyes puffy and lip quivering. Sunshine noticed one of Crim's pillows tucked under her elbow—it probably still smelled of her. "O-or y-y-you both could c-come in?"

They took their cups and one of the carafes. Yuki shut the door behind them, yellow light from the parlour filtered through the papered panels. They sat on the bed, all five of them, Li-Li drawing her knees up and placing the pillow over them before laying her head on it. Princess rubbed her back affectionately. Laal, finding a brush thrown on the floor, picked it up and ran the few strands of red through her fingers, mouth tight.

How had things gone so awry? Crim gone, Mentor returned but wrong, and these *things…What are we to do about these* things? Laal sighed in response. Head thumping, Sunshine threw herself back into the haphazard pile of cushions, bolsters, pillows and stuffed animals. One deep breath, and she was awash in the scent of Crim, in the memory of days just passed but already missed, in the certainty that they had lost so much already, and would lose more. Most certainly.

XXXIII

"Wh-where are you *going*?" She exclaimed, dashing across the parlour to slam the door in Princess' face.

"Out." The little brat stated, trying to push her aside. "Move!"

"Laal s-said to st-t-stay here!"

"Right before she stepped out the door. Now *move!*"

Princess managed to shift her this time, but the exchange had caught the attention of Yuki, who appeared at her side with lip curled. Putting themselves in front of the door, they crossed their arms.

"We stay here."

"And what? Wait for one of those patrols to go past? Wait for them to hear us in here?"

"They've no reason to come in. No reason to disturb us," Yuki said. "If you go out *there*, however, with your charming attitude you're bound to catch someone's attention."

"I need to see the others."

"N-need?" Li-Li scoffed. "You w-want to run off again. Leave us, p-p-probably."

"That's still under consideration." Princess bit her lip. "You can come with me. Both of you. I'm not running this time, I swear."

"We're not going with you. Not a chance. Right Li-Li?"

Something about Princess's demeanour gave her pause. Was she *worried?* The way she bit her lip told Li-Li she was hiding something, but she also seemed desperate to get out the door. Like she had something important to do.

"Where a-are y-you going?"

Princess's expression softened. She looked hopeful, grateful. "The Minaret. I swear, I'll be back before Laal and Sunshine. And you can still come, of course. Just don't tell anyone what you see—"

"What we see?" Yuki frowned. "What are you hiding up there?"

Needless to say, their curiosity got the better of them, and a few moments later Li-Li and Yuki were skulking through the tunnels after Princess. She refused to tell them what she and her minions had stashed in the Minaret, but insisted that it was important. Life or death important.

"I swear if this is just another barrel of moonshine—"

"*Shhhh!*" Princess stopped dead and threw an arm out to steer them against the wall. "They're coming."

Li-Li could never tell if the Ifram that passed were ones she had seen before, or new arrivals. They seemed to be everywhere now, scuttling about, clicking and chattering noisily. Always surrounded by a Sidhe escort that had expanded to include not just the Reavers, but dozens of volunteers. For every denizen of the Mountain that mistrusted their new friends, there was another in awe of them.

The rest of their guests had disappeared, for the most part. Now and then small groups and lone travellers would pass through, and pass quickly, barely stopping for a ramble about the Marketplace. Li-Li had seen them around the Ifram, seen the way the hair stood on edge in species that had hair, or the way features twitched and hackles rose. Other species disliked the newcomers; that much was obvious. Not for any particular reason, either; there were, of course, groups that liked or disliked each other for political reasons, but no-one seemed to have any history with the Ifram. They simply distrusted them on sight.

As Li-Li watched this cluster pass by, she wondered if she was harbouring some kind of deep-seated prejudice. Not for the first time. As the weeks had gone past, her apprehensions brought with them a helping of guilt. Was she being unfair? After all, these people had done nothing to harm any of them. What if they were, as had been said to them, only looking for allies? Only another people just as curious as the Sidhe, finally making strides to connect with the rest of the universe?

One of them turned, enormous head tilting. Did it have eyes? If so, they were pointed in Li-Li's direction. She quailed, pressing herself closer against the cool, firm rock of the wall. Clicking, chirping in her brain. She shut her eyes, praying it would not hurt like the first time. It didn't, instead subsiding into a low hum. Was this its hello?

"Hello," she whispered back. Yuki, at her side, turned to frown at her, but she was focused on the Ifram. It started, head bobbing up and down for a few seconds, then noticed the group was getting away from it and scurried to keep up. Li-Li smiled.

"What was that?" Princess demanded, eyes wide.

"I d-don't know. I th-th-think…I don't know if i-it saw me, but it n-n-knew I was huh-here," she babbled. "I th-think it was b-b-being fuh-friendly."

"Friendly?" Yuki echoed.

"We should go back."

"What?" Li-Li grabbed Princess by the arm as she tried to pass.

"I can't risk it. If that thing follows us—"

"He won't."

Princess put her hands on her hips. "Oh? *He* won't? How do you know that?"

Li-Li let go of her. "I don't. I j-just didn't get that i-i-impression f-from him."

Her companion took two more steps back the way they had come, halted again, then whirled and marched onward. "Let's hope you're right."

*

She tried to ignore them. As they stamped up the Minaret stairs (Princess loudest of all, like she wanted to warn people they were coming), Li-Li could hear the beats of the dormant hearts in the Tomb. Felt their dreams and thoughts wash over here like a warm current, hairs standing on her arms. At her place behind the others, she smiled to herself, stifling a giggle. They had almost driven Crim mad every time she passed, those hearts and those thoughts. Why was this funny to her?

"Stay here," Princess ordered. "I'll call you in."

Yuki turned and cocked an eyebrow at Li-Li, who shrugged. If she listened hard enough, she could hear their hearts, too. The hearts of all the Sidhe around her. It was not common to do this, as the sound was quite deafening, but for an instant she dropped her walls and let it in. The cacophony. Yuki's, closest of all, was unsurprisingly fast, like a tiny storm in their chest. Princess' in the next room slow and steady. Her own fluttered a little. By the noise, Li-Li could tell that all of Princess' friends were in the next room.

She moved her head, trying to hear better. All of them? Yes. That seemed like enough beats.

*

Princess' head popped round the door. "You swear to tell *no-one about this*?"

"Swear." Growled Yuki."

"On pain of absolute death?"

"*Death!*" Li-Li squeaked, suddenly unsure. Princess laughed like she was joking, but something in her eyes-

Bim dropped down in front of her, grinning. He had clearly taken up the bed immediately to the right of the entrance; his clothes and paints were scattered all around it, with belts slung over the edge of the platform. Ola was there too, greeting them and acting *very* friendly. Li-Li got the distinct impression they were screening them. Twice more, they were asked for their word. Twice more secrecy was demanded. Gia, who had been lounging by the fire, stood up, hackles half-raised and pinning Li-Li with her eyes.

"Yes! Of c-course! What in the w-w-world are you hiding up—"

"Keep your voice down!" Princess hissed, brushing past her cohorts to take Li-Li's hand. Yuki followed watchfully. "I'm sorry, really. You'll understand in a minute. Just...just *shush*."

She led them across the Maker's quarters, past the warm fire and the chicken slowly roasting. Past the jugs of wine and water, open books and used paints. Someone had clearly been living here for a while.

The panels around the rightmost bed were half-closed, with the window next to it open and sunlight shining through to illuminate the brown knee of whoever was sitting on the bed. Princess edged up the steps and pressed a finger to her lips as she pushed the rest of the panel aside.

"That's just—" Behind her, Yuki gasped.

Lilith sat on the edge of the bed, robes untidy, hair askew. She seemed drawn, tired, her cheeks sunken, lips dry and her eyes ringed. Still she beamed out at them, looking happier than Li-Li had ever seen her. The bundle in her arms moved, and a tiny hand gripped the front of her gown.

She could not speak, so Yuki said it for her: "Is that a *baby*?"

Lilith giggled. "Yep."

"This-this is *absurd*! I can't believe you! We all knew you were sneaking out but *this*!"

"Keep your voice down, Yuki." Princess' voice was dark with warning.

"I *will not*! You lot have always been full of shit but to go out and snatch some poor mortal child—"

Lilith burst out laughing. Princess, still not amused, bared her fangs at Yuki, daring them to approach her friend. Li-Li shook her head and turned to explain to them: "Yuki, it's *her* baby."

They froze, immediately shutting up, Princess' claws lowered an inch. "What?"

"Th-this is clearly L-Lilith's child. Look at him."

The infant by his size was just a few weeks old—probably born shortly before Mentor returned. Yet as Li-Li edged closer he turned his head and looked straight at her with comprehending far beyond that of a mortal his age. He smiled and she returned the gesture. Yuki, right up against her shoulder, peeked uncertainly at him.

"A trueborn?" They finally deduced. "Like Mother's children?"

Princess nodded. "Trueborn."

"I conceived him. Bore him. Birthed him. He is mine," said Lilith, gently extracting a strand of her hair from her son's iron grip.

"Hah!" Yuki exclaimed, then threw a glance back at Bim and Ola. "So which one of you was it?"

Li-Li, also curious, turned. Bim and Ola, looking nervous, both shook their heads. She frowned at them. Bim, looking offended, added: "We don't have that kind of friendship."

"His father is mortal," Lilith explained. "You're right, we do go Outside from time to time. Sometimes I went to visit him—he was handsome, kind and—well, this happened."

The baby began to fuss. His mother offered her breast. Princess sat down next to her and patted the empty spot at her side for Li-Li. She joined them, still struggling to understand what she was looking at.

"I-if he's trueborn," she thought aloud. "Not s-s-sired…th-then how is h-h-he Sidhe? W-w-without a god?"

Princess rolled her eyes. "He has a god, otherwise he would not be Sidhe. The Making is not necessary to create a Vessel."

"Wh-what?"

"Do you know of the First?"

"Of c-c-course!"

"How were they made?"

"They j-joined with their g-god!"

"But how? Why?"

239

Li-Li looked at Yuki, who also shrugged.

*

"It's the part they don't teach us," Ola chimed in. "In the beginning, the god entered the First without a Making, uninvited. The First fought it, tried to push it out. They were expelled from their village—they were possessed, after all, constantly babbling to themself and falling to the ground in fits. Desperate, they wandered high into the mountains surrounding their home. There, they met a shaman who had spent a lifetime speaking with the gods, a man who saw them for what they were. Using his ancient magicks, he helped them to push out the unwanted deity, though the effort killed him."

"They returned to the village the next day, and showing their friends and family that the demon was gone, were accepted back with open arms. Their mother and sisters laid out a feast, and invited all the other houses to come and bear witness to the miracle of their child's safe return."

But something had followed them down the mountain, wearing the shaman's skin. It tore the earth up from under them, spoke to the river so it burst its banks, set the forest around the village on fire. When at last the people were driven out—or those that had survived at least, it came to them and demanded its Vessel back. It told them it was their god, the maker and the keeper of all the land that they lived on. How dare they begrudge it one body when it had given them so much?

"The mother laid her hand on her child's shoulder, and begged for them to receive the god once more. The First refused. They challenged the god, called it a demon. As the ground began to shake again, their brothers took hold of them, and the god laughed. 'If my Vessel does not come freely, make it as this.' He gestured down to the shaman's withering form. 'Loosen its tether upon its body, so that I may enter. You will do this, or all of you will be sent back to the mud from whence I moulded you.'"

"So the First was taken, and anointed with oils, dressed in finery and placed on an altar surrounded by drums and singers, they endured the goodbye usually reserved for sacrificial animals. Throat cut, blood pouring over the flowers encircling them, their life ebbed away drop by drop. Stubbornly, they held on, feeling the eyes of the god staring lustfully at their body. At last, of course, they could go on no longer, and slipped. At their side, the shaman gave a hoot of victory, and dropped dead. The god entered its Vessel, dragging the First along with it. 'For your insolence,' it told them. 'You shall stay here forever with me. You shall live on this mountain with my voice in your ear, watching this village be rebuilt, watching the people who raised you and the people who knew you live and die. Again and again, people will come and go, and you shall watch them, but never again be one of them.'"

*

"Ahid never needed to be made," Lilith explained. "Because there was never a mortal soul in his body. His god did not need to oust anyone in order to gain a Vessel."

"So…he's just a god?" Yuki said.

"Part of one," His mother replied. "But also his own person."

"I don't understand."

"It's complicated." Princess laughed.

"But…but th-this could be the f-fuh-future of our kind!" Li-Li exclaimed, standing suddenly. The baby opened his mouth and wailed. "S-sorry. If we c-c-can just have children th-then why take v-v-Vessels! Wh-why go through the m-Making if—"

"Trueborns are not created like mortal children," Princess interjected. "They are exceedingly rare. We could never make them at the rate the gods demand Vessels."

Lilith tittered. "Make them?"

"You know what I mean!" Princess, also laughing, continued: "Supply and demand."

"Maybe the gods would understand?" Yuki ventured.

"Did you hear my story?" Ola shoved them playfully. Yuki still snarled. "You suppose that was the only god with a temper? No, we produce Vessels to keep them complacent."

"Wh-what about this n-n-new god?" Asked Li-Li. "The Ifram one?"

"The one that promises to keep all the others out of our business?" Princess said. "What for? You think it's making a promise like that for nought?"

"It has its own uses for us," Lilith agreed. "And it doesn't like the other gods. Hence why he can never know about this little one."

Li-Li looked down at the child again, and was once reminded of another infant. Another mother soothing her crying child. Outside, the wind rattled their house, rain belting against the walls and driving sheets of mud down the slopes not far from where they huddled around a waning fire. The infant bawled and bawled, his little throat worn from the effort, his tiny, frail body shaking. Their mother had tried to break his fever, but still he boiled. Their father stood at the door, knowing well his son would not make it through the night. So small. So very small.

Little Ahid, now playing with the buttons on his mother's sleeve, smiled up at her again.

She would die for this child.

XXXIV

The steps were slick, narrow and steep. She slipped almost a dozen times as she groped her way down, down. Far deeper and further from the church walls than she expected. She put her hand out as her foot once again skated over a patch of slimy lichen, catching herself on the rusted rail before she managed to dash her head. It groaned, one of the fixtures hanging loosely away from the glistening brick, but held her up, the firelight in her hand throwing shapes up and down the tunnel. She grumbled and stood slowly, directing the light back down. It glided away obediently, showing her the last few stairs and the puddled floor below. There was a door there, just a little further on.

One of the hinges was broken, and the other two nearly fused solid, but Crim managed to drag it open enough to squeeze through. As expected, this was the entrance to the catacombs proper, and just a few steps ahead the imposing walls fell back slightly into rows and rows of carven shelves.

"Why am I down here?" She whispered to the peering skulls as she passed, wondering if any of them would answer. "He sent me down here. What for? For Mother?"

They looked on in silence, some no more than bones in a narrow cubby, others laid out in their stone beds like they were merely sleeping, draped in their favourite robes with rings on their fingers and crosses on their necks. Boxes no doubt filled with possessions had been laid next to some of their owners, too. But for the most part she had naught but the company of yellowed skeletons.

The passage forked. She halted, directing little floating flames down one way and then the other, checking the walls as though expecting to find some sort of signage.

"I don't even know what I'm looking for." She sighed. Then blinked. Something had moved to her right. She jumped as it shifted again, turning and ready to fight. *Someone* had sat down behind her. A portly man was perched on one of the lower shelves, smiling at her.

"Hello."

"H-hello." Cupping her flame close, she approached. The light danced through his cloudy form, refracting strangely as it passed through to hit the back wall. "You're the first I've met down here."

"We don't get many visitors." The ghost explained. "I suppose people are shy."

"Oh…what is this place? Why is it separate from the rest of the graves?"

"Ah." He winced. "This is for those of us born in the parish who…erm…*aren't suitable* for burial in hallowed ground."

"How so?"

"Most of us pissed off a priest one way or another. Plenty of the unbaptized, too. Heathens, heretics, pagans."

"I don't understand."

He raised an eyebrow at her. "You aren't Catholic, are you?"

"I don't even know what that is."

A laugh, deep and jolly. He patted the shelf next to him. "My name is Matthew. I was a monk, once. A devout follower of our God. I pledged my life to serve him."

"Crim. I…I lived here once, too. A long time ago. On the lake."

"By the lake?"

"*On* the lake."

"Ah!" Matthew snapped his fingers. "A pagan! I should have known! Those tattoos—no Christian would sport anything like that."

She tugged at her sleeve, adjusting it down over her forearm, then jolted upright. "You can see—um—you can see through my disguise?"

"Disguise?"

I guess dead mortals see better than live ones. She smiled, then repeated nervously: "I'm Crim. I lived here—on the lake—a long time ago. Longer than I can remember. But I was stolen and kept elsewhere by my captors. I came back, but everything is changed. My home is gone, and this strange town is here. I found my father, but he is like you."

Matthew took a long moment to understand why she was gesturing at him, then gasped. "It's like one of the old stories, isn't it? The child taken by fairies returned, to find everything gone. OH! Oh! You poor pet!"

Crim blinked at him. "Fairies?"

"That's what we would call them, now. Though I always thought they ate the ones they took."

Crim shuddered. "Not me."

"But you say you found your father, child. How?"

"He's here. Well—he sometimes appears here—on the road. He walks from the lake to the big gates. The townsfolk are all afraid of him, but he only looks mean. He's always been harmless, really."

"I just called him 'The Man'."

"Yes! That's him!"

"Ahhh. The poor fellow. I wonder how long he's been marching that same march, waiting for you to come home."

Crim's heart twisted in her chest, she managed through the pain: "But I'm here now, and I found him at the gates this very night. Something is bringing him here. Not me. Something else…"

"Someone else, I'd say, Dear," Matthew deduced. "And someone precious, if even the sight of his daughter cannot bring him rest."

"When he looked at me, I saw my mother."

Matthew pondered for a long moment, studying her. "You know, I thought you seemed familiar, though I've only seen her once. It's the hair; hers is black. Does that sound right?" When Crim nodded slowly he stood—he was a lot shorter than she had expected. Gesturing for Crim to follow, he let the way back to the fork and pointed down the passage she had not taken. "Second right and then down some stairs. That's where they throw any remains they find and can't identify. A bit of a mess but I reckon she's down there. She never wanders out."

"Second right?"

"Uh-huh. People are starting to wake up now, so you can ask again if you run into trouble—hello Martha!"

A worried-looking woman floated past, rocking a new-born baby in her slender arms. Crim offered her a nod. "Hello."

"Oh and—" Matthew stopped her before she could march off. "Stop by again, will you? If you have the chance?"

*

The way became narrower now—the walls and shelves began to tilt inwards as the rock tapered into almost a point overhead. Remains littered the floor, or had been confused and misplaced by those passing through. By the looks of things, Crim guessed that these were probably older—or at least less important than the ones on the main passage. The spectres she passed mostly confirmed this, in their outdated dress and faded appearance. Those that could speak whispered greetings in ancient tongues. At least, she guessed they were greetings; she could not read their minds.

"Girl." One woman called, seated in a nook with three of her grandchildren. "What are you doing down here? This is no place for you."

"I…I'm searching for someone, I suppose."

"Hold up your light. Let me get a look at you."

Crim did so, drawing the flame closer to her face and willing it to burn more white than red. The aul one sucked her teeth as she took her in, then nodded.

"Just a little further on, Love. Down the stairs and she'll be on your right."

"Yes. Thank you." Crim bowed and trotted onward. *She'll be on your right.* Her mother? Was she so close? Her heart fluttered. The old woman had only looked at her face and known who she was here for. Matthew had known as well, after he thought about it. Did she resemble her so much?

These stairs were worse than the others by far—broken and slick, with barely enough room for her to pass. She braced herself against either wall as she descended, the way dim at first, with roots poking through the sagging ceiling. It was close and damp and cold, with thick grime all about. She complained loudly to herself and the roused dead as she went. Some chuckled their agreement. One, lounging in a cubby being overtaken with weeds, tried to catch her as she lost her footing, and they both laughed at the futility of it as she rubbed her bruised arse. It got worse and worse as she went on, until she thought even she might suffocate.

About three-quarters of the way down, though, the air changed, becoming fresher, though tinged with the sour smell of thriving livestock. A homely glow rose up to meet her, along with the rich aroma of burning pine. She suddenly found herself not at the bottom of that half-rotten staircase but on a threshold, in a low porch made of wattle and daub. A curtain of thick hide hung in front of her, the orange light spilling round the sides and underneath. This she pushed aside to reveal a round room hemmed in by low beds. A fire burned in its place at the centre, smoke wafting up through a hole in the thatching. A sound rang in her ears, and Crim turned to scowl back the way she had come. Children laughing as they ran past, their shadows falling through the doorway a dog yipped after them. Pigs grunting as they snuffled along the ground, the nanny goat bleating as she was milked. She knew this; knew all of it, and as she faced the fire again a melody met her. A sweet voice carrying a lazy song. It drew her forward, and the flames seemed to grow the closer she came. A woman sat on a squat bench, hands busily working, gaze fixed downward. She grew bigger as Crim approached, until she could only reach up and tug at the blue sleeve of her tunic. Still humming, louder now, words forming on her lips, the woman pulled Crim up into her lap and showed her what she had been polishing: a slender torc made from twisting bands of bronze. It was cold around her neck.

"Still a bit big. But you'll grow into it *Mo Chroí.*"

Crim twisted to look at her, foot catching a rib bone underfoot and sending it bouncing against a pot. The house was gone, the hearth disappeared and her mother with it. She tottered and slumped against the wall, vision blurred and doubled. She gripped the edge of a wooden shelf, blinking and willing herself to focus on what was in front of her. The cubbies were even smaller here; small squares built into rows upon rows of crumbling oak. She was drawn unquestioningly to the one third up from the floor, and had to crouch to look into it.

Her mother was surprisingly intact; only a few of the smaller bones appeared to be missing, but she would not miss them. With trembling hands, Crim picked up her skull and stared into her eyes. Once green and shining, they now stared hollowly back.

"You've been calling him here, haven't you?" She said. "You don't belong here. Why would anyone put you in this place?" Crim set her down and shrugged off her outer robe. Laying this on the floor, she meticulously collected her mother's remains—every digit, tooth, ring and scrap of fabric she could find—and bundled them into it, skull last of all. Using the sleeves and sash to secure everything, she lifted her into her arms. "Come on. It's time for both of you to rest."

*

Making sure to say goodbye to Matthew on her way, Crim carried her mother up out of that dank, dark hole and back out into the crisp night air. It was past the small hours now, and the sky was not quite so dark. Many of the spectres wandering among the stones above ground had lost some of their shape, glow fading to a slim silver outline. James' forefather, who had clearly been watching the catacombs vigilantly, walked silently with her right to where the lines of the graves ended, eyeing the bundle she cradled to her chest curiously.

"He's still there," Crim said aloud, her guide nodded. He, too, was faded; the tombs and statues behind standing out more clearly through his image. Was her father like this? She picked up her pace, not wishing him to dissipate before she could return her mother to his embrace. Her father's ghost, stubborn in death as in life, still clung to his form, but small strings of steam rose from him in places. Crim almost ran to him, but was too afraid of dropping her mother, and checked herself. He reached out a hand as she slipped through the gates, touch cold and faintly wet, hand drifting from her arm to the balled and knotted robe.

"I have her," Crim promised. "She's safe."

With a nod, he led the way across the square and past the pub. All was quiet now, and no-one saw her pass. She was grateful to find the town asleep, and loosened her grip on her cargo. Still, she cast an eye about now and then, nearly daring some brave fool to try and take her mother from her.

She followed her father out of town, along the road that hemmed the lake where they had thrived. A path meandering to the left brought her under the shelter of the trees, hiking gradually upwards. The Mountain loomed there, somewhere above the canopy. She felt its pull, and cast her eyes downward, to the remains swaddled against her breast and the figure leading the way. Had she followed him up this path before? In eons past had they hunted and gathered in these woods? Images like dreams drifted in and out of her mind. She saw a clearing, just a narrow break in the trees blanketed in long, whispering grass. Near lost her father, but a narrow line in the weeds brought her to his side. He had stopped, staring ahead; the ground rose steeply in a high bank, and the path turned to follow it, but they had halted completely now. Part of the bank bulged outward; a low hump thrust out among the sea of green grass. Crim's father fixed his sharp grey eyes first on the bump, then on her, and she understood. Laying her mother down gently, she dug her fingers into the earth that covered the hill and burrowed into it, tossing aside whole fistfuls of dense brown soil, not stopping until she was almost elbow-deep and her nails scrapped across smooth grey stone. The years had hidden this from the world, so her parents' tomb remained fairly intact. Even this slender portal stone was hard for her to move, as it was wedged firmly down into the earth so that she had to ease it up and outward inch by inch, careful not to disrupt the structure. She vaguely wondered if the whole thing had been built by her brothers. They had always been handy, all four of them.

*

It opened into a narrow hole, which, taking her mother up again, she squeezed sideways into. Another stone just a few steps in proved easier to push away, and toppled inward and down into a low chamber. Summoning another flame, Crim tossed it upwards, where it cast its light down onto three piles of remains. The largest, undoubtedly, belonged to her father—a full skeleton swathed in rich green robes lying on a dark fur cloak. An axe lay at his side and a spear and shield were propped against the wall over his head. A few vessels nearby no doubt had once contained some of his favourite foods, trinkets and probably even his paints as well as the remnants of a goose and a cow's skull. The robes to her left, dyed deep blue and scattered with gold jewellery and a whole collection of different-sized knives, she realised were her mother's. In the muffled dark, she knelt amongst them, and diligently arranged the bones she had rescued on top of her cloak and under her tunic, trying her best to make it seem like she had not been disturbed.

"Well. Here you are," she whispered, laying a hand on her mother's skull, thumb stroking a small crack in her forehead. "Back where you belong. And you—" Crim turned to her father and picked up his skull, cupping it carefully in her hands as she had her mother's. "No more terrorising the neighbours, alright? I…um…" She put him back down before her body gave up, and she lay curled in the centre of the tomb, the weight of her own fate crushing her into the dirt. There, alone, she shuddered and felt the burden of her immortality settle on her back, wrapping around her, trapping her in a vice-like embrace. "I have to leave you now," she told them. "You belong here, together. But I don't. I'm not dead. Not alive, either. I can't stay." Crim looked into their faces, as though trying to find some solution, some salvation in those empty sockets. "I want to stay."

She huddled there, cheek pressed to the cold earth below. She pushed her fingers through the soil of her home, breathed the air in like her mortal life depended on it, sniffed at the breeze and perked her ears to the stirring of dawn. Curled there in the muck, she wished for someone or something to deliver her back into her parents' arms, where she might find peace. But doom seldom responds to wishes, and overlooked the mewling Sidhe. At last, with eyes

249

parched, she sat up and wiped her face on her sleeve as she tied her robe back around her waist. It was only then that she remembered to look at the other pile.

Some sort of animal. That was what she found. Its bones laid atop a bearskin with undue reverence. Jars and bowls placed around it she supposed had probably held foods and small belongings the same as with her father and mother. There was a bronze axe head, too, and a decayed wooden shield, like one might give a child not yet seasoned for battle. And a tunic; a deep crimson tunic with a belt. The more she looked, the more she found things that were familiar; a knife made by one of her sisters, a ring made by another, and she was sure one of her brothers had given her the belt. Last of all had come from her eldest brother— the skull of the bear that had almost devoured his sister.

"And you—" With renewed clarity, she lifted the dog's skull from her old cloak. A black dog with bushy ears. Her father had gifted her to his youngest daughter as a whelp and taught her to train her. The hound had since then never left her side, even in death. Crim patted her head, fingers imagining soft dense fur where now there was greyed bone, "Oh, Meara. How could I forget you, old friend?"

Though her heart was against it, Crim laid Meara back down where she had found her, urging the loyal hound to guard her parents in her absence. The three of them had earned their rest, after all. But she did pillage her own grave; the axe head, knife, bear skull and a few other trinkets she tucked into her belt and pockets. Finally, kissing her mother and father one last time, she crawled back out into the meadow.

*

Night had faded to shades of grey, and to the east streaks of pink and orange and gold ebbed upward behind white puffs of cloud. The lake below burned with the first embers of sunlight, and the mountains opposite appeared black. Crim clambered up the slope and sat on top of the blanketed dolmen hugging her knees, surveying for a while her old home; the rustling grasses dotted with thistles and wildflowers, the lush green treetops marching right down to the nearest shores of the lake—glimmering ripples lapping against stony banks, mountains and hills formed a jagged wall to her right where birds now rose from their eyries to chase the morning mayflies. On her left, the stark edge of the forest marked the beginning of fields past which the road streaked, branching off here and there to wander into town, or to find the large stone bridge that spanned the river which drained the lake. Beyond this bridge a broad, bald knoll sported the largest house Crim had ever seen—one large enough to accommodate the entire town, even without the smaller buildings that surrounded it, all fenced in tightly and seemingly accessed only by a narrow lane. She presumed this was where the infamous lord and lady dwelt, keeping watchful eyes over their domain.

This was her home. And yet not her home. The land had changed, their little island had sunk. Others had moved in and torn up the trees. All those she had loved now lay silent in the earth. She did not belong here. Crim knew this, and sniffed loudly into her elbow.

A movement at her side, and she looked up to find her father lounging on top of his own tomb, his figure fading in wisps of white steam as he grinned up at the sunrise. Crim took him in for as long as she could, smiling faintly herself as his own song rose to meet the day—a silly little thing he had written himself about a robin and a bluetit fighting over a worm. He used to sing it every morning, back then. Even as he was carried away by the wind, white puffs rising to join the lumbering clouds, his voice seemed to grow, until it was the only company she kept on that lonely hillside.

XXXV

Everything was wrong. All wrong. Mentor's return and the arrival of their Guests had spurred a wave of unease and unrest throughout the Mountain. People on edge, watching each other with suspicion and the newcomers most of all, but daring not to voice their concerns, to question the presence of the Ifram and their purpose. Others, delighted by the arrival of the Ship, had formed a fast alliance with the strangers, and escorted them through the Mountain in armed units, challenging anyone that crossed their path, or even looked at their new *friends* in the wrong way. They denounced the gods, and praised the new deity that still lingered, watching all from the detached safety of the Maw, his brilliant light blinding believers and non-believers alike, so that few now wandered up to the Lake or the Gardens. Sunshine felt the usual peace of her home now balanced on a chord that could snap at any moment, and said as much to Laal. They agreed that the younglings should not return to their dormitory, kept them close in the safety of Crim's room. Even Princess obeyed for the most part though she still disappeared. Li-Li observed that though her time away became shorter and shorter, she always returned looking agitated and jumpy.

Sunshine met her in the passage this evening, and seeing the tears standing in her eyes pulled her inside, stroking her golden curls with the fondness that they had cultivated over the months they had survived without Mentor, now bloomed into sorority by fear. She brought her into Crim's dark, cluttered room and sat her down by the dressing table.

"What's wrong?"

"I passed some on the way here," Princess said, hugging a pillow to her chest. "Three of them being escorted by Hyeong and some other Reavers. He…"

"Did he hurt you?"

She shook those pristine ringlets. "No. He grabbed me, though. Said I was threatening our visitors. I didn't…I hardly even *glanced* at them. He just threw me against the wall."

252

Sunshine gently removed the pillow from her hands. Rested her head on Princess' knees and started to hum. Something wordless and nonsensical, from the recesses of her mind, but comforting nonetheless. Princess sighed.

"There's something…something *wrong* with him, Sunny. I don't know what. Don't know why—but his eyes were like pits."

"I know," Laal called them the *dead eyes*. A curse that seemed to be infecting more and more of the Sidhe the longer the Ifram stayed. A madness. "Don't talk to him. Don't talk to *them*. Don't even look at them."

Princess gripped her shoulder. A little too hard. "Are you afraid?"

"Yes."

"What can we do?"

"Nothing, Youngling. Not for now."

"Can't we get rid of them? Send them home?"

"We do not know how kindly they might take that. And we do not know their strength."

Her lip quivered, but Princess fell silent. Sunshine could feel her terror—it rippled through her in waves, at times rising to a panic that caught her breath, and she would utter something like a sob. Little chin crinkling. She kissed her cheeks.

"Nothing will happen to you, Love. I won't allow it."

*

She left Princess napping with the others after a large lunch, her arm around Li-Li. Yuki, their ever-reluctant third, sprawled on their back and snoring loudly. Mentor had demanded that Laal and Sunshine join her again, so they reluctantly donned their weapons and their armour to escort her and Mother.

At the top of the High Stair, they met the trueborn—Onaldi, Seti and Yamanu hardly left their posts outside Mother's chambers lately, and seemed to have set up camp in the hallway adjacent to them. Three bed rolls were spread out in one of the corners, with cups, plates and utensils scattered about. The trio looked exhausted, turning to greet them with sunken eyes and hollow cheeks. Sunshine wondered if they were eating and drinking properly, and Laal silently communicated the same impression to her.

Seti blocked their path, blade hissing from his sheath to point at them. Sunshine almost laughed, but his eyes were hard.

"Why are you here?"

"We've been here," Laal responded flatly. "Several times, in fact. Do you not remember?"

"Mother is with our guests. She does not wish to be disturbed."

"Calm yourself, brother," Yamanu chimed in. "This is Sunshine and Laal. You know them. Their mentor must have sent for them."

"They can tell me that, then." His sword swayed in front of Sunshine's face. She pushed it aside. At this any composure he had left broke, and he lunged, point pausing where it tipped her throat. Laal gasped.

"*Seti!*" Onaldi bellowed, leaping to her feet. "Have you gone mad?"

"Why are you—*aaah!*" His sister had his wrist now, and twisted it. The weapon clattered noisily to the floor. He hissed at Onaldi as she held him.

"I am so sorry," she offered. "Mother wants us to watch the stairs at all times. She demands that we question anyone who passes. I do not understand why. Seti is only following orders."

"He just takes those orders far more seriously than us," Yamanu added, not moving from where he reclined, picking at a bunch of grapes.

"I am not hurt," Sunshine said, rubbing the place where the blade had touched. "It's fine."

Onaldi took her brother by the ear and dragged him away to his bed, presumably for a scolding. Yamanu gestured them on with a forced smile.

"What was that?" Whispered Laal.

"I have no idea. Just keep moving."

"Did he…?"

"I'm fine. Not even a scratch."

*

Mother's chambers were crowded. They always seemed to be crowded lately—large as they were, the presence of three Ifram with their sprawling insectoid bodies left little room for everyone else. They were guarded by three Reavers—Hyeong, Nashoba and Ayo, who sat on the couch opposite Mother and Mentor. Their guests did not sit, Sunshine had learned, nor did they lie down or lounge in any fashion, so they gave the impression of being perpetually vigilant. The constant presence of an armed guard accompanying them only added to this. It was as though they always thought they were about to be attacked, but why?

These three in particular seemed important. They looked no different from any of the others, but Sunshine now recognised the senseless chatter of their minds. They were always with Mother, and rarely roamed about in public. If they did go to on tour, they would have a full entourage with them, all armed to the teeth and ready to stop all who tried to approach.

Sunshine and Laal had no intentions of going near them, yet still they watched closely as they went to sit on either side of Mother and Mentor. The creatures clicked slowly as they went, and the Reavers straightened in response. She could have sworn Hyeong's lip curled at her for a second. Surely they did not perceive her as a threat?

"As I was saying," said Hyeong, still eyeing them strangely. "Our Guests have a desire to see the Market today. They have heard much about it from their crew, and would like to see your wares. They also hear that there are other visitors there."

"Not likely," Laal muttered.

"What?"

Laal, taken aback by the intensity of his stare, stammered: "I…I mean we don't have many other guests this week. I suppose it's normal for the Market to have a lull—"

"That's better, as a matter of fact," Nashoba cut in, his low, level voice drawing the other Reaver's attention away from her. "Less to watch for."

Sunshine cocked an eyebrow. "Watch for? Like what?"

"People with lesser senses of hospitality," Ayo added, smiling.

"Right."

"They will need an escort, of course," Mentor nudged her. "Girls, you will go with them."

"Us?"

"Yes, you."

"Surely there are more Reavers who would—"

"There are," Hyeong interrupted Laal. "But I know how well you've mastered your *draoi*, and Sunshine knows how to handle that sword. We can rely on you to deal with any trouble that comes your way. Correct?"

"What kind of trouble?" Laal pressed. "They are as safe at the Market as anywhere else—"

"Let's hope so. Now, as a *thanks* for your assistance." Hyeong stood and reached over to lift a silver cloche from the table; under it was a bowl full of wriggling grubs. Fat, white things with blue nubs for legs and twitching black heads. "They have brought a delicacy from their homeworld—lachyuu larvae. These are a particularly expensive type from the southern continent."

Out of the corner of her eye, Sunshine saw Laal physically recoil. These things were enormous—the length of her hand at least, fat and slimy. She looked up at their guests. Did they eat these things, truly? She had never seen them eat or drink anything offered, and now understood why. Very few cooks under the Mountain specialised in insects.

With a golden tongs, Hyeong selected a particularly plump specimen from the bowl (which some had already escaped and were busily making their way off the table), and extended it to her. Sunshine clamped her mouth shut, craning her neck back as far as it would go. He tutted.

"Let's not be rude."

Mentor elbowed her again. *"Sunny!"*

Skin crawling, she held out a hand and grabbed the larva around the middle; it was cold, squishy and slick. As it writhed in her hand, it proved exceedingly difficult to hold onto, and she suspected it knew what was about to happen next. To her surprise, its fat head turned up to her with something akin to fear emanating from its beady little eyes. Disgust overcome by guilt, she hesitated again.

Mentor's voice rang through her mind this time, loud enough to disrupt all other thoughts: *Eat it!*

Laal, who had taken one rather quietly, met her gaze and nodded. As one, they lifted the unfortunate creatures to their mouths. They were too big to swallow whole, so instead they bit off their front ends, sticky blue blood and stringy innards exploding down their chins as their teeth made short work of the gooey exterior. The grubs squeaked horribly in their last seconds, both halves squirming spasmodically, little mandibles pinching in vain at the insides of Sunshine's cheeks. She gagged, bile rising into her mouth, but kept her lips pressed tight as she chewed. It was bitter and horrid, and did not go down without a fight. She forced the tail down more easily, but not without a deal of thrashing. Mentor pushed a cup of water into her hands, shushing aggressively. She drank it gratefully, shivering and retching as she imagined it squirming around in her stomach, tiny mouth tickling the walls. Laal, with tears streaming down her face, doubled over and pressed a palm desperately to her lips, throat still working to push the last of it down.

Hyeong laughed, the darkness in his expression breaking momentarily. He clapped Nashoba on the back as he stood, and winked at Sunshine.

"Don't worry, you'll get used to them."

*

They were never quiet, the Ifram. As they strode along passages and corridors, their gold-tipped, stiletto-sharp legs *tap tap tapped* sharply. Occasionally, they would brush those bladed forearms together, too, producing a squeaking scrape that itched the inside of Sunshine's head. When they were not chattering, their minds remained active, buzzing incessantly on the edge of hearing. The Reavers appeared immune to all of this, but Sunshine and Laal, who walked behind, shared regular agitated looks.

The further they went, the more Sunshine managed to distinguish the Sidhe who were happy to see their guests and those that were not. Like a tide, whole groups would ebb and flow closer or further away, some with excitement and admiration in their eyes, others with fear and loathing. The latter were not helped by the Ifram or Reavers' reactions—the visitors clicked and snapped angrily at them, and the Sidhe guarding them bared their teeth, stroking their weapons. At this they quickly retreated; none seemed of any real danger, and Sunshine began to wonder once more why an escort was necessary.

It all became so much more apparent once they reached the Market. With all the other visitors gone, only Sidhe and Ifram remained—both groups eyeing each other with varying levels of wariness and distrust. As Sunshine passed, she earned a few scowls from familiar faces, and smiled back. She could not blame them, really; she felt just as uneasy, but there was something else in the air. Something more sinister.

She reached out, touching the minds of her peers. Fear, uncertainty. Those were to be expected. Some, however, had feelings that went deeper: anger, hatred, loathing, disgust. She picked up her pace, moving closer behind her wards. For no reason, she told herself, it was just easier to navigate through the crowd.

Whisper and Gibber were the first ones to truly surprise her. Seated either side of a wobbly table just next to Kata's shop, their eyes went wide at the sight of the Ifram, and Gibber began to mumble. Her sister, ever careful of her, immediately jumped down from her stool and made to leave her away.

Hyeong stepped in front of them, a strange sort of amusement on his face. The twins halted, holding hands tightly. Nothing was said aloud, but Sunshine had the distinct impression they were under interrogation.

"Let them pass," she demanded. The Reaver looked at her and laughed, but fell back into his usual place at the front of the entourage. He watched the sisters unblinkingly as they retreated.

"What was that about?" Laal hissed as they picked up their pace.

"No idea. Let's be on our guard."

*

Adik was on the porch that wrapped around the walls of her shop as they passed, leaning on the balustrade with a cup of tea in one hand, directing her mentees with the other as they rearranged some of the flags and streamers that decorated the way up her little hill. She waved to Sunshine, Wren and Caius following suit. Tal, hand raised to wave, paused and balled her fingers into a fist instead. She had seen the Ifram, and looked in no way pleased that Sunshine and Laal were with them. Leaving her work on the ground, she jogged down the creaking steps and right up to Laal.

"What are you doing?"

Sunshine edged closer.

"We were asked by Mentor," Laal explained.

"Your mentor has you acting like bodyguards for *them?*" Tal shot the Ifram an angry glance. They bristled, Reaver drawing closer around them. "I told you something's not right about her."

Laal nodded, now looking nervous. The attention of the Ifram and the Reavers was on her now, and Sunshine sensed they were not feeling friendly. Her hand went to her sword. If they touched a hair on her head...

"We'll talk later," Laal attempted, patting Tal on the arm. From her vantage point, Adik was now calling to her youngling, no doubt sensing the tension in the air.

"I don't want to talk later." The girl insisted loudly, straightening to glare at the clicking beasts. Sunshine had to admire her courage.

"No," Hyeong said. "Let's not talk later. You have something to say to our guests, please, go on."

Tal looked the Reaver dead in the eye, and Sunshine could tell she was probing him. For some reason, he seemed to allow it, too. "Oh Hyeong. You're not like this. You were never like this."

"And what do you know about me?"

"More than you can recall yourself, I presume. Because you've lost yourself. To them." She moved to square up to the Reaver, not breaking his gaze. He was so fixed on her that he did not notice the flash of the dagger sliding out her sleeve. Laal cried out, and at the last second Hyeong made to grab her, but too late. She darted past him, under Ayo's shield, and was on the nearest Ifram in the blink of an eye. Adik screamed for her to stop, vaulting from the porch high above as the pieces of her cup tinkled down the hillside. None of them moved fast enough, and the blade sank into the side of the beast soundlessly.

An ear-splitting screech filled the whole cavern, springing from the mouth of the victim and taken up by all of the surrounding Ifram. Tal stood back as it lurched, clearly expecting it to fall, but it did not. Instead those bladed forelimbs extended and, rearing up on its hindmost legs, it brought both of them down on her. The first sliced clean through her shoulder and all the way down to her chest, the second lopped off the lower part of her other arm as it almost cut her in half. It hit her spine and stuck for a moment before the beast managed to jerk it free. Tal made no sound, nor did she even attempt to flee as those blades rose again and again, hacking her to pieces. Standing in her remains, oblivious to the dagger in his side the victorious Ifram stamped its spiked feet and hissed loudly at Adik, who was now being held back by Wren and Caius wailing incoherently.

Sunshine could not hear her, however, could not even hear Laal's muffled sobs at her side. Her ears were ringing, her stomach churning as she stared helplessly at the bloody mess seeping into the floor.

XXXVI

"Hey."

Hands on her shoulders. Shaking her. Her eyes fluttered open, then closed. Still dark. Someone wanted her awake. They could wait. Could stop making noise. Cold hands, she shrugged them off and turned on her side. The bed sagged. Someone standing on it. Someone kicked her in the ribs.

Li-Li yelped, now wide awake. To her left Yuki sat up, rubbing their eyes, blue tangle of hair standing on end. They made to grab her assailant, missed, groggily sat back and grumbled.

"Quiet, both of you!" Princess whispered, hauling Li-Li up by the arms. "Wake up!"

"What are you doing?" Asked Yuki, studying her with one open eye.

"We're going for a walk."

"A walk?"

"Yes?"

"You and your servants?" Yuki sneered back. They did not like being woken. Especially not by Princess.

"*Friends*. Yes."

"And you want us to go with you?"

"Yes."

Yuki laid back down and pulled the blankets up to their chin. Princess made a face.

"Li-Li tell them to get up!"

"Yuki aren't y-you c-c-coming?"

They rolled over to face her. "You want to go with them?"

She nodded.

"With Princess?"

Yuki still had a hard time comprehending her newfound allegiance with Princess' group. Still grumbled and moaned every time they were dragged along

260

on one of their 'adventures' (as Princess called them). Still went, nonetheless, following Li-Li wherever she led. She assumed they secretly hoped to be brought to Ahid, as the baby had clearly stolen their heart as much as he had hers, but they would never say as much.

"You d-don't have t-to come."

They stood, still wrapped in a woollen blanket, and kicked open one of the bedside compartments. Sunshine and Laal had cleared some of Crim's belongings out of them for the younglings, though most of the room remained untouched. They did not speak to Li-Li while both of them dressed, did not break their silence as Princess ushered them—creeping, tiptoeing—out of the bedroom and into the dark passage. It was still very early, and beams of pink light were just starting to creep down the shafts and windows in the Mountainside, the sunrocks still sleeping and the starstones dimming. Yuki not greet Bim and Ola, whom they met in a dark passage that sloped Maw-wards. Did not question their purpose again, just stayed by her side.

*

"Wh-where are we go-going?" Li-Li finally questioned, turning sideways to squeeze round a narrow bend. She had not even known this tunnel existed, and clearly she was not alone—they did not meet another soul as they went on their way, twisting, turning, wriggling and ducking their way. Once or twice she tripped on wayward rocks, hardly able to see her feet in the dark. Yuki, already grumpy, did not bother to offer any light.

"I found this a few weeks ago," Bim said somewhere further up the line. "It leads into one of the burial chambers to the back of the Tomb. One they didn't block up properly."

Sure enough the further they went the louder the steady *thrum thrum* of the Tomb became. Louder, louder, the muted thoughts from lost souls hummed through her head. Flashes of memory. Visions of the inside of a sarcophagus, skeletal fingers groping feebly at the lid. Weeping, hardly audible. A trapped scream. Words, thoughts, pleas. She shut her eyes tightly and took a deep breath, feeling another swoon creeping up on her. Taste of copper, and a thin trickle of blood ran from her nose.

"Are you all right?" Ola had caught up to her, and laid a hand on her shoulder.

"Fine," she managed, spots dancing across her vision.

"Don't like tight spaces? Here—take my hand."

His hand was large, warm. She gripped it like a lifeline anchoring her to the physical realm. It probably hurt having her squeeze like that, but Ola did not complain. Instead he continued to speak to her, filling her mind with silly stories and jokes as they went on, pushing the noise away.

Somewhere behind she was sure she heard Yuki growl.

*

"Here." Bim pushed the ragged edge of a faded tapestry aside and hugged a marble statue of a leopard-faced god as he stepped around him, muttering apologies. Ola held the dusty fabric aside as he ushered Li-Li through.

"You're pale," he noted, frowning. "If you wish to go back to the dormitory…"

Li-Li wondered how she could have gotten paler, and shook her head. "I'm f-f-fine, r-really. Better now that I'm ou-out of th-that hole. Thank you."

He grinned. "Still, if you need to—"

"She said she's fine," Yuki snapped, shoving him aside as they stepped out of the statue's embrace. "So leave her be."

"*Yuki!*" Li-Li hissed, trying to look apologetic as Ola retreated back to Bim's side. "Don't be *rude*!"

"You don't need his help."

"I *did!*" She shot back. "I c-c-couldn't suh-see back there!"

Yuki pouted. "You could have asked me."

"And you could have st-t-tepped in, but you d-didn't. Suh-so, stop th-throwing a strop! If you're g-g-going to be this wuh…way all day just l-luh-leave!"

They stared, aghast. As her words sank in, Yuki's round little face morphed through a handful of expressions; shocked, hurt, angry, then settled back into their usual scowl. They blinked, edge of their mouth trembling, then stormed away.

"Yuki!" Li-Li moved after them, then stopped, well aware that the others were watching. They were not the reason she stayed, however. As much as she loved Yuki, she could not stand them lately. They had always been grouchy, suspicious, downright argumentative at times, but *never* towards her. Perhaps because for a long time the two of them had only had each other. Perhaps they had squashed their true nature down so as not to drive away their only friend. But now they both had the chance to make new friends, Yuki had turned from loyal, protective and sweet to downright possessive. Much as Li-Li had tried to excuse it in her own head, she could not allow it any more. She enjoyed her time with Princess and the others, and would not let even her best friend rob her of that. So she balled her fists and turned to the others, forcing a smile and a light-hearted tone. "Well, where are w-we g-g-going?"

"You're sure you don't want to go after them?"

"S-sh-sure."

Princess linked her arm. "I doubt Yuki will ever like us, Li-Li."

"They w-will," she replied. "They just n-need t-ti-time."

She shook her golden curls. "Uh-uh. As long as we're taking your attention away from them, they'll hate us."

Li-Li blushed. "They need to learn to…to sh-share. I c-c-can't just ignore ev-ever-everyone else."

"Hmmm…"

"Suh-So this is where a-a-all of you ha-have been h-hi-hiding."

They stood in the Maker's apartment, which was looking more and more like a den for Princess and her friends; the four beds had been made up with colourful bedding, rumpled and strewn about from being slept on, dirty dishes were scattered about on the trays, floors and bookshelves, with a few clean plates sitting next to a basin of bubbly water, robes and paints and jewels had been tossed to and fro. Li-Li found herself standing on one of Princess' petticoats. Kicking it meekly away, she peered up into the nearest sleeping nook.

"Y-you really made a home h-h-here. Was this wh-wh-where you d-disappeared to all the t-time?"

"Sometimes," Princess affirmed. "There are others. We will show them to you in time."

Li-Li tilted her head. "Why are yuh-you sh-showing them t-t-to me a-at all?"

"Because we're friends now."

"You don't th-think I'll t-t-tell?"

"No. Would you?"

"No."

"Well then, as long as you promise to keep all of this secret—" Those round little cheeks turned pink, and Princess skipped around what was clearly her dais to where a pile of bedding had been clumsily arranged under one of the windows. "I...I know it doesn't look as comfortable as Crim's bed but, um..."

"But it's safe," Lillith, who was busy nursing her son, put in. She jerked her head to the opposite wall. "There's a place for your little pet, too."

Sure enough, there was another mount of blankets and pillows for Yuki. More hastily thrown together, she noticed. Li-Li pursed her lips at it. "B-but why? Wh-what's this all for?"

"If we can't leave the Mountain, we at least want to keep away from those *things*," Bim told her. "From here we can both stay out of their sight, and observe what *they're* up to."

"And if we need to get away we have a choice of escape routes," said Ola. "Like the one we showed you."

"Get a-a-away?"

"I've seen how you watch them, Li-Li," Princess half-whispered. "You sense it too, don't you?"

"I...don't n-n-know what y-you m-mean."

"Danger. You sense danger. You can't explain it. It's like every bone in your body is telling you to get away. Only you're not sure if you *could escape* them if you tried. So you freeze. You just gawk at them like helpless prey. You wonder if you could fight them, but daren't try. You want them gone from here."

Li-Li wondered if they knew all of it. The dreams and the visions. The swoons and that sickly feeling when the Ifram drew near. A sickening fear. "It's unfounded. It's si-silly."

"It's not silly," Bim interjected. "We've all heard what happened to Tal."

"She attacked them..."

"Don't act simple," Princess scoffed. "You've seen it too, haven't you? You've dreamt of it, I know."

"What?"

"The end. The death, destruction. The Mountain destroyed."

Li-Li's head reeled. How did Princess know? "That was j-ju-just a dr-dream."

"A dream we *all* had?"

All of them? Bim nodded, Ola too, then Gia, Lilith bit her lip and hugged Ahid closer to her breast. "It happens."

"Even if it is just a dream," Princess said, not wanting to argue. She waved the others down as some of them looked less than pleased. "You'll stay awhile, right Li-Li? Stay with us for a few days."

"I…I've never…"

"You can still see Laal and Sunshine. Still study and do your chores. But just come back to us at night. Please? Just a few nights?"

"Mentor w-will wonder…"

"And you *mustn't* tell her where we are." Princess turned deathly serious. "Laal and Sunshine is one thing, but Mentor *cannot know where we are.*"

"Mentor?"

"Yes!" Surprisingly agitated now, Princess grasped both of her arms, squeezing. "Please, even if you leave now, swear to her you will not tell her!"

"I wo-won't!" Li-Li swore.

"And will you stay? For a little while?"

She looked at the bed they had made for her from what they had to spare. Someone—probably Princess—had even filled two vases with flowers on either side. "For a little while."

*

She stayed a while. Four days to be exact. Four days away from Mentor and the others. Away from Yuki, too, since they both stubbornly let their feelings stew, refusing to apologise and even speak. She had seen them once or twice and not even offered a greeting. The air between them was cold. So cold in fact that she did not think she entered Yuki's thoughts at all, or at least assumed that her doings during their separation were of no interest to them.

How naive she was. To assume that they had forgotten her. That they would leave her side so easily. The truth was that they kept an eye on her at all times, and knew exactly where she snuck off to when her chores were done. Not that she was very secretive about it—stealth just was not in her nature, and she was careless about who saw her slip into the minaret stair. She did not even stop to check if she was being followed.

*

"Peaches!" Lillith cheered, snatching one out of Li-Li's basket and taking a large bite, the pit *cracking* as her teeth drove straight through it. She offered a tiny morsel to Ahid, who despite still looking very much like a young human infant had almost a full set of teeth, and surprising motor skills. He took it from his mother and eyed the lump of fruit suspiciously before sucking on it. "You were in the Gardens today?"

Li-Li sat on one of the cushions by the oven and began to sort through the fruits she had procured. Some would become tarts, others she handed out to her friends with a shy smile. She tossed Gia an apricot.

"Yes, f-for the a-a-afternoon."

"Did you see Yuki?"

She sighed. "B-by the shore."

"Still nothing?"

Shrug.

"Fuck 'em."

Princess hefted a banana skin across the room. It struck Lillith in the cheek with a sharp *slap*. The baby laughed. "What she means is: I'm sure they'll come around, Li-Li."

"What I meant was 'fuck em'."

"Anyway, you don't need to worry about what they—"

Bim stood up. Ola's hand went to the knife at his belt. Li-Li felt it too, and shrank back against the wall. The basket toppled noisily. Ahid shuddered and began to cry, Lilith quickly wrapping him against her and raising her spear. Someone grabbed her. Princess. She was stronger than she looked, though that should not have come as a surprise, and lifted her bodily out through the window, hopping over the sill and crouching next to her on the narrow veranda.

"Lilith?" She peeked back into the room, hand ready to pull mother and child out with them, then her eyes went wide. "Oh no."

Li-Li looked too now, that sense of foreboding anchoring her to the boards below. They had all sensed them before they arrived, but only Princess had moved in time. Now the two of them were safe while the others stood facing two Ifram escorted by a trio of Reavers.

"What are you doing up here?" A voice that was strangely distant. Both amused and agitated. The Reaver kicked some of the fallen fruit aside as he approached. Bim, Ola and Gia were all standing now, fingering their weapons and looking frightened. They formed a wall between Lilith and the new arrivals. Surely they were no match for Reavers?

Princess' gaze was fixed on Lilith, clearly willing her to flee with them. The latter seemed to be frozen in place.

And their guests…the two Ifram, like most of their kind, carried two metal pipes across their backs, one longer than the other. As Li-Li watched they each manoeuvred one of these into their hands and pointed them at the trio blocking them.

Some sort of weapon?

Princess nodded, her fingers trembling against the wall. Talking now inside, low voices. Nobody moved a muscle.

"I told you we're baking!" Bim quavered, nervously glancing at the pipes. "See? Fruit! There's flour in that sack over there! And here's a pan—"

"I didn't say you could move, any of you."

"Are we not supposed to be here or something? It was never a problem before."

"You've been missing for days."

"And if we have been here? Where's the harm in that?"

"No harm I suppose. Though there have been *rumours,* Bim. People talking about our guests here. People who want them gone. Some of them are meeting in secret, we hear. Plotting against them. We can't have that."

"We've no argument with them," Ola responded flatly. "Now leave us be."

"Leave you be?" The Reaver was sounding less friendly and more sinister now. The hairs on Li-Li's arms stood up. Lilith was finally moving, edging closer to the sill. Princess looked ready to yank her over at a moment's notice. "You mean we're not welcome here? Our *guests* aren't welcome here?"

A long silence. It seemed neither Bim nor Ola knew exactly how to respond. Finally, Gia cut in:

"I mean, if they want some of the tart…um…"

The Reaver laughed. "That's more like it. And who was making it? I see five seats here. But only three of you. Where are the rest of your friends?"

"Um."

Li-Li shivered. There was another sound in the room. It had been quiet before, just on the edge of hearing, but now it turned sharper. Minds moved, edging towards her. She pushed them away, and the noise rose again. A loud *hissing.* No. A *snuffling* and *sniffing.* Like something was trying to follow her scent. A board creaked just inside the window. Lilith's elbow appeared above them.

"There's no-one else here, I told you!" Ola exclaimed.

Then, the words none of them wanted to hear: "What have you got there, Lilith?"

She did not respond, but did not need to. Little Ahid, also sensing those groping thoughts, suddenly burst into tears.

*

Li-Li put her arm around Princess, who was ready to jump up to her friend's defence, and dragged her down until they were both lying prone on the walkway. Inside, there came the *thump thump thump* of someone hurtling across the room. A shout. A roar. Two bodies crashed against the wall, cracking the glass with the impact. Ola growled and the Reaver snarled, grunted. A bang as someone struck the metal oven. Bim gave a shout, barked something at Lilith, who whimpered and scurried away, desperately *shushing* her son. Another scuffle. The Reaver had darted back to the centre of the room, and Li-Li allowed Princess back up so they could look through the window. Lilith cowered in the corner now rocking a wailing Ahid. Ola was picking himself up off the floor, clutching one dislocated shoulder. Blood poured out of the claw marks on his wrist. Bim was now struggling with two of the other Reavers as the first grabbed Gia. She kicked and snapped at him even as he punched her. Even when his teeth sank into her neck. Ola bellowed something in his mother tongue, finally raising his blade. He leapt at one of their assailants.

A high-pitched shriek, enough to shatter even a Sidhe's ears. A flash of red light erupted from the end of one of those metal pipes with a slight *pew,* hitting Ola in the chest, flinging him back against the oven. He did not make a sound, just slumped into a heap on the floor, a smouldering hole where his heart should be. Gia saw too, and screamed. The Reaver holding her, looking equally shocked, lost his grip as she threw herself at Ola. She touched his face, babbling senselessly and trying to pick him up. There was no point. They had all felt it— he had left them. Li-Li clapped a hand over Princess's mouth as the cry lodged in her throat found her voice.

Stop. She willed Bim, but he was already turning on the Ifram who had fired. Practically ran into the second blast. It took his leg out from under him, and the next took off the top of his head. Gia, still shrieking nonsense, tried to stand, tried to fight, but the other beast had already trained his weapon on her, and silenced her instantly.

Quiet! Willed Li-Li, pinning Princess under her, palm still clamped against her lips. *Please, be quiet! They'll find us!*

Lilith was still in there with the baby. As she struggled with Princess, Li-Li urged her to come to them. Lilith did not respond, her mind a mess of panic and fear. She did not even resist when one of the Reavers grabbed her.

"You had no part in this." Li-Li heard him say. "You or this child. I do not wish any harm to come to either of you. Please, come with us."

Princess's fist connected with her nose. She felt it shatter. Pain. Princess' face showered with dark blood. She tried to grab her arm but the next blow got her in the side of the head. Dizzy, Li-Li found herself being shoved aside. Princess was standing up now, ready to vault through the window in defence of her friend. Half-blind and choking on blood and mucus, Li-Li could only think of one escape. She took Princess around the waist and lifted her with all of her might then, using the windowsill as leverage, she threw them both backwards over the railing. They struck the roof below so hard that she was sure her spine would shatter, but still she gripped her. Held her tight as they tumbled, sending loose tiles to shatter below. Below. Li-Li caught a glimpse as they rolled over the edge. Guessed it was at least fifty metres to the ground, and just closed her eyes.

XXXVII

Laal dropped a bowlful of chopped scallions into the pot and absently stirred them in, a pungent, gamey aroma rising up from chunks of chevon cut with hints of garlic and paprika. There was enough for six, but then she always made too much; Mentor was unlikely to join them this evening (she had not graced them much with her company since returning), Yuki was in one of their dark moods, and would likely only poke at their bowl until everyone else had finished. As for Princess and Li-Li…Sunshine leaned aside to peek through the crack in Crim's door. They were both still bedridden.

*

Her thoughts drifted back to that day. Yuki bursting into the apartment, tripping over Princess' dragging feet as she dangled barely moving from their back, Li-Li in their arms completely paralysed. Dinner had hit the floor in an instant, as Laal pulled the wounded up onto the table. Princess groaning and whining as she probed her shattered arm and leg, one side completely bruised and scratched, sliver of eye bloody in its cracked socket. Li-Li could barely be heard, could not even writhe as they turned her this way and that, Laal praying as she kneaded the bones of her neck back into place. Sunshine stroked her hair and told her she would be fine—she was Sidhe, after all, and would mend in time—Li-Li sniffed helplessly back.

"What happened?" She demanded, perhaps a little too harshly.

Yuki, pulling at their hair in distress, reached out to stroke Li-Li's cheek, but swiped it away as soon as she sobbed. Their tunic was smeared with her blood in the front and Princess' in the back. They tugged at their clothes, inspecting the dark patches.

"Yuki, please." Cooed Laal. "We need to know. Did someone do this to them?"

270

"I-I don't…I don't know." The words thick and stunted. It occurred to Sunshine that she had never seen them cry before. "I wasn't with them, I only…I *felt* her. She called out to me. She couldn't move. By the gods: she can't move!"

"She will in time. Her neck is broken for now, but I've set it right. Her body will do the rest."

Sunshine pressed: "You didn't see anything? Hear anything? Was there no-one around?"

"There were plenty around. All around them. Smith told me to take them. Helped me some of the way. She's gone to speak to Mentor now."

"People all around and not one of them knew what had happened?"

"I didn't really ask. I just took them and, well…"

"You did well, Yuki," said Laal softly. "They should heal, but their limbs need setting. Princess' eye—" She bent over to inspect the damage, shushing Princess softly. "The eye itself is fine. She doesn't need a new one."

"Perhaps one of them can show us?" Sunshine suggested. "Princess, can you try?"

Princess whimpered, a watery trickle of blood now running down her temple as she closed her eyes. Sunshine sensed her opening up, the low hum of her mind edging outward. She met her halfway, embracing the images as they were released: the Temple, the Minaret stairs, something like an apartment. Blurs. Noise. Screams. She was falling backwards, the cavern roof rising away…

"Can't," Princess grunted through gritted teeth. "*Can't.*"

"It's fine, Sweetheart." Laal pressed a steaming cup to her lips. "Here; this will help you sleep."

With much help Princess drank, spluttering and moaning as Laal eased her back down.

"What happened?" Yuki blurted angrily, shaking Princess even as she began to drift. "You didn't show us anything!"

"*Yuki!*" Laal rarely used force, but she tossed them aside now. Yuki hit the wall and slid down it, staring up at them both with a dazed expression. "Princess has done her best. We will have to wait…to wait until—*ugh!*"

As Laal reeled and caught herself against the table, Sunshine felt it too. An assailing avalanche of images and sounds. Jumbled at first, doubling back on itself and jumping from vision to vision. Then arranging into order. Sunshine was standing in the apartment watching Princess and her friends laughing, all of them sat round a furnace. They came through the door unexpectedly, the four of them. Two of their Guests and two guards. For some reason, she was watching them through a window. There was a conflict—a disagreement. A flash of light and two of Princess' friends now lay dead on the floor. A third followed shortly. The fourth cowered in the corner hugging something to her chest. At her side, Princess almost screamed. She silenced her. Pulled her away from the window. And then they were falling, falling…she thought they would never stop, but abruptly they did. She hardly felt the impact, but she heard Princess yelp as she finally let her go. Heard her cries of agony as she writhed beside her. Why was she always so dramatic? It didn't hurt at all. But they would hear; one was already on the balcony, staring down at them. He would catch them—she had to move. Had to take Princess and run. Find Mentor or Laal or Sunshine. Any second now she would get up and lead the way.

Any second now. I'm trying any second now. Princess, please wake up! Run!

Sunshine took her hand; it felt so frail somehow. Limp and unmoving, her slender fingers cold. Her eyes still moved as she stroked her powder pink hair, fixed in a startled stare.

"I saw, Li-Li," she assured her. She used her teeth to open her wrist, and offered the thick trickle of blood to the youngling. Laal did the same with Princess, though it would only speed up their healing a little. They really needed someone like Mentor or Mother to mend them, but Sunshine did not think that wise. "We both saw. You did well—you saved Princess. And Yuki saved you. You're safe now. We'll guard you, and Laal will fix you. Come on. Let's put you to bed."

*

"I said *will you feed Li-Li?*" Laal interjected, hands on her hips.

"What?" Sunshine blinked. Found her tying her sash around her waist. "Where are you going?"

"I need to talk to Smith. Apparently something similar happened to one of her apprentices just two days ago."

"Another attack?"

"Seemingly." Laal opened her apothecary cabinet and began sorting through vials and jars, arranging them into a worn wicker basket. "There have been rumours…"

"Rumours?"

"About what they want. Why they're here. Some people are starting to think we'd best send them on their way."

Sunshine nodded. Defacing the Temple and denouncing the gods had been questionable. Random acts of violence were inexcusable. She peered back into the dim bedchamber. Someone—probably Princess—was mooching about within, sniffling softly in pain. So many of them had been ready to welcome their guests. Despite their unusual ways and appearance, they had tried so hard to consider their ideas and the change they brought, but now that two people she loved were hurt, she only wished to see their backs, and that feeling was rising among the Sidhe.

"At least, take some food." Taking a lidded container from another press, she began to ladle stew into it. She urged this and one of the warm, round loaves on the table into Laal's basket. With a kiss she added: "And be careful."

Laal nuzzled her. "I will. You know I'm smart enough not to cross them."

"Hah. I know."

But as the door closed behind Laal, for once she doubted her ability to take care of herself. None of them knew what might set off these creatures. And as for the kinslayers that escorted them…

"*Urk.*" Princess slumped down by the table, ejecting her out of her concerns. She was looking better day by day, yet nothing like herself; her usually-perfect curls were an unbrushed mass of frizz, she was wearing the same robes Sunshine had put her in the first time she had risen, her face, hands, ears and feet were unpainted and grimy, most of all her deep blue eyes seemed to have lost their light, and swam behind unshed tears in a red, puffy face.

Sunshine slid a bowl in front of her and broke some bread, hoping the divine smell of Laal's food might spur her to eat. Princess only looked vacantly down into the thick brownish-red broth, the edge of her cherubine mouth twitching downward. Sunshine sat back down into her own chair and proceeded to dip hunks of crunchy crust into the stew until they were soft and juicy enough to swallow with hardly any chewing.

When she was done she took both bowls away, though Princess' remained untouched. She used her fire to reheat it and placed it on a tray along with some bread and water.

"Help Li-Li to eat, will you?" She requested. "I need to go out."

The youngling was aware enough to take it, and shuffled back into the darkened room. "Li-Li. Dinner." Though her voice rang as she said it, Sunshine noticed it was hollow, devoid of its usual music and life. Princess had lost most of her friends in a single day, and no-one had heard from Lilith since the incident, so she supposed her mood was understandable, but still she had an unrelenting urge to shake her out of it, to drag her back out of her mourning and into the light. She would even take her sass if it meant some return to normalcy.

She edged over and peeked round the doorframe. Princess had Li-Li under the arms and was hoisting her up into a seated position. The other girl, with limbs still mostly immobile, let her head loll back against the wall, smiling sweetly as a spoon of hot stew was pressed to her lips. She ate slowly, talking gently to Princess about minor things, maintaining that little grin the whole while, but the tingling and burning as her body mended itself no doubt bothered her, and her eyes betrayed this.

*

"You weren't followed?" Whisper breathed, checking this way and that as she shut the barn door behind them.

"No. I took the back passages like you said, and looped around a couple of times for good measure," Sunshine replied, producing the smooth, blue-grey stone from her pocket. The one stamped with the likeness of a bull's head. "You gave me—"

"Yes. I remember. Come on."

Whisper brushed past her, ignoring one of the stallions who had been roused by Sunshine's arrival. He lipped at her sleeves as she passed and snorted indignantly when she walked on. Sunshine patted his nose sympathetically as she followed. Beyond all the stables and stalls the hay bales were stacked three high and three deep, without any obvious way to the back wall. Whisper turned sideways, crouching to slip through a slight gap between two stacks. She was shorter, and made it through rather easily, but Sunshine emerged into the cramped hollow with pieces of straw dangling from her bright coils. Whisper quietly removed a few before hunkering down to pull back a mat on the floor. Under this was a hatch that opened over a ladder descending down into a yellow glow. Sunshine hesitated.

"You can turn back whenever you like. All we ask is that you keep our secret."

Exhaling a puff of air, Sunshine lowered herself down on to the cold, clean rungs. The Ifram had hurt the younglings—she had to make sure they paid. Others no doubt agreed with her. A whole group of them now sat on the floor muttering. Silver rose to greet her, and introduced the four other elders that Sunshine was unfamiliar with. Smith and Hammer, needing no introduction, smiled. The rest were a mix of old and new faces, some greeting her with enthusiasm, others with suspicion. She presented herself warmly and sat. They spoke for hours, all of them, well into the night. Sunshine listened more than she spoke, and when at least no-one had anything left to say, Whisper invited them to sleep—it was now too late for any of them to be seen in the passages without drawing attention. Sunshine found a corner near the twins and wrapped herself tightly in the scratchy brown blanket she had been given, one hand gripping the knife in her belt.

At mid-morning Kiri, Silver's mentee, fell down the ladder, knocking over an empty wine jug as he threw himself into the middle of their circle. Everyone sprang awake at the racket, Sunshine, along with a few others, holding out their concealed weapons in anticipation of an attack.

Breathless and wide-eyed, he exclaimed: "The Forum! Mentor, They have Lilith in the Forum!"

*

The Menagerie was large, with several different exit leading out to various points both in and outside the Mountain. Their group took it in turns to leave their little hideout, with Silver and Kiri leaving immediately for the most direct path, all taking their own route down to the Forum. Sunshine found herself looping through a round, rough tunnel all the way back to the Foyer. It was here, surprisingly, that she met Laal coming up from a nearby stairwell. Her lover seemed just as surprised to find her there.

"Enjoy your evening?" Sunshine asked, kissing her on the cheek. She smelt of incense and wine.

"Yes. How are the younglings?" Laal eyed her curiously.

"Quiet."

"No trouble?"

"Two of them are invalids. The other watches Li-Li and won't do anything else."

"Hm. So did you hear about…?"

"Lilith? That's where I'm headed."

Seemingly pleased with this response, Laal finally took her arm. "Lead the way."

*

The Forum was in no way full, yet as they entered the air felt dense, imposing. On the opposite side of the Pit, the lights of the Market burned and glittered brightly, but here the lamps and braziers seemed to struggle to provide even the barest illumination. Where Mother stood on the overhanging podium was darkest, so that the glow of her eyes was almost frightening. Sunshine imagined that she looked angry, or at least upset, and prayed for Lilith's sake.

The prisoner—for there could be no denying that this was some sort of trial, sat on the lowest bench with two Reavers flanking her. Her wrists and ankles were tied to her waist with ropes made of woven Sidhe hair—a substance only the teeth or weapons of a Sidhe could break—and Half a dozen Ifram stood nearby in complete silence, and Mentor sat on the opposite bench next to Hyeong.

Silver was currently having a heated exchange with the Reavers, neither of which seemed willing to let her near her youngling. It was the first time Sunshine had seen her looking so afraid. In one last desperate attempt, she reached out a hand to Lilith, only to have it swatted away with the broad side of a blade. Defeated for now, she went to sit by Kiri.

Lilith was frozen. In the gloom, she seemed as a statue staring off into the light of the Market. She only moved at a single sound, a sort of squeak which rose up from the bundle in her arms.

Laal's grip on her arm tightened. As that squeak came louder this time, more of the crowd's attention was drawn to that bundle. Many gasped.

"Sunny. Is that…by the *gods!*"

"A baby." It was. A tiny thing with plump cheeks and big brown eyes, he laughed and bounced as his mother spoke to him, completely oblivious to their predicament.

"He must be trueborn. Look at him." Laal was leaning forward, smiling, eyes bright with fascination. "No mortal child that size is so aware. At least now we know why Princess started sneaking off again."

Sunshine laughed, secretly relieved that her underling had a good reason for her antics. For once.

Mother raised a hand, and all but the infant quieted. He was too busy pulling his mother's hair and gurgling. Lilith nuzzled him. She shook visibly as Mother spoke.

"We come here to bear witness to Lilith. She is accused of conspiring against the Ifram, our beloved guests, and of meeting in secret to partake in acts of terrorism against them—"

Silver's mouth fell open, she sprang to her feet and was pulled down by Kiri. There was no defying Mother, not even now. She could be killed for even trying. Lilith turned finally and caught her mentor's eye, shaking her head. Even she knew she was beyond help.

On the podium, something strange was happening; Mother said no more, but descended the steps, nodding to Hyeong as he ascended to take her place. A chill ran down Sunshine's spine.

This isn't right. Laal's fear soaked her thoughts. *Mother should be the one to judge.*

The rest of the court seemed to agree, and a ripple of unease spread through the benches. Some voiced their concerns aloud and were *shushed* nervously. Sunshine glanced around, sharing anxious looks with those nearby. What was going on?

*

Hyeong, ignoring the stir, grinned up at them. He bowed, like an actor taking to the stage, and boomed: "Brethren, when the Ifram came to us a few short moons ago, it was an act of friendship. Friendship that, I am sad to say, we have failed to properly reciprocate."

A murmur. Scattered scoffing. Whispered insults.

"They came to us offering friendship, promising peace, asking only for our cooperation. And what have we given them in return? Suspicion. Accusations. Hostility. Attacks on innocent Ifram tourists just a few metres away from where I now stand." He pointed behind himself to the Market.

"That was *one* incident!" Someone shouted, jumping up. They shook their friends off and continued: "What about all of the attacks on *us*? What about the

277

banning of our gods, the defacing of our Temple, the threats from *your Reavers* to their *own kind*! What about Tal!"

"Tal," Hyeong shot back. "Was a terrorist. Be careful of who you sympathise with, Ryusei, you could land yourself in trouble."

There was something about the way he said that. Something about the lowering of his voice and that shark-toothed grin of his that made Sunshine feel cold. She willed Ryusei to sit back down. Willed him to be silent. Thankfully, he stopped, and allowed his friends to lead him out.

"As for the gods," Hyeong continued as though the interruption had never happened. "Our new friends have opened our eyes, have they not? They have shown us their own deity, and let us know that we need never be slaves to the old gods again! That means that we never need to partake in a Making ever again." He was tiptoeing down the steps now, pointing at Lilith as she rocked the baby in her arms. "That means we *must never* partake in a Making again."

"I told you!" Lilith spat. "I did not 'make' him! I conceived him, I bore him. He is *mine*! My flesh and blood. My *son!*"

"And here he is, another unfortunate vessel for a false god." Hyeong jerked his thumb at the guards, and in an instant they had Lilith by either arm. She kicked and snapped at him, but he took the infant from her arms easily. "So we must make an example of you."

Silver was out of her seat at once, rushing to help her youngling as she was dragged up onto the podium, but Mentor intercepted her. She whispered something into Silver's ear, pointing at Mother, and the frantic elder paused. Kiri, at her side now, begged with the Reavers to let his sister go.

"If we do not embrace change," Hyeong continued. "We will never grow. If we do not rid ourselves of our impurities, we will never be free. And we will never be good, so long as we allow sinners to walk free." One of his geom slid smoothly from its sheath as he cuddled Lilith's son against his shoulder. Silver cried out, and was held by Mentor. The prisoner, held in place as she was, could only watch as he drove the point into her heart. It was forged by Smith, made of truesilver, and sliced through her with ease. With a croak and a jerk she died, and was thrown down the steps into her mentor's arms.

The babe, feeling his mother's passing, began to bawl, and Hyeong hummed gently as he shook and wiped the blood from his blade.

"Shhh, Ahid," he cooed. "My quarrel is not with you. After all, you never asked to be born."

A collective cry rang out; so clear was the Reaver in his intent that all of them saw it before it happened. With Lilith's blood still dripping around his feet, he casually dropped her son off the edge of the outcrop. Ahid's descent into the Pit was never-ending, and for as long as the Mountain stood his cries seemed to echo up, haunting the Forum and the Market and anyone who entered those places, until they were abandoned and there were no ears left to hear him anymore.

At his demise even Mother rose—though not without her usual grace and poise. Sunshine suspected there was something more to the straightness of her spine, to the hands balled up against her sides, but she did nothing. What could any of them do? There was not a Sidhe made yet who could sprout wings and fly.

The clamour that arose once people regained control of themselves was chaotic, but died down just as quickly. For the Reavers turned, brandishing their weapons and their *draoi*, what Ifram there were unslung their weapons from their backs and pointed them at the crowd. Shots were fired, and a few charged to meet the challenge of the Reavers who had betrayed them, but the majority were as horrified and heartbroken as Laal and Sunshine, and they fled.

XXXVIII

There was no pain. No sensation. Nothing. As she lay there, Li-Li vaguely remembered where are arms were, her legs, her fingers and toes. How did she move them before? She tried to wriggle. Tried to curl and uncurl ever little digit. Did she succeed? She did not know.

Princess was usually there, too. Sometimes—usually when she thought Li-Li was sleeping, she would lie down next to her, either just by her side or with her arms around her. Most of her days were spent sitting by the desk, however. Sitting in a trance, staring off into space. Occasionally, she would play with Crim's paints and jewellery, smudging her face and hands without much design and laughing at her reflection in the mirror. Li-Li wondered if Princess knew how unsettled this made her feel, watching her friend slowly unravel while she lay prone in the bed of someone she had already lost.

On that day, they woke up without Laal and Sunshine. She hardly noticed until she grew hungry. Li-Li raised her arm and inch, watching it flop back down onto the covers. Soft humming caressed her ears; Princess was happily arranging one of Crim's drawers, sitting on the floor with its contents all around her, easing each piece into line with all the others. None of them were particularly important belongings—mostly souvenirs and bric-a-brac Crim had accumulated from the Marketplace. Li-Li doubted her efforts would ever be appreciated by their owner.

She groaned as loudly as she could manage, foot twitching as she tried to bend her leg. If only she could sit up. Thankfully the movement jerked her blanket, and a small vial of lavender oil rolled down the steps. Princess raised her head.

"Good morning."

"M-morning," Li-Li managed. Still trying to move her body, she felt toes and fingers, wrists and ankles spasming. Her eye twitched involuntarily.

"Are you in pain?" She had Princess' full attention now, and the other acolyte crawled across the bed to touch her brow. "Laal left some medicines out. I'm sure I could find—"

"No. No p-p-pain. Is th-there anyth-thing to eat?"

Princess fed her, bathed her, clothed her and brushed her hair. In times when she was clearest, she spoke. In fact, she spoke on and off all day. Mostly about Lilith and the others; about their adventures together. It was through these stories that she confirmed Li-Li's suspicions about their longest absences: from time to time they left the Mountain, wandered out into the mortal world and explored and revelled away from the watchful eyes of the Elders. Other times she talked about Yuki, Laal, Sunshine, Mentor, about her rocky relationship with them and the rest of the Sidhe. Only once did she speak of Crim.

"I hope she never comes back, Little Mouse. For her sake, I pray she stays far away from this place. It's easy to feel lost as a Sidhe among mortals, but here I reckon she felt completely hopeless."

In the middle of the afternoon, there was a stir in the air. Li-Li thought she had imagined it initially, but Princess eased her limp body away from her and went to the door. She found Yuki on the other side, who passed her and approached the bed looking anxious. They had not been what disturbed her, and were clearly feeling the same prickling chill that had disturbed Li-Li and Princess. A sickly feeling settled in her stomach; a weighty foreboding.

It hit them all at once, like a blow to the head. For an instant, Lilith's presence flared in their minds, burning bright and fierce, then it disappeared into a black pit. Li-Li felt as though she was falling, falling down into the darkness and saw the roof of the Forum flying away from her.

"Aa-aaah!" Princess' wail brought her back to Crim's room, and she was her collapse against the doorframe, fingertips digging into the polished wood. Yuki, in a rare moment of empathy towards the little brat, left Li-Li's side and took her into their arms. Stroking her golden curls, they stared wide-eyed at Li-Li over her shoulder.

She shook her head, despair squeezing her heart. There was no denying it. After days in captivity, the Ifram had finally disposed of Lilith. She raised her hand to cover her face, none of them even noticing what she had managed. Lilith had been executed, but what of little Ahid? She had not felt him leave. Had they spared him? Did they still have him?

Li-Li prayed to the gods that they did not.

Laal and Sunshine returned not much later, both of them shaken and agitated. Laal slammed the door behind them, only for Sunshine to open it again and glance up and down the darkened corridor. When she shut it, she turned the key that until then had always sat untouched in the lock, and pressed her back up against it.

Reaching out to steady herself against the table, Laal sat down. Yuki eased Li-Li into the chair opposite her. Princess was still lying on the bed, staring at the ceiling and not responding.

"No-one leaves these rooms," Laal instructed. "Not without permission and *never* alone. Do you all understand?"

"We understand," Yuki affirmed.

"Princess?" Asked Sunshine, still holding the door shut behind her, like she was afraid someone would come bursting through at any moment.

"In there. She hasn't moved since…"

"Wh-what happened?" Li-Li reached out to Laal with her one good arm. "Lilith i-is sh-she…is sh-she—"

"Dead," Sunshine rasped.

"He just skewered her like some beast," whispered Laal, staring at the table cloth. "There was no trial, she was unarmed, bound. Could not even fight him."

"Ahid?" Yuki asked hopefully.

"Gone."

"No!"

"Hyeong tossed him into the Pit," said Sunshine, a growl rising in her chest. "He never stopped screaming."

"*No!*" Yuki's voice cracked. They stamped their foot, breath hitching into shrill gasps. "He's just a *baby!*"

"I know, sweetheart," Laal managed.

They turned, fists raised and, finding nothing else to smash, punched a hole right through Crim's door. "*He's just a BABY!*"

Yuki disappeared back into Crim's room, where they could be heard but not seen. Between bouts of senseless rage, Li-Li heard them speaking softly to Princess.

Days passed into weeks, and each time she woke Li-Li felt stronger. First, she began to move her head and neck, turning to look at Princess as she talked, smiling and chatting with as much energy as she could muster. The latter was silenced by grief for the most part, but could be coaxed out of this for brief moments. Moments when she would laugh and talk and get up from the bed to roam about the apartment. It was a giddy, light sort of happiness that never seemed to stick, and she returned to her stupor just as easily.

Next came her fingers and toes—she would wriggle them all day, and Princess seemed cheered by this. She would challenge her to hold various objects around the room, giggling at her success. Wrists and elbows came soon afterwards, then weeks later her shoulders. Li-Li did not say it, but she worried her legs would never heal. Even as she finally began to drag herself out of bed and crawl around, with all of her being she wished for her legs back.

Laal and Sunshine were delighted by her progress. Delighted, but as she edged closer and closer to the door, and joked about how much she wanted to go outside they became nervous. Truthfully, she really did want to visit the Menagerie and the Library—she had not seen Bart in a long time, after all. It would be good for Princess too; she was sure she, Princess and Yuki could make it there and back without incident, but the two elder Sidhe refused firmly, describing the unrest that now pulsed through every passage and tunnel under the Mountain. At one point, Sunshine even locked the door in front of her.

"I'm sorry, Sweetheart," she said, looking uncharacteristically sad. "It's not safe."

"Wh-why?"

Laal and Sunshine shared a glance.

"Our Guests are becoming more sceptical. More unpredictable."

"Clashes have increased. An Anointed was killed just the other day," Laal elaborated.

"Whisper told me they may be looking for you," added Sunshine.

"Looking for *m-m-me*?" Li-Li squeaked.

"They know you were there. In the Minaret. You and Princess both. One of the Reavers identified you."

"If they know you were with Lilith, that you were visiting her…If they see you as a threat…" Laal stroked her hair. "We can't protect you if they turn. Those weapons of theirs are like nothing we've ever seen before. Not even Smith knows how to defend against them. And they have the Reavers at their beck and call, too."

"Not to mention a growing hoard of Sidhe admirers."

"Suh…So I j-just hide here?"

"That's all you can do for now. It's the only way we can keep you safe."

*

So she stayed. Locked in the apartment indefinitely with Yuki and a vacant Princess. Wasting her days away by reading some of the books from Crim and Laal's extremely varied collections. Dragging herself to and fro in an anxious dance across the parlour floor. Trying in vain to stand on her own two feet.

Laal and Sunshine were spending more and more time away. Neither of them ever spoke about what they were doing, but Li-Li felt their unease, their paranoia and their anger. It seemed as though each time one of them returned they were more wary, less willing to leave the safety of the rooms themselves. And they absolutely refused to let the younglings out.

Not that Princess wanted to go anywhere. The loss of her friends had completely drained all sense of character from her. Gone were her haughty smiles and sniggers, her scoffs and sneers. Even her whimpering and whining had been silenced. All that remained was an empty shell.

*

She grunted, hauling herself up shelf by shelf until she reached the gap from which Laal had handed her a tattered apothecary guide. Taking the slim journal from between her teeth, Li-Li tried to brace one arm against the bookcase to give herself the last few inches necessary to slip it into place.

Arrogantly, she tried to then take some weight onto her legs. It was worth a try after all. Surely, kneeling like this on her knees would be easier than standing completely?

No. Her knees refused, sending her hips wobbling until she flopped sideways, hitting her elbow jarringly on the bedframe as she went. Li-Li hissed, bending and straightening her arm until the tingling sensation went away. She examined the ceiling of Laal and Sunshine's chamber—the smooth white plaster and patterned borders. The single lamp that hung from a chain, forever glowing in varying shades of orange-yellow. Unlike Crim, their bed was raised on four sturdy rosewood legs, the headboard and baseboard carved with some distinctly Mesopotamian-looking figures. Everything was neat and orderly, from the garments in the wardrobe, separated in half and arranged by type, to the shelves carefully dotted with statuettes, vases and various treasures, to the two armour trunks set side-by-side and gleaming with fresh polish. Li-Li rolled onto her stomach and slithered over to these, opening each lid to find them empty. They were always empty these days. Sunshine and Laal no longer left the apartment dressed casually; they left fit for war. According to what they told the younglings, this was becoming the trend under the Mountain.

She saw up against the two trunks, rubbing her thighs and calves. At least, she could feel some of the friction now. She bent each leg at the knee in turn, which was only achieved by manoeuvring them with her hands, and practiced moving her toes and ankles.

Li-Li thought of calling Yuki—they often helped her to stand, balancing her carefully against themself and letting her try to walk. Like an infant first earning its legs. Then she remembered that they were gone, too. Against her pleas, and against their elders' demands, they had started to sneak out in the afternoons. They were determined to gain some intelligence on the Ifram, and had taken to crawling through disused tunnels in order to get around the Mountain unchecked. It was dangerous, and silly, but there was little Li-Li could do to stop them, and she would not tell on them, so she was left more or less alone every day now.

More or less alone…except for Princess.

*

Princess…It had been a while since she checked on her. She had been lying on Laal and Sunshine's bed reading for most of the afternoon.

Princess? She must be hungry. Or at least a little lonely. She adjusted her legs again so that she could resume her struggle across the hard, cold floors, even managed to shove the bedroom door shut behind herself. She was halfway across the parlour when a chill swept over her, and she turned, looking around the room for the cause.

Was someone watching her?

No.

Someone outside?

No. Whatever had stirred her unease was definitely in the apartment. Definitely close.

Definitely...Her eyes fell on the door to Crim's room, which was open a crack. Her stomach twisted. She had gotten quite fast on her hands, and was there in a flash.

"Princess?" She knocked three times.

Another wave, stronger this time. This time tinged with panic. No one answered. There was not even a stir from within.

The sliding door hit the far end of the frame with a clear *snap*! As she thrust it aside. No. This was all wrong. "Princess!"

The smell hit her first. Acrid, coppery, pungent. Strong enough to make her eyes water. Li-Li clapped a hand to her nose and mouth, cringing back. Staring into the gloom, she could see nothing. Sunshine had lit the lamps in here in Crim's absence, and they glowed much the same as her own, but in vain; the whole room was filled with a dark haze. A black, choking shadow. Li-Li dragged herself through it, feeling it brush against her skin like cold dust. She reached the foot of the bed without knowing it, her hand hitting the first step with a tap that seemed far too sharp and clear in this ominous quiet. Raising herself, she was finally granted enough illumination to try to make sense of what was in front of her. Princess was there, and it looked indeed like she had not moved from where Li-Li had left her. In fact for an instant, Li-Li thought she looked peaceful, lying on her back in Crim's bed, the covers around her waist, her arms spread wide.

The covers...Li-Li choked. Then gagged, clear bile running down her chin to drip onto her hands. She fought the urge to vomit. The covers...The covers looked black, shiny. Gleaming pools of blood turning thick and sticky where the fabric could absorb no more. It was still coming out of her, pouring out of Princess' open wrists in steady streams, thick and dark and horrifying. One of Crim's knives, barely bigger than a letter-opener, lay by her right hand, still looking immaculate in the midst of the crime it had just committed. Li-Li could hardly bring herself to look at Princess' face, but she had to. The bedding squelched sickeningly under her weight, and by the time she reached her friend her entire front was drenched. It stank...oh it *stank*, but she had to look at her. Even with the ruined sheets around her, even in the oppressive dark, Princess was beautiful. Her cherubine face plump and pale, cheeks still rosy. Her rosebud lips, usually fixed in a pout, now parted, revealing the pristine white points of her perfect teeth, with those little canines hardly big enough to be those of a

Sidhe. Last of all, Li-Li looked into her eyes, as big and blue as the ocean, staring wide and round into nothingness past long golden lashes.

*

There was still light in those eyes. The realisation struck Li-Li suddenly, and, somehow balancing on her knees, she eased her arms under Princess' prone form, lifting her into her lap. The movement seemed to rouse the latter, for she blinked and looked up at her.

"You're going to be fine," she blurted, tearing the hem of her skirt and trying desperately to tie it around one of Princess' gushing wrists. "I'm here. I'm here, Princess. I can save you—"

"No."

She hardly heard it, and most certainly did not acknowledge it. Another strip of fabric, pulled as tight as she could manage, went over the wound. "I can save you."

"No," Princess breathed. She lifted her arm just enough to caress Li-Li's face. "I'm sorry. I love you."

"I love you, too." That light was fading now. Her cheeks were sinking. Those golden curls had lost their lustre. "Let me save you."

"This is my liberation. Let me go."

She knew it, really. Knew Princess had been dying, little by little, for the longest time. Though the pain of it threatened to crush her, she knew in this moment, the best thing she could do for her friend—for her sister—was to say goodbye. She kissed her, and with her last ounce of strength Princess let out a little laugh. Li-Li watched her leave, watched that last glimmer leave those cerulean eyes. She turned almost grey, her skin dry and flaking. Her hair, eternally shining and golden, had lost its shimmer and now appeared almost white and brittle. Li-Li dared not move for fear of breaking her, but knelt in the damp, reeking sheets, holding the body until the others came.

*

Yuki appeared first, looking shocked and pale. They tried to put their arms around her. Tried to take Princess from her embrace. A gust of wind knocked them back, sent them back out the door and over the table into the far wall. They looked hurt as they righted themself. Li-Li did not care. She needed to hold Princess. Needed to keep her there. Everyone needed to say goodbye.

Her wrists…Li-Li sobbed, finally, turning one and then the other to inspect the straight, deep gashes she had made. How long had it taken her to bleed to death? How much blood did a Sidhe have? Li-Li looked down at the bed, completely soaked and pooled in places. She buried her face into her hair, breathing her in.

"Li-Li?" Sunshine's voice made her jump. She was standing in the door now, Laal behind her, Yuki nearby panting and sweating. Had they run to fetch both of them?

"I-I-I don't un-understand!" Li-Li blurted, hugging Princess to her breast. "I d-d-don't know wuh…wuh…what happened! I w-was r-ri-right in the n-next room!"

"It's not your fault," droned Sunshine, gaping down. Her eyes were misty, wide as she took in the scene before her. The mess. Yet she did not seem surprised. Only sad.

"I d-don't know…I don't n-n-know…Wh-why didn't—we c-c-could have helped!"

"No. You couldn't, Li-Li." Sunshine, still looking dazed, eased herself down onto the bed shakily. Leaning over, wincing as she braced a hand against the blood-soaked mattress, she brushed Princess' cheek with her fingers and shivered. Li-Li knew; Princess was so cold already. "None of us could."

"W-we *could have!*" She cried. "Why d-d-didn't she c-call us! We c-c-c-could ha-have helped!"

"No." Closing her eyes, Sunshine's face scrunched up as she spoke. "She was already gone, Li-Li. I should…I should have known it would end like this."

"E-end li-like this?" Li-Li was confused. Sunshine was talking like she *knew* this would happen. If she had known, why hadn't she stopped it? "Why are y-you a-a-acting like th-this is *nothing*? D-don't y-y-you *care* that she…she's dead!"

"Li-Li…," Laal whispered sharply. A warning.

Sunshine did not react; she was too preoccupied with the knife at Princess' hand. "Truesteel…This must be one of Crim's."

Li-Li whimpered, eyeing the red garnets set into a filigree handle. Definitely Crim's taste. "What d-do we do? Wi-with her I m-m-mean?"

"Nothing, Sweetheart," answered Laal thickly, pointing at the body in her arms. "Look."

Princess' face, already cracked and dry, now was crumbling apart. She gasped in horror as she watched it; first a few large flakes wafting on an unfelt breeze, then more and more smaller pieces fell away. Panic in her heart, Li-Li tried to hold her tighter, but her fingers pressed through Princess' form as it turned into naught but ashes. Drifting, grey ashes that collapsed into a pile on the bed and all over her lap. Li-Li summoned the voice to scream, and fell into Sunshine's arms.

Princess was gone. Lost to eternity.

XXXIX

"This is…nice," Aoife said at length, turning her mug of tea by the handle absently as she glanced around the threadbare room. Her eyes fell on the rusted, grimy artefacts laid out with reverence on a lopsided chest of drawers.

Crim nodded, pretending to enjoy her own drink. Laal had always insisted on filling her up with tea whenever she was injured or down, and all it had ever done was give her more motivation to become well again. She hated the stuff.

"About my mother…"

"It's fine. I hadn't intended on staying much longer, anyway." She did not mention the heated conversation she had had with Aoife's mother, the accusations that had been thrown at her. The demands of her husband to *get that demon out of my house!* The woman was perceptive, and the longer Crim stayed under her roof the more suspicious she became of her, until one day, for just a moment, she let the veil slip. She was sure Eileen saw her then; truly saw the Sidhe hiding behind a human mask. She leapt up from her chair and let out such a roar she woke the whole family. Crim had felt it too; a palpable power emanating from the woman. She dared not challenge her.

So Seamus had to push her out the door, looking apologetic and scared (more of his wife than of Crim). He managed to convince her to allow him to put together a bag, with some scraps from the table and a ragged blanket, and then sent Crim on her way.

Luckily, she had not needed the blanket or the food. Her claim that she had been looking elsewhere for board was not entirely untrue; she had been speaking to Comhnall Meagher about it only a few days prior while she helped him to mend a keg. He insisted they still had a spare room, and she could have it if she promised to give a hand about the pub and his father's land.

"There's always plenty to be done. So you'll earn your keep. We could always do with a hardworking pair of hands." He grinned, turning the patched drum right-side-up. "All you need do is ask."

So that evening she had walked straight up to the bar and asked. Comhnall handed her the key from his pocket like he had been expecting her.

"Take your time getting settled. We can talk work tomorrow…Did she feed you at least?"

*

Aoife left after an hour, taking the awkward silence with her. Crim walked her out to the main road and turned the opposite direction, heading up the hill towards the big house. She had spent some time surveying the enclosed estate, stalking about the high walls and hedges that kept it safe—from what she could not decide. The mortals that lived there never noticed her; she made sure they did not as she watched them strolling around manicured gardens, riding horses around a small pen, using long hammers to knock small balls under arches in what she understood to be a very boring game.

These were different from the ones in the village, somehow. It took her a while to pick out all the differences, but there were many, though they looked much the same. They spoke differently and acted…the best word she found to describe them was 'stiff'. At least the ones in charge were—they had a number of servants who appeared more or less the same as the locals she knew. There were servants from elsewhere, too, and Crim wondered how they had ended up in the kitchens and stables of a house in the middle of the mountains. Had they travelled here? Or been taken?

Sometimes, when her curiosity got the better of her, Crim would scale the walls. Usually when it was darker and quieter about the grounds. There was a maze of tall hedges that she particularly liked, with a mossy statue of vesta at its heart. She would sit there until night fell and then creep towards the house to look through windows (she did not like her chances of remaining undetected when she was too close to them in the full light of day). Somehow, she knew that the ones who slept in the higher rooms were the ones in charge, not only of the house, but of the entire valley. This was why the villagers spoke of them so often, why they were so afraid of offending them even from their humble little hearths. Crim wondered what might happen if they defied them.

*

She had promised Comhnall, the younger Meagher she would help him this evening; one of the Murphys was getting married today, and he needed every one of his family members and her to pull their weight. Crim cut her snooping short, dropping down from the veranda where she had been lounging at the first twinkle of a star and racing back (not too fast—she did not want to startle anyone out on the road).

Meagher's was already packed, and filling up to the brim now with the wedding party, including bridge and groom, who were seated in her favourite booth in a little nook partially hidden behind the curve of the bar. It had its own little fireplace, and she eyed them grudgingly as she passed. Tying an apron around herself, she nudged up next to one of the sisters to help with the dishes.

She had disliked the pub at first, with its noise and crowds and reek of pipe smoke that wreathed everything like ghostly tendrils. Disliked the patrons—the men that leered and the women that glared while their children climbed all over the tables and chairs. Disliked the worn upholstery, the yellowed curtains and scratched varnish. Working here had changed her mind on most of these points, however. She learned that most of the customers were merely curious of her; seeing her regularly brought out their true nature, and she found them pouring out their life stories over the bar soon enough, to which she listened intently. So intently that some would slip her a coin or two, or invite her to dinner at their house. Honest people, most of them. Knowing this painted the whole village in a better light, and she soon began to look forward to her shifts. Soon she felt at home.

*

Diarmuid poked his head round the door, caught her eye and smiled sheepishly. "Erm…you've got a visitor."

Crim frowned back. "I think you're mistaken."

"No. She asked for you specifically," he insisted, coming over to lean on the counter. "Said she was from the house, she did. Another servant I'm guessing? Stout girl. Persian…probably?"

Crim started, the plate in her hands slipping back into the water with a racket (but thankfully not a crash). "Laal?"

Diarmuid blinked. "I-I don't know. Didn't quite catch her name."

"Where is she?" Already out the door and marching towards the common room, he had to jog after her. He finally caught her by the elbow while she was staring about the room like a mad woman.

"I showed her upstairs. She said she would wait—"

Thinking about it later, Crim wondered if she scared him with how quickly she moved. How she was away from her and leaping up the stairs faster than his eyes could follow. Thankfully, neither he nor anyone in the pub that night ever brought it up.

*

Laal stood up from her seat on the windowsill when the door opened. For a split second, the two of them just stared at one another, before throwing themselves into a crushing embrace. Crim heard her laughing in her ear, that breathy little titter followed by lips against her cheek. She pressed her face into her shoulder, stroked her cream-coloured hair, kissed her.

"I never thought I would see you again," she whispered, her breath coming short and painful in her chest.

"Same here. You left and I never even got to say goodbye…I—"

"I'm sorry for that, you know. I wasn't leaving you. Any of you I just…"

"I know." Laal petted her head the way she had always done, and pinched her cheek fondly. "I know. It wasn't fair. Any of it. And we knew you were miserable, you know. Right from the start. I'm sorry that none of us ever helped you, or stood up for you."

"No. I didn't want you to. There was no way you could help." Crim shook her head, clearing some of the giddy haze away. "But how are you *here*? I don't even know how I found this place, I just sort of *arrived*."

"You didn't find your way?"

"No."

"But this is where you lived, right? Before?"

"Yes. Somehow I feel like I was brought here."

"Hmm. Or perhaps you just found it without meaning to."

"Perhaps. But *how did you find me?*"

"*I* didn't. Smith did. She assumed you would go back to where you were born, and her and Hammer both seemed to remember where you were taken from. Probably something the elders all know. Either way they told me this should be my first port of call and...well..."

"Here I am."

"Here you are." Laal fixed her scarf—which did not need fixing, and made her way over to the chest of drawers, where the spoils from Crim's grave still lay proudly on display. She picked them up one by one, handling each with great care. "What are these?"

"They're from before. I found them buried next to my parents."

"Your parents?" Came the shocked response. "You *have* been on an adventure."

"You could say that."

Unable to make small talk any longer, Laal finally blurted: "We need you back Crim. At the Mountain—"

"No. I'm not going back. I'm staying here."

"You don't *belong* here!"

"I belong here more than anywhere else. This is my home."

"*We* are your home!" Laal exclaimed, thumping the tarnished wood. "We're your family!"

"My family is long dead, Laal."

That hurt. Laal's face moved to cover up the pain, but Crim knew it, and hated herself for it. "So what is your plan? To waste the eons away in this place? To haunt these woods and these hills until the world changes or ends?"

"Yes."

"And what about us? You don't care what happens to us?"

"Of course I do! How can you say that!"

"We *need* you, Crim!"

"Don't be silly."

Laal let out an exasperated huff. "Mentor returned, Crim."

"See? She will take care of all of you."

"No. She came back *wrong*, Crim. I don't know how to explain it, but we cannot trust her. And she brought *them* with her. These *creatures*—oh I don't know how to describe them. They came in a ship that floats in the sky, they defiled the Temple and the Tombs. And now they have begun to slaughter anyone who defies them. They executed Princess' friends like animals and then Princess...poor Princess..."

"No." She did not like the weight in those words.

294

"She died in your bed. By your knife."

Crim clutched at her chest. How tight it felt. She was sure her heart had stopped for a moment. The room swam. "No."

"Please listen to me, Crim."

A sickening, heavy feeling settled in Crim's stomach as Laal showed her. The Ship, the defaced gods, the insect-like chattering Visitors. It all felt familiar, though she could not tell how.

"What makes you think I can help?"

"Gibber."

She snorted. "*Gibber?*"

"She told Sunshine to find you. Demanded it. Sunny said she told her *clearly* and *in full sentences* that you were the key. That you would save us."

Crim remembered Gibber the day of the Making. How purposefully she had acted. She had not spoken, but she had been different; like she knew exactly what she was doing and why. "I don't know, Laal."

"Just a few days. I'm begging you. Come back. Look at what they've done— what they're doing. If you don't think you can help, I'll let you come back here and never bother you again."

"You're not bothering me. I just…" It had been weeks since she had felt it. The Mountain looming behind her, shadowing the village, the woods, the lake, everything around it. Closing in with slow purpose, like a beast ready to swallow her whole. She shivered, suddenly cold.

Laal's hand was warm and soft. Her face full of love. "Please, Crim. Just give us two days."

XL

Li-Li was walking. Finally walking again. As she watched her take ten jittering strides across the parlour, part of Sunshine's heart felt healed. The youngling looked brighter, too—happier and more energetic.

She focused on Li-Li as she made another lap. Focused on that light, warm feeling that filled her when she watched her regain her strength. That sensation dwelt far too close to the wounds in her heart, however; the old scars of Crim's disappearance, the gaping hole left by the loss of Princess.

Her eyes fell on the door to Crim's room. Li-Li had broken it in her desperation to save her sister, and one side stood partially buckled and leaning off its track. Laal had locked it and filled the gap between the doors with scraps of wood. They had managed to salvage some mattresses from one of Smith's friends and a curtain from Adik and made a haphazard sleeping nook for Li-Li and Yuki by the wall of the parlour. No-one was to enter that room by Laal's command, and now only ghosts slumbered in the gripping dark.

Li-Li stumbled, one of her knees twisting grotesquely. Yuki was up in a flash, steadying her. They tried to ease her back down into one of the chairs, but she refused, rubbing the joint rather aggressively. Her usually sweet face always seemed so angry lately, and Yuki's was drawn and harrowed.

"Take a break."

"No." She pushed them away.

"You're doing great, Li-Li. Don't overexert yourself." Yuki patted her shoulder. The wrong move.

Li-Li snarled, plucking one of the crutches Laal had carved for her from against the wall and jabbing it at them. "St-stop *babying* me!"

"I'm not, I just trying to—"

"I d-don't care! I didn't a-a-ask!"

Sunshine, seeing them wince and hang their head, attempted: "Li-Li don't be so harsh."

The youngling shot her a glare, but her forest-green eyes were damp. Sunshine shut her mouth, and nodded at Yuki.

Leave her be.

Shaking their azure nest of hair, the retreated back behind the curtain to their sleeping nook. In all the commotion, none of them had heard the door open until Laal spoke:

"What's the matter?"

"*Nothing,*" Li-Li grumbled, leaning heavily on the crutch and daring not to bend her knee.

Laal met her eyes, and Sunshine shrugged. They both sighed. The younglings would get through this. They all would. They had to.

She reached into her lover's mind, letting her joy at seeing her swell up. Laal smiled sweetly, but kept her thoughts closed. Sunshine thought she looked uncomfortable. Shakily, she swiped the scarf off her head and ran the shimmering silk through her plump fingers, examining the pattern.

"What's the matter with *you?*" Sunshine asked. Laal rarely hid her feelings from her.

"I went…um…I went with Smith."

"I know. You were gone longer than I expected. We missed you here."

"I missed you too."

"Did you find the fungus?"

"What?"

"You said you were looking for some sort of mushroom?"

"Oh. That. No." Laal giggled suddenly. "I found something else."

Another laugh out in the hallway. Quieter, deeper. Sunshine heard someone whisper: "Am I the fungus?"

She stood. "Who was that?"

Laal was smiling now. *Really* smiling. Ear to ear. "I found her."

Crim stepped into the room, and Sunshine's breath left her body. At first, she tried to blink her away, for surely this was a vision, a fiction? Perhaps Whisper wearing a guise? She forced herself to look closer, and Crim waited patiently as she was probed, blushing slightly.

She held out a hand and Crim took it. The same strong grip. Those same soft hands, but different. The ink on them, usually a blurry blue, now looked stark and black. Her face was changed too—where once it had been smooth and flawless, it now sported scars. Mortal scars, probably gained in her youth, scratches mostly, but the right side was marred by deep claw marks that reached to her neck, where some beast had undoubtedly tasted her. A bear, probably. Usually Sidhe consciously erased all of the flaws they had gained while mortal; scars, marks, even those aspects of gender that did not suit them, but Crim had actively remembered and redrawn these markings into her skin. Jarring though they were, they suited her better than her blank features—added to that savage beauty that until now Sunshine had only caught glimpses of.

"Can I hug you?"

Laughing again, Crim threw herself into Sunshine's arms. Was she stronger now? By the gods, she squeezed tight enough to crush any of them. Sunshine relished it, caressed her, nuzzled her, pressed her lips to her warm skin. Laal joined them, unable to hold back. When had any of them last been so happy?

"What's she doing here?"

Standing behind Laal, Crim recoiled visibly. Sunshine cringed, feeling the heat of Li-Li's glare, which was not even directed at her. She was angry. Irrationally so. Sunshine's blood boiled in solidarity, but she pushed that sensation down. How could this youngling, who so adored Crim, be so enraged at seeing her live and well.

"She's here to help," Laal shot back, looking less than pleased at her attitude. "To see what we can't do about Mentor, the Visitors and all of this madness."

Putting what was perhaps too much weight on her crutch, Li-Li narrowed her eyes at them. "Do y-you know wh-what they are?"

Crim shuffled her feet, hurt and confused by this confrontation. "No."

"What they c-c-can do?"

"No."

"What they've d-d-done here? H-how m-many they've killed? How many m-m-more they plan on sla-slaughtering?"

"I'm getting an idea."

"D-do you know why i-it's up there, wa-w-watching us? What it wants?"

"What *what* wants?"

The youngling cast down her only support, and wobbled as she threw her arms in Crim's direction. "She didn't even see the ship!"

"It was behind the Mountain when we arrived." Growled Laal. "And that does not matter. What matter is that Crim *is here with us alive and well when we need help*. Not to mention she has access to the hidden sections of the Library, a close relationship with Bart and—"

"I can stay in the Patriarch's Tower."

"…and she can stay in the Patriarch's Tower." Laal started and turned. "What?"

"I'm not supposed to be here, and I don't want people raising questions about why I'm here and what I'm up to if they see me. From what you've said, Laal, people are paranoid, and our guests are not afraid to shoot first and not ask questions. It's better if I'm hidden, at least until they're gone."

"Crim…"

"Not to mention what's left of the Patriarch's personal collection is up there. It's only a few journals and scrolls, but it could be useful. His vision was legendary; maybe he saw something about these Visitors that can be used against them."

Sunshine folded her arms, anger still surged through her, washed around her as it poured from Li-Li (who was now standing remarkably steady) but now it was tinged with guilt. Sunshine knew that in her heart of heart, Li-Li was overjoyed to see her mistress. The youngling never wanted Crim to go away again, and now that she was talking about not even spending one night with them, she felt a pang ring clear through the parlour, emanating from Li-Li.

In a clear, hopeless voice, the youngling asked: "You're re-really not back a-a-re you?"

Crim shook her head grimly. "No, Little Mouse. Just two days and you'll be rid of me."

"Just g-go if y-y-you're not staying."

"*Li-Li!*" Sunshine barked. She had let her go on long enough, thinking the youngling would quickly burn out and ease her assault. She had gone too far; though Crim tried to mask it, the hurt of such spiteful words bled through into her expression.

The shame was rising in the younger Sidhe's chest, yet she still attempted one last jab: "She doesn't c-c-care about u-us."

"I do," Crim quavered.

Sunshine caught Li-Li with her glare. She went rigid, feeling the strength of it, tottering more dangerously on her uncertain legs. She said no more, and hung her head.

Sheepishly, Crim asked: "At least let me hold you a minute?"

Sunshine, still caught in the middle of them, wished for Li-Li to allow it. And there it was: a crack in her angry façade. Eventually, she nodded, and tried a few steps towards the door. Crim smiled her crooked smile and met her halfway, before she could stumble or trip. Li-Li did not melt into her the way Sunshine had expected, but allowed the embrace for a long minute before pushing away. Yuki came out of hiding for a hug, too, for once looking gladder than Li-Li to see her. Laal, remembering their secrecy, pulled the door sharply to. Sunshine just took it all in as they stood there. Two days. Not nearly enough time to spend with her dear friend. A blink and she would be gone.

*

They had dinner that evening, all five of them; Sunshine, Laal, Crim, Yuki and Li-Li. Yuki appearing less and less impressed to see Crim, kept their silence while a defrosted Li-Li gushed and wept all over her. The meal had helped calm her, and the wine. She was behaving more like her gentle, calm self. The youngling even tried in vain to convince her mistress to stay, but was only met with firm refusals from a stone-faced Crim.

"Bu-but why c-c-can't you!" She insisted, and Sunshine felt some of her own frustration in her voice. "Tell me!"

"I found my home, Little Mouse. I was never truly at home here, as much as I love all of you. I've never belonged under the Mountain."

"None of us do," Yuki added abruptly, surprising them all. They and Crim shared an understanding nod. "I've been remembering more, lately. Ever since meeting Lil—meeting the others. Hills, mostly, and low houses. The rains and the storms that would tear the walls apart. My mother…Aaah…If I could find those hills again, I would be gone, too."

"Hills…" Laal mused. "No. My village was rocky and dry. There was a cliff too, I think. Not very high."

Sunshine thought hard, sitting and staring into her bowl. She dug around in the recesses of her mind for a long while before adding: "There was a lot of dust in my last few years. It had always been hot in summer, but for some reason it got worse and worse. At times, it was so dry it was choking. My mother wanted to leave, but father refused. He told her to be patient: change would come. Then the rains would come and the grasses would grow. And the herds would come back to graze. My brothers used to hunt them."

At the other end of the table, Li-Li had fallen silent. Sunshine had heard her descriptions of her home many times before, the stories of her sisters and her cats and the sloping forests they used to run through. No doubt she was mulling through those precious memories, and considering if she could escape back to that place. She stirred at length.

"Oh. I m-miss m-my sisters."

*

After dinner, they played cards and drank well into the night. Crim won most rounds, of course, but taught Li-Li a few tricks in the process while Yuki watched on. For a few brief hours, things took on the visage of normalcy, and in some moments Sunshine even forgot their troubles. Forgot the demons roaming their halls, Mentor's madness, the sense of encroaching doom. She even tried to convince herself that Princess was out there somewhere, causing trouble in the Market maybe, or wandering the Mountainside with her friends.

They had never quite managed to wash the blood out of Crim's bed, and the scent of death still hung heavy and black in the room. Sunshine was glad she had decided to stay in the Tower—Laal had told her about Princess, of course, but she did not need to see it. As the night wore on Li-Li and Yuki slipped behind their curtain at the end of the parlour, Li-Li granting Crim a quick glimpse of their old futons, and their belongings packed into bags and trunks around them. Yawning, the two younglings crawled under the covers, cuddled together and soon fell asleep, leaving their elders to share a few stilted words.

True to her word, Crim left eventually. Sunshine and Laal tried once more to dissuade her; offered her a futon by the younglings, and even a place in their own bed, both of which she refused. Sunshine fancied she eyed the door to her own chamber as she did so. Had the reek taken up the whole apartment? Or was she questioning her decision?

"I'll come to you in the morning," Laal said heavily. "Bring you some breakfast. And here—some of the things that were in your wardrobe. I have washed them, so they shouldn't smell of…of…"

Death.

Sunshine placed a hand on Crim's shoulder. As one they forced a thin smile.

"Will I be able to see it from the Tower?"

"Yes," replied Sunshine. "It orbits the Mountain. And you should be careful; there are patrols. Not just those things, but Sidhe who are loyal to them as well. Don't let them see you."

301

"Right." Crim hugged the blanket to her chest. "Whisper, Gibber…do they know I am here?"

"We hadn't a chance to tell them," Laal explained. "Or Smith. No-one knows."

"I would like to see them before…um…"

"We'll pass on the message," Sunshine promised. "Just stay away from the inner halls."

"Yeah." Shuffling her feet, Crim was now unmistakably reluctant to leave. Sunshine's heart lifted, but she pushed it back down. It was no use getting her hopes up.

"I can walk you to the Narrow Stair, if you wish," she offered.

Crim shook her head. "I shouldn't be seen with you. Of course I don't plan on being seen at all. But at least if I'm alone you can feign ignorance. No…I…I should go."

She kissed and hugged each of them, and even pressed her lips gently to the foreheads of the two sleepers, patting Li-Li's head fondly. Laal tried to reach for her again as she passed, but Crim kept her eyes forward as she strode out the door.

*

"How do we go back?" Sunshine asked, burying her head in her hands. "I feel like everything is just slipping away from us, never to return."

Laal, brushing her hair, paused, resting the comb on her shoulder. Sunshine felt it tap tap tap. "We don't. There's no going back."

"I can't lose Crim. Not again. And especially not right after…"

"After Princess?"

She sighed. Laal finished combing and began to massage oil into her coils. Sunshine rested her head back against her breast. "Is there any way to convince her?"

"There are a million ways," replied Laal. "None of which I think will work."

"Do you have the stones?"

"Isme and Viper should have them ready in a day. Enough time for us to imbue and set them," Laal explained. "Yuki and Li-Li can help now, too."

"You think they can handle it?" Sunshine's mind drifted back to Li-Li's swoon so many months ago when they had last tried to imbue some Espers.

"We'll give them some of our blood this time. *Before* they do it. That should get them through one. We can supervise them, of course."

"Do you think, maybe, when she sees them she'll—"

"No. Don't do that. Don't get your hopes up."

XLI

She had forgotten how high the Eyrie was. Forgotten the cold sting of its stairs under her soles and the wind whistling through gaps in the masonry. Even with her lantern, lit by Sunshine, it was dark and eerie. Did the memory of the Patriarch still live here? She shuddered. Sidhe spectres were far more powerful than mortal ones, though far less common. Some of them could speak and manipulate their environment almost as well as their fully-aware counterparts. When they were angry, they were difficult to subdue.

The door was ajar when she finally reached it, pressing her palm to the splintering wood, it swung heavily open. Inside, a lazy fire flooded everything in red light. To her left a large, buckled four-poster bed sat unmade and unused; Crim had made a nest for herself out of blankets and cushions in the corner, where she lounged with a book on her knees. She looked up as Li-Li entered and grinned.

"Little Mouse."

A flush rose to her cheeks. What anger she had felt upon seeing her mistress had long since fled. Now Li-Li was full of a confusion of joy, sorrow and shame. Hindered by this, she lingered by the bedpost.

"Come on. Let me see you." Her mistress reached out her arms—uncharacteristically warm and welcoming. Li-Li knew she was trying very hard to be affectionate—knew Crim was probably just trying to make the most of these moments together, but instead of reciprocating she edged over and sat on the floor. She did not wish to be held just now. Crim only smiled, unphased by the slight. "You've grown."

Li-Li tilted her head. "I-it's only b-b-been a fuh...few months."

"Yes, but you're different now. I see it in the way you move. You've found your strength; some of it, at least."

She eyed her mistress suspiciously. Was this really the same Crim that had left them? Had she also somehow been compromised by mind-controlling demons, like Mentor? She was different—there was no denying that. Even the way she looked had changed: her face seemed softer, rounder, more like a human's while still maintaining its ethereal glow. Her eyes, still that rich emerald green, were deeper. And her skin—where it was not dotted in tiny freckles it was pockmarked and dented with scars both deep and shallow, the most striking of which took up most of the right side of her face, neck and arm, like she had been clawed and chewed by some ravenous beast. She seemed happier and sadder all at the same time.

"Where di-did you go?" Li-Li asked. Laal had told her, naturally, but she wanted to hear about it from Crim. She had told them over dinner the previous night, but Li-Li wished to hear it again.

"Home. That is; the place I was born."

"W-was it eh-everything you wanted?"

"No. Not at all. Everything I knew or loved is gone. But…"

"B-b-but you s-stayed? You *wh-w-want* to stay there?" She could not keep the frustration from her voice. Nor the accusation.

"It's hard to explain, but it just feels *right*. That place. Like it's where my soul resides."

Crim had never spoken of souls before, or any sense of belonging for that matter. Li-Li studied her again. Her mistress looked and sounded the same in tone and shape, even if parts of her had altered, and she could not sense anything off about her. Could she really have evolved so much in such a short time?

"D-do you think I-I could, um…I m-mi-might e-e-e-ever…?" Li-Li pursed her lips and gave up.

"I think we all should," said Crim, inferring the rest with a comforting grin. "Go. Out into the mortal world away from this prison. Rediscover ourselves and find some purpose. Or at least some happiness."

"Betray th-th-the g-gods?"

"Yes."

Li-Li looked into the fire. Was there still a home out there for her? From a locked box in her mind, she drew out images of her family—her sisters darting around the village, her mother mending the walls of their house, her father splitting wood, one of the cats trying in vain to herd her kittens. The hills and the shady forest paths and the stone idol sitting in his shrine.

Fear.

Pain.

Death.

She gasped, nightmare fluttering away as Crim dragged her into her arms. She was usually so good at stopping before that part. Usually shooed it away.

"They did that to you, remember," Crim whispered. "The gods stole everything from you. You owe them nothing."

"Unh," she whimpered. Now that Crim was holding her, Li-Li felt herself melting into her. She was so warm. So very, very warm.

"Li-Li. Tell me what happened here. What are those things? What happened to Mentor and the others? Why is the Temple defaced?"

"I th-thought—"

"Yes, Laal and Sunny told me plenty. But I want you to tell me now. Tell me what you've seen and what you know."

Li-Li took a deep breath, willed her tongue to obey, and told Crim the whole story, from Mentor leaving to her abrupt return to the Visitors and their demands. She brushed over the topic of Princess; those memories were still too painful to relive, the more she spoke the more her words seemed to flow, until her lips and thoughts began to work together. She found herself saying things she had not admitted to Sunshine, Laal or even Yuki. Especially not Yuki—they would only worry.

"When the swoons came, did you see anything?"

"N-no. I'm n-n-not like Mother or the P-Patriarch. Nothing I suh…see makes sense."

Crim frowned. "Tell me."

She chewed her lip. "I g-get senses m-m-more than anything. Gut f-f-feelings."

"Fine. What's your gut telling you?"

Li-Li paused. Thought about it. Crim showed no signs of hurrying her, so she ventured inward under her patient gaze.

"I-it's all ruh-wrong. They…those th-things are wrong."

"The Visitors?"

Nod.

"I wonder how we can get rid of them." Crim stood and went to the window. A few shards of glass cracked under her feet, but could not pierce her skin, rather, her bare soles ground them to white dust. The moon was just coming out, silver and full. The ship hung on the other side of the Mountain, but part of its hull could just about be seen peering around the upper slopes. "Something tells me asking politely will not move these guests."

An idea struck Li-Li at once, and she leapt up. "Bart. H-he knows things. Th-things that we d-don't! M-maybe he ca-can help. Maybe he ha-h-has some idea of what they a-a-are, h-how to make them guh-go."

"Correct," Crim responded. "I would like to see my old friend before I leave. Whisper and Gibber too. Smith, Hammer...I...I know I shouldn't, and I won't try, but just a glimpse would be nice."

"You w-w-won't come with muh-me?"

"No. Much as it pains me. I can't risk being discovered."

"I d-d-don't know. I've n-not been out of the ap-apartment before today, and the L-Library is in the h-h-heart of the Mountain. And I don't n-know how to explain all th-this to Bart—"

"Does he not know about them? About what's going on here?"

"H-he doesn't leave the li-library, and th-they n-n-never go-go in. I expect he's h-heard some of it bu-but probably not all."

Crim poked at some of the stained glass spikes still clinging to the steel framework of the window. "Then tell him. Tell him everything. Once he understands I'm sure he'll have some answers for you. But be discreet about it. We don't want to put him in danger. Or ourselves for that matter."

"R-right." She made to leave.

"Li-Li?"

"Hm?"

"Take Yuki with you," Crim ordered. "Call them. Meet them in the Temple before you go anywhere."

"Right!"

"Li-Li?"

"Huh?"

"Could you...do my paints?"

She laughed, touching the satchel at her hip. The one heavy with pots and brushes and cloths. She had thought Crim had only asked to be painted as an excuse to talk to her, once she saw her, she had forgotten all about it. "Y-you're serious?"

"Yes. Please."

Her heart felt heavy all at once. Crim hated being painted, or *had* at least. Was this part of her goodbye? Li-Li swallowed a sudden lump in her throat. "Sure. Um…C-could you sit by th-the f-f-fire?"

*

Crim sat, and was still the whole time, their chatter ebbed into awkward silence as Li-Li mixed her paints. Moving slowly, careful to find the exact shades of blue and red and grey-white. She knew her mistress' usual patterns well, but this time, armed with a brush, she worked to refine them; first masking her whole face in flat, corpselike grey, then painting her lips and eyelids jet black. Two red streaks went under each eye, and one above, with her hairline traced in deepest blue that came to a point at the centre of her forehead, followed by three dots to the tip of her nose. From her mouth poured the remainder of red like a stream of blood ending bluntly between her collarbones. Her neck became stark white— whiter even than her usual complexion, with two thin blue lines extending around from the edge of her jaw to the back of her neck. Li-Li, best as she could, tried to refine the whole visage, and as she scooted back to examine her work she had to admit she had done a fine job—still, even without the clumsy, finger-smudged paint, Crim looked unnerving and savage. Even as she smiled. Those straight white teeth, sharp even for a Sidhe, with wicked curved canines underneath the flashing green of her eyes.

When she was done, Li-Li fetched a cracked hand-mirror from the writing table and handed it to her mistress. Crim eyed herself thoughtfully, fingers tracing the faint lines of a claw mark on her cheek. At length she asked: "Will it last?"

"I um…I-it could last a f-f-few d-days probably."

Crim tossed the mirror onto her nest of blankets. "Good enough. I need to meet Laal later. Something urgent, she said. Until then I want to have a look around."

"Crim!" Li-Li blurted, then clapped a hand to her mouth, blushing. She had never called her by name before.

Her mistress' face lit up to her surprise, and Crim pushed her hand away. "Go on, Little Mouse. It's high time we spoke as friends."

Her heart fluttered. "Y-y-you sh-shouldn't—um—you pr-promised Laal and Sunshine th-that you wo-w-wouldn't—"

"That I wouldn't be seen. And I won't," Crim stated. "There are paths all around the Mountain, Li-Li. Tunnels running like roots behind the walls and under the floors. After this is done, you should explore them for yourself."

"I d-don't think—"

Her mistress took her hand and squeezed it between hers. Li-Li, suddenly warm, looked aside. "I'll be fine. Just make sure you talk to Bart. And make sure *you're* not drawing attention to yourself, Li-Li."

Something about the warmth of her hands and voice, the softness in her face, overcame Li-Li's senses, and for an instant she forgot herself, bent her head down and pressed he lips to Crim's cheek. Her mistress started, and when Li-Li moved back she found only shock in those bright eyes. She quailed, yanking her hand away, and was gone before Crim could speak.

*

Bart was poking at the fire when they entered. He sensed her, and Li-Li felt the gentle hum of his greeting in her head as she sat down. Using tongs the size of her entire body he moved two more logs into the flames, then turned with robes rustling over the dusty floor.

"You have been absent, Little Mouse."

"And me," Yuki added.

"Yes and you. I hope you've been keeping yourself out of trouble."

"Mostly."

"I expected you would be maintaining your mistress' collection. And her duties."

"Y-yes," she admitted. "I'm sorry, Bart th-there w-w-was a lot—"

"Absent a long time, and not just you. The Library has been very empty as of late. And even the ones that do enter are subdued," he rambled on, picking up a stack of books off a side table and lumbering slowly down an aisle. Li-Li jumped down of the sofa and trotted after him. "I thought you had gone the same way as Crim. Thought you had left us. Only when the rest started filtering out did I understand that something was amiss. But I am tethered to this place, and cannot go far beyond the threshold, and no-one will speak much about it. So I have been an anxious wreck for many weeks, worried about all of you. Then I felt…I felt…"

Li-Li, hearing the catch in his voice, pressed: "You know about P-Princess?"

A sharp snort. He did not look at her, but busied himself with finding homes for the books under his arm. "Your little friend confirmed it, of course."

"Yuki?" She tilted her head, puzzled. Yuki never seemed to enjoy their time in the Library. She tilted her head at them. They shrugged.

I wish Princess were here.

"Yes. They did not like her much, did they?"

"N-no."

"I did," Yuki interjected, turning red. "I mean I didn't *hate* her. She was a handful. But I miss her now."

"Strange, how someone's passing—even someone one is not fond of—can paint things in a different light."

"Huh?" What else had Yuki been saying to him? Li-Li got the distinct impression these two had seen each other more often and more recently than she had. What did they have to talk about?

"Oh, but never mind that." Bart faced her finally, though when he smiled his eyes remained sad. "I am delighted that Crim is well."

Li-Li snapped her jaw closed, suddenly aware that it had fallen open. "H-how d-d-did…?"

Bart winked. He always seemed to just *know* things. No wonder Crim trusted him so much. Was he already aware of their guests? Li-Li suddenly suspected he knew much more than what they had told them. Probably far more than any of them did about anything.

He bent down, the red-brown mahogany of his eyes warm and friendly as ever, yet somehow also steely. "Tell me, Little Mouse. Say what you came to say and ask what you need to ask. Only do it quietly. The books can only muffle so much."

Li-Li scooted forward, feeling safer in the shadow of Bart's hunched form. He smelled like the books; old and musty, the end of his plaited beard tipping her head as she told him all about their Guests. About what had happened in the Tower and with Princess. Finally, she told him about Crim.

310

A deep rumble in his chest met the end of her story. Something between a growl and a sigh. He hunkered down even lower, joints creaking and talismans clinking.

"These creatures," he whispered. "Tell me about them again. Do not rush. Say it all."

She began again, only this time from when Mentor left as this seemed the most appropriate place. Bart's fingers were calloused, tickling with coarse hairs and scratching with short nails as they pressed to her temple. There was a slight pressure in her head accompanied by pulsing, like someone was rummaging around pushing things aside in search of answers.

"B-but Mentor wasn't r-r-right. We could see it; L-Laal better tha-than the rest of us. Wh-wh-when she looked over I-I—"

"Stop." His word firm, gentle and final. Bart stepped away; his hands heavy on her shoulders. "I should have paid more attention, Child. To all of you. I've spent so much time in this Library I forget there is a world outside. I am sorry."

Li-Li blinked up at him. "Bart?"

"These Visitors, Little Mouse. Nothing good will come of them. In eons past my people met them, and welcomed them into our homes as friends—just like the Sidhe have done here. And now…now…well…"

"N-now what?"

"I believe I am the only one left," he managed, grimacing. "I trusted them. More than others I knew. Far too much. When they began to act suspiciously, I excused them. They do it little by little you see; eating away like a slow cancer. They get inside people's heads and—well, before I knew it we were their friends, then their servants, then cannon fodder in their wars, their minions, cutting down others who did wish to associate with them, then when we began to question things—to defy them—that's when the culling started. A few of us managed to escape, but they hunted us to the ends of the galaxy."

"Lykourgos f-found y-you."

"Yes. On a rocky moon orbiting a desolate star. Feeding off moss and rodents and cowering in the shadows at any sound. He found me and brought me here. And here I have remained safely for four thousand of your years."

"Your people?"

Bart shook his head sadly. "I stopped asking eventually. When I realised I was clinging on to false hope."

Li-Li took Bart's hand—or, rather, his gnarled old finger—and squeezed. She thought about saying sorry, or some other words of comfort, but none of them seemed enough. She did not have more than a few seconds to hold him before Bart stood, and with a roar like a maddened beast stamped his hooves.

"But we must not let them win!" He thundered. "Not again! I cannot let them take another family from me!"

Frightened by the noise, she fell back against the shelves, and when he reached for her, backed away. When he saw this, just as quickly as it had started, the madness left him, and Bart's face softened. He brushed a knuckle against her cheek. Li-Li squeaked: "B-B-Bart?"

"It's nothing, Little Mouse," he said gently, moving past her and back to tend the fire. "Think not of it."

"B-but…you suh-said…"

"Think not of it, Child." Picking up the poker, he turned some coals near the back of the hearth. "It has been a long while since the pain of it all has struck me so. That is all."

"I'm sorry."

A laugh. "No. Do not be sorry. It was not you that caused it."

"What a-are you g-g-going to do?"

"I am going to put some more coals down here," He responded casually. "And then I am going to make some lunch. Would you like some?"

"N-no th-thank you." Li-Li eyed him suspiciously. Yuki, now at the edge of her seat, jerked their head towards the door. "And after that?"

Bart smiled. "You should stay a while in the Library. Sit in Crim's old office. Peruse the shelves like you used to. It has been so long since you were here."

Sensing she would get no more answers from the old minotaur, Li-Li looked into the flames and sighed. "I s-suppose I'll have a luh-look around."

*

Yuki wanted to leave, but Li-Li took Bart's suggestion and led them to Crim's office. It had been left more or less untouched since she left, though some efforts had been made to tidy her mess. Li-Li sat at the desk, and Yuki on the battered couch.

"Did h-h-he tell you a-anything?" She asked. "Did you suh-see any of hi-his int-t-tentions?"

They hesitated. "I…um…not exactly?"

"Wh-what does that m-m-mean?"

Poking at a hole in the seat, they thought. "He's definitely going to do something about them. I just can't tell what."

"I knew it." She stood.

"Don't!"

"What?"

"This is important to him, Li-Li," Yuki explained. "Those things killed his people. He doesn't want us to intervene."

"If he d-di-dies?"

"I got the impression he has accepted that."

Could she really do it? Lose Bart so soon after Princess. "But he's our friend."

"That's exactly why I think we should respect it."

Much as it pained her, Li-Li understood. She huffed in resignation and began to sort through some scrolls in the open drawer by her elbow. "I wi-w-wish we could g-go back. B-before a-all of this."

Messing their already messed hair, Yuki followed her lead and started adjusting the pile next to them on the couch. Shakily, they added: "Yeah. Me too."

XLII

She had counted a dozen so far—a dozen scuttling, chirping creatures roaming the passages and halls of the Mountain. In spite of her promises to Laal and Li-Li, she had found herself wandering ever inward, using the secret tunnels to find herself behind a statue in the Market, in the walls of the Hall, under the floor of the Arena, stepping out onto the lowest veranda encompassing the Temple. From these vantage points, she was able to stalk her subjects unnoticed—both Visitor and Sidhe alike.

It seemed the Reavers had fallen into their favour, along with a host of others. She found Hyeong and one of his friends escorting a couple of the creatures around the Gardens. Nashoba also stood to one side in the Market, overseeing as his wards mauled some rugs. He looked considerably less pleased by his duties, but still stood to challenge anyone who ventured too near, grey-gold eyes flashing.

*

The latch was stiff; fused together with rust and dirt. Crim pulled her sleeve down over her fingers and wiggled it until it moved more easily. The fabric helped to muffle the scraping of both parts, and she made sure to hold the hatch shut as she listened for people on the other side. It moved outwards and upwards, brushing against something soft—a tapestry, by the feel of it. She inched it open, ready to retreat at any sign of movement. Once there was enough space to peek under, she did so; found herself looking at a narrow, tiled walkway walled on one side and punctuated by slim arches on the other, each of which seemed to lead out onto a small balcony.

She knew this place. It was just above the Forum and seldom used now that Princess and her friends were no more. Crim crawled out of the cramped tunnel and stretched as she stood, her joints cracking. It was almost as dark as the unused passages up here, but still she stayed to one side of the nearest opening, leaning against the sculpted pillar as she considered the crowd below. There was not many of them; five or six small groups seated here and there on the broad benches, mostly ignoring one another but occasionally calling out to an acquaintance in another circle. The nearest cluster seemed to be making jewellery—she recognised two of them from her time in the Menagerie. They had been friendly with Whisper and Gibber, so she wondered if perhaps they could get a message to them. Were they trustworthy? Could she even trust the *twins* at this stage?

Lowering herself onto her rear, she scooted out towards the railing and pulled her hood down over her face. Anyone who looked hard enough would recognise her, but she would not be long. Focusing on the nearest familiar face, Crim send a gentle nudge of greeting. The other Sidhe sat up, looking around.

Eyes down. She urged. *I do not wish to be seen.*

The girl gave a slight nod and lowered her gaze, pretending to concentrate on threading beads.

Do you know me?
No.
Good. I need to speak to Whisper. Can you deliver a message?
Who are you?
That's none of your concern. Will you give her my message or no?

The girl's eyes darted from side to side. Crim knew she had located her and was suppressing the urge to look up. She slid back into the shadows, ready to break off and retreat to her hiding place.

Right. I mean: yes. I'll help.
Tell her: "The Cardinal has gone to roost."

Confusion. *What?*

I cannot explain. She will know what you mean.

Who? The girls head jerked. Crim was faster. She was already clambering back through the hatch, tugging the tapestry into place and welding the catch closed. No-one would follow her this way.

*

She wandered a while longer, allowing the abandoned tunnels to lead her this way and that, up and down and all around the spaces between places in the Mountain. At last, when she was finally beginning to feel tired and hungry, she came across a metal door that was cold to the touch. The temperature had been dropping steadily up to this discovery, and the air was thin. Crim suspected she had passed the snow line, and was proven right when, after a few moments of heating from the inside, she unbolted the door and shouldered it open, sending a whole heap of snow tumbling down a steady slope. Kicking some more drifts apart, she left the door open and stomped out to where what might once have been a path turned sharply left, descending in a slender shelf to a wide-open space that ended abruptly in cliffs on all sides. In the centre of this space lay the Tarn; a circular, ice-covered lake she had hiked up to only once before. She laughed to herself, realising that Sunshine of all people had shown her the hard way up to it, and then laughed again when she remembered how ungraceful she had been on the ice.

Stumbling slightly where the snow gave way, Crim edged along the path, hopping down a sudden drop that was either a ledge or steep stairs, and found herself immediately knee-deep in the cold stuff once she struck level ground. She also shoved her sleeve-wrapped hands into it, right past the elbows, giggling childishly. She liked snow. Liked the pristine white and the soft crunch of it. Liked the stillness and the silence of it. Even the cold, sharp and biting, was somehow pleasant, though she wished she had brought gloves and a scarf. Sidhe do not suffer in the heat or cold quite so much as mortals, but they *do* feel it. Ignoring the numbing pain, Crim began to pick up whole handfuls as she went, using her heat to make it melt through her fingers, and even tried to make a little snow figure, as she had seen children doing in books (she had very little memory of snow from when she had lived, and supposed it must have been rare). The figure was small and lop-sided, and his head fell off as she backed away to admire her efforts. Leaving him decapitated, she edged out onto the lake.

Sunshine had wanted to skate. That day, she had come back from the market with the notion that she would enjoy it, having listened to Iluak romance about playing with his brothers on frozen shores. Full of excitement, she had told Crim and Laal to bundle up and follow her on a trek towards the top of the Mountain. Laal, having more sense than the two of them, had given up after just a few minutes of shivering and returned home, but Sunshine had been determined…right until the second she fell and could not get up without Crim's help.

Smiling to herself, Crim carefully shuffled her feet, letting that little bit of momentum build into a slow glide that carried her into the middle of the glassy surface. She tried to lift one foot, and immediately found herself tilting forward, other leg slipping out from under her. When she tried to plant her foot again, it skidded off to the other side and she only just managed to turn as she fell so that she landed on her back rather than her face. Still, she slid further, laughing out loud. Unlike Sunshine, she simply let herself drift to a halt, splaying her limbs out and sighing up at the stars. The Sun was retreating under her little world now, gone to sleep in the jagged underbelly of their microcosm. The Moon had not yet awoken, so all that was left in the pink-and-purple sky were the stars, stars that glistened in technicolour or twinkled in white, that clustered in galaxies or drifted alone, stars that—

Were interrupted by the hulking bulk of the orbiting Ship.

Crim grumbled, scowling up at it. A reminder that she had no time to waste playing in the snow. She had to get back to the Eyrie and hope Whisper had gotten her message.

A short tunnel led away from the ice-covered tarn and out onto another narrow path hemming the snow-clad slopes, this one slightly more sheltered but also precarious. Crim huffed and puffed as she kicked and stomped her way through the cold—not necessary, as Sidhe have no need to breathe, but it helped to vent some of her frustrations. All the while she felt the Ship behind her; imagined scores of eyes staring down at her, the *click click click* of a thousand voices. She picked up her pace, wishing above all else to get away from it. Luckily, the way from the Tarn to the Eyrie was not very long, and she soon found herself looking at the broken ramparts and desolate buildings within the Keep sitting just below her, toeing at the edge of the path in search of a way down. Surely it had to branch off somewhere?

The answer was no. The path did not branch off. She had made it almost to the other end of the walls before she stubbornly decided to try her luck where it did not seem so steep. Sliding, jumping, tumbling in a series of missteps that would have easily killed a mortal—especially the ten-meter drop onto the circling wall—she reached the centre of the Keep in a fraction of the time it would have taken to walk around, and with a dozen new scratches and bruises.

*

Someone was here. Most definitely here. She felt them the second her foot struck the lowest stair. Froze. Reached out, expecting Whisper to greet her. When no response came Crim hesitated, wondering who could have found her here—perhaps those eyes watching from on high had not been imagined. Suppose some of them were now waiting for her? She shuddered. Or some of the Reavers, sent by their new masters to retrieve her? She should never have left this tower. Should never have tried to contact Whisper. Now she had put them all in danger.

She stopped trembling, allowing a familiar heat to expand in her belly. Her anger spurred her forward, tramping up the stairs loudly. She would fight them, whoever they were. Better to die fighting than to bow to those beasts.

"You took your time."

Sidhe are not prone to cardiac arrest; their hearts do not beat. As mentioned before, however, their bodies have a hard time giving up old habits, with result under certain circumstances hearts, lungs, stomachs, any organ still in the body, would react as though it were still expected to do its duty. When a voice rose up to greet Crim from the dark recesses of the Patriarch's chamber, she was certain she would expire from fright, and even clutched her chest, tottering back against the wall.

"Wh-who's there?" She gasped.

"It's been a while, Crim." Familiar yet unknown, the voice had a mocking tone to it.

Remembering to be angry, she summoned her fire, and sending it out to the hearth and the scattered handful of lamps, threw the room into a warm glow. Gibber, who was seated at the writing desk, blinked in surprise. Gibber—and yet not Gibber—her eyes cunning, her expression knowing, her smile devious.

"Who are you?" Crim demanded again, barring her teeth at the intruder.

Gibber scoffed. "Do we need to go through this *every* time?"

"What?"

"Oh…but I suppose this is the second time. Or is it the first?" Gibber tugged at her robes. "Perhaps the first like this?"

Crim snarled. "Explain yourself! Who are you and what have you done to her!"

"Her? Ah! This?" Gibber touched her face, then seemed to discover her hair and began raking her fingers through it thoughtfully. "She's in no danger, Crim. I'm only borrowing her for a while. I needed to talk to you."

She tilted her head, squinting at the stranger in her friend's body, pushing inward and finding an impenetrable wall blocking her. She bounced off it and disassociated; separated from reality. It was like she was both here in the room, and not there, and everywhere all at once. Gagging, Crim shoved herself back into her own head, filled every micron of her body right down to her feet planted firmly on the hard wood below.

This was *not* Gibber. Not for the moment, anyhow.

"It's you, isn't it?" She finally realised. "From before? You showed me what I needed to see. You helped me escape!"

"I gave you the motivation, nothing more," Gibber replied.

"What are you?"

"You know that."

She did. She had sensed it that other evening, looking up into the dragon's maws she was made acutely aware of her immortality.

"So it's true? You're the dragon? I'm your Vessel…you're my…" Crim patted herself down, suddenly frantic. "But how—how are you in Gibber? Are you not in me anymore? How am I still here if you're not—"

"Don't worry, I'm still holding you together. And I'm still with you. I can't leave. Once bonded, a god cannot leave their Vessel unless it perishes."

"But how can you be both *here* and *there!"*

*"*I am a god, Crim. I can be in many places at once."

"Oh. Ah!" Crim took a deep breath, still pressing her palms against her torso, measuring its firmness. "Yes, that makes sense."

"I tried to talk to you before, you know. Tried to explain. But trying to create my own form took more out of me than I expected. I could not even hold my shape, never mind speak," Gibber explained.

"Don't gods make things all the time?"

"Some of us are better at it than others. And we actually make far less than you would assume—more like we mould what's already there. We're not the Creator."

"Creator?"

"I can't explain, and you would not understand anyway."

"Hmph."

"Besides, I did not come to tell you the meaning of life. I came to tell you what to do."

"Typical."

Gibber looked affronted at first, but then chortled. "Humour. Interesting."

"I hope this is about that thing in the sky."

The smirk melted from Gibber's face. Instead, she looked sad. Terribly, terribly sad. "I came as soon as I could, or as soon as I could guess—time is hard for us to measure—but once I saw that thing floating over the Mountain, I knew I should have come sooner. You need to get rid of them, Crim."

"Well, I know *that*. But it's not so easy. We need to think of a way to convince—"

"No. No convincing." Gibber stood up; fists balled. "Listen to me Crim: I have lived a hundred lifetimes. A hundred different versions of this. I have seen that thing arrive and I have seen what it will do. Seen what those beings will do in the name of their God—whole civilisations wiped out in the blink of an eye, or broken down and enslaved in His name. They are *righteous*, they are *ruthless* and they are *bloodthirsty*. It is only a matter of time before they turn on the Sidhe—before they destroy this Mountain and everyone in it. All this I have seen."

As she spoke, an onslaught of images and sounds struck Crim—flashes, snippets of what her goddess had witnessed. Eons and eons worth of suffering; people she knew, people she did not yet know, people she would never know, all of them miserable. The lucky ones she saw dying; the unlucky she saw in chains. She reeled, stumbling over to the heap of blankets just in time to collapse completely, cold sweat standing in beaded drops all over her body. The fire dimmed. Some of the lamps went out.

Bringing herself to hands and knees, she convulsed, and for the first time she could remember brought up half of the contents of her stomach onto the floor. Not a pleasant experience. No wonder mortals tried so very hard to avoid falling ill. She wiped at her nose, which burned unpleasantly, and spat the last few mouthfuls of acrid bile out before speaking.

"They have done all this?"

"Have done, will do, may do. Are currently doing," Gibber affirmed.

Crim burped thickly. Leaned back against the pleasant cold of the stone wall. "There are more of them? Out there?"

"Many more. I cannot be sure of their numbers, but there are dozens of other ships."

"Do they have no home of their own? Why do they do this?"

A shrug. "I have searched. Probed their minds. They are different. I cannot tell how, but I am unable to read them as well as others of your kind. I only feel their malice, and witness their atrocities."

"But you know how to stop them?"

"No. I do not. We have tried, you and I. Dozens of times. None of them successful." Gibber hesitated, considering her, then added: "They will take the Mountain, that much is certain."

"What?"

"Beyond that, the story always changes. But the Mountain will be theirs sooner or later."

"And the Sidhe?"

"That depends on what you do next."

"What *I* do next?"

Gibber approached, extending her hand to help Crim up. "Your people are vulnerable, Crim. Some do not sense the danger; some are too afraid to do anything about it. Others are already enslaved. But they *can* still be roused. Can still be saved. And *you* know what to do."

"I do?" Crim frowned, waiting for Gibber to tell her, feigning ignorance. But her goddess was right—she already had an idea. Had been sitting on it for days, since Laal had come to her in that pub, since she had seen the fear in her eyes and felt the hopelessness in her soul. She had spent the time returning and her short stay trying to ignore it in truth. Part of her knew it was the only way to get rid of their Guests. Another part wished the solution was not so clear. "No…I don't want to do that—"

"You don't have a *choice*, Child. It's you or them," Gibber spat. "It's not a matter of what you *want* to do, but what you *will do.* There is no choice."

"I can't. It's too much. Maybe we can—"

"*No.* There's no negotiating with these creatures, Crim. You have seen what they can do. There is no choice."

Her head filled with cries. Screams. Bodies burning. People being hacked apart. Whole cities levelled. She retched again. "I can't…"

"What about Sunshine? And Laal? You'll let them die?"

"I-I…"

"Yuki?"

"I can't—"

"And Li-Li?"

Her heart twisted. *No. Not Li-Li. Sweet Li-Li.* "No."

"Do not get angry at me, Child. I am not the one threatening them."

Crim was trembling now. Rage burning red-hot through her, a crimson glow casting tall shadows against the corner. Smoke and fire and seething heat emanating from her in all directions. Through all her eyes glowed a fierce and vivid green, and she gnashed her pointed teeth. With a false calm, she uttered: "They must be destroyed."

Gibber nodded grimly. "That is the only way. The *only way,* do you hear me?"

"The only way."

XLIII

"How are the younglings?" Asked Whisper, whacking one of the floor mats with a stick and sending puffs of dust floating up to the rafters. They had strung lines back and forth across the roof of the barn, and used these to hang out blankets, clothes, anything that needed drying for the few refugees now living in the cramped den under the floorboards. Most of them were victims of the Ifram's brutal punishments, nursing injuries ranging from a few cuts and bruises to missing limbs. Whisper never turned anyone away, and they all did their part to nurse the wounded back to full strength.

Two had already died down there; both younglings that neither of them had known very well. One boy had come in barely hanging on, a charred hole in his chest where one of those accursed weapons had struck him. None of them knew what to do with such injuries—they were deep, cauterised by the heat of the beam, and when someone was hit in the chest as that poor boy had been, it usually obliterated their heart. Not even blood from one of the elders had helped him, and he was gone by the time they got him down the ladder. The same elder told them she had seen someone shot in the head, and they had dropped immediately, their brain completely cooked.

The other poor child Whisper had to sedate. She was carried in on a makeshift stretcher wailing, flesh torn apart by wicked gashes from head to toe. The blanket covering her so soaked in blood it had stuck to what was left of her skin. Gibber hummed to her as she gently removed it. So stunned had all of them been by the sight of so much blood that they failed to notice one crucial thing; her right leg was missing, hacked off from just above the knee. Surely those bladed forearms could not do such damage? Sunshine heard some of the others muttering such things around the deathbed, and reminded them that Tal had been shredded to pieces in front of the whole Market.

Those two they had burned, high on the cliffs near the Maw, which they could reach from the Menagerie through one of many small tunnels. They all suspected the visitors on the ship floating high above had seen them, in fact Sunshine was sure she had felt several pairs of eyes on herself that night, and several shook their fists, shouting challenges at its pristine white underbelly. Sunshine had only sat and stared into the flames, clutching a bloated skin of wine. They had to get rid of these creatures, before they were all naught but ashes. How? She tilted her head back as she drank, watching the ship surface glimmer in places she suspected were windows. How could they be rid of them.

A glint on the other side of the fire. A pair of pale eyes watching her intently. Sunshine had shivered, wondering what made Gibber seem so thoughtful. The latter grinned.

*

Whisper's face appeared in front of her. Sunshine started out of her reverie. "Huh?"

"I asked how Li-Li and Yuki are?"

"Ah. They're—" She could have lied and told Whisper they were fine. Instead she huffed. "They're scared. Laal and I are terrified *for* them. After what happened in the Minaret, we didn't want to let them out at all for a while."

Whisper nodded. "I'm not sure any of should be out lately. We haven't been out of the Menagerie in months."

"Gibber is fine with that?"

"No. But it's for her sake that we stay here. Sometimes she…um…she doesn't…you know."

Sunshine knew. If Gibber had one of her outbursts around those demons…her thoughts wandered back to that poor girl, unrecognisable with her torn up face. She shuddered. Had it really been wise to let the younglings out today?

A girl came running up, a tall lanky youngling with turquoise hair and serpent's eyes. She shook Whisper by the arm.

"Mistress!" She panted, looking startled. "Someone gave me a message for you. I don't know who, though. I never saw them. We were all just sitting in the Forum and I felt someone greet me and I turned around but I couldn't find where they were and they told me not to and—"

"*Breathe*, Aalari." Whisper patted the girl's hand. Her arm had gone quite white where her fingers pressed.

"They said um…a robin? No. Some sort of bird."

"Sparrow?"

"No."

"Finch?"

"No." Aalari rubbed her shoulder nervously, suddenly noticing Sunshine.

"Flamingo?" She offered.

"Smaller. What's a red bird, Mistress?"

"Cardinal, I suppose?"

"Yes! 'The cardinal has gone to nest'!"

"Gone to nest?" Sunshine repeated. "I thought it was *roost*."

Whisper furrowed her brow. "'The cardinal has gone to roost'? But Crim's the cardinal. That doesn't make any sense, Aalari. Crim's gone."

"Err."

"Sunshine?"

"Eh."

"Crim's gone, right?"

"She did go."

"And she's not here anymore?"

"Um."

Whispers face lit up. "She's here! She came back! Cr—" Thankfully, she caught herself and whispered: "Crim is in the Eyrie, right?"

Giving in, Sunshine nodded. "And it sounds like she needs you for something."

"I need to find Gibber. Aalari, come."

With that, she dashed out of the barn, her confused underling trailing behind. Sunshine picked the mat up from the floor where she had dropped it. She folded it neatly and draped it over the empty stable door. "She didn't come back."

*

"You said you'd be careful," Laal scolded, pouring Crim a cup of green tea.

Crim sniffed the stuff distastefully, but took a polite sip. "I was careful. No-one saw me."

"Aalari saw you," Sunshine said.

"She did not, and she doesn't know who contacted her."

"It was reckless," Laal continued.

"It was necessary."

"What did you have to say to Whisper that was so important?"

"I know she's been mobilising some people. Her and Smith have their own little factions, but they seem to be working towards the same goal. I wanted to make sure they would be on our side."

"Be on our side *when*?"

"When we do what needs to be done."

"Which is *what*, Crim?" Sunshine asked, not liking her tone.

"I'm still working out the details."

Laal clicked her tongue. "We don't *need* to do anything. At least not as far as I can see. And there's no use aggravating—"

"You haven't witnessed it. You haven't seen what will happen if we do nothing, or if we fail. It is necessary."

"And you have?"

"Yes."

Laal sat up, eyeing her. "You're sure of it?"

"Very."

Laal was not certain of Crim—the shadow in her eyes betrayed this much. Sunshine stood behind her and laid a hand on her shoulder.

She would not lead us astray.

Plump hand pressing against her skin, soft and warm. *I know. And yet…*

A knock on the door. Two short raps and three long taps. It eased open. Li-Li and Yuki entered, each with a satchel at their hip. Once the door was closed they stood there awkwardly, and Li-Li asked Crim:

"D-did Bart visit y-y-you?"

"No."

"Oh."

Yuki mussed their hair. "Did any of you see him?"

"No," responded Sunshine.

"Why?" Laal added.

"He um…he l-left the Library."

Crim stood up. "*What?*"

"What happened?"

"We t-t-told him about th-the I-Ifram…"

"He seemed to know something about them," Explained Yuki. "He said they're the ones that destroyed his kind."

Laal gasped, clapping a hand to her mouth in horror. "No!"

"Where did he go?" Crim was round the table, and had Li-Li by the shoulders before anyone could stop her. "What's he doing?"

"He…um—"

"Don't tell me he's going to challenge them."

"Um!"

Yuki's little fingers were stronger than they looked. Five of them clamped around one of Crim's arms, tearing it away from Li-Li. "We couldn't stop him."

"*Shit!*" Crim spat, kicking a small cauldron across the room.

"How long ago did he leave?" Sunshine continued the questioning.

"This afternoon."

"I meant to see him today," Muttered Crim. "I didn't have time. It took me so long to get the message to Whisper and then I…got side-tracked. If I had gone to the Library with Li-Li I could have stopped him."

"We can search for him. Reach out to him," Laal offered. "I'm sure he'll be in contact with one of us if he's—"

"Still alive?" Added Yuki.

Li-Li whimpered, hugging her bag.

"What have you two got?" Sunshine met no resistance as she lifted the leather flap. Stuffed inside were three books and at least six scrolls. "You took these from the Library?"

Crim looking closer and closer to a mental breakdown, whirled around. "You *stole* from the *Library*?"

"Borrowed," Yuki corrected. "And you'll thank us later. In these bags is all the information we could find about the Ifram. Every last morsel."

Not so far gone that she could not look impressed, Crim plucked out one scroll and carefully rolled it out onto the table. On it, in clear blue and red lines, was a cross-section of a familiar shape.

Laal tilted her head as she examined it. "Is that the ship?"

"It is!" Crim had gone from distressed to strangely excited.

"Suh…so you're n-n-not angry?" Li-Li squeaked.

Sunshine laughed, stroking her silky pink hair. "Crim is never angry at *you*, Little Mouse."

They did not hear anything about Bart that day, nor the next. Crim, previously determined to have her business done and leave them in just two days, stretched this out to three, then four, then a whole week. She still slept in the Eyrie, and spent less time with them and more time going about her own suspicious business—part of which they all agreed probably entailed searching for the old minotaur. Li-Li told them she was hunting her own food, cooking it over the fireplace in the Patriarch's bed chamber, scouring the Forest and foothills for secret ways under the Mountain.

"There's a dungeon down there," Laal pointed out. "It was covered up after the Patriarch fell and his opponents were released. Mother sealed it herself with spells."

"You don't think she opened it back up?" Sunshine imagined the horrors that lingered down there. The chains, the instruments of torture, the ghosts trapped in the walls. "The ones that are missing…you don't think…?"

"I do think." Her lover curled up against her. "I think it's getting worse and worse."

It was the evening of the eleventh day. Crim had returned for dinner, looking haggard and hopeless. In each of their hearts, they all feared the worse for Bart, but now none of them had the strength to talk about him aloud.

Nonetheless, Sunshine caught the glint in Li-Li's eyes as her mistress came through the door, and the dimming of that light when Crim shook her head for the millionth time. Crim then fell into her usual chair, watching idly as Laal put the finishing touches on their meal. The table was set, and baskets of bread and fruit had been set out, along with a vat of thin soup and two jugs of sweet wine. Sunshine had arranged some candles around all of it; some tall and slender, others short and fat, all warm and bright. Crim picked at a bunch of grapes, nibbling numbly at each in turn, in their own time each of them let out a sigh.

Li-Li turned to the door before the knock came—two heavy thumps and then footsteps retreating. No-one moved at first, then Yuki, who was closest, cautiously turned the latch. They paused, looking at first up and down the passage, then down. Li-Li let out an uneasy whine as they bent down to pick something up. They backed into the room and kicked the door closed, struggling under the weight of an enormous wooden box. Li-Li edged away, tugging at the sleeves. Sunshine felt the same unease as they approached. It only lasted a few seconds, but she felt as though time were moving at a snail's pace.

"Don't put it on the—!"

Too late. It had already been set on the table. As it was released, something apparently was triggered, and panel by panel, top to bottom the box opened, emitting at first a horrid stench, then a handful of flies, and finally Barts severed head rolled out to lie among the bowls and candles and flowers as a sort of macabre centrepiece. They all remained frozen, Laal with her hands covering her face, Yuki studying their hands like they had somehow done this, Li-Li hugging herself. Sunshine was pinned to her seat; the back of the head was to her—the ragged flesh and exposed bone of the cut that was fairly clean. She would have liked to presume he had not suffered, but one of his horns was gone, splintered off near the base. It would have taken great force to break it like that. She wondered if his face was battered, yet dared not look. Crim's expression said it all—she stared into the eyes of her murdered friend, shock steadily building into white-hot rage.

"I'll kill them," she snarled. "I'll kill them all."

XLIV

Crim left without eating. She did not return the next day, nor the day after. Yuki asked if she had disappeared back into the mortal world, but none of them thought so. They felt her still around the Mountain, and heard rumours of her from reliable sources. Li-Li thought about going to the Eyrie to visit her, but refrained. Crim need to be alone now, and had ordered none of them to follow her as she stormed out the apartment door. Laal and Sunshine both feared she would do something rash and get herself killed—just like poor Bart—but that did not seem to be the case.

Li-Li strongly suspected she was plotting away up there. She had some sort of idea for the Ifram, they all knew. Whisper was in on it, and Laal suggested Smith had been visiting the Eyrie in the evenings as well. Li-Li only wished that Crim would share with them. When the time came, would they be asked to help?

*

She whittled the hours away in the Library, Yuki usually in tow. The books they had taken were mostly useless—whole encyclopaedias and bestiaries stolen from a trusting old minotaur for nought—so they now scoured the shelves and cubbies of lesser used sections, desperate to find more information on their unwanted guests.

It was strange now without Bart; she made sure to pass by his parlour every day—his presence still lingered there, in the oversized and moth-eaten furniture, in the ash-coated hearth almost large enough for her to walk into (easily large enough for Yuki), in the tins of tea and coffee and biscuits dotted around the room. There were traces of him elsewhere, of course, but they quickly turned stale, and the Library began to feel colder and colder. There were fewer people here as with most public places under the Mountain following the Sidhe's arrival, and the ghosts gradually became more common than the living, floating from shelf to shelf, turning this way and that looking for familiar faces that no longer visited. Li-Li and Yuki greeted all of them, as Crim and Bart had both insisted.

They started each day searching the bookcases, and quickly retreated back to Crim's study. Reavers rarely entered here, and they had never seen an Ifram enter, but times were uncertain and dangerous, and neither of them liked the idea of having to explain themselves.

*

"I'm going to see Viper and Esme," Yuki announced. They remembered to put their book and notes aside as they stood, but forgot the three scrolls in their lap. These now bounced and rolled away, giving them a good chase as one ended up in the darkness under the couch. The two elders had been their only regular contacts outside of the apartment since Bart's death, and seemed to have taken it upon themselves to try and keep up his hospitality. They were poor cooks, but always left part of their meals aside for the younglings' lunch.

"If i-it's more of th-th-those meat p-p-pies—"

"Don't worry I'll dump them." They winked, causing both of them to frown. Yuki then blushed and scratched their head. "Right…I'll—um. I'm going."

Smiling to herself, Li-Li returned to her notes. Or lack thereof. She was not finding anything of any help for their predicament, much like most days. She reached over to inspect Yuki's paper, and found only a doodle of a manticore in blotted black ink. Sighing, she got up and stretched, placing the cork back into Yuki's ink bottle and wiping off their quill. Bored of this cramped, dim room, she took it upon herself to look for more material.

*

Another book hit the growing heap with an audible *whump* and a spray of thick yellow dust. With two more stacks to go, Li-Li picked out Zephyr's *Of the Species* and flipped through idly, scanning the illustrations for anything that resembled the Ifram. She had already checked this particular volume a dozen times, and couldn't tell why she expected to find more information.

Nothing. Another to her pile. She rolled a scroll out across her eclectic notes and brought her forehead down onto it, groaning loudly for good measure. Eyes protesting the sight of more words, they squeezed shut tight, one tiny muscle making her lid flutter with strain. Strange, little mortal things they held on to.

*

Rustling from the walkway above. Li-Li imagined another Sidhe might have wandered in here to drive themselves mad over journals and bestiaries in search of what was not written. Surely she and Yuki were not the only ones looking for answers? The boards creaked lazily underfoot. But why did they drag their feet so? One of the tables rattled, and three scrolls *thunked* hollowly to the floor.

"Pick th-those…" She jerked her head up in time to see the tail-end of their robe disappear behind some shelves. A scroll rolled forward just enough to stick out from under the balustrade. Already frustrated by her lack of progress, Li-Li swore one of Crim's 'big' swears. Chair screeching out from the tableside, she stormed up one of the four ladders that led to the narrow wooden catwalk. Hemmed in by slender writing desks on one side, and a long bench on the other, she almost had to turn sideways to where the reams of parchment were slowly unravelling. Gathering and wedging them into a desk drawer, she took the next set of steep stairs onto the main floor.

"Hey," she called down the aisle. "D-don't you n-n-know how to pick up—
"

Movement to her right. Li-Li spun to see the same white skirt float out of sight.

"Hey!"

Nothing at the end of the row when she got there, but a misplaced page led her down another. Further and further into the labyrinth she meandered, lured by rustlings and rumour. When a tower of tomes tumbled, she was there, but her tormentor was not. Growling half-words to herself, she carefully reassembled it, ready at this point to give up the chase.

Just two cases down, a shadow disturbed the lamplight. Li-Li focused on her task, ordering each book according to size and focusing on it. The figure edged forward to peer at her, a long, slender arm snaking along one shelf. She froze. One of *them*?

Turning startled her visitor, and a half-dozen volumes were knocked out of place as the appendage (not an arm, really) whipped bonelessly away. Letting out a dismayed cry, she took off again after it. Yuki would be better at this, would have it caught or cornered already, but she was slow and ungainly.

*

The Ifram was gone. As Li-Li zig-zagged up-and-down aisles and back-and-forth across rows all signs of it faded. She tried to reach out with her mind, but only got so far before giving herself a headache. She had scared it off. She hated connecting with them anyway, hated the sliminess and the senseless noise inside their heads.

Ahead the shelves ceased, and she strode into a space littered with chairs and couches, peppered here and there with side tables and coffee tables, illuminated by an assortment of lamps. Here she gave up her pursuit, and fell back in defeat against an old case.

*

The lamplight caught something reflective from across the way. Gold sequins lining a sheer white veil. A head peeking at her from the dim, blue-grey arms wrapped around each other apprehensively. She was half the size of her male counterparts, not even reaching to Li-Li's shoulder, and clearly far more timid. They took a moment to study one another. This creature was short, soft-looking, with rubbery limbs and smooth, shimmering skin. Her eyes were four: two large, pale blue with broad crescent pupils, and two smaller in between. The back of her head was bulbous, ovular, and undulated with each shallow breath. This balloon-like dome tapered into a stout, rounded beak that *click-clacked* in curiosity as they loitered. There was a slight pattern to her skin, Li-Li noted, and it shifted and darkened as they stood there. She wondered if this creature could camouflage herself? Is that how she had lost her? Had she been *playing* with her? Luring her away then hiding in plain sight? Everything about this little one drew a sharp contrast to her male counterparts. Soft rather than rigid. Afraid rather than vicious Cephalopodic rather than insectoid in anatomy. Frightened yet curious. Li-Li stared and she stared right back.

"Hello."

Her guest let out a high-pitched *purr* of greeting, but remained mostly behind the shelf. Li-Li backed until she found a rickety stool, where she slowly sat down

333

and placed her hands on her thighs, palms upward. Did this creature know what a smile meant? She tried it anyway.

Four smooth tentacles uncoiled, and the Ifram edged cautiously out from the safety of the books. She blinked four milky-blue eyes at Li-Li. Considering her approach. Li-Li tried patting the chair next to her. Her guest's skirt fluttered, and she caught a glimpse of another cluster of appendages coiling and uncoiling rhythmically.

"Or you can stay there, if you prefer."

Chirp. One step at a time, it moved. Carefully sliding over to her, head tilting this way and that as she studied her for any sign of danger. Li-Li remained still, relaxed, smiling.

Purrrr.

"Hello."

The Ifram's arms rippled happily against her sides, the tiny silvery pearls on her sleeves *ticking* against one another. This close, Li-Li could see that she was actually dappled in patterns of grey, blue, white and black. Her eyes—which appeared flat blue at a distance—actually had a faint turquoise hue accented by navy around elongated pupils…Li-Li could only guess that the chirping, trilling and rattling of that beak formed some sort of speech. As she touched the other's mind, she was of course unable to discern any recognisable thoughts, only a sense of intrigue, excitement and bubbling nerves. Unlike the males, she felt no foreboding, no nausea, no searing headaches at her touch. In fact, she was rather excited.

"Li-Li."

Chirp chirp?

She planted a hand on her chest, trying to project the concept with all her might. Conjured up the best image of herself she could paint. "Li-Li. My name is Li-Li."

Those four little tentacles curled and twirled, her guest letting out an animated series of whistles. Li-Li could have sworn she glowed slightly. Somehow, she had made herself understood. To her surprise, a vision of a violet sunrise flashed unbidden in her head. The Ifram was trying to tell her something as well, but she could not see it.

"I'm s-s-sorry I don't un-understand."

The light dimmed; her guest lowered her arms. *Disappointed.*

"Maybe you can show me? In one of the books."

Head tilt. *Confusion.* Li-Li jerked her chin at the shelves. The Ifram shrank slightly. *Apprehension.*

Assuming she had misunderstood, Li-Li hurried over to one of the cases and picked a hefty volume from over her head—near concussing herself in the process. She opened it in front of her guest and slowly flipped through the pages. Uncertain at first, the little Ifram was drawn in by the script, and even more so by the colourful illustrations—these she prodded and stroked curiously. Nothing seemed to catch her interest, however, so Li-Li showed her another, and another. They were now gradually making their way down the row.

Still sensing some perplexity, she elaborated: "Most of our names come from things in this world—flowers or the sky or ideas that we like," she explained, handing a book over to the Ifram (who staggered under its weight and needed three arms to hold it). "Maybe you can find something you recognise."

The visitor moved each page delicately, clicking her beak rhythmically. This volume had dozens of carefully pressed flowers and clipping fixed to its pages, and she made sure to stroke each of them one by one before moving on with a flick of her tentacle. Every now and then, she flickered with a soft blue glow, and let out a quiet whistle of delight. It seemed she liked flowers. When she came to one in particular, she flashed all of a sudden with a few sharp *click click clicks.*

L-Li leaned over. "Th-that's a snowdrop…it's a little w-wh-white flower. About this b-big."

The Ifram patted it lightly and *trilled,* blinking up at her.

"Snowdrop?"

Chirp-trilllll!

Li-Li knew it was not her true name, but wondered if it was the closest her guest could find, or simply a name picked out of necessity. However, as they spent more time together, it became apparent that she *enjoyed* being called Snowdrop. In turn, Li-Li learned that she had been dubbed something similar to

'*Pink Flower*', though she could never quite picture what that meant—only that it was said with equal excitement. And that was enough for her.

XLV

She was plotting something—something she disliked. As she glowered up at the smooth underbelly of the Ifram's ship, she once again tried to swallow the foul taste in her mouth. Gibber lingered in the corner, by the remnants of the Patriarch's bed, which she had smashed to kindling following Bart's death. Her goddess rarely spoke to her now, not since they had agreed on a course of action, but she still brought Gibber up to this accursed place, endangered her every day by passing the scurrying hordes of Ifram and their vermin Reaver guards. Crim resented her for it, but also resented herself for hesitating. The longer she waited to take action, the smaller her chance of success, this she knew, yet Gibber watched over her with all the weight of the responsibilities she did not want to accept.

"Another was executed today," her goddess, using Gibber's voice, announced.

"Just one?"

"Do you no longer care about 'just one'?"

"I care about everyone. Every single one of them."

"And yet you waste time up here. Hiding."

"Planning."

"The longer you plan, the tighter their grip becomes."

"I don't even know how to get up there."

"Then find out."

"How?"

"One of them would know."

"You expect me to just *ask*—"

"No. They would not tell. I expect you to *take* the information from them."

"What? Kidnap one? Torture it? If the others found out—"

"Then you might finally be forced to act."

She leaned on the windowsill, crisp air cooling her face. "And how do I catch it?"

"Enough 'how', Child. Only 'do'. Put your robes on. Brush your hair. Nothing gets solved like this."

*

Li-Li was in the Library as usual. Unusually, Yuki was not with her. She had been spending time alone there lately, and the time she spent grew later and later. They had asked her about it—Laal was quite worried she would get caught—but she insisted she was searching for something to help Crim, that she was close to a breakthrough. She had begged for their trust, and Crim had helped to wear Laal down enough that she would *only* allow her to travel to the Library and back, preferably with someone else to escort her. Naturally, Yuki often accompanied her, but lately they were growing weary of research, and would retire back to the apartment after a few hours.

Crim's study was empty. She peered through the dust-coated glass panel, and turned the handle to find it still locked. Curious. Had Li-Li not said she would stay in here? It was safer than the reading areas; the Ifram never entered the Library, but one could never be too careful. She knew one or two of the Reavers liked to read.

"Little Mouse?" She whispered into the shelves, senses perked for any movement, any indication that Li-Li had only stepped out to find some material. She was not in the nearby aisles, nor at any of the desks in the adjacent reading area. There was not a single residual sign of her. "Li-Li?"

Crim crept further in, entering the stuffy maze of shelves and stacks and scattered furniture, squinting through the flurries of dust that fell lazily through the air. Her mind went ahead of her, feeling the floors and the shelves and the sparse bric-a-brac for a sense of the youngling. She was nearing the furthermost wall of the Library before she picked up anything; a faint glimmer, a sparkling in the haze ahead. A misplaced scroll, held open to show a sketch of the anatomy of a Kyedhen's wing. A strand of pink hair caught between pages. A patch of lavender-coloured paint from someone's foot, right next to a rolling ladder. This Crim clambered up, onto a noisy metal balcony. A shorter set of rungs to the next level, then the next. She climbed and climbed until she was looking over most of the bookcases, and spared a thoughtful glance back to the ring of arches that surrounded Bart's parlour. Giggling from above tore her eyes away.

"Little Mouse?"

Soft hushing, like someone trying to soothe a baby. Crim gripped the rail of the next ladder and jolted as though a bolt of electricity had shot through her. Shaking this off, she ascended to find Li-Li facing her. The youngling seemed startled, nervous, and even a tad defensive. Her hands were balled at her sides, as though prepared to strike her mistress. Crim frowned.

"Am I…disturbing you?"

"I-I w-was looking for—um—fuh-for more information."

"Did you find anything?"

"N-nothing!" Li-Li glanced over her shoulder, and splayed her arms wider.

"Who's your friend?" Crim did not approach, but pointed to the white skirt peeking out from behind Li-Li's leg.

"No-one."

"Hello? Why are you hiding there?" Crim took a step forward. Li-Li stiffened.

"She's sh-sh-shy."

She had never seen the youngling act so suspiciously. Firmly, she stated: "I am only being friendly."

Crim took another step, but this time Li-Li moved as well. With a swing of her arms, she threw a gust of cold air across the balcony. Yelping in surprise, Crim found herself lifted backwards. She hit the latticed floor, tried to brace against the oncoming wind, only to roll comically back and down the hole she had just climbed through.

"*Oof!* Li-Li what the *fuck!*"

A pale face appeared above her. "Sorry! I d-didn't think it w-wuh-would be that st-strong!"

"Why would you do that in the first place!"

"I'm *sorry*! She's just *really shy*!"

"*Who!*"

Li-Li disappeared for a minute. Crim heard her whispering something to her timid friend. No voice answered her, curiously enough. She popped back into view.

"You h-have to p-p-promise no-not to react."

"React to *what?*"

"Promise first!"

"I *promise*! Now may I come up?"

"You w-won't react?"

"I won't react!"

Li-Li backed away from the ladder. "Come up."

Shakily, perhaps with a slight concussion, Crim edged back up. Li-Li was still standing protectively in front of her companion, but a smooth little arm wrapped around her waist, and four pale blue eyes peered fearfully at her mistress. Crim froze, still crouched by the ladder, remaining at eye level with the sentient cephalopod.

"What is that?" She asked measuredly.

"You said you wouldn't—"

"I am not reacting. Yet. I am asking: what is that?"

"This is Snowdrop."

"*What* is she?"

The Ifram cowered out of sight. Li-Li spread her arms and planted her feet, creating a wall between it and Crim. "She is my friend."

Her mistress slowly picked herself off the floor. "She is one of *them*!"

"She's n-not like the o-o-others."

"How so?"

"Sh-she's gentle, and k-ki-kind, and she means no h-harm."

"And how do you know this?"

"I know *her*."

Crim took a step closer. Li-Li did not back down. Crim was shorter, and could not see past her. "Introduce me, then."

"You wi-will not h-harm her!"

Realising how she must seem, Crim took a breath, quelled her rising temper, painted a smile across her face, and backed away. "I will not. Just introduce me, okay?"

Apprehensively, Li-Li turned aside. Not completely, but just enough for Crim to see behind her properly. "This is Snowdrop."

Crim blinked at her. "Um?"

The rest of the walkway appeared empty at first, and Crim immediately, fearfully, wondered if the Ifram could fly. Or else had the damned thing climbed down the bookcases? Then the image before her distorted just a fraction, and something blue appeared floating in the air. An eye, peeking out through glassy tentacles. The creature had gone transparent.

"You're s-s-scaring her!"

"She's invisible!"

"I-it's just ca-c-camouflage," Li-Li explained, unperturbed. "Like an oct-t-topus."

Still fixated on Crim, the Ifram uncurled another arm, and a second little eye appeared to study her. Sighing again, she crouched down and let her mind reach out to their guest. This female was easier to infiltrate than the males, and met Crim with equal intrigue. Unlike her counterparts, there was no sliminess, no animosity to her thoughts. They were not as clear as another Sidhe's or a human's, but Crim could pick out distinct emotions and sensations being communicated to her.

Snowdrop truly was afraid. For some reason, this sent a pang of guilt through her body. She reached out a hand, the visitor quailed.

"Hello."

Blink. Blink. Eyelids moving in succession.

"My name is Crim." She was speaking as gently as she could, but her anxiety made her volume flutter. She probably said her name a bit too loud.

Whimper.

"I'm not going to hurt you. I promise."

Surprisingly, Li-Li laid a hand on Crim's shoulder. "This is my friend."

The Ifram lifted her head completely at this, four eyes staring wide.

"Yes. I'm a friend."

Chirp?

"That's right."

A third arm unravelled and, turning greyish before the rest of her, meekly stroked the back of her hand. It was warm and soft and gentle. Crim immediately felt a soothing wave pass over her, and her heart stirred with something akin to fondness.

Yes. We are friends.

XLVI

Sunshine melted down into the boiling water, eyes on the ceiling as the candles she had lit painted patterns on the jagged rock. The grate at her toes was scalding to the touch as magma roiled in its vent far below; she planted her feet against the metal, energised as it scorched her skin. Once out of the water her soles would heal quickly enough. For now, all she needed was the burn. She dunked her head under and watched the seething red glow of the Mountain's core awhile, and surfaced to find Laal watching her.

"We need to talk about Crim."

"We do?"

"She's been here far longer than she promised—"

"And we are glad to have her."

"We *are* glad."

She patted her soaked hair. "But."

"*But* she's spent the whole time up there." Laal jerked her chin in the direction of the Eyrie. "Plotting."

"She'll come up with something soon enough." Sunshine grabbed at her ankles, trying to pull her in to the steaming pool. "Come here."

Her lover kicked at her. "Not now."

"Why not?"

"*Stop it!* You're not listening!"

"I will once you get in here."

"*Ouch!*" Her toe had tipped the surface, and she jumped back. Was the water really that hot? "No! Just *listen* a minute!"

Sunshine sighed, dropping her arms with a loud *splash*. She had really wanted to enjoy her bath in peace. "Fine."

"I think…I-I can't explain it. This afternoon I just got this…This *feeling* in my chest; it was like a weight. At first, I thought it was nothing but it went deeper and deeper." She pressed a palm to her heart, pushing at where it must have formed. "It was *dread*. Dense, dark dread that burrowed its way through me. I couldn't escape it. I still can't."

Word by word, dread seeped towards Sunshine. She began to feel cold, immobilised, like she was frozen in ice. "*Oooh*."

"Whatever she's planning up there, I do not like the feel of it."

Hot water in her hands. *Hot, not cold. It is hot.* She splashed it over her face, ignoring Laal's gasp. "We have to trust her."

"Why?"

"*Why?* She is our sister! She has never done us wrong before!"

"I'm not saying she will do us wrong. Not on purpose."

In that rare instance, she was unfathomably angry at Laal, so angry that the pool began to froth. "I will not speak like this about her."

"We need to."

"I will *not*. Not now."

Laal sat cross-legged a safe distance away from the boiling water. "We cannot let her go unchecked, Sunny. She probably does not know or desire the doom she is bringing. We can *help* her."

"The water is fine now. Please come here."

Gingerly, Laal tested the temperature, then slowly undressed. She slipped into the pool right up to the neck. Sunshine wrapped an arm around her, and Laal draped her legs over her lap, nestling against her shoulder. Should she really trust Crim so dearly? *No.* She felt it in her heart. There had always been something *off* about Crim. A darkness lurking inside. Nothing conscious, but always there. She wholly believed the younger Sidhe could be leading them all blindly into danger. Much as she loved her, she knew Laal was right.

We need to keep an eye on her.

*

They stayed like that—silent, wrapped around each other in the Grotto—for the better part of the evening. The next morning they lay in bed in much the same pose, not even sharing their minds. Until Laal announced that she had plans to meet Gnat by the Swamps to hunt for frogs. With a chaste kiss, they parted, and Sunshine felt the weight of her absence alongside a newfound panic that the trouble with Crim might drive a wedge between them. That feeling grew and slithered around in her gut all day.

Mother and Mentor rarely called for them anymore. They had never been able to decide if the Elders sensed their distrust of the Ifram, or they had simply lost their usefulness. Without any summons from Whisper, Sunshine was left to whittle her day away at her own time. She kept busy, of course; she had always had a knack for finding and picking up odd jobs, and people were glad to have her on hand. Most of all she loved to craft and sew, and today found herself lingering around the Market in search of something to keep her hands busy. Here was where Adik commandeered her, and set her to work at fixing beads, sequins and other adornments to some of her commissions. Sunshine had an eye for detail, and could imagine brilliant and elaborate patterns on a whim, so the seamstress valued her help. She had often helped in making the scarves she ordered for Laal, but left the more difficult work to her superior.

Adik seemed lonely, presumably still feeling Tal's loss—the boys were sweet, but could scare fix a button. She spoke to Sunshine tirelessly as they worked, and Sunshine happily distracted her from her grief.

"You should open your own shop you know. I could use the competition," Adik urged her for the umpteenth time.

"I'm too lazy. You know that," she responded. "Besides, you have Unma to keep you on your toes."

The dress maker scoffed. "I would hardly call her *competition.*"

"Really?" She used an old charcoal pencil to sketch out a mandala on the sleeve of a lime-green jacket. "Laal got a beautiful scarf from her just a few days ago. Perhaps you've seen it—with the lavender detailing?"

Adik grunted, but did not reply. She was now distracted by a potential customer, who was currently touching some of the swatches of fabric on the counter, clicking curiously. Another Ifram stood a few feet away, tilting his head and chirping at his companion.

"Would you...like something?" Adik ventured.

He looked up at her, head concealed as usual by one of those bulky helmets. Two of his appendages upheld a square of silk brocade, which he ran through his fingers as he clicked. Clearly intrigued by her work, he glanced between it and the seamstress before offering it back.

"I can make something for you," she explained.

"Yes," Sunshine chimed in. She stood up and tugged at her shawl, making her way slowly beside Adik. Her sword hung heavy at her waist—she carried it every day now. Though she dared not to reach for it, this was comforting. Out of the corner of her eye she could see Adik's scimitar propped against the leg of the heavy wooden counter, unsheathed. "She made this shawl, this skirt for me. And all the garments you see here."

Click click click click click. Curious. He put the piece of cloth back down. His companion rapped a pointed foot against the floorboards, clearly impatient and unimpressed.

"Keep it."

Chirrrp?

Adik held it out to him. "It's just a sample. I can make another. Keep it. And please come back if you change your mind about getting something made."

He took it with a breathy *trilling* and returned to his friend, holding it out proudly. The other simply *clicked* and walked on.

Sunshine smiled at his back. She hoped it appeared natural. Fingers twitching, she spread her palms firmly against the tabletop, suddenly heady with fright. "I don't think they know much about fashion, Adik."

"No, apparently not. At least not the males."

"Hmm."

"That little one has been about a lot, though."

Sunshine blinked at her. "Little one?"

"Oh? You haven't seen her?"

"No?"

"There's a little female that likes to come by in the evenings. She doesn't buy anything, either—I don't think they understand the concept. But I've let her sit and watch me work a few times," Adik explained.

"I was beginning to wonder if they even had any females."

"Same. You should drop by and meet her. Such a sweet little thing. Sticks to Li-Li like glue."

She started. "To *Li-Li?*"

"Aye. They seem to have an…understanding. I'd like to say friendship, even. Crim was with them last night, as well. I'm surprised you haven't met her."

"Li-Li...friends with—" She struggled to find the words. "You said *Crim*? And there was Crim warning the rest of us to be careful!"

Adik frowned. "The little one is different, Sunny. Not a bad bone in her. Not that any of them seem to have bones. Not all of them could be awful, anyway. I don't think the one we just met was, either."

Eyeing the door, she had to agree. There had been something charming about that Ifram, about the way he played with and stroked a mere scrap of material like it was the most beautiful thing he had ever held. She was glad Adik had given it to him. Was glad to have seen the good side of even one of them.

Mentor called for her later, as the yellow sun rocks were fading and the meek blue-green glow of the star stones began to stir. They met in the halls beyond the High Stair and walked to the Arena in relative silence, Laal's revelation about Crim creating waves in Sunshine's mind that she struggled to contain.

Pointing to the Armoury, Mentor ordered: "Go. Pick our weapons. Be quick."

Sunshine never really thought about the training swords she picked—she always picked the same two stout gladiator swords that hung in cracked scabbards from a shelf four rows to the left. These, paired with matching shields, imitated her own blade the closest, though the iron blades were far heavier and clumsier than that of their truesteel counterpart.

She trotted back out with the equipment in her arms, feigning a grin as she passed one sword and shield to Mentor. She had not been summoned, had not sparred with Mentor in months. Certainly not since the Ifram arrived. What was the reason for this sudden attention?

With a swipe of her blade, Mentor cut a clean line in the sand, and backed away to her starting point. Sunshine clanged hilt against clunky shield and skipped into place. Mentor said nothing, face an expressionless mask. For the second time in just a few hours, Sunshine's insides went cold. She opened her mouth to ask a question.

A twitch of one foot. That was all the warning she got. She could not even form words as Mentor leapt at her, but she did let out a cry of fright, lifting her shield to catch the blade arching overhead. It screeched over the tarnished bronze sun and Mentor growled and manoeuvred her own shield against Sunshine's, thrusting her shoulder behind it and knocking her aside. Sunshine did not allow herself to be knocked—she did not trust what Mentor would do if she hit the ground—regaining her footing in time to parry another blow. Mentor was hot on her heels, eyes seeing past her, teeth gnashing.

"Mentor?" She panted finally, darting to put some distance between them.

"Fight me."

"I am glad to train with you. However—"

A tendril erupted from the ground, spraying dark waxy leaves into the air with the speed at which it moved. It lashed at her legs, but Sunshine was swift enough to jump over it, slicing it in half as she went.

"Fight."

"I didn't know we were using *draoi*."

The thing split into multiple slender woody vines, all of which slithered immediately over the sand for her feet. With a stamp Sunshine sent a rippling wave of fire outward, which devoured them easily. Hissing from behind told her Mentor had not been quick enough to dodge it.

"What is the purpose of this, Mentor?" She attempted, watching her opponent rub cool water over the soles of her feet. "We have not trained in so long."

"Enough of this," Mentor grumbled, retreating back to one of the pillars. "Get your sword."

"*My* sword?" Had Mentor gone mad? They never trained with true weapons. It was too dangerous. "I don't understand."

"You do not need to understand, girl. Only do what I say."

Sunshine backed off, right up against the opposite wall. Mentor had retrieved her kataras from their sheath by the pillar, and now swiped them in the air experimentally. She could not take her, both of them knew as much. Did that mean Mentor meant to kill her? Had she found out about Whisper? About Smith? About Crim?

"Don't you understand?" Came the cold, measured challenge. "I'm giving you a chance to defend yourself."

It was no good; she was trembling from head to foot. Sunshine was no coward, and an accomplished fighter, but there was no hope in this fight. Nonetheless she set her training gear aside and hefted her truesteel sword and blazing shield. The light of the golden sun on its front caught Mentor's features, illuminating only dead eyes and set features.

Sunshine toed the edge of the circle, then, ignoring the lump in her throat, took her position opposite her teacher.

Once again a jerk of her foot gave Mentor away, but she moved far faster this time. Like she was no longer playing. Sunshine rolled out of her path, eliciting a huff of indignation and a spring to block her path. With such an effortless hop, Mentor could clear the entire arena, and Sunshine with horror found herself face-to-face with her would-be killer.

"Defend yourself."

This burst of flame was not as controlled as the first. It engulfed Mentor with terrifying ferocity. Still, Sunshine could not find the heart to do harm, and it was brushed aside as soon as the elder realised it was merely uncomfortably warm. By this time, Sunshine was trying to make her way out of the circle for the exit— if she stayed she was dead. If she ran, she was probably dead, too, but she prayed Silver or someone passing might come to her rescue.

"That's *cheating*!" Mentor roared, flinging a net of thorny vines at her. Spinning as she ran, Sunshine kicked a fireball back to deal with it, now finding the voice to cry for help.

"Silver! *Silver*!"

Mentor darted for her, cut her off on her way to the door, foot raised. Sunshine felt her organs squished together by the force of the kick, which sent her flying into the circle. She coughed, tasted blood, and just had a split second to snatch her sword up before Mentor pounced again. Darting herself, she had not the energy to make it more than a few paces, and the elder had already altered her course, bounding off the pillars like a cat, cold eyes pinning her in place. She landed on Sunshine's upturned shield, sending her to the floor once again.

"Please!" Sunshine begged, tears leaking from the corners of her eyes, wriggling under her weight, arm straining to jerk the shield side to side as Mentor stabbed under it, trapped like a mouse under the cat's paw. "Silver! Help! Silver!"

An edge sliced through her left side like butter, the pain red-hot. Blood flowed freely from the gash. Mentor really *was* trying to kill her. Desperate, Sunshine twisted enough to get her legs under the shield as well, and with the full force of all four limbs thrust it up and away from her. Mentor went with it, but she did not wait to see where she landed—the Armoury door was still open, and Silver's chambers were just on the far side. If she could just make it…

The pain was too much. She was losing blood too quickly. She felt herself slowing, Mentor's breath on her neck. She cried and cried for Silver, to no end. She had no choice, at the end of one of the rows she turned suddenly, catching a glimpse of Mentor running, bounding nearly on all fours after her. With a grunt, she grabbed the metal cabinet next to her and tipped it on its side. Mentor tried to stop, tripped and managed to fall next to it—but he right leg was trapped, and Sunshine was no longer fleeing. Instead she was on her, using her whole weight to keep Mentor to the ground, thighs pinning her arms to her sides, shield to her neck, the edge biting but not sharp enough to cut. Her sword gleamed as she raised it over her head. She paused.

"Do it."

She paused.

"Sunny. If you let me live, I'll try it again. Do it."

She gaped down at Mentor, seeing the sudden change in her. Gone were the dead eyes and the false smile. For now she was lucid, clear. Was it a trick?

"What happened to you, Mentor?"

"These things get into your head, not everyone's, mind you. They plant seeds there—to make you think they're your friends, to make you believe what you know and what you love is wrong. So that you betray your own kind. I was weak. I let them in, then led them here."

"You were different."

"I know. When they're in control, it's like you're a prisoner in your own body, to a certain extent. The rational part of you is put in a cage."

"But you escaped? You're here now?"

"No. Don't let that stop you. I could lose control at any moment. I've been working little by little to fight it, but it always wins in the end. You *must* stop me."

Sunshine's fingers clenched around the hilt. "I understand."

*

As she made the long trek back to the apartment, Sunshine kept her weapon in hand. Every few steps she would glance at it, wondering if she had done the right thing. Only time would tell—for now she only had to face the others.

Laal, sensing her approach, met her at the door, kissed her sweetly and said something about the mushrooms she had found. She stopped, however, when she saw Sunshine's face.

"What is it?"

Taking her lover by the arm, she led her inside, where the others were waiting. To her dismay, she found that Crim had chosen that of all evenings to join them. The latter was watching her with false calm, a facade that cracked the instant Mentor stepped into the room.

"What's she doing here?"

"Crim, sit down."

"I asked a question."

"And I'm asking you to sit."

She sat. "Answer me."

"Mentor is herself again."

"For now," Mentor cut in. "Only I don't know how long it will last. I told Sunshine to do away with me, but she's much too good for that."

"I'll help."

"*Crim!*" Laal gasped.

"She brought them here."

"They were controlling her," Sunshine explained.

"Are they not now? How can we be sure? What if this is a ruse, and she's here to spy on us?"

"Crim's right, Sunshine," Mentor concurred. "I might think I'm in control now, but it could just as easily be a trap. I don't know what you're doing here, and I don't want you to tell me, all I want to do is protect you—"

"You ca-can't protect us i-i-if you're d-dead," Li-Li chimed in.

"She could help us. She knows more about them than anyone," Sunshine said with false cheer. "Crim if you talk to her—"

"No." Something had been coming over Crim in those brief moments; Sunshine could see it like a shadow building around her. When it finally reached her eyes, they took on an eerie glow. When she moved her hand again it hit her knife, which struck the floor with a solitary *tink*. Their eyes all went to the noise reflexively, and that half a second was all she needed. She was across the room and throttling Mentor in the next blink. With her hands wrapped around their teacher's neck, they all witnessed the change in her features; her mouth opened to reveal large, jagged teeth, growing impossibly wide below shining eyes, her fingers, now long and taloned, scraped rifts in Mentor's skin. Her victim hung, pinned against the wall and passively allowing her own demise.

It was Laal who acted first, followed by Li-Li. They pried Mentor from Crim's hold and escorted her to the table. Yuki remained frozen in place, but growled loudly at Crim as she tried to pursue. Sunshine took it upon herself to say:

"Leave, Crim."

Her features shifted back to normal, and she had the audacity to look stunned. "You're making me leave?"

"I am."

With a quick look up and down, a hurt *tch*, Crim wheeled. The door crashed shut behind her.

At the table, Mentor rubbed at the claw marks on her neck. "You should listen to her more."

XLVII

Snowdrop came to the Library every other night. In the beginning, Li-Li would walk back and forth, searching and calling for her much like their first meeting. A faint jingle of sequins or drop of a book when she came near was all the response the little Ifram would give, and she would find her in a different spot each time. Like a particularly arduous game of hide-and-seek that sometimes lasted hours.

Crim and Yuki (who had since been gently informed of her new friend) accompanied her from time to time. Her mistress, despite her outward misgivings quickly took to their guest, and helped her to find books and illustrations to her liking. Snowdrop seemed to have no real understanding of what anything they showed her was, but appreciated the colours and patterns in front of her with a pure and childlike wonder.

*

As the days wore on, and Li-Li grew tired of searching for her, she would sit at one of the tables on the uppermost level and work until Snowdrop came out of hiding (usually after everyone else had left). Only by doing this did Li-Li realise how very afraid Snowdrop was. Crim and Yuki noticed too.

"This place is for everyone, you know," Crim said one evening. Snowdrop was still cowering by a bookcase, semi-transparent and glancing about. "You have as much right to be here as any of us. You don't need to hide 'til the coast is clear."

Snowdrop purred quietly as she spoke, arms crossed in front of her.

"I'm not angry with you. I'm just saying we could meet at the entrance, or somewhere easier to find. Perhaps my study? It's secluded, but I still know where to find you, no-one will bother you—at least I don't think so—and if they do you tell me and I'll deal with them."

Her stance relaxed a bit, emphasised by soft *cooing*.

"Here." Crim pulled something from her pocket. "It's a key."

Snowdrop eyed it, still cooing. She ventured forward to stroke the brass decorations around the handle. She clearly did not understand what it was.

"You use it to open the door. I can leave it somewhere near the study, if you don't have pockets. Do you know what pockets are?"

Blink blink.

"I think it's best if she just meets us by the door," Yuki suggested. Crim and Li-Li both nodded.

Blink.

Li-Li patted the empty space next to her. "C-come. Sit."

*

She could not *sit* quite so much as *perch*. Li-Li watched as she clambered up onto the chair, the ends of her limbs dangling limply towards the ground. Since she was not strong enough herself, Crim pulled the chair back in under the table.

"I fuh…found this," Li-Li announced, placing a botany manual under Snowdrop's nose. "It's g-g-got a few more p-pressings—look, th-this is a daisy."

Click click click. Trill.

"You can touch it. It's dry, but see—" Li-Li carefully traced the outline of a petal with her finger.

Still *trilling*, Snowdrop lightly caressed the flower with one appendage and hummed with light.

"They grow…oh a-a-almost eh-everywhere. At l-least some s-suh-sort of them."

Chirp chirp chirp.

"My sister's daughter used to pick them and put them on our beds."
Chiiiirp?

Li-Li roused herself out of the memory. Snowdrop had turned the pages herself and found a wrinkled flower with a huge cluster of petals. One of the leaves had not been stuck down properly, and poked out from the paper. The Ifram played with it carefully.

"Ch-chr-rysanthemum," Li-Li read aloud. "It s-says this particular wuh...one was picked in s-s-s-southern China."

Click click?

"It's the r-region I come fr-f-from."

Click?

"Sorry I-I don't n-n-nknow much about it. I d-don't r-r-remember."
Click click chirp! Snowdrop patted the book with two arms.
"This is a b-boh-otany book. It doesn't have c-c-countries."

Chirp click?

"I-It's only about flowers. I'd need a ge-geography book...one ab-about my home world."
Chirp chirp chirp chirp... Snowdrop was staring down at the words scrawled in black ink, drawing over them now with intense focus.
"Usually, our books will focus on just one topic. We have ones with lists of things—dictionaries or encyclopaedias—but those don't give much information."
She stared up at her.
"I t-take it your wr-r-writings don't fo-follow the same r-r-rule?"

Click chirp?

"Y-your, um...your books? Your...what do you h-h-have?"
Click click. Concept unknown.
"Do you not make these? Anything like this? Writings." Crim nudged the manual. She and Yuki were both leaning forward, intrigued by the Ifram's reaction.

Snowdrop pushed it over the table to her. The ideas of *make* and *write* whirling around in her mind. Confusing.

*

"*Uh…*" Crim lifted her portion of the table, surprising her guest. Almost all of the tables and desks in the library were built in such a way—with compartments for writing materials. Out of the corner of her eye Li-Li caught Snowdrop struggling with all four arms to find the catch on her segment, and then fighting get her own open. Giggling, she reached across and swung it up for her. The Ifram's four eyes went wide at the sight of quills, styluses, pencils, brushes, colourful pots of paint and ink, small blocks of wax and carving knives, tightly-wound rolls of paper and parchment and papyrus and stacks of thinly-cut slate and wood all laid out neatly in their own sections. Overcoming her shock, she clicked and trilled happily at them. Snowdrop awkwardly picked up a quill, mirroring Crim's movements, and coiled another tentacle around one of the ink bottles when she saw her uncork one. Checking that it was not dry, Crim placed all of her instruments back on the desk as Snowdrop still poked at the treasure trove before her, and unrolled a small scrap of vellum.

"We use this," Raising the quill, Crim allowed her guest to admire it before dipping the nib. "And this stuff. It's called ink—it's like a dye." The idea of a dye was familiar, at least. "Put it on your quill. Just a drop, or else it will splotch. Oh—a bit too much—I like to use a corner to…"

Chirp! Chirp! Chirp! Chirp! Snowdrop flashed blue as she watched her wipe a blot of excess ink off on the paper. Fascinating.

"So you have point at the end, and if you use it like *this…*" She traced the first syllable of her name in one bold line. "Each of these represents one of the noises I make. If I put them together in this order, I can write my name."

Her guest was almost blinding now, wriggling her arms and chirping as she watched Crim making lines and dots on the page.

"If we put these markings in different orders, we can make different meanings. If we do this a lot, it becomes one of these." She prodded the book, now lying forgotten in front of them. "So we can share a lot of information with each other."

Still strobing with luminescence, Snowdrop clicked at the quill and ink bottle she now held. Amazed.

"Do you want to try?"

Trill?

"I c-can show you. H-here." Li-Li took a piece of paper out from Snowdrop's drawer and helped her close the lid. Her guest sat back, arms curled into her body, blatantly afraid to damage or get in the way of anything. "Come on. P-p-put the bo-bottle down. Like Crim's. Can y-y-you open it?"

*

With a vigorous tug and a *pop!* The stopper came out, spraying them both with navy-blue droplets. Li-Li gasped and wiped at her face, rubbing some out of her eye to find Snowdrop slouched right down in her seat and slowly going invisible again. Unsure how to comfort their little guest, she laughed. A tad too loud and too merrily—Yuki cocked an eyebrow at her, but Crim, catching her intention, joined in quietly. Snowdrop, startled at first, *cooed,* then sat up. Understanding that they were not angry at her, she began to dip her arms into the spatter dotting the desk (and frankly the two of them). The ink did not stick to her smooth skin easily, but she managed to stain one entire limb blue. Copying their giggles, she raised said limb to inspect it.

"I w-w-wouldn't—" Too late; the Ifram had smeared blue streaks into her face. "I-is that f-fun?"

Coooo! Fun.

Crim snorted. "Okay. Now try like I did...just a little. Can you help her, Little Mouse? I don't think she has the motor skills. Yep, perfect. Now try to—"

Snowdrop scrawled a long, wavy line across the page, and some on the table.

Fun.

"Aha! You did it!" Li-Li clapped.

Chirp! Chirp!

"Can you do this one?" Crim tapped the first part of her name again.

Clicking with concentration, Snowdrop put the quill to work, and produced a wobbly replica devoid of spatial awareness.

"Wow, you really…" Crim was interrupted by further *clicks* as her guest insisted on copying the rest. Again, without much understanding of how the characters should be spaced or sized. Some of the lines didn't even connect. "Oh! You did my whole name!"

Trillll! Fun. Proud.

"Here." Crim handed her own page over to her. "Why don't you take this. Practice copying it, and I'll show you some more next time?"

Li-Li pulled another blank slip of paper from the desk. Snowdrop flashed, enough to make her wince, and curled both scraps of paper into a neat little roll. Happy. She tucked them away under her veil.

Coo… Gift.

Crim laughed. "It's not a gift. It's homework."

Gift. Snowdrop slipped three of the slender gold cuffs from one of her arms and placed them on the table.

"N-no, Snowdrop. Th-th-there's no need—"

Gift! Her guest wrapped three tentacles around her hand and pulled. Li-Li allowed it, not wanting to hurt her by resisting.

"I-it's just some p-p-paper, Sweetheart. It's n-not like those…"

Snowdrop placed the cuff on her thumb and pressed the malleable gold together until the ring was closed as tight as she could manage (which was still not tight at all). *Gift.*

XLVIII

It had been days since she spoke to Laal or Sunshine—the longest they had gone without communicating since she ran away. Even Yuki and Li-Li were painfully distant now during their sessions in the Library. She did not dare go near the apartment, not near Mentor. How could the four of them trust her again so easily? Mentor clearly did not even trust herself.

"It is what they do," Gibber said as they tended to a gaggle of miniature cockatrices. "They have weapons, I assure you of that. The Sidhe have already been shown some of them, but the true danger they wield is the poison they place in people's minds. The hatred, the paranoia, the idea that all of your loved ones are against you."

Crim grunted, nodded. "You're getting too comfortable, you know."

"Huh?"

"Whisper is *right there*." She jerked a thumb over her shoulder. "There are Sidhe all around us. And you have the nerve to speak through one of us at this very moment."

"It is the only way I can speak to you."

"Find another way."

"I am trying."

"Good."

"Are you even listening to me?"

"Not really. You're just spouting the same sermons I've been hearing for weeks."

"And yet you still waste time. You still do not take action."

"Here we go."

"What?"

"I'm feeding the chickens. *Ouch!*" If there is one insult to a cockatrice, it is being equated to any lesser fowl. She rubbed her ankle, already swollen and greenish-black with venom. "Little fucker."

"You have a plan?"

"For the thousandth time: Partially."

"Best make it wholly, so you may be rid of these vermin and their god."

"Holy?"

"What?"

"Never mind."

*

Someone was waiting atop this stair. Crim sensed their presence as soon as her foot hit the lowermost step. Had they watched her emerge from the Narrow Stair? Either way, they let themselves be known. Partially. She came up, fighting against the sleepless wind, palm pressed against the inner wall of the tower. They welcomed her.

The Patriarch's bedchamber was in disarray. Much more so than before her stay. She had never been the tidiest of residents, but now, with all that was on her mind, cleanliness came last. Strewn clothes, overturned pots of paint and ink, torn papers all littered the floor. The hearth was scattered with discarded bones, shells, husks off nuts—enough for the rats that scurried around it to feast. The pile of blankets and pillows she called a bed surrounded by plates and cups. Most of the four-poster bed had been further broken down into firewood and piled against the wall, so that only the grey, torn mattress lay on the floor. The head and footboards had been propped up comically on either side of Crim's 'bed'.

The books, however, the scrolls and the tablets and other material she had pilfered day by day from the Library, were tucked away with reverence on the shelves. Not neatly—not even in any way that resembled a system—but Crim would never betray Bart by mistreating them. Presently, Mentor stood in front of these shelves, browsing.

"You." Crim felt her hackles raise. Heard the hiss in her voice. She did not even try to restrain it.

"Yes. I came to talk. Nothing more." Her teacher flipped open one broad-paged journal. "Still, if you choose to tear me apart instead, I wouldn't blame you."

"I should have killed you in the apartment."

"I know. The others should have let you."

"You let them in."

"I know."

"You betrayed us."

"I know."

"Bart...Princess. So many have died because of you."

"I know."

Fangs still on show, Crim flexed her extended claws. She was sure she had meant to say more, but Mentor's sorrowful acceptance of her accusations disarmed her. Was she doing this on purpose? Another trick?

The elder examined her critically. Like the old Mentor, eyes bright and cunning. "How long have you been turning feral?"

She looked down at her talons, ran her tongue along her jagged teeth, narrowed her gleaming eyes. "I had never done it until I saw you that night."

"You have a temper. I always thought you'd manage eventually. You know not many Sidhe can do this, let alone remain in control? I'm glad I could teach you, if not inadvertently."

It was certainly Mentor's brand of praise. "What did you come to talk about?"

"I want to help."

She laughed. "You've helped enough."

"That's true, and I don't even know if I'm really helping now. I couldn't tell you if this was another trick." Mentor sat on the floor. "If you wish to kill me, I will allow it. But so long as I am here and clear, I will try to help you."

Crim retracted her claws, then her teeth. Her stance fell apart, and she sat opposite Mentor on her bed. "I don't trust you."

"You're a smart girl."

"But you know them better than anyone else."

"I do."

"Then tell me: how do we get rid of them?"

Mentor inspected the chipped paint on her feet first, then the fireplace. Crim clicked her fingers, stout flames springing up from between the coals to fight for fuel.

"You have to kill them."

She pulled a blanket around herself. "Thought as much."

"I don't just mean one or two, Crim," Mentor pressed. "Not just the leaders— even if I knew who they were. Not just enough to scare the others away. The ones in that ship are just a drop in the ocean compared to the rest. There are *millions* of them. If even one manages to get word back to their home, the others will come. At that point there's no hope for us."

"Can any of them be turned?"

"No. To be honest I don't think any of them even have individual thoughts, or personalities. It's like they all share a mind."

Snowdrop had a personality. Crim was fairly certain she did not think like the others, as well. Could she kill her? "All of them…"

"You're reluctant. I understand," Mentor added her own flare to the room; slender green fingers of fire that danced behind Crim's squat soldiers. "But I also know you. I know you understand what needs to be done, despite the weight it might have on your conscience. I trust you more than any of the others to do it."

"I already knew, really. I was just…"

"It's not a pleasant task."

"No."

Mentor stood, snapped a few pieces of timber into twigs and fed them to the fire. At the promise of food the flames began to mingle, casting a multicoloured glow across the room. Squatting in front of them, she allowed Crim the time she needed to think. There was no false positivity, no sugar-coated words. She was really behaving like herself. Crim was almost fooled. Trustworthy or no, this was an opportunity for information.

"How do I do it?"

"The ship," replied Mentor promptly. "Most of them stay up there, out of sight. There must be thousands. They only allowed us up once, and even then we were not given a tour. I had to estimate. The others can take care of the ones down here."

"Others?"

"Whisper, Smith. I'm fairly certain Adik and Silver have their own cells. Hyeong and his Reavers quelled a few movements quietly, but the Mountain is humming with unease. You must feel it?"

Crim nodded. They all felt it. "How many are on our side?"

She had meant to say *on my side*, but if Mentor noticed her mistake she did not mention it. "I can't say for sure. At most half of the Sidhe. Though I feel that is a generous estimation."

"Right. How do I get up there?"

"Do you know the Blue Stair?"

"Barely." Rarely used, the Blue Stair branched off one of the paths from the Forum and led to a door hidden in the rockface above the Front Gate.

"The path beyond it leads to an outcrop just between the Source and the Maw. There is a…device planted near the edge. It will lift you up."

"Without anyone being notified?" It sounded very much like a trap.

"They don't think any of us are smart enough to figure it out. Or brave enough to try it. Either way both sides are unguarded."

"Right…" Luckily, Crim knew someone far more reliable than Mentor. Though she spoke to her well into the night, probing for ever more information, forever eyeing her for any signs of deceit, she filed everything she learned away into a neat little corner of her mind. To be confirmed later.

*

The others had already retired to her study when she arrived in the Library the next afternoon. She took some of her moments alone among the shelves to wander back to Bart's Parlour; the point at which the lowermost rows converged, each of them spanning out from the bases of the seven arches that punctuated its walls. The ceiling here was lower than the rest of the Library; domed and frescoed with visions of heroic minotaurs battling cyclopes and centaurs and griffons. They had cleaned the furniture, with the help of some other admirers. The drawers and cupboards and side tables, they found, had mostly been filled with plates of cakes and biscuits for his guests. Cabinets by the fireplace held his centuries-old collection of cups and saucers in varying sizes and patterns, all washed lovingly and locked away for good. The fireplace they had cleared and swept and scrubbed, and Crim now found to her aching delight that someone had filled it with flowers.

Giggling to herself, she did the one thing she had never dared do while Bart was alive; she clambered ungracefully up onto his chair—the one object in the room no-one had the heart to touch. It was still peppered in crumbs, spotted with tea and fuzzy with coarse hairs. She hugged a pillow, which still stank of him, and wondered what he would think of what she was preparing herself to do.

*

Her study was not nearly large enough for four people. Even if one of those people was a four-foot creature that could shrink herself down to two feet. Snowdrop was currently scrunched up on the couch with Yuki, whom she was still rather fearful of at times—the youngling treated her with indifference for the most part, and poorly-concealed suspicion when their mood turned foul. Li-Li, sitting at the desk, had her nose buried into a runic scroll, a splotch of dark ink on her lip where she had been sucking on her quill.

With no-where else to sit, Crim picked up the volume she had been struggling through for days and dropped to the floor with a bookcase at her back. Snowdrop watched with intrigue as she crossed her legs and opened the pages across them, after a moment's observation slid down from the cushions and settled next to her, legs wriggling happily on the cold boards. Crim nudged the book onto her left leg so that she could see better; this one had no illustrations or pressings, and was only written in tight black scrawl, but she summarised each section for the little Ifram, who listened intently.

"I have a question for you, actually," she whispered at length. Yuki and Li-Li could hear if they wanted to—they were only two feet away—but the latter knew not to listen, and she eyed the former with a warning. Snowdrop, surprised by her sudden change of tone and volume, tilted her head, then mirrored Crim by leaning in and *purring* adorably. She was so little, so sweet. Could Crim truly betray her like this? "About that ship. The one in the sky."

Chirp chirp. Snowdrop pulsed nervously with yellow light.

"You know it? The one you come from?"

The Ifram was shrinking considerably now, glowing a faint champagne colour. Li-Li turned in her chair and shot Crim a glare. She was fiercely protective of her little friend, and Crim could not blame her.

"I'm just wondering how you get down here. Are there stairs, or a ladder...?"

Chii-chirp!

"I don't think she likes your questions," Yuki said.

"Crim," Li-Li cautioned.

"Well it's by the moon," she continued. "It never comes down, so how does she come here every day? Unless you're staying in the Mountain?"

Flash. *Chirp.*

Crim took that as a 'no'. "So how do you get here?"

"Stop. Sh-she doesn't w-w-want to t-talk about it."

"Could you show us?"

She was turning transparent again. Even Yuki shook their head at Crim. Reluctantly, she dropped the subject. They read for another hour in silence, Snowdrop hovering on the edge of visibility, until they all sensed someone else nearby. The Ifram sat up suddenly with a little squeak and melted into the bookcase.

*

Li-Li stood. "Wh-who do you think th-th-that is?"

"No-one pleasant," responded Yuki.

Crim was on her feet too, she edged up next to the door and peered out the patterned glass. She could just make out several figures moving below the balustrade opposite. "I can't see who."

They all glanced to where they knew Snowdrop should be, straining to make out her shape in the candlelight.

"W-we should check?"

"I will," Yuki volunteered.

"N-not alone. I'll g-g-go t-too."

"It's probably just some other younglings coming to clean."

"If someone sees you, they'll ask for Li-Li," Crim pointed out. "Everyone knows you two come together."

"R-right! We're a t-t-team!"

Yuki's ears turned red, but they agreed. Crim continued to peek out of the gaps in the etched window, and saw them split in opposite directions, Li-Li with far more confidence than Yuki. As they moved to find better vantages, the group of newcomers moved further out into the lower floor. Crim bristled as a Reaver sauntered into view, carefully sweeping the empty tables around him as his wards ambled to and fro. His partner stayed behind the two male Ifram, one of their firearms ready at his chest.

Come back. She urged the others, palm pressing against the glass, nose millimetres from it. *Come back!*

Should she go after them? Would Yuki and Li-Li remain out of sight? Could they convince the Reavers that they were here on mere errands? Her other hand drifted to the handle.

Something smooth and soft wrapped around it. Snowdrop's arm, gone cold with fear, held her hand away from the door. She was not strong enough to physically restrain Crim, but something in the gesture convinced her that going out right now would be suicide for the both of them. Hating herself for it, she crouched against the door instead and turned her key in the lock, ready to brace her back to it should anyone try to force their way in. The glass she had enhanced herself to resist most attacks, but the hinges she mistrusted. Snowdrop sidled up next to her, one little limb still gripping her hand. She let the candles go out and vaguely wondered if this was how she would meet her end—huddled in the dark with the wife of the enemy.

*

"Th-they're gone."

"What were they doing?"

"I d-d-don't know."

"Is Yuki not with you?"

"No."

"Oh…I'm sure they're fine."

"R-right."

"Let's wait for them. Pack your bag and theirs. I don't think we should come here anymore."

"D-do you think th-they w-w-were looking for…?"

Crim studied Snowdrop, who had gone back to her usual colour—if not a chalkier version. She was still curled up in the corner by the door, eyes downcast. "Were they looking for you?"

The Ifram tucked herself in more, moulding to the shape of the corner. *Afraid.*

"I don't th-think she's su-s-supposed to be h-here."

"No," Crim agreed. "Why are you afraid, Snowdrop? Will they hurt you?"

Whimper.

"We can't leave her alone."

"Wh-what do we do?"

"She needs to get back to the ship. Unseen. We could…escort her?"

"W-we can't g-g-go up there."

"She should be fine once she's aboard, right?"

Snowdrop stared up at her with pitiful blue eyes. Crim could not deny that she wanted to protect her, but she also wanted to see how she reached the floating vessel.

She extended her hand to their guest. "Come on."

*

Yuki was patrolling the long passage leading to the main Library doors, and whirled once they heard footsteps.

"The Reavers took their visitors out this way. I don't know which entrance they used to get in."

"Doesn't matter. We need to get this one back before someone realises she's missing." Crim patted Snowdrop where her shoulder should be. The Ifram clung to her leg trembling.

"Back where?"

"Up the Blue Stair. Mentor told me that's where they come in and out."

"*Mentor* told you?"

"I th-thought you didn't tr-t-trust M-Mentor?"

"I don't. But she offered me intel and I took it. Now is the perfect time to see if she was being honest."

"If w-we're wrong. If we g-g-get caught with…"

"Yuki, can you scout ahead? Click your fingers if you see any Reavers or Ifram," Crim ordered. "Li-Li keep a look out behind. I'll take her and hide her if necessary."

"I duh…don't know…"

Did Li-Li mistrust her with her friend? "I'm the only one remotely strong enough to fight the Reavers. Their friends…none of us know where we stand with them. But I'm also counting on the two of you to fight as well, should we need you."

Li-Li pulled a knife from the folds of her robe and tucked it up into her sleeve. Yuki followed suit. "Of course."

*

The Blue Stair was unoccupied—their footfalls echoed loudly up and down the smooth marble well. Except for Snowdrop, whose little legs whispered gently

366

over the dipped steps. As Mentor promised, it led by a tall door out onto a narrow path hemmed by a dark wall on one side and sheer a sheer drop on the other. They went in single file here, Li-Li hugging the smooth rockface. Yuki, strutting ahead, dared not look over the edge.

Mercifully, this opened into a broad-mouthed cave in the Mountainside and a short, sturdy overhang on the cliff side. Crim noted that there were benches in the cave on either side of a well-used firepit. The overhang, though mostly bare, was far more intriguing thanks to its new decoration—a slender white podium topped with a black stone. Snowdrop pulled her to this, four arms reaching up to the stone, which sat just above her head.

"This is how you get up there?" Crim deduced. "How on earth—"

Yuki gasped. Li-Li gave a yelp, remaining stuck to one of the benches well away from the drop. Even Crim staggered back as a beam of blinding white light suddenly engulfed the Ifram. A trap! A weapon? If she was in pain, Snowdrop did not cry out, but vanished.

"What happened to her!" Yuki wailed.

"I don't know!" Crim waved her hand through the air where she had stood. "She touched it herself—you saw that? I did nothing."

"I-it must be the w-way uh-uh-up!" Said Li-Li, feigning calm. "Sh-she wouldn't have g-g-g-gone near it i-if she th-thought—"

"What if she didn't know?" Yuki shot back. "The others might have known she was here and boobytrapped it!"

"No...no." A shrill laugh escaped Crim. "Li-Li's right. Think of their weapons. They shoot light, right? This must be more of their *draoi*. I'm sure she's fine."

"Y-yes...she's...she is...f-f-fine?"

XLIX

Whenever Laal was truly absorbed by her reading, she twirled the hairs at the nape of her neck. Sunshine watched as she did this for the umpteenth time in the centuries they had been together. Even when she turned her attention back to her shield (still smeared with polish), she kept her on the edge of sight. Occasionally, she would read to her, but only things about battles and voyages and daring expeditions. Today she was reading something about fungi, and Sunshine could not even pretend interest in that.

"Circles."

"What?"

"You should rub it in circles. You're going to get streaks that way."

"I know how to shine my own shield!"

"Yes. You shine it as well as you shone your sword."

Sunshine picked up her weapon to inspect. "What's wrong with my sword?"

"Look at the pommel."

"There's nothing—oh. I missed that."

Rolling her eyes, tiny smirk on her lips, Laal returned to her book.

"Why don't you read something more exciting?"

"Such as?"

"I don't know…the one with the sailors fighting monsters. And the woman with snakes in her hair."

"Apollonius is over there if you want to read it."

"I want *you* to read it."

Eyeroll. Smirk.

A knock on their door interrupted Sunshine's thoughts of reading all afternoon. Without another warning, Mentor entered. Sunshine did not spare her a glare—they had let her back into their lives, partially, but she had not yet earned free roam of the apartment.

"A word, girls." She shut the door at her back and folded her arms. Without any preamble, she said: "Crim has a plan."

"She does?" Laal asked warily.

"Since when have you been talking to Crim?"

"We have been…consulting."

"Conspiring?"

"Yes."

"I thought Crim wanted to kill you?" Added Laal.

"She did. I expect she still does, but I've proven my usefulness in providing information on our guests."

"What information?"

"About their ship, their habits, their weaknesses."

"And you did not think to include us in this?" Sunshine sloppily wiped the last of the polish off her shield and stood.

"We are including you now."

"And where is Crim?"

"She's waiting for you. I don't think she feels safe coming in here anymore. Not since her Ifram friend disappeared. She said it would be best for you all to come to an agreement…Outside."

Crim met them by the stone that stood in the clearing just before the Gate, on edge and watching the shadows with suspicion. She accepted Sunshine and Laal's embrace stiffly.

"No-one followed you?"

"No one, Crim. How have you been?" Laal replied tenderly. "I'm sorry about your friend."

"She was more Li-Li's friend, really."

"Maybe she's still alive?" Sunshine added optimistically.

Crim offered a wry smile. "Maybe. Either way I've nothing to hinder me now."

"Hinder you?" Repeated Laal.

"Come."

She led the way down the slopes to the edge of the Mountain, then silently stepped out of sight. Laal and Sunshine followed, hopping down a bank and immediately finding themselves next to a misty road softened by a full days' rain. Sunshine started to shiver as soon as the night air touched her, breath puffing out before her in white clouds. She and Laal both pulled their cloaks close, but Crim seemed rather unbothered.

"Where is this place?" She hissed through chattering teeth.

"Control, Sunny," Laal reminded her. "You only feel the cold because you remind yourself."

"I can't think of anything else!"

Laal rolled her eyes.

"There's a village down by the lake," Crim explained, already marching ahead. "They have a tavern with a fire. We can talk there."

"Fire is good. But again; where is this place?"

"It's where I grew up."

"Oh." Sunshine nudged Laal. "Is this where you found her?"

"Yes."

"Well, you managed not to freeze to death before."

Sunshine let Crim lead on, falling into step beside Laal. She envied Crim in that moment. Envied the muddy road and the rustling trees that still held echoes of her past life. Envied the sight of the lake where she had once dwelt with her family. Even envied the folk she had met, that might well be descended from her brothers and sisters. After all, Sunshine could not even picture her mother's face.

*

The tavern was unexpectedly large for a town so small; ten ragged booths wrapped around the outer wall, hemming in a helter-skelter collection of chairs and tables, all-encompassing a rather impressive bar with tottering stools and worn counter. The barman seemed to know Crim, and ushered all of them to a rather well-concealed nook of a booth against the wall opposite the door, enclosed by a curve in the bar. A small fire provided welcome warmth to Sunshine, which she huddled next to, quite sure she was turning blue. The barman even handed her a woollen blanket along with her ale, for which she thanked him profusely.

"Not be hearing it, Love," he said, blushing. "Can't have guests sitting there shivering like that, what would people think!"

Plates of hot food—a vat of stew, a beautiful white cod, bowls of potatoes and vegetables along with a whole loaf—were placed in front of them, and Diarmuid cheerily announced that he was at their service exclusively for the evening (not without a longing glance at Crim, who offered a smile as reward). Sunshine quickly decided she liked this place. The locals, wreathed in pipe smoke and all rather well-oiled, eyed them with curiosity, but only smiled politely when she met their eye, some even raising their glasses and offering small words of greeting. It was warm and peaceful and homely. She could not blame Crim for sneaking back here when given the chance (which she had clearly done, often).

Laal seemed equally impressed, helping herself to a rather large cut of the fish and a heaping plateful of boiled vegetables.

"So…" She began. "…why are we here?"

"Because we can't talk in the Mountain. There's too many of them skulking about, and we can't be sure of how much they hear. How much they know," Crim explained. "Besides it's easier to think here."

She certainly agreed with that. Now that she was Outside, it was like a haze had been lifted from her mind. "I never noticed it before, but they brought a sort of noise with them, didn't they? Like a constant droning?"

"I felt the same way when I came to find Crim," Laal concurred through a mouthful of fish and peas. She was uncharacteristically ungraceful in that instant, and Sunshine adored her for it. "It was like being shown everything anew. Like this little voice in my head had been silenced, and I could finally listen to myself again."

"Do you think it's part of their power? Perhaps it's what's making the others act so strangely? Mentor, Mother, the Reavers?"

"We can't be sure of that," Crim replied. "But I think that is the case, to some capacity, yes."

"I see it as more of an attempt to disarm us," Laal proposed. "Some sort of conditioning, so we don't see the threat…"

"Whatever it is, it's powerful," said Crim. "Strong enough to catch Mentor."

"And Mother," Sunshine added.

Laal pushed her food around her plate. "If it they overpower Mother…what hope do we have?"

Diarmuid had come back to check on them. Crim flashed him another grin, so that the boy blushed and turned away. "Very little…but we must try."

The weight of her intentions was already turning their little corner dark. Sunshine felt trapped under it. Still she asked: "Try what?"

"To get rid of them."

Laal, appetite lost, pushed her plate aside. "Whatever you're planning, I presume I'm not going to like it."

"I don't either, I promise you, Laal. I doubt any of us will like it."

Sunshine checked that the mortals were not paying attention—currently all three of them were subtly turning their awareness away from their conversation. Only one woman happened to glance up as she turned, but returned to her friend's story just as quick. "Out with it then."

Crim untied a pouch from her belt, ensured they were not being watched again, and carefully unfolded it on the table. Laal nearly leapt up with fright, but held on to the arms of her chair for anchorage. Sunshine felt her spine snap straight with a *crack*.

*

"Put those away!" Laal exclaimed, shoving the spiky little stones back into Crim's hands. "These are innocent people!"

"They're not imbued," Crim pointed out, setting the three carbuncles back in the centre of the table. They were each about the size of an egg, circular, and knobbly. For now they were clear, with a swirling black cloud at their core. Sunshine knew that this would take on colour once it was infused with *draoi*. And that colour would mark them as lethal.

"Is this really necessary?"

"We need to be sure they're gone. All of them. We can't have any getting back to the others."

"Others?"

"Mentor told me: that ship is only a small portion of their entire population. Only a small sample of what they're capable of. If the rest come for us, we're done."

"This is horrible," Laal whined, wincing at the sight of the carbuncles and the thoughts of what they could do. "Too horrible. Surely there's some other way—"

"There isn't," Replied Crim. "Believe me, I've driven myself half-mad over it. Spent all these weeks up in the Eyrie thinking. Scoured the Library for other options. This is our chance at survival."

"At what cost?"

Sunshine picked up one of the stones. It was deceptively hefty. "You think three is necessary?"

"We need to be certain it's done."

"One for me?"

"Uh-huh. You, Yuki and I are the best ones to do it."

"Sunny!" Laal exclaimed. "You can't be...you're so easily convinced!"

"I've seen enough of us die. I've seen what they've done to the rest of us—torn us apart, enslaved us, made us afraid in our own home. I believe what Bart said about the genocide, and I believe Crim now."

"Remember Princess, Laal," Crim pressed. "Remember Lilith and Ahid. Bart. Tal. I don't want that happening to anyone else."

"Neither do I. It's just...*horrible.*"

"They were horrible first," Sunshine said bitterly, mind full of golden curls and blue eyes. The never-ending cries of a falling child. She took out her handkerchief and wrapped the carbuncle up tightly in it. "It must be done."

*

Crim downed the rest of her ale. They ate their meal slowly. As the regulars began to trickle out, Diarmuid came over to join them. He sat next to Crim and turned as red as her hair, though she hardly seemed to notice. Sunshine made an effort to be nice to him, especially since Laal had stopped speaking.

"How's the family?" He asked Crim over the rim of his glass.

"Fine. My father is well now."

"Good. I've seen you before, haven't I?"

"Yes," Laal responded shortly.

"Are you another cousin, then?"

Sunshine gaped at him. "Yes?"

"I know meself. Big family. Folks from all over. Sure my cousin's married to a Greek lad." He bounced his knee and glanced at Crim. "World's getting smaller, eh?"

She smiled. "Yes. It is."

Laal set her cutlery neatly across her plate. "We should really be going."

"What where to?"

"Home."

"I doubt you'll be getting home in that dark." He produced a key from his pocket. "Have you anywhere in town to stay?"

"They don't," answered Crim. "I hate to ask, but—"

"Not at all! Only we've not much space to spare, it being Saturday evening. You don't mind sharing the room?"

"We're cousins. We can share the bed. We're used to it."

"It's the best thing to do in this cold! Though don't be doubting I'll give you enough bedding."

He was such a sweet boy, really. Sunshine beamed at him. "We don't doubt you, Love."

L

"Do you think they eat?" Yuki mused, sucking at the last few pieces of meat left on their turkey leg.

"Th-they must…m-m-mustn't they?" She replied, eyeing the pork skewers she had ordered for herself. They were a bit too spicy, though she would never admit it. Instead, she displayed more interest in the simmering vegetable hotpot between them, trying to match each bite of meat with an equal one of mild broth and rice.

"Never seen them do it, though." They licked the leg, and then their fingers, smacking their lips happily.

"I c-c-can't imagine it's q-quite the same ah-as us." Li-Li braved another nibble. "N-nuh…not with those beaks."

"Hmmm…what do they have inside?"

"Guts, I im-imagine."

"Huh? No, I mean…do they have teeth? Teeth and a beak?"

"I d-don't know, Yuki."

"Ask Mentor."

"Sure."

"Maybe they don't chew at all. Maybe they just…" Yuki tilted their head back and mimicked dropping the entire femur down their neck. "…like a bird."

"Uh-huh."

They bit down on the bone with an awful *crunch.* Li-Li winced. Crim liked to do that as well. *Crunch crunch crunch.* "What's the matter?"

She tore an entire chunk off the skewer and immediately regretted it. Hints of black pepper, cumin and cardamom rushed up her nose. The chili did its best to tear a hole through her oesophagus while turmeric and coriander cheered it on. She coughed and barely managed to wheeze: "N-n-nothing."

"Not nothing. You're staring off into space all day, and you ordered the pork skewers because you weren't paying attention and now you can barely swallow a bite. What's wrong?"

Li-Li sat up. "Fine. I'm th-thinking about Sn-S-Snowdrop."

A tiny muscle next to Yuki's left eye twitched. "Me too."

"Do you think sh-she's a-a-a-alive?"

"No."

"Hm." They had not heard from the Ifram since that day in the Library. Not since she disappeared into a column of light. Li-Li had searched the shelves and the stacks and the alcoves, had asked everyone she trusted to keep an eye out, had sat in the cave atop the Blue Stair for hours and hours watching the sky. At times, she would even reach out with her mind, groping at the noise in that accursed ship despite the agony it caused. All for naught.

"What do you think of Crim's plot?"

"I p-prefer n-not to."

"We don't have to do it, you know. I haven't touched the stone yet. We could say no."

"I wo-w-won't leave her."

"Won't leave Crim." Yuki spooned broth over their rice and mixed with far more force than necessary. "Laal said something similar, even though she's *disgusted*. Surprising. I always thought Laal was the more sensible of the three. I suppose that's my own bias overcoming my senses."

"A-and what do y-your senses t-t-tell you?"

Yuki leaned forward, planting their palms firmly on the table. In spite of their diminutive stature, they towered over Li-Li. "She's lost it. She was always a little unhinged, but this mission of hers is *suicide*. You must see that?"

"I don't!"

"Only a *lunatic* would think this is the only way!"

Li-Li threw down her spoon and looked away. "That's your op-opinion. Yuh-y-you're entitled to it. You a-a-aren't being forced to f-f-f-follow her either, you n-know. You c-c-can wa-walk away."

"I can't. Not while…while all of you are in danger."

"Hmph."

"What if Snowdrops still up there?" They attempted at last. "We can't possibly let her die with the rest of them!"

Two Ifram stalked past, one holding up a beaded bracelet and jangling it as he went, *clicking*. Li-Li watched them all the way to the entrance, where they turned right down a passage. Dishes clattering on the table, she pushed her chair out and made after them. "You're r-right."

"Li-Li? Oi!" Yuki dashed after her and took her by the arm. "What are you doing?"

"Searching for our friend."

*

"No! Absolutely not!" Yuki stared at the ship. "We're not going up there!"

"Aren't you c-c-curious?"

"No!"

"A-aren't you wo-worried about Snowdrop?"

"Not half as worried as I am about us right now."

"Don't say that. I-if she's u-u-u there, you want to f-find her, too."

"Yes. I do. I don't want her to get caught in Crim's mess. But…Li-Li if we get caught—"

"They're f-fuh-friends, remember? Surely th-they won't m-mind? We're j-just visiting."

Yuki mussed their shock of blue hair. "Wouldn't say that. I…"

"W-wh-hat do you think th-they'll do?"

"Kill us." They insisted. "But, Li-Li, what are *you* planning to do?"

"Just a puh-peek. I s-swear. We won't touch a-a-anything. If w-we can't fi-find her, we l-l-leave. Unseen."

Yuki wavered.

"I'm g-g-going either way, Yu-Yuki. W-with or without you."

"Ugh. How do we get up?"

"S-s-same as them, I guess." Li-Li took their hand and led them over to the pedestal. "She sh-sh-showed us h-how."

They tugged her. "Let's do it at once. We don't know where we're going, after all."

"Right." She held up both of their hands.

"On three?"

"N-n-nope!"

It was nothing like the tug of a Doorway. As soon as their hands touched the stone, Li-Li felt warm all over, then her vision went blank, and for a split second she forgot who or what she was. It only lasted a few moments, before her eyes opened to a bright chamber decked from floor to ceiling in geometric patterns of white and gold. The floor below seemed to be made of glass, below which narrow pipes could be seen sending up sharp beams of white light. She squeezed her eyes shut, trying to adjust. *Gods,* it was so bright in here. Blinding. How did those creatures stand it? Her eyes, even her lids ached. Only when she put her hands to them did she realise Yuki was gone.

"Yu...*Yuki!*" She spun in place. "Yuki!"

Stumbling down the steps from the podium, half-blind in the searing white, she did a lap of the empty room. It was no use, of course. They were not there. With panic uncoiling in her stomach, she decided on one of the three doors leading out. Another, silvery-grey stone much like the one on the podium was attached to the wall beside it—touching this opened the door with a soft *whoosh.* Beyond was a long, equally bright corridor. Another door led off to the right, and one also faced her. Trembling, Li-Li made for the one on the right first—the stone next to this turned red and let out an accusatory *beep beep beep* at the press of her palm. She jumped and hurried on.

*

Every corridor in this ship looked the same. This was the conclusion Li-Li came to as she combed another section—or what she at least *thought* it was another section. She couldn't tell. There were platforms at a few points that moved up and down; she had taken a three of these to different levels, but lost count of just how many ups and how many downs there had been.

Yuki was still nowhere to be found. She had taken a few minutes to cry in a corner, and now was determined to find them. No matter what. Not a single Ifram passed her, and she soon stopped checking corners and squeezing into nooks to listen for suspicious sounds. It was like there was no-one home.

Another down. Another door. Another long corridor. This one had smaller doors at smaller intervals. Most of the ones she had tried had been locked.

"No harm in trying..." She pressed her palm to the nearest one. It beeped once and *whooshed* open. "...Oh?"

Li-Li popped her head in, and at once failed to comprehend what she saw. To her right, a round glass pod stood open, a thick greenish liquid bubbling slightly within. There was nothing else in the room, save a shallow pool opposite her, filled with the same substance. An Ifram stood next to this, dangling two of its lower tentacles over the lip. It was small, yellowish in colour and naked, and far more gelatinous than its male counterparts. The little female looked up as the door opened.

And shrieked.

*

Pain in her temples, like someone had jabbed her in either side of her head. She peered out under her lashes, waiting for movement. With no sign of anyone in the room, Li-Li tried to stir, only to groan with agony. Lying still again, she ran her tongue over bloody teeth and cracked lips. She managed to roll her head to one side, which caused her shoulder to throb, to find that she was still lashed to the same stained table. At her feet was a desk, and a door that led to a row of cages—one of which she had briefly occupied. She knew the door to the stairwell was on her right, but the wall to her left was the real focal point of the dank, dark chamber. On hooks and shelves. Nailed to the wall and propped upright. Hanging from the ceiling on long chains that ended in rusty manacles. Instruments of torture left on display like prized possessions, ranging from the very simple to the utterly deranged. Li-Li had learned most of their names over the past days, along with their bite.

Her bonds were woven from Sidhe hair—she could not break them, nor the truesteel brackets that held them to the table. The wood itself, softened by eons of fluids, was not as sturdy. She had been scraping at the fixtures in all of her fleeting moments of rest. Now she wrapped her broken and battered fingers around them, tugging.

The roar of pain as she strained nearly ejected her from her body, but she persisted, laughing hoarsely as one arm jerked loose, then the other. She picked a chisel up from the small table by her head and hacked at the parts holding her legs down. For as long has she had lain here, she had worked to set herself free. Now she sat up and searched for the next step. The door was surely locked, and there was nothing in the cells save the crumbling remains of their last inhabitants and a family of rats. She slid over, legs dangling.

"What the fuck do I do now?"

There might have been a key in the desk, but she disliked her chances of getting anywhere unarmed. From the shelves, a large truesteel sickle winked out at her. *Perfect.*

Her feet gave from under her. She fell through the air. The sickle winked mockingly as her face connected with the shelf.

*

A boot nudged her shoulder. Not hard; just enough to wake her. The second time was a bit rougher. She remained facing the wall, knees hugged up to her chest.

"I said *up!*" The heel this time, it came down with enough force to make her move. She uncurled. Before she could raise herself hands clamped round her arms, hoisting her until she stood, filthy and cold, facing him. Hyeong smiled his shark-toothed smile as he held her there. "See? It wasn't that hard, was it?"

Li-Li remained mute. She had not spoken to any of them since they tossed her in this damp, filthy place, since they refused to tell her where Yuki was. Even when they tried to beat the words out of her, she did not utter a sound. She let five whole days and nights pass in silence, staring at the walls and ceiling instead of eating or drinking, letting her mind drift out in search of Yuki, and finding nothing. No matter what they did, she would not speak.

"Mother wants to see you."

Cold in the pit of her stomach. They had threatened her with this. Told her they would let Mother and Mentor know she had been snooping where she was not wanted. Said Mother would rip her limb from limb. Li-Li had heard the stories, or some of them at least. Enough to know that she should be afraid, that she didn't stand a chance if Mother decided to end her existence.

And she devoured him. On the steps of the Forum, she ate him piece by piece.

"And I suppose you still have nothing to say?"

She pursed her lips tightly shut. Speaking meant giving away why they were on that ship, meant exposing herself and Crim, and incriminating everyone around them. She would rather die. Hopefully swiftly and painlessly. Though she knew now that was a dream.

"*Tut tut tut.*" Hyeong gave her a shove towards the door, she hit the frame, shoulder screaming again, then lurched through. Nashoba lingered in the shadows of the broad, sloping stairs, arms crossed and silent as always, though she thought she saw the hard line of his mouth twist at the sight of her. Just a little. He gestured upwards and fell into step in front, leading her up through the previously-unused Dungeons. There was little illumination save a few untended star stones, wavering as their energy slowly sapped away over time. The steps were shallow, and roughly three strides wide, leading them around and around in an endless spiral with cells and guard rooms opening this way and that, as well as the occasional store room and theatrical torture chamber. Li-Li guessed that it took them all night to climb to the top, though her fussy mind and wobbling legs might have exaggerated that somewhat. There were others down here, she knew that. She had heard and felt them over time, now as they passed each door she put out feelers, seeking Yuki, or any sign of them. All she found were a few desperate spirits, a few hopeless ones, and a few empty husks.

They stopped climbing, finally, and a steady *thump thump thump* on a cast-iron door from Nashoba had it creaking open to reveal the faces of two other Reavers, both of whom eyed her with contempt.

"Delivery for Mother," Hyeong sneered behind her. "A lost little lamb."

They sniggered, copying him, and together heaved the bar off another iron door at the opposite end of the guard's mess hall. Hyeong bowed to them and sauntered on. Nashoba made to go after him, but then seemed to remember that they were escorting Li-Li—their prisoner, and looped in behind her.

"See down there?" He whispered in her ear, pointing down the passage. His voice was the same deep, grating rasp she remembered. The one her mistress so enjoyed. "The kitchens are that way, and the Hall beyond. Perhaps, if you hadn't been so nosy, you could be enjoying a nice hot meal with your friends right now."

In the Hall? Li-Li rolled her eyes. She could hardly remember the last time she ate in there. Her and her friends much preferred each other's company to everyone else's.

He chuckled darkly as though he had made some sort of joke, air hissing through those shark's teeth, and turned right. "Unfortunately, you're going *this way*. To the High Stair."

"If only Crim knew what you were doing to me."

A low growl. A soft shove on her good shoulder. "Move."

The way to Mother's chambers was abandoned, cordoned off by guards at regular intervals. These passages were hardly used at the best of times, but now they met not a soul, Hyeong, Nashoba, and Li-Li stuck between them like a convict on her way to the gallows. She managed her expression into one of stone, but inside a frantic fear threatened to burst forth.

Run. It said. Nashoba had made one mistake—she knew if she could just make it through the kitchens and beyond the Hall, those passages led directly up to the apartment. It would be a long sprint.

Her ankles twinged in response. They were still healing. Hyeong's sledgehammer had assured that there would be no running for quite a while.

She walked instead, one shaking leg in front of the other, the flagstones hard and cold underfoot. The High Stair loomed ahead, lit up blue by large star stones. Hyeong dashed forward, up the first flight and turned to face her, giggling.

"Here we go!"

She stopped short, Nashoba's heavy footfalls ceasing right behind her. Even if she got away from Hyeong, he would catch her. She was sure she would *rather* Nashoba catch her—he was by far the sounder of the two—but had no desire to see how well-placed her faith was.

The steps zig-zagged back and forth on themselves one hundred times, the tap of their feet echoing up and down to announce their arrival. No doubt Mother knew she was coming. Li-Li wrang her hands and cleared her drying throat. Would she ever come back down?

*

A single shaft of onyx jutting out from the inner wall of the Mountain, reaching up to the rocky ceiling. There was no need for light stones here; a narrow gap in the Mountainside filtered light from their miniature sun and miniscule moon towards them, throwing an oblong spotlight across the black marble floor. In this pool of light stood two guards. Not Seti and Yamanu, as they had always been. Ifram this time. This did not bode well. Where were the Trueborn? They never left Mother. As the trio approached one of them held out an arm and Li-Li flinched. The device he held emitted a yellow beam and *bleep-bleeped.* He turned to Hyeon and clicked.

"Mother wanted to see her. She's one of the two from the ship."

Two. So they had found Yuki. So where were they? Had they already met with Mother? Were they already…?

"*Move!*" Hyeong yanked her arm. "She awaits."

Her legs no longer worked, so walking up to the ebony doors proved a challenge. She tried to focus, wide-eyed, on the dark wood. Tried to admire the handiwork and the detail of each barely-visible grain that ran from top to toe. Her feet caught one another and she tilted forward, but Nashoba caught and steadied her as Hyeong laughed, still dragging her forward. He rapped several times excitedly.

*

"You have been *told—*"

Hyeong cowered away from the door. Li-Li leaped forward past him to the familiar face emerging from the golden light of one of Mother's smaller chambers.

"M-m-m-Mentor!" She threw herself into her teacher's arms. Mentor enfolded her without hesitation, exhaling in a weary sigh.

"Hyeong, Nashoba. You will wait out here. Mother only wishes to speak to Li-Li."

The two scowled at Mentor's ordered, clearly offended. Hyeon opened his mouth to protest, but his friend clapped a heavy hand down on his shoulders.

"We will wait," Nashoba concurred, leading him away.

Mentor had Li-Li now, and steered her firmly inside, shutting the door closed tightly and turning the lock. She did not speak as she sat her down on the recessed sofa. Not a word even as she turned to fetch Mother.

"Mentor?"

Halting, she did not look back at her. "I cannot speak to you right now, Child. Not before Mother has had her say. Please wait here."

There was something *wrong* in the way Mentor spoke, her speech strangely lilted and cold. She strode out of the room with a smile, not one of encouragement. Not that Mentor had ever been the most affectionate person, but Li-Li had always trusted her, always known she would keep her safe.

That trust was not there now, and that icy dread crept into her veins again as she realised. Her teeth began to chatter. She felt ill.

Where is Yuki?

The velvet cushion by her elbow toppled off the seat, causing her to start. A snake thicker than her thighs was slowly sliding out from behind her. He raised his head, groggy and obviously as surprised by their meeting as she, took a good long look at her and yawned, revealing the two long, venomous fangs that Mother had gifted him long ago.

"Y-you must b-b-be Apep, then," she guessed. "I've h-huh-heard about you. F-from Mentor, Crim…a-all of them."

He looked up again and flicked his tongue, the rest of his body still emerging from his little nook between the seat and back of the sofa.

"I-I'm Li-Li." Her teeth still chattered, but somehow the serpent made her feel more at ease. Somehow, his eyes were calm, kind. As his tail finally coiled up to meet the rest of his body, he began to move again. Not onto the floor to find another hiding place, as she expected, but into her lap, curling the upper half of his body into a loose knot and letting the lower portion stretch out on the seat. He rested his head on her knee, content. "If I d-didn't nuh-know any better, I'd s-s-say you were t-trying to comfort me."

He stuck out his tongue, and said nothing.

*

They did not have to wait long for Mentor to emerge from the next room, peering strangely at Li-Li, expression unreadable.

"She will see you. Alone."

Should she stand? How, with the snake still resting in her lap? She could not find the strength anyway. Mentor's glare struck an electric fear in her, and she forced herself up from the sofa, poor Apep rolling to the floor. He did not complain, but slithered away. As she made her way over to the door, she reached out to Mentor, seeking some sort of comfort. Expectedly, she was left feeling alone and hopeless for her fruitless attempt. Mentor stepped past her, but lingered on the threshold as Li-Li entered.

"Leave us." Mother's voice was low, calm, but stern. No one questioned what she said. Except, perhaps, for Mentor.

"But I—"

"*Leave. I wish to speak with your pupil alone.*"

Mentor frowned, looked in Mother's direction as if to say something else, but then clearly thought better of it and skulked out the doors. Defeated as she was, she voiced her displeasure by shutting them firmly.

This chamber was much smaller, a step bringing her down onto a tiled walkway hemmed by small black columns banded in gold. A window no doubt fathoms above let in a golden fall of sunlight that illuminated the steaming Roman bath. It was here that Mother sat, long arms hanging lazily along one side, scented leaves and flower petals kissing her gleaming skin, the rest of her submerged in pure white milk.

"*I—*"

"*You were not yet invited to speak.*"

Li-Li's mouth snapped shut immediately.

"Come. Sit. Wash yourself first. You stink."

She rocked in place. Mother was inviting her to bathe with her? Did this mean she was safe? Or did she just want her to be clean when she ripped her throat out?

"I will not have you standing here spreading that stench around my chambers. Take a sponge and soap from there." Mother pointed to a small cabinet nearby. "Quickly. I am losing patience."

*

Li-Li sprang into action. The sponges were large, soft; the soap she chose dotted with grains of sugar and fragrant. A king cobra peeped out from one of the urns as she shut the press. Curious, friendly. He had not been placed there as a trap, but curled back down to sleep once he had greeted her.

Undressing in front of Mother was a strange experience, helped immensely by her superiors' interest in the small water snake that had joined her in the bath. Out of the corner Li-Li had the honour of observing her playing with the creature, lifting first one leg and then the other out of the milk to let him coil around. All play stopped when she turned and lowered herself opposite them. The hot milk felt divine against her wounds—though it burned at first, this quickly subsided into a slight tingle. Li-Li guessed that it had replenishing properties, and prayed that it would heal at least part of her.

With the sponge and the soap she scrubbed. First her matted and crusted hair, then her stained face. As she reached her shoulders the task of washing became increasingly more difficult, and she thought she might faint when she had to bend for her toes. At this point Apep joined them, looping around a nearby column to first inspect the milk, then her. His cold nose tipped her injured arm, little tongue flicking out against her flesh. She understood he was trying to comfort her, and smiled a teary smile at such a sweet little creature. He draped himself lazily across her shoulders.

*

"First, I will tell you what you are charged with." Mother boomed at once, startling both of them. Even the water snake looked up. "Then I may ask you some questions. Finally, when I am satisfied, I will decide your fate. Do not lie to me—it will serve you no good. Understand?"

She nodded frantically.

"You were found by the Ifram guards in the chamber of a female on a restricted deck of their ship. You had arrived there via their transportation technology after following two of them out of the Mountain and witnessing them using it. You were not invited onto the ship, but proceeded to make your way onto it and snoop around without anyone's knowledge. Because of your behaviour, *I* have had to defend this entire Mountain against accusations of espionage and endangering our guests by not keeping a proper eye on my subjects. I have denied all allegations and tried to show our *friends* that we have zero tolerance for such things by punishing you and your co-conspirator. Thankfully, the Ifram are so far pleased with how I have handled the situation, and are no longer threatening retaliation."

Li-Li gulped. Her head was spinning. She could hardly stay focused on Mother with the sound of her own blood rushing past her eardrums.

"Pleased as they are with *us* as a whole, however, they are still *not* pleased with you. That is to say: they still want you dead."

And there it was. She shut her eyes even before Mother said it, knowing what was coming.

"What do you have to say for yourself, Li-Li?"

What did she have to say?

Well, if they're going to kill me anyway: "They're m-monsters. All of thuh-them. And a-as long as y-y-you align yourself wi-with them, you're a monster t-t-too."

Mother's hand struck out faster than she could see; she only felt the sharp wind that came along with it. In the back of her mind, she told herself to close her eyes, not to witness her own murder, but instead they went wide, hands gripping the sharp tile, bracing for impact.

*

An angry *hiss!* A weight gone from her shoulders. Apep had leapt between them, gifted fangs gleaming in the sunlight as he aimed for the Mother's throat. Mother grunted, catching the snake in her two hands she stood up, milk cascading off her muscular form and *twisted.* With a hideous, wet noise, innards spilling down into their pristine white bath she twisted him apart, tossing head and body in opposite directions. Dark blood splattered all over Li-Li, the parts that had dropped down between them slowly turning the milk a revolting pink. She gaped down at it, then back up at Mother, who was picking bits of snake from between her fingers, gold eyes burning bright.

"A-a-a…*Apep!"*

"He disobeyed me."

Li-Li snivelled.

And then Mother had her, was lifting her bodily out of the water. Li-Li sobbed, but did not fight. What was the point? She would probably split her in half like her supposedly-beloved familiar.

She was on the floor now. Against the wall, stars dancing in her eyes. Had Mother thrown her? She felt the tiles behind her tender head. Yes, she had thrown her. Tears were streaming down her face.

"Please…*p-p-please just end it!"*

"Get out."

Li-Li rolled onto all fours and tried to crawl into the corner. Fingers like iron had her by the hair now, yanking her back. She hit the doorframe heavily and heard her left wrist *snap* as she tried to catch herself. The pain was a distant memory.

"Get out!"

"M-M-Mother!"

But Mother was on the other side of the room now. "Enough of you! *Out!"*

Panting, she watched as Mother picked up the upper half of Apep's body from where it had fallen behind a fern, and realised her punishment was over.

I'm free. Not dead. Free.

*

She fell across the apartment through the door, still bawling like a scolded child, heart galloping away in her chest. Battered but alive. Hyeong and Nashoba were gone; there was only Mentor standing there waiting.

"Come here." Mentor held out her arms, a plain blue robe in one hand.

"No."

"You're starkers."

"No!" Li-Li backed against a pillar, naked and battered. "Y-you left me d-d-down there! W-with *him! You left me in there with* her!"

"I had to. Li-Li. I had to let them think I was complacent."

"She tried to kill me!"

"No she didn't!" Mentor retorted. "If she wanted you dead, you would be in pieces."

Like poor Apep.

"Who do you think convinced her not to, eh? Who spent *every night* after those things left *begging* her to spare you. Feeding her stories about you being curious about—no—*fascinated* by the Ifram."

Mentor tossed the robe at her feet. Not letting her out of her sight, Li-Li retrieved it, tying the sash loosely around her tender ribs. Her teacher strode away, and she started at the sight of Onaldi lingering nearby. Surely she must have heard? If so, she gave no sign, but stood silently in the pool of light with an arm around—

"*Yuki!*" Fresh streams of tears spilled down her cheeks, and she rushed to embrace them. "You're a-alive! B-but...oh...Y-Y-Yuki..."

They were unrecognisable, their face swollen and bloodied, and purple where it was not bloody. They had a bandage over one eye, and a long gash had been stitched haphazardly shut from their jaw to the back of their neck. What sections of skin were visible were stained green and yellow by old bruises, purple and black by new ones. Welts and punctures marked them from head to toe. They leaned heavily on Onaldi, one of their legs broken and the other also noticeably burned under their matching robe. They groaned up at her, unable to speak.

"They'll be fine," Mentor assured her. "Blood, a few days' rest, some food and drink, and all this will mend. You're both lucky to be alive."

Li-Li did not respond, not feeling in the least bit lucky. She guided Yuki's arms around her and balanced them. They were lighter than they looked. "C-c-come on, le-let's get you huh-home."

LI

She watched as Laal slowly ran a whetstone over the edge of a set of small, curved knives. Watched the spark as the stone hit the blade at the start of each pass. Watched the candlelight flash across the etched truesilver and finely-sculpted truegold handles whenever the weapons were moved. A brown leather belt lay on the table, slotted with narrow sheaths, ready to be tied to Laal's waist.

The weight of the scabbard at her own hip reminded her of what they were about to do. What the others had talked her into. None of them had ever used their weapons for anything other than training or hunting, (except maybe Mentor) but tonight if their plans went awry (Sunshine had imagined a dozen ways in which they would), they might finally be put to proper use.

"Here. Might want to do your sword, too."

Sunshine glared at the stone placed in the middle of the table, like this was what was now tearing her conscience asunder. Not the fact that she and Laal were so prepared to end thousands of lives for the sake of theirs. Not the fact that they had all agreed to it *so quickly*. Nor the revulsion she now felt towards all of them.

Now she and Laal sat across the table from one another, and also worlds apart. They had hardly spoken since the tavern, since their plan had been put into motion. Laal was still not happy with it. Sunshine was not either, but she saw Crim's logic. Saw that there was no other hope. What had happened to Li-Li and Yuki only solidified her hatred for the Ifram, and her certainty that they would stop at *nothing* to subdue all Sidhe, perhaps even all life. She did not want to speak—she was angry, scared, choked by guilt and grief—but as the time drew nearer there came a mortal panic that Laal would never understand…

"Laal?"

"Hm."

"If we…If something happens up there…"

"I know. You told me. When they catch us do not hesitate, because they won't."

"No. Not that." She cringed. Had she really said that? It was sound enough advice, given the circumstances…"I was going to say; if I don't make it—"

"*Sunny!*" Laal whirled to look at her. "Don't you dare say that!"

"But I have to, Laal. Now let me finish will you?" With a deep breath she blurted: "If I don't survive this, I want you to—to understand…To know how much I love you."

That beautiful face twisted, and Laal's throat bobbed. "I know you love me. I love you too. And I'm sorry but I won't let anything happen to you. You are not permitted to think about it."

"Laal…you can't deny the possibility that *not all of us—*"

"*All of us!*" Laal barked, startling her. "All of us are surviving this night, Sunny!"

"But—"

"Don't even suggest that!" A little tear streaked down her cheek. "Don't you dare."

"I'm sorry." She stood, and with an ease not a thousand lives or a thousand sins would ever take from them, swept her into her arms. "I'm not trying to upset you. But we have to face facts."

"I'll face facts if it happens. Not now. I just want to enjoy now while we can."

*

The ship loomed silently overhead, sleek lines and polished hull warping and reflecting images of stars so that the night sky seemed distorted. As she had had ensured countless times, there were no discernible windows, just one gigantic solid mass of metal watching over the peace of the Mountain. Still, she felt eyes on them.

At her elbow, Li-Li shivered, and Yuki hugged her one-handed with a faraway look on their face. There were five people present, huddled on and around benches in the cave just a few yards away from the transportation device, yet not a sound could be heard. Now, at the brink of it, Sunshine sensed that they were all questioning their purpose here. She uncurled her fingers to inspect the carbuncle glowing yellow in her palm. Strange to think that such a small thing would soon determine who lived or died before dawn. Turning it idly, she pondered (not for the first time) her right to hold that kind of power in her hand.

At once, Crim sprang up from where she had huddled on the ground, and ducking further behind the rocky mouth tilted her head, listening carefully. Sunshine perked her ears up, too, and nodded as they locked eyes. Footsteps, following the same skirting path as they had, approaching slowly. Crim looked down and the prints they had neglected to cover, and swore under her breath.

"What are you hiding for, Crim?"

"I…was just resting, Mentor. I've been hunting. In the Forest."

A weak lie. Crim was usually a better spoofer than that.

"And what did you catch?"

"A hare."

"You don't like hare."

"No, I don't." Crim hesitated. "That's why I left it. Something else will get to eat it now, at least."

"Crim?"

"Yep?"

"Why are you all here?"

Sunshine tucked the stone back into her pocket. Stepping forward to meet Mentor, she interjected:

"Just sitting…and…"

"It's unnerving, isn't it?"

Crim, now behind Mentor's back, cocked an eyebrow at her.

"I don't know what you mean, Mentor."

She jerked her head towards the ship. "That thing. Hanging there. Like it's watching. Like it's waiting."

Sunshine glanced up, then back at her. "I think it's beautiful."

"Don't bullshit me."

Her heart leapt in her chest. Their confidence in Mentor had been rocked again, but still she wanted her with them. Was she lucid again? Or were they caught? "Um…"

"I've been watching you. All of you," Mentor declared loudly, peering around the rocks concealing Laal, Li-Li and Yuki. They two younglings had left their seat and were cowering in the back of the cave, healed by blood but still hurt. "You didn't think anyone would notice you skulking about under the ship? Or sneaking off to that mortal town?"

Behind her, Crim's eyes went wide. Concern for the mortals? Or them? Or both?

Sunshine willed herself to stay focused on Mentor.

"Mentor, we're just curious. We swear."

"No, you're reckless. The lot of you. You underestimated your foes and have raised their suspicions."

"I don't know what—"

"*Don't bullshit me, Sunny!*" Mentor snapped. "I know tonight is the night. I know what you're going to do. That's why I'm here now—to make sure you don't fuck things up more than you already have!"

"I-I…What?"

Laal rose, and stood before the acolytes. "Mentor, please. You need to understand; we couldn't tell you—"

"The Ifram are our enemy," she finished, with a nod. "Are insidious, dangerous, vicious. No-one knows this better than me. I am saying it now to prove I'm not under their sway. When I first met them…it wasn't like I said to everyone. It was never *pleasant,* they never *welcomed* me. That's just what they made me believe. They took me…*somewhere*. They did…*something*. Until I forgot who I was and what I stood for. Until I was moulded into their willing ambassador to our people. I handed the Mountain and its secrets over to them, and now their poison runs deep."

Sunshine shifted, not sure what to think of this sudden switch in character. As she had seen that time in the Arena, Mentor seemed clearer now; the glow returned to her eyes, the vivacity returned to her sharp features. Could she really believe the old Mentor was with them now? The one that was always on their side? "Mentor, are you…?"

"I'm myself. I see things clearly. For now, at least; you know it never lasts long." She balled her fists. "I have to fight it every hour of every day. For you, and the other younglings that stray. But while I'm here—while I'm myself again—I'll help."

Laal perked up. "How?"

"Well, I don't trust myself to go with you. If I go back to being hazy again I'll only put all of us at risk. So I'll stay here while the five of you go up there. I can't do much else but remind you where you're going." Mentor crouched down and traced an oval in the dirt. Crim and Sunshine hunkered next to her, watching carefully, while Laal and the others maintained a safe distance, listening all the

393

same. "As Li-Li and Yuki should remember, the teleportation pad over there leads you to a chamber in the lower section of the vessel—let's say around here—they don't think we're smart enough to get up onto their ship, *or* find our way around it *or* understand the schematics they leave lying around in the Mess Hall, so you should be able to get from here to the engines—here, here, here—without any trouble. They don't post guards *anywhere*."

"Th-that's right," Li-Li interrupted. "I d-didn't see a s-s-soul until I wa-wandered into one of their r-r-rooms."

"I practically landed on top of two," Yuki remarked, wincing.

"The engines are where you want to go—there's one on the third level, opposite another teleportation chamber…just here."

"Li-Li, Yuki," Crim interrupted. "You do that one and get out."

"But—"

"No discussion!"

"Another two floors up in the same place."

"That's ours," Sunshine declared, throwing an inappropriately casual wink at Laal, who scowled.

"If you disable both of these, they'll be crippled. To be *truly* effective, you will need to destroy all three. The last one is on the seventh floor, but it's the most risky. It's right next to the bridge."

"That's my one."

"You can't go alone, Crim!" Laal objected.

"This is my idea. One person is less likely to draw attention. I can…distract them if there's a problem."

"Crim…"

"There won't be a problem. Mentor's giving us all of the intel. Right?"

"Correct."

"H-how do we get d-d-down?"

"Get back to this room—or one of them," Mentor instructed. "There's one on each floor, as far as I know. I don't understand how they…*direct* you, so you might end up in the middle of nowhere. But it'll bring you back to the Mountain."

*

Still tucked into their corner, Li-Li and Yuki squeezed each other tighter, the trauma of crossing the Ifram still fresh in their minds.

"And what next?" Laal pressed. "What happens once the ship is done with? Some of them still be here, after all. With those weapons."

"You have more allies than you think, girls," Mentor informed them, smirking. "And I've already spoken to some of them. Win or fail, there's already an army mustering in the Mountain, ready to pick up where you've left off."

Crim lit up. "Allies?"

"Most of them have just been waiting for an opportunity to strike. This is it."

"And this will be our rallying cry," Sunshine mused, grinning in spite of herself. A flicker of hope had taken up residence in her heart, dispelling all doubt.

"Exactly."

"What about you, Mentor? When the fight begins, will you—"

"I can't promise you anything, Sunny. But I hope to help. I'll fight to remain clear, if nothing else." Mentor stood and brushed the dust off her knees. "I'm proud of all of you, just so you know."

Those words stung the corners of Sunshine's eyes, and before she even knew what she was doing, she yanked Mentor into a hug. "Thank you, Mentor. Thank you for everything. We love you no matter what."

Mentor grumbled something back, but endured the gesture, and Sunshine only stepped back when Laal was there, squeezing her tight. Next came dear, sweet Li-Li, blubbering and unable to form words, then Yuki who said nothing, Crim was last of all, with muttered thanks, who received a jab on the shoulder in return. For the briefest of seconds, Mentor turned, seeking a sixth pupil, only to drop her arms and sigh.

"Let's get those vermin."

*

Bright. Much too bright. Sunshine winced against the searing lamps that filled the room with their white-hot glow. Passing a hand over her eyes did nothing, did not even dispel the colourful dots now scattered across her field of vision.

"*Shit.*" Crim jabbed two knuckled into her sockets and rubbed. This proved futile, and she ended up shutting her eyes completely for a long while. "How can they stand this?"

"Do they not have night in their world?" Laal groaned, droplets coating her lashes.

"I d-don't remember it b-be-being this bad before?"

"No, they've upped the ante," Yuki growled. "I still remember the inside, though. It just goes around in a loop."

"Ri-r-right. Out, to th-the o-other end." Li-Li was gesticulating. Sunshine could not focus on her hands. "U-up two fuh-floors."

Crim, still groping blindly, found the wall with her palm. "Go. Like we planned. Don't deviate. You and Yuki take one engine. Sunny and Laal the other. Don't even wait to regroup here; just plant it and get out."

"Crim?"

"I'll be fine, Li-Li."

"We don't want you to go alone, Crim," Laal scolded.

"I don't want any of *you* going alone."

"I could."

"No. You and Sunny stay together. I'll be *fine*, I swear."

Sunshine took Laal by the elbow. "She'll probably have better luck sneaking around alone, Love."

She bit her beautiful lip. "But what will happen if they catch her?"

"The same thing that will happen to any of us if we're unlucky," Yuki cut in. "There'll be no holding back this time."

With that same sorrowful look on her face, Laal kissed Crim's cheek. "If you die, I'll never forgive you."

Crim guffawed. "You too."

Seventeen. That was how many times Laal turned to check behind them since they had boarded the ship. Sunshine got her by the wrist and tugged her on.

"There's no-one behind us."

"I know," she hissed back. "I'm worried about Crim."

"She can take care of herself. She's crafty. Vicious sometimes, too. Pity the Ifram that crosses her."

"Hm." Laal peeked over her shoulder again. "Still—if she gets into trouble…If she can't make it back to the transferer-teleporter *thing*—we should have agreed on a rendezvous point."

"Stop it."

"I can't."

"You have to. Stop *worrying*. That's what will get us caught, you know. I need you at full faculties. You and that brain of yours."

Laal groaned.

A large, bulky door came into view as they rounded the next corner, and they let out a unanimous sigh of relief. They had made it to the engine room unhindered.

"I hope Li-Li and Yuki made it this easily."

"*Laal.*"

"Right. You're right. Of course they did. They know the ship better than we do, after all."

Sunshine snorted.

"Oh, that was a bad joke."

"Laal."

*

The door hummed open on unseen hinges, disappearing into the walls on either side. Beyond was a room blessedly dimmer than the rest of the ship; desks and glass panels displaying schematics and illegible messages were set at regular intervals, each *humming* and *beeping* to its own beat. Laal, ever the student, seemed to forget her worries for the moment, staring fixedly at the nearest one.

"This looks like the engine." She prodded one of the spinning images in the margin, and it appeared on the main screen as a full, three-dimensional model. "Amazing. I have no idea what any of this means."

"There's a first." Sunshine hefted her carbuncle in one hand and nodded to the full-sized engine. It stood a good ten metres high and was surrounded by various platforms and walkways leading all the way to its crown. Shaped like an hourglass, it burned with a pale blue light at its core, which flared into purple, then fuchsia at either end. It emanated power, pure power. She felt the pulse of it from her heart to her fingertips.

"Laal. As soon as I plant this we need to run," she warned.

"What? But you said there was no one—"

"There *is* no-one behind us. But we need to make sure we're as far away as possible when this thing blows. Preferably back inside the Mountain."

"Yuki and Li-Li—"

"Are smart enough to do the same."

Laal gulped, now forgetting about the desks and the screens, her aquamarine eyes wide as Sunshine placed their carbuncle against the vibrating gold base. The stone fizzed slightly as it adhered to cold metal, yellow glow at its core now *throbbing* with intent.

"It won't go until we're off the ship, that much I can guarantee."

"How far?"

"That much I *cannot.*"

*

"W-we need to g-g-*go.*"

Yuki bent over one of the desks, trying to make sense of the scrawling glowing across its surface. Like the others in this room, what it said did not mean anything to them, so like the others it cracked and broke under their fist.

"Y-*Yuki!*"

"It won't go off 'til we're back on solid ground."

"Th-that doesn't mean you sh-sh-should—"

With a snarl, Yuki took the next table by either side and yanked so that the veins stood out on their neck. Lifting it in a shower of sparks and broken glass, they threw the whole thing against the wall, where it met with another panel to a loud *crash.*

"*Yuki!*"

"You should try this." They sneered, gesturing to the few pieces of furniture left intact. "It's very therapeutic."

"Yuki, stop it!"

Another tinkle as a screen hit the floor. "I told you, it won't—"

"What if they c-come!" Li-Li squeaked, eyeing the door fearfully. "They m-must have huh-heard."

"Let them. I'll do the same to those bastards."

"Let's *go!*"

"Just two more."

"Yuki, I c-c-can't go b-back."

An agonised expression passed over their features, and Yuki considered the desk in their hand, still attached to the floor on one side and smoking. Each broken wire sent a current of electricity up through their arms as they smashed and punched and tore. They drank it up, that power, forgetting all the pain and fear this place had brought them not long ago.

Li-Li. Poor Li-Li had been there too. Had been tortured and traumatised the same as them. It was easy to forget. She had so quickly gone back to just being Li-Li that they forgot more often than they liked to admit. Now she was standing here, terror in her eyes, clutching her skirts and worrying at the fabric as she turned once again to look at the door.

Yuki placed the desk carefully back down. *Idiot. Get her out of here!* They reached for Li-Li's hand and she started when they took it, for a split second, she regarded them with pure fear.

"Idiot." They nudged her towards the door. "Come on, let's go."

"Y-yeah."

She followed, hand trembling in theirs, pressed right up against the wall as they hurried back down to the transferal chamber. Both of them kept eyes on the narrow doors, ready to run as soon as one opened. None did, as expected, and they made it to the nearest teleporting room intact. As the machine droned, pulling them off the damned vessel and back to the Mountainside, Li-Li let out a laugh of relief and fell against Yuki, hugging them close.

"Made it."

"Yeah. Made it."

*

Truth be told; she had no clue what she was looking for. She was almost certain she was getting close to where Mentor had marked the engine rooms, but none of the doors would open. Crim found herself still walking in circles around the ship trying to decide where she was going. The doors on either side of her all looked the same, and there was neither sign nor map to point her in the right direction. Not to mention she was running out of time—the carbuncles the others were placing on the engines would not be activated until all of them were off the ship, true, but there was only so long they—she—could remain aboard undetected.

She went up a floor, maybe she had miscounted? Another loop around a same-ish hallway, past the same narrow doors. Li-Li had told her what she had found behind one of those doors—a startled female—and looking at them now distracted her with thoughts of Snowdrop. Was she here? If she opened every door she passed, would she finally find her, alive and well? If she tried, and put their mission in danger, could she save her as well?

Can't do that. Crim caught herself pausing before one of the cabins, fingers twitching to touch the stone in the wall and barge in. She balled her fists and marched on.

*

The next level of the ship was the smallest, as the giant oval rounded out. No doors immediately as she exited the lifting machine, only sleek walls and floors as far as she could see. Moving counter clockwise brought her to a large set of reinforced doors, and Crim caught her breath. Somehow, she knew this was it. Unlike all other rooms on board, this opened easily at the touch of an illuminated panel, and she stuck her head round just enough to see inside.

Ifram. Six of them, all preoccupied with glowing panels and instruments. They chittered as they worked, seemingly oblivious to the intrusion. One of them had an image of the Mountain marked out in red lines rotating in front of him, and was zooming in on various points as he spoke to his counterpart, who prodded a square slab of glass in his hands.

It's amazing how quickly one's courage evaporates when faced with a roomful of foes. Now, eyeing the weapons on the Iframs' belts, Crim's resolve to destroy them, to fight any that faced her, seemed futile, foolish, a suicide mission. She decided it best to simply leave quietly.

Her fingers found the panel once again and pressed. For some reason, it moved like a button this time, and gave under pressure only to emit a shrill *"boo-beep!"*

Every head in the room turned to the door, so she spun on her heel and ran.

LII

"That's it. I'm going back up." Sunshine stood. They had found each other by a sourceward obelisk, in the shadow of which they watched and waited for the last in their party. They all knew they should be putting as much distance between themselves and the vessel as possible, but had not the will to do so. As she tried to manoeuvre past the others, Laal caught her by the belt.

"Don't."

"Crim—"

"Give her more time. She'll make it."

"I can't. I can't stand waiting around like this."

"Right now I see two possibilities," Yuki offered. "Either she makes it back, or she's dead. No point in you dying too, just because you couldn't wait."

A tiny tear rolled down Li-Li's cheek at this. She wiped it away and turned to look at the ship. Yuki shut their mouth.

"The c-c-carbuncles wo-won't w-w-work while sh-she's u-up there, right?" She asked feebly.

"Not unless we tell them to," Laal replied. "But if this goes on too long…if she's already captured or dead, it might be best to decide on how long we should wait."

"You mean to decide how long before we give up on her?" Sunshine shot back. She regretted her tone immediately; Laal did not deserve such disrespect.

Thankfully, Laal gave her an equally horrified look. "Exactly."

"Crim's practical." Despite the cold silence, Li-Li was now treating them to, Yuki spoke as bluntly as ever. "If it was one of us up there, she would say the same as you, Mistress. She would understand."

Sunshine crossed her arms and huffed miserably. "You're right. Both of you."

Laal jerked her chin up at the moon. "Leave it 'til he turns yellow, then we'll need to move. We've waited here too long already."

"Crim…" Li-Li managed shakily.

"We can't," Yuki responded gruffly.

"No. C-*Crim!*"

Sunshine looked to where Li-Li was now pointing. Sure enough, there was Crim emerging from the white beam of the teleporter, alive and well.

"Wh-why is she r-r-running?"

Laal leapt up. "She's not alone." At once, she had Yuki and Li-Li under the arms. "Get away, all of you! Into the Mountain!"

"Laal?" Li-Li, still rooted to her seat, looked to each of them in fear.

*

The name had barely formed on her lips when the sky lit up. First with one explosion, then with the other on the far side of the ship. They seemed to ripple towards one another, the strange, reflective metal of the hull crumpling inwards before being forced back out by blue and orange flames. A third ball of flame burst forth from the middle, rolling out to merge into one roiling storm of fire. The sound came last, an ear-shattering *boom* as the whole structure flew apart, most of it vaporised into a million billion specks of dust. A few in-tact chunks crashing into the trees and rocking the side of the Mountain. Each of them moved fast as they could, forgetting the others in their panic, darting and leaping and sliding out of the path of any missiles, oblivious to the ground rippling and tearing behind them, sinking into an enormous crater with the force of the blast.

As soon as it happened, as soon as they heard it, it was over. Just like that, the vessel was gone. One by one they made their way to the lip of a giant, smouldering bowl. They looked up to find the heavens blessedly empty. The stars blinked back into view even as the last shards burned up in the air.

Laal felt Sunshine's arm around her shoulders. She was cheering. Something about how they had done it. She shook her head, not sure what they had achieved. She did not feel as though they should be celebrating. She furrowed her brow and stared harder. They were *wrong*, those stars, Sunshine eventually stopped and followed her gaze. Li-Li and Yuki were nearby, looking rather shaken but otherwise unscathed. They asked what the matter was, and she told them she did not know. Sure, there was the Maiden, and the Heron, and all the others that she had missed while the ship had sat in front of them; there was just something about the whole scene…

Then the sky rippled, the stars dimmed, and she found herself staring up at the underbelly of a ship. Not the same ship. This one was far, far bigger. It took up the whole mouthward horizon—the curve of its pristine white hull enough to engulf their entire microcosm. It was rather flat on top, with structures like towers and buildings jutting up from the surface.

Presently, a tiny door opened in its side, and three specs appeared. They flew at speed away from it. Little black orbs with red dots for eyes. Laal did not like the look of them.

"Run!"

*

Trees whizzed past in a blur or green and brown, dead leaves and needles cast upwards in their wake. Li-Li's arm hurt as she was tugged this way and that, deeper and deeper into the dense Forest. A glance back confirmed her suspicion that they were rapidly moving away from the Mountain.

"Wh-where are we g-g-going?" She demanded, trying to pull Yuki back. Her arm was going to rip out of its socket at this rate.

"Outside." They answered shortly, half-lifting her over a fallen oak.

"Mentor t-told us to g-go b-b-back!" Tripping, she flew a few feet, held up by sheer momentum, and stumbled back into step ungracefully. "T-to the Mountain!"

"Fuck that. We're dead if we go back there. No. We're going Outside. Where there are millions of mortals to hide us."

One of the streams that fed the River rushed along on their left, made deep and swift by meltwater trickles from the Mountain-top. Ahead, the distinct sounds of Swamps rose to meet them; croaks, chirps, cries and even a low growl or two. Li-Li groaned.

"Y-Yuki, slow down," she commanded, digging in with her heels; the soil here was already damp and soft, gathering around her ankles as she planted herself firmly.

Yuki growled at her, Li-Li's head jerked back with shock. They turned, and with two hands attempted to yank her onwards. Both of them were surprised by Li-Li's strength as she stubbornly refused to take another step.

"Damn it, Li-Li!" They spat. "What are you doing!"

"Wh-what are *you* d-doing! We can't leave them all to d-d-die!"

"If we go back, *we'll* die with them!"

"And w-we should!"

Yuki gaped at her. "You want to go back and die for nothing?"

"I-I want to g-go back and d-d-die *with our friends.*" She cast an arm Swamp-ward. "Not r-run ah-away to hide am-am-mong humans like a c-c-c-coward!"

"I thought you were afraid?"

A hysterical laugh. "I'm *terrified,* b-but I still know what's r-right. H-how can you expect me to l-le-leave them? Mentor and Sunny and Laal a-a-and—"

"And Crim."

"Yes and C-Crim!"

*"*But you would leave me."

"Wh-what are you t-talking about!" She snarled, throwing up her arms.

"If I refuse, you would go back without me, wouldn't you?"

"That's not f-fair."

"What isn't?"

"M-m-making me choose."

Yuki turned and stalked away. "There's no choice. Crim's there, so you'll go running back into the arms of death."

Let them go. Let them go. But she darted forward. "Yuki, *please!"*

"I can't let you die, Li-Li." They rasped. "But I know it's also wrong to pull you away if…if that's what you want."

Yuki shook her off as she reached for their arms, the cuff of their sleeve tearing off in her hand. She sobbed. "Y-Yuki."

They took two steps, then seemed to hesitate. Li-Li took the chance to throw her arms around them, and to her surprise they turned into the embrace. For a long while she just stood there, holding them to her, not caring how stiffly they endured it, not heeding the long sigh that escaped them, not giving in as they tried to pull away.

Yuki touched her cheek, and for the first time she saw tears standing in their eyes. Only for a single breath—with the next they kissed her.

It came as no surprise, really, though Li-Li cursed her luck that it had to happen now, of all times. Choking as she did so, she wrapped her arms around their neck and just forgot for a minute why they were here, why she was crying, why they had been running, and what parting meant. Their lips were soft and warm, they smelled nice, that was all that mattered.

*

Just as quickly as it happened, they pulled away, and she moaned their name one last time, resisting the hands that raised to push her aside. It did not immediately register that their attentions were now turned skyward, nor did she recognise the urgency in their voice.

"What is that?"

"Wha…" She jumped. A red eye, peering down at them from above the treetops.

A high-pitched whine, and a beam of light shot past them, striking the ground with a small flash and leaving behind a blackened hole ringed by burning leaves. They both screamed. Once again, Yuki grabbed her arm, and once again she found herself sprinting. Another flash, and the smell of smoke, and she no longer needed to be pulled. They ran hand-in-hand, branches whipping at their faces, feet sinking further and further into the sodden earth even as the air turned muggy and stale.

With one leap, they were now knee-deep in stagnant water, swathed in white mist that soon became a veil as they waded further, urged on by the songs of toads and crickets as well as an urgent, primal fear. Above the sounds of creatures, far above was an unfamiliar drone, and a pale glow that sought to permeate the fog. Moving as one, they wove their way through the reeds and grasses, carefully moving away from the searching Eye while remaining under cover. But they did not know this area as well as Laal, and soon found themselves at the edge of their depth, not trusting any of the spongy tufts around them to take their weight, and unwilling to try their luck in the deeper parts, they turned in a small circle, panic holding them tightly together.

Presently, a log glided past, close enough for one yellow eye to consider them hungrily. For its own sake, however, the alligator decided not to try them for dinner, but pulled itself up onto what could only be a solid finger of an island a few meters away in search of something less likely to disagree with him.

A streak of red, an outraged hiss, and he collapsed down, dead. Li-Li, already partially up out of the sludge, made a break for it. With a shout and a curse, Yuki quickly appeared alongside her.

"Shit! Shit! Shit! Shit!"

The shelter of Swamps was slowly waning as they raced along one narrow spit of land, the fog was drifting apart, the trees did not lean in so far, the reeds seemed sparser. Behind, an angry Eye could be seen floating above the murk, gaining steadily on them. Another blast, far too close this time, which turned a single pool of grey water to steam on impact. To Li-Li's dismay, another swathe of water came into view ahead. She almost slowed down, but Yuki shoved her from behind with both hands. Hard.

"Swim!"

A mortal could never have moved through the mire they were now immersed in; they would have immediately been pulled under and drowned. For a Sidhe, in this very instant, being reduced to human speed was just as much of a death sentence, and Li-Li found herself bidding the world goodbye as yet another beam sliced through the mud at her feet, singing her flesh and increasing the temperature from icy to boiling point in the blink of an eye. She could see neither the bank ahead, nor the Eye above, nor Yuki, whom she hoped was still by her side. Deciding the mortal fear of drowning was now less important than the very appropriate fear of being blown to smithereens, she took a deep breath (which she did not need) and dove under the surface. It was awful; suffocating and unyielding. Debris brushed past her, and she dared not open her eyes, but groped blindly with her hands until they finally reached a solid wall. Somehow, Yuki had gotten there ahead of her—their hands burst through the muddy surface as they sensed her near. With both arms under hers, they hefted her completely out, coughing and whining as she forced her legs under herself, propelling her forward even before she could scrape the mud from her lids.

All of a sudden, Yuki was steering her aside, almost looping back around the edge of Swamps towards the Mountain. Still blinking pieces of dirt out of her lashes, Li-Li did not question them until she found herself behind pressed against the bark of a tree. Yuki had found a dead Elm, and was shoving her down into a hollow in its trunk. She wiped her face with her sleeve, finally able to see again.

"Wh-where are we?"

But Yuki had disappeared back outside. She crawled forward just enough to see them standing in the middle of a clearing, arms held wide and raging at the sky. The Eye circled overhead, now joined by another, the pair seemed to watch petite Sidhe curiously.

Li-Li's voice had left her. She mouthed their name as they raised their hands, lightning pouring forth from their fingertips. With a roar, they lashed out at their pursuers to a deafening crack. Fire erupted from the branches the bolt struck, and two red eyes mocked them from the smoke. She bounded forward with a cry, some silly part of her ready to knock them out of harm's way.

Two flashes of light. One smoking crater. The Forest set aflame.

*

Laal cried as she tripped over a felled branch, coming down hard on her hands and knees. Sunshine, ducking past the clawing briars, was with her in an instant, lugging her upright as much as the tunnel of twisting twigs would allow. Those awful red Eyes had found them huddled together by a standing stone, and reduced the limestone monument to rubble. Now they were fleeing for their lives, hoping against hope for the Gate to appear in front of them, even though with every twist and turn through the dark Forest they knew they were lost.

The stones were their best hope; every time they neared one Sunshine yelped with joy, but they all looked the same and she did not know the Forest well enough to tell whether they were simply looping back to the same clearings. Laal knew, of course, but she was too frantic to remember, panting and questioning every sound that met her ears.

"Let's rest here a bit," Sunshine suggested. "We can get our bearings and try for the Gate again."

"They know we're here," Laal breathed. "They know we'll make for the Gate. If they don't catch us out here, they'll have us for sure the second we set foot inside. We're dead, Sunny."

"Our friends are in the Mountain, Love. Remember? The allies Mentor told us about. They won't allow it."

Laal only shook her head, peering wide-eyed through the long thorns poking at their heads. The sky was quiet for now, and no burning beams of light were being fired at them. "Where are they now?"

"I don't know."

"Where could they *be*?"

"Hopefully, they are asking the same question."

"Did you see how many poured out of that ship? The others—"

"Will be fine. We'll all be fine."

"But—"

"*Shut up!*" Sunshine scolded, even as she kissed her. "Please. Let's just go home."

Laal pouted, features still fixed in fear, but stopped her catastrophising. Sunshine kissed her again; just a brush this time, and scooted backwards ungainly out of their shelter.

"What are you doing?"

She jerked a thumb up to the treetops. "I'm going up there."

"What? No! They'll see you!"

"Possibly. Possibly not. But we need to figure out where we are and where the Gate is," she replied, one foot already planted into a protruding knot. "I'm not waiting around for them to find us."

*

In the brush, Laal *huffed* in displeasure, but said no more. Sunshine was glad of it; the oak she had chosen was tall, girthy and crooked, with plenty of sturdy limbs and burls. Altogether the easiest to climb in their vicinity. It was not the climbing she needed to concentrate on, but the eerie silence stretching out among the trees. The peace of the Forest was disturbed, and anything with any sense had now found a place out of view.

She found a family of owls clustered together in a darkened nook, and nodding her apologies for startling them, deftly swung upward and away. The branches were tapering off now, and she had a hard time finding ones to take her weight. Finally, she sat in the saddle of two diverging limbs overlooking most other trees as far as her eyes could see. There was a stone up the slope and to her left, peeking just above the surrounding leaves. Sunshine judged it was just a half-hour walk from where they were, and carefully mapped their path in her head. The Maw was just above the white obelisk, meaning that if they used it as a waypoint and continued on towards the jagged gap in the Mountainside, they would quickly fall across the Gate. They would have to cross the River, which was still fairly fast at this point, and that would take time and effort, but as long as they did not encounter any more Eyes, they could be home before very long.

Dropping back into the undergrowth (but blessedly missing the brambles), she found Laal already halfway out of their little nest. Crouching to pick a crumpled leaf out of her ruffled hair, Sunshine gallantly helped her to her feet before pointing mouthward.

"There's a stone right there. It's over the River, but we can make it if we hurry."

"Run?" Laal guessed.

"No…No I didn't see any Eyes nearby, or signs of anything else coming this way. We can walk. Take it easy."

"Save the running for when we have to."

*

Roaring water charged closer as they followed the same diagonal, heading directly for the standing stone, and then onwards towards salvation. They were both tired, frightened, and were not really in the mood for talking, so pushed forward determinedly, saving a touch here and there for one another—a brush on the arm, a hand to the back, a brief acknowledgement.

I'm still here. Keep going.

As she picked her way through the undergrowth, Sunshine let her thoughts wander ahead. What would happen when they reached the Mountain? Would they be safe? What of the others? How would the Ifram retaliate in the aftermath of their sins?

"Ahh!" Laal gasped as she lowered herself into the rushing torrent of the River. The water was icy, and as Sunshine dropped in from the sheer bank, already to her hips, the passing floods hit her like incessant blows. With their strength depleted, they would have to be careful crossing. Not that they could drown, of course, but they could be swept away, swept right into those searching red Eyes. She linked arms with Laal, bobbing cautiously forward, and of course Laal, by far the shorter of the two, was floating before long. She was also far more buoyant, loved water and began to tug Sunshine forward, giggling.

"Don't be such a chicken!"

"I am a *frozen* chicken!"

"Just remember what Mentor taught you. Breathe, and exhale the chill away."

Teeth rattling in her head, Sunshine could not even concentrate on inhaling, never mind the rest. "Help me get across, will you!"

With a role of her eyes, Laal paddled backwards, took her in her arms like one saved from drowning, and swam them both across the icy, pummelling cascade. The bank on the other side was a straight drop down, with half a meter to spare, and Sunshine had to be hefted up by the rear only to fall face forward on the damp grass, spluttering and shivering and cursing. Laal simply climbed out and sat on a rock while she dried, looking as graceful as ever and rather refreshed by the whole experience.

"How much farther?" She asked.

Sunshine picked a twig out of her hair. "Not far to the stone. To the Gate...I can't tell."

*

They could not linger long; the fear of those menacing red lights drove them into the undergrowth as soon as they were dry. The slope of the Mountain steepened here, and they half-crawled up in silence. Here and there they caught rumour of the life that still dwelt among the trees; a badger peeking out of his den, a rabbit flitting back to her burrow at the slightest sound, even a small group of deer huddled together in the shelter of a fallen tree. Laal *tut tut tutted* at them. A large doe grunted back.

The tree line appeared over the lip of the hill—a few sparse boles wreathed in moonlight, and they picked up their pace. Checking first, they broke their cover to find themselves at the foot of the immense granite block. Laal sighed with relief and pressed her forehead to the cool stone.

"Where now, though?" Sunshine muttered, eyeing the angle of the stone, and its position relative to the Maw. Making a line with her arm, she looked to Laal for help.

"Well...If we take the slope of the Mountain into the equation...." Laal strode a wide circle around her, finger to her cheek in thought. Then she drew a line down the slopes to the midpoint between the two markers. "Around there?"

"You'd better be right."

"I'd better."

"We should make for the next stone, anyway. That should stop us from getting lost again."

"Agreed. And that should be—"

*

410

They were interrupted by a loud *hoo-hoo!* And a large brown owl appeared over the branches behind them. Swooping up to perch atop the obelisk, he spread his wings and let out another sharp *hoot!* At once, Laal grabbed her hand, but Sunshine was already moving.

"Let's go!"

Not a second later, a flash of red light struck the stone, blowing a chunk out of the edge they had just dove around. Laal and Sunshine, already among the trees, spared a glance back to see their feathered comrade reel out of the way of the oncoming Eye. Thankfully, the demon was far too interested in them to do him any harm.

Another beam burst through the branches as the Eye ducked below the canopy, zipping and diving after them. A third followed, fourth, fifth. The sixth caught the outside of Sunshine's arm, and grinning her teeth she barrelled on through searing pain, pushing Laal ahead. Thankfully, the creature did not seem too used to navigating such dense woods, and they managed to get several trees between them simply by swerving around the larger trunks. The odd scraping noise notified them that it was actually colliding with some of the limbs above, though not enough to hinder it much.

*

Moonlight ahead. The second standing stone reared up as the Forest gave way again. They slid behind it. This time the Eye did not try shooting it, but shot over, not allowing them a moment's rest. Laal let out a cry of dismay as a beam whizzed far too close to her face. Making better use of the next batch of trees, they managed to lead it into a greater number of sturdy limbs. One even proved strong enough to send it reeling aside as one concussed. This bought them precious seconds to lengthen the distance between them.

"Sunny!" Laal shouted, and her heart leapt into her throat, assuming she was hurt. But no, Laal was pointing ahead, to the next break in the Forest, and the standing stone glowing white. They let out a *whoop!* In unison, feet pumping beyond their limit at the sight of the Gate. The Eye buzzed angrily above, as though to remind them that it was still there, shooting through whole branches to reach them.

Sensing their urgency, the Gate began to uncoil as soon as they hit the soft soil surrounding the obelisk. The Eye shot at the metal and surrounding rock in vain—for nothing of this world or any other could destroy what the Mountain had made. Still yards away, Sunshine launched them forward with a great leap, and the two rolled over the threshold even as the Gate snapped shut at their heels. Again, the Eye let out a furious *BZZZZT!* And shot at the glittering truesteel. It was useless as it had been the first time; the Gate glowed red-hot where it was struck, only to cool and gleam again.

In the shadows of the Porch, Laal burst into tears, and Sunshine held on to her tightly, whispering comforts and showering her with kisses. So overcome with relief were they that they did not hear footsteps coming up behind, or the unsheathing of blades.

"Welcome home," said Hyeong.

*

"Hush," Mentor commanded, clapping a hand firmly over Crim's mouth. "They will hear you, girl. Bite your hand if you have to, but stay silent."

Crim squirmed in pain as she pulled the makeshift bandage tighter around the scorched wound in her thigh. A moment's hesitation had been more than enough for the Eye to land one of its shots, and just like that she had been at its mercy, lying in the mud staring up at it as it moved in for the final blow. Mentor had appeared out of nowhere, dropping out of the trees above it with her *katars* out. As it turned out, sturdy as the thing looked, one swift blade to its glowing core was enough to kill it, and both the creature and Mentor fell to the ground together. Then it had simply been a matter of picking Crim up and dragging her up into these isolated caves. The wound would not heal easily—the heat of the beam had cauterised the edges, but left the centre gushing blood. Mentor offered her a drink of blood, and that helped a great deal. She was no longer at risk of bleeding to death, but she would be vulnerable for a while.

"There. That will have to do for now." Mentor thumbed the torn edge of her shirt and favoured Crim with a rare smile. "You'll live, Crim. For now, at least."

Urk came the response, and her student flopped back onto the cold stone.

She stood, and crept back to the mouth of the caves. Few knew of their existence—a hive-like network of tunnels that led to concealed entrances into the Mountain—and rightly so. They were only meant as an escape route, and had never been needed as far as the eldest of them could recall. In fact, generations passed not even knowing that they were there, save the very elite. At her rise to power, Mother had ordered all of the elders to map them.

"It is folly to assume we will always be safe here; fate has a way of punishing such oversights."

It seemed their secret had not been revealed to the Ifram—as Mentor peeked out, there was no sign of any of them, nor of the monstrous Eyes. They could not stay forever, of course—just long enough for Crim to rest.

*

Crim snored, twitched, swore, then put a hand to her leg, eyes fluttering open as she wondered why she was in agony. Mentor sat nearby, staring into space, but immediately roused at her movements. Scooting over, she removed her hand from the bloodied wrapping.

"Shhh. Be careful. Don't move it too much." She helped her sit up. "How is it?"

"Sore."

"Do you think you can walk now?"

She gingerly bent her leg, wincing as the effort pulled at severed nerve. "I can walk."

"Good. Here." Mentor lifted her so that she stood back against the wall. "Let's see."

Crim hobbled from the wall towards her, hopping a little bit as her face screwed up and she began to sweat. "Ta-da?"

Shaking her head, Mentor put an arm around her, guiding Crim's hand over her own shoulders. "I suppose we'll have to take it slowly then."

"Take what slowly?"

Jerking her chin into the blackness of the cave, Mentor explained. "This is part of an emergency network of tunnels throughout the Mountain. If I remember the way correctly, we should be able to make it to safety undetected."

"No-one else knows about these?"

"…All of the elders do."

Crim pulled back. "That includes Mother."

"Yes, it does."

"And you don't think she would have told our guests about these tunnels?"

Mentor's mouth pulled into a tight line. "I can't be sure. But I believe we stand a better chance in here than we do out there."

Crim considered this, remembering the Eye, how relentlessly it had pursued her. The relentless sting of her injury flared up in response. She hissed. "Then lead the way."

*

The tunnels were broad enough for them to proceed without much stooping or side-stepping, and branched out at regular intervals in different directions—some leading left, some leading right, some sloping upwards and some down. For the most part, they seemed to move straight ahead, with Mentor stopping at the odd junction to get her bearings. At occasional crossroads was a small, round room with doorways leading in various directions. Each of these doorways was labelled with a rune, the meaning of which was lost to Crim, but no doubt her guide could read them, for Mentor never stopped for more than a few minutes.

"Who built these?" She eventually asked, eyeing the five arches snaking off into the dark.

"The Patriarch, most likely," Mentor answered. "Though most of our records from before his time are lost."

"Destroyed?"

"Probably."

Mentor brushed the edge of her *katar* with one finger, staring down one darkened tunnel with intense concentration.

"Did Mother really kill him?"

A sigh. "Yes. She killed him. On the steps of the Forum, which once housed his throne."

"Because he was evil?"

"I don't know about evil...cruel, yes. Vicious, yes. Megalomaniacal, yes. But looking back I truly believe he thought he was doing the gods' will. However twisted."

"Sounds evil to me."

Mentor gave a thin smile. "Yes, I'm not surprised."

"Did Mother really...um..."

"What?"

"Nothing..."

Another sigh, deeper. "You want to ask if she ate him?"

"Um…"

"She did. Part of him, at least."

Crim gawked at her. Had she really just heard that? Had Mentor just verified all the twisted rumours people whispered regarding Mother's ascension?

"Oh don't look at me like that, Crim. I know what they all say. So does Mother," Mentor spat. "She cut his throat, drained him dry, and ate his heart. By doing that, she gained his power and his authority."

Not knowing what else to say, Crim simply responded: "Oh."

"I suppose no-one ever told you the rest, though."

"The rest?"

"No, of course not." Mentor fixed her with those violet eyes. "After Mother was done, she cast him down the steps in front of his throne. And do you know what those nearest did? The Patriarch's trusted guards and advisors? How they reacted to their lord being thrown from his seat of power?"

"N-no?"

"They finished him. Mother ate his heart, true, but *they* tore him limb from limb and *devoured him.*"

Crim recoiled at the thought. She knew some of the people Mentor spoke of; many of them still dwelt in the Mountain under Mother's command, some occupied the same positions, while others had retired to simpler lives. To think that they might—

"Ugh." She shuddered.

"Don't be so squeamish, Crim. There may yet be more of it now that we have disturbed the peace once again."

"'More of it'?"

"Indeed." Without explanation she stood, and jabbed a *katar* down the leftmost passage. "Come. This way."

*

Her leg still throbbed, though not nearly as much as before. She still needed Mentor's help from time to time, when the pain became too much, but with one hand to the wall, and the other to her thigh, Crim made it most of the way without incident. At one point, she tripped up some stairs, and the healing tissue flared up in response, resulting in a flurry of curses and her having to sit down a good long moment to recuperate. Mentor waited patiently at the top of the steps, but did not move to help. Soon enough she was back up and carefully hopping to meet her.

*

An eternity of shuffling and limping and hobbling, and she swore the way ahead was becoming brighter. Sure enough, as they rounded one last bend a crack could be seen in the dark stone, through which orange firelight spilled. Mentor put an eye to the narrow opening and signalled for Crim to stay quiet.

"Good," Mentor announced, pressing a palm to the crack. With a creak and a crunch, the rock split outwards from where she touched, and folded to either side, revealing a narrow opening leading into the Mountain. Relieved, Crim heaved herself into the glow. The light took up most of her vision for a time; all those hours in the dark tunnels meant that even the faintest gleam assaulted her eyes like a burning glare. She blinked impatiently, spots dancing before her, finally having reached safety.

"What?" As the glare faded away, she found standing in a long column of moonlight, the doors to Mother's chamber on her right. "Mentor, where did you bring me?"

Crim took two steps back, stumbled, only to be caught by her trusted Mentor. "I brought you to the safest place I know."

"You brought me to *her!*" She wriggled, but could not shake off the hands now clamped on her shoulders.

"Shush! Crim! Shush! Someone might hear you!"

"Let me go!"

"Where to? To your room? To Whisper, or another of your friends? They would catch you as soon as you get down the High Stair!"

"And where would they bring me? To her!" Crim jabbed a finger back at the rearing black doors. "Just as you are! At least if I get away from you I might have a chance-!"

She made a desperate dash, but Mentor intercepted her, held her tight enough to crush her very bones. Crim wailed in dismay.

"Stop it, Crim! She is not who you think!"

"What? Not their ally? Not their puppet? Not the one who sold us to them?"

"No! Not at all!" Mentor shook her. "Crim; she is the one who sent me to help you!"

She froze. "What?"

"Mother wants them gone as much as anyone else. Yes, she plays their games, pretends to obey and revere them. She has done all of this to lower their guard—to make them think we are harmless so that we might get rid of them in one fell swoop! She is the one who sent me! She provided the carbuncles! She is the one who convinced them to let Yuki and Li-Li walk free, so that they might join your mission!"

Crim blinked. "What?"

"*Trust me*, Crim."

"I…" A voice in her head told her not to, but it was small and distant, drowned out by the need to believe her. Besides, she was too injured to resist. "I trust you."

"Good girl." Mentor kissed her cheek. "I would never lead you into danger."

LIII

Mother's chambers were the same as she remembered; extravagant. A new lion-skin rug now adorned the floor of the seating area, and she had acquired some more ornaments, nick-knacks and vases. As the doors closed behind her, Crim caught the luscious scents of vanilla and honey coming from the baths, and also the sound of hushed voices. It seemed Mother was entertaining company.

Mentor made her way over to the couches and flopped down with an exhausted grunt. Crim followed suit, limping across the room to sit next to her. At once, the weariness of the past few days overcame her, and the fought the urge to sleep. She looked around.

"Where is Apep?"

Mentor started. "Who?"

"Apep!"

"Oh…" Waving a hand dismissively, Mentor replied: "He's probably sleeping in one of the ferns."

But Crim could neither hear nor see nor sense the gigantic snake anywhere nearby. She had half a mind to get up and search for him, but the ache in her leg was too much again, and the weariness in her bones stayed her other limbs. Instead, she let her head loll back against the cushions.

*

A sharp jab in the ribs woke her, and Crim sat up to find Mother seated opposite, staring at her with that unreadable expression she so often wore. Beside her Mentor rolled her eyes.

"Mother asked you what happened, Crim."

"Oh…um…" Averting her eyes from Mother's golden-yellow stare, Crim did her best to explain her suspicions, plans, events on the ship as well as what she knew of what happened after.

"And what of the others, Crim?" Mother asked plainly, once she was done (or rather, once Mother had decided she was done).

She bit her lip as her heart sank. "We all ran, Mother. We broke off into different directions so…I do not know."

"You have not heard from them? Any of them?"

"No, Mother."

Those golden eyes flashed to Mentor, who also responded: "I thought it best to split up. To try and make it to safety in pairs. If the enemy were forced to choose who to chase, then perhaps the rest would have a greater chance of survival."

"So you were prepared to let some of them die?"

"Not willing, but *prepared*, yes. If the rest could survive."

Mother only stared, and said nothing.

"Did…" Crim ventured, flinching as she turned to her. "Did any of them make it back?"

"Yes."

Next to her, Mentor exhaled loudly and relaxed. "Are they all safe?"

"No."

"But…"

"None of you are safe. I'm sorry, Priya, but the others were all captured. They were all questioned by the enemy."

Crim felt ill, and at once a cold swept over her. "What?"

"So now the Ifram know exactly what you had planned, and exactly who took part in the plot to get rid of them."

She thought Mother's composure broke for an instant. For a split second, something like anger washed over those fine, hard features.

"What are you saying?" Mentor pressed.

"I'm saying: I cannot save you."

The doors swung open, and Nashoba marched in, followed by the other Reavers in their group, and four Ifram soldiers carrying rifles, which they held to the backs of their prisoners. Hyeong appeared last, making his way over to Crim with quick strides, and dragging her out of her seat.

"No!" Cried Mentor, reaching for her arm just as he pulled Crim away from her reach. One of the Ifram was upon her in an instant, jamming its weapon against Mentor's stomach and chittering menacingly. All semblance of her usual calm collapsed as she understood his command. "Neferu!"

Mother truly winced this time, and turned her face away. "I cannot help you, Priya. Not this time. You have gone too far."

"Neferu..." Mentor choked, allowing herself to be led into line by the Ifram. "Please."

Hyeong threw Crim to her knees next to her friends. Immediately, they scooted together, arms around one another and tears running down their cheeks. They had all been brutalised, and Sunshine's leg appeared to be broken and set deliberately apart using steel rods. Laal's beautiful face was crisscrossed with cuts and pockmarked with blistering burns. Li-Li was battered and bruised beyond recognition, and drenched in blood.

Where is Yuki?

Mentor fell down next to them, and Sunshine pulled her into their little circle. They were allowed this moment; the clumsy kisses, the hushed *I love yous,* the desperate tears. The last acts of the doomed.

*

Neferu balled her fists against her thighs, and cleared her throat before she stood to face the condemned. The ache in her heart was harder to quell, as the guards tore them apart and forced them to kneel for their sentence, she looked into each of their faces and saw the hatred for her burning there, alongside the crippling terror that held them in place.

Most of them, at least; both Crim and Sunshine had to be held in place by Nashoba and Ayo, respectively. They screamed at her, cursed her, tried to burn and bite and scratch their captors while simultaneously pleading for their friends.

"Mother! It was me! It was my plan! I tricked them!"

"I set the carbuncles against their engines! I fuelled them with my own fire! They were only a distraction!"

"Mother?" Hyeong's voice interrupted their pleas. He stood, blades at the ready, the Ifram's appointed executioner. He smiled politely and raised his eyebrows at her. "Your orders?"

"Yes." She looked to Priya—to Mentor—last, though it took all of her courage to witness the loathing in her lover's face. The betrayal. "All of you are here...are here because of your part in a plot to do harm to our friends, the ever-gentle Ifram. You are guilty of destroying one of their vessels without provocation, which has resulted in the loss of one thousand two hundred and eighty-seven innocent lives. This has been rightly labelled an act of terrorism, for which the penalty is death for all of those involved. There shall be no half-measures, no parley this time, especially considering that this is the second offense for some of you—"

Li-Li sobbed.

"Rather, your sentence shall take effect immediately."

For just a second, Crim and Sunshine finally fell silent, astounded. The next instant they began to fight again, invigorated by the promise of their imminent deaths. With a *crunch*, Ayo's fist connected with Sunshine's jaw, and he pinned her down with a foot to the neck as she crumpled to the floor. Nashoba had no need for such measures; he was strong and large enough that Crim's efforts to free herself went mostly unnoted.

*

The soft whisper of one of Hyeong's long knives slipping from its sheath. The soft whimper of Li-Li sobbing in the arms of a Reaver. The subtle rattling of Laal's frightened breath that harmonised with Sunshine's snarling. Crim seething, frothing at the mouth in Nashoba's arms. Worst of all; the look of unbridled hatred that contorted Priya's features. The loathing that seeped into her from the one she loved most in all of eternity.

"You'll pay for this, Neferu," she swore. "Perhaps not with your worthless existence, but with your soul."

I already have.

But she continued: "We will die here, but you will continue. You will rot in your guilt till the day that this universe—*urk!*"

Even Neferu jumped when the blade shot through Priya's neck. The crunch of her vertebrae as it entered seemed delayed, and only caught up to what she was seeing when the point erupted from below her chin.

"*Urk!*" Blood sprayed from her mouth as she choked on her last words.

"*Urk!*" As Hyeong pulled back she toppled forward, palm to her throat in a useless attempt to stop the stream that spilled from the wound. The black tile of the floor turned liquid with it, and as the pool ebbed ever closer to Neferu's toes she bit back a cry. Forcing herself to remain composed, she made through the door to the baths and slammed the very wall closed behind her. There she allowed her façade to break, knees buckling as she quietly vomited into one of her dozens of exquisite urns. Jadis (Apep's successor), was roused from her sleep by the steaming pool and raised her emerald-green head to blink up at her indignantly.

"What have I done?" Neferu whispered to the serpent. "Oh, what have I done?"

LIV

This was not real. As the Reaver held her back she reached for Mentor, ears ringing with Laal's hysterical screams, throbbing with the undercurrent of Li-Li's weeping. Blood flowed out of Mentor's neck. So much blood. Her legs were already wet with it, her hands slipped as she tried to crawl forward. To help her. She could still help her. Mentor could not be gone so easily. A trick. It was a trick. Hyeong had switched his truesteel blades for mortal ones and now was torturing them. Of course. Mentor was…

"Cold," she croaked. She was so cold. And grey. Like all the colour had ebbed flowed out of her. Just like Princess. Laal's shrieking reached its crescendo.

"*Shut up!*" Hyeong roared, first to all of them, then directly into Laal's face. Before any of them could comprehend what was happening, Hyeong had her, gripped Laal roughly in both hands and shook her, but she did not stop. Not even a blow to the stomach could silence her. "SHUT UP!"

And just like that, she shut up. The room fell silent. Eerily silent. They tore their collective gaze away from Mentor's body to see Laal still in Hyeong's hands, head dangling at a most unnatural angle. For the longest time, she could not understand what had silenced Laal. A broken neck was not enough to stop a Sidhe. It was like her mind had chosen to see everything else except the hilt of the knife firmly embedded in one of Laal's eyes. The most beautiful eyes. One still shone at her now, but not for long before it was dimmed by death. Just like that, what once was aquamarine, flecked with hints of topaz blue turned to dark brown, and her hair, her perfect hair, lost its glimmer too, fading to black. Finally, the rich copper colour of her skin became ashen and devoid of all lustre. Only then did Hyeong drop her.

-

423

"Laal?" Li-Li squeaked. There was no need for anyone to hold her; frozen in place as she was. A little tear left a wet line down her cheek. "Laal, we have to go. Laal…Laal I want to leave. I want to sit by the fire, Laal. I want rice pudding. Laal, let's go. Laal? Laal!"

Finally unhinged, she screwed her face up to cry again, but had no more tears left, instead shedding droplets of blood which fell unseen into the veritable ocean now all around. Her speech left her, all except for the names of those around her, and of course her beloved Yuki. She chanted them where she knelt, seemingly passive until she felt Hyeong's fingers at her shoulder. With a cry, she elbowed him, and he clapped her loudly over the back of the head, grabbing a fistful of her hair as she tried to squirm away. Their names came more desperately now, like a prayer for help. Still, she swung with her elbows, feet skating in the crimson puddle as she tried to stand. He was too strong, and pulled over and over and over at her hair, his other blade sang into view, and the cold of it at her throat turned her prayer into a cacophony. Li-Li dug her claws into this forearm and the others into his thigh, ripping into him as she twisted and bucked. She could not stop him, but fought even as the knife sank into the smooth flesh of her throat. Hyeong let out a howl of triumph when he felt her warm blood spill over his hand, ignoring the fingers now embedded in this wrist. He laughed now when she wriggled, and twisting her hair tighter around his fist proceeded to twist her head with it, forcing it aside with one hand as he sawed away with the other. The light faded from Li-Li's features long before he was done. Long before he held her head up like a trophy and tossed her body aside. The only sound in the room was his cackling, and even the other Reavers looked away.

She leapt up, not sure what she could do, only knowing that she would kill him. If she could just reach Hyeong…and she did. If she could just get her hands around his throat…and she did. If she could just…

*If I could just…*Pain. Unequivocable. Unrelenting pain. Hyeong was smiling at her, his face millimetres from hers. *Why is he so happy?*

Pain. He held up his knife to show her that it was coated with blood. His hand was sticky with it. Some was even smeared across his face. Pain. She released him to clutch her wound. Pain.

LV

It all happened at once then. A banging on the doors, so hard the room shook. A shower of splinters, some that looked like arrows, that sent both Reavers and Ifram diving for cover. Flashes of light. Scraping of metal. Cries of pain. An Ifram collapsed not far away, opened from shoulder to hip, and she noted with some interested that his blood was blue.

Blood. So much blood. She remembered that she was sitting in it. It was warm. Was some of it hers? Her leg hurt. Turning to look at it brought a new wave of agony.

That's right. Hyeong had surely been aiming for her heart, but missed this time. Instead, he had torn through her guts so that she would die a slow, painful death. Pressing it did not help, but she did so nonetheless.

*

All of you. The others lay around her, lifeless and cold. Mentor had fallen face-down, but the others stared up with glassy eyes. She kissed each of them in turn, reverently returning Li-Li's head to her body where it belonged. She, most of all, looked like she had turned to wax. Soon they would all be dust.

There was a crash somewhere, and Hyeong hissed at someone. Another Reaver, interestingly. They were fighting. All around her, Reavers and the intruders clashed and fell. The Ifram were gone, all save the one who had fallen, no doubt fled back to their ship. Clever, really, leaving the Sidhe to kill each other.

*

"Come here." Someone had her now. They tried to pull her up but she wailed. "Oh, look at you…I've got you."

Smith. Of course it was Smith. She hefted her up over her shoulder and smashed a Reaver's head with her club in in the process. Then, calling to some of the others, she made a hasty retreat. Silver and Hammer appeared behind, running full tilt away from the commotion. She tried to look beyond them, but moving hurt too much. Nonetheless she heard enough shouts and cries of pain to get an idea of what was going on. There were other footsteps as well, some in front, some behind, some coming from either side. Some were met with gasped greetings, some with blades and screaming. Some simply kept on running.

*

Her eyes fluttered back open, and they were jogging through the tunnels, which were now ringing with the sounds of battle. A cry, and an elder fell against her. She yelped back, but whether friend or foe the priestess was dead before she hit the ground, Silver and Hammer hopping over her. A fireball whizzed past their heads and Silver threw one of her little knives, which stuck a young man who never summoned another flame. None of them even paused, Silver simply recalled her weapon and kept running. She had felled five assailants by the time they reached one of the larger chambers, and Hammer three. Of course she could not see what Smith was doing, but she guessed her numbers at two.

There was another brawl here; dozens of Sidhe exchanging blades and blows. She turned her head this way and that, pain in her stomach engulfing her, awareness fading with every movement. Eight were defeated that she saw, and three others joined their party, though she did not know them. Two took their places ahead of Smith and one at her side, who touched her cheek and felt her wound rather ungently, *tutting*.

"We need to go, now."

*

Down, down they ran, and a black haze now bordered her vision. The pain was still there, like a distant memory. At the same priestess' command, they picked up their pace, barrelling through the hoard to where she could not tell. She wished they would leave her. Wished she could go back and die with her friends instead of down here in these caves.

"Shit!" Smith barked, jerking and shuffling as another undoubtedly tried to stop her. Silver, Hammer and the others were all engaged as well, by the sounds around her. Silver killed one and he fell under Smith's feet, causing her to stumble. A grunt, and she suddenly turned stock-still. As Smith collapsed, she fell from her shoulders, and the entire bulk of the larger priestess came down on her.

Pain. Unbearable pain. She slipped from the brink of consciousness.

*

They were still moving when she drifted back to the world of the living. The caves were darker now, more cramped, full of damp, stale air and dripping water. What few starstones dotted the low ceiling set the dark rock all a-glitter, and glowing clumps of frogfungus peeked out from moist, warm corners. They were below the Mountain now, though now far, for the heat was still bearable.

The shoulder she was slung over jostled more than before; her stomach bounced against bone in such a way that she should have been blinded by agony, but she was not. The world was slipping away, or she was. She could feel her grip on her body loosening.

"Here," Silver ordered, rather close to her now in the confined space. "Just up this way a little."

Turning, they jogged up a rather steep passage, so narrow that her bearers resorted to single-file, which turned sharply again to the left near its end to throw them into grey light. She squeezed her eyes shut with a grunt, as the brightness sent coloured dots dancing behind her lids. Kept them shut at the sound of shouts, the clang of metal once again and whizz of arrows sailing through the air. More fighting, and banging at wooden doors. It seemed their allies were besieged in this place, and slowly losing their claim to it at that.

"This way!" She could have sworn that it was Whisper, though she had never heard her shout so loud. "We need to fall back! This way! Hurry!"

She bounced and bumped up three or four steep steps, and Silver muttered something. A question.

"I don't know. I'm sorry. I was in the Menagerie when it all started and...well...I just ran. There was more of us but...I lost them."

Nothing more was said. Her bearer stepped forward, and she felt a familiar jolt. It was the pull of a Doorway, but *more* somehow. Her stomach did a somersault, and she dry-heaved until she blacked out once more.

LVI

Wherever they were, it was hot and muggy. Insects, small and large, filled the air with their buzzing and bumbling. The earth below was soft reddish-brown, kicked up and indented by dozens of feet; booted, bare, some crawling, some walking, others that had been dragged left deep ruts behind.

They left the rocky hollow and stepped out into the greenish-gold light of a rainforest in mid-morning, already steaming and humid, there was still some air to breathe; it could be heard in the leaves, if one listened hard enough, listened past the chattering and hooting and chirping of its creatures. The dirt trail, over many bumps, banks, protruding roots and hollows, let into the trees, through multi-coloured flowers and bushes.

"Did many make it?" Hammer asked, their brow already dripping with sweat.

"I led a few here," answered Whisper hoarsely. "I lost count. And you saw— most of the other Doorways were open, too. I'm…optimistic."

"Stay optimistic. This one's going to need it."

Viper, walking behind Silver, took one glance at their cargo and groaned. "No. I don't think she is."

"Don't let the others see. Come this way. Quickly." Hammer led them off the path and through the dense tangle of roots and ferns.

"No," Whisper sobbed. "*No no no.*"

"Shh, child. Let's take a better look." Viper hugged her as Silver knelt down and unshouldered her burden.

"Oh," she choked. "Oh Crim. Ah…I'm so sorry, Little One."

"This is a nice spot. Peaceful," Viper remarked. "Let her rest here."

More whispered apologies, and they eased her back among the roots of a tree, which cradled her there even as she failed to support herself. One by one, they turned away, seeking other survivors and better news. So, they left her reclining peacefully in a bower of twisted roots and dripping vines.